In only a matter of days, 9/11 and the destruction of the Twin Towers will be rivaled by a lone-wolf terrorist attack on America. Atlanta is targeted as Ground Zero for the most horrifying plague in modern times.

Alnour Barashi stared down from the window of the Sun Dial Restaurant, 73 floors up in the Westin Peachtree Plaza, at the weekend throngs below. At the crowds strolling through Atlanta's Centennial Olympic Park, people perhaps headed for the CNN Center, the massive Georgia Aquarium or the World of Coca-Cola. *Americans, a nation of infidels.* He imagined all of them—men, women, children—writhing in agony. Dying.

His determination and patience had been rewarded. The prize: a recombinant Ebola virus as easily transmittable as the common cold. It was something known in the field of microbiology as a chimera virus, named after the mythological fire-breathing creature with the head of a lion, body of a goat and tail of a snake.

He leaned back in his chair, closed his eyes and considered what he was about to unleash. In the 14th century, bubonic plague, the Black Death, swept through Europe claiming more than twenty-five million lives. Death was excruciating. Victims often endured a week of continuous, bloody vomiting and decomposing skin before gasping their final agonizing breaths.

Now, Barashi mused, it would be America's turn. Payment had come due. *For its arrogance, for its imperialism, for its brutality. For its dismissal and humiliation of us. For its crusade to project its values onto our culture and our religion.*

But no more. Of that he was certain. He held the power: the Black Death of the 21st century.

Praise for Plague

"A page-turning thriller rooted in today's world of political unrest. This all too realistic fiction will suspend your belief in the safety of home and the assurance of government protection. *PLAGUE* will keep you up at night long after you've finished it."
—John House, MD, author of *So Shall You Reap*

"If you love thrillers and haven't read Buzz Bernard yet, I suggest you stop what you're doing and rectify that right now. *PLAGUE* grabs you around the throat and squeezes, with believable characters, a realistic plot, and non-stop action. One of the best thrillers of 2012."
—Al Leverone, author of *The Lonely Mile*

"An all-too-believable nightmare tale about the horrors of biological terrorism. Buzz Bernard will keep you up at night wondering *What if?*"
—Tom Young, author of *The Mullah's Storm, Silent Enemy*, and *The Renegades*

"Fans of the late Michael Crichton should check out Buzz Bernard's PLAGUE. This bioterrorism thriller is a real page-turner."
—Cheryl Norman, author of *Rebuild My World*

"A delight for thriller readers. Intense, edgy, full of twists and scary plausibilities. A totally unexpected protagonist and a brilliant cast of characters. Fans of Michael Crichton, Robin Cook and Stephen Coonts will want to pick up H.W. "Buzz" Bernard's PLAGUE, but not before clearing all decks and fastening their seat belts."
—Donnell Ann Bell, bestselling author, *The Past Came Hunting*

About Buzz Bernard's Previous Novel, *Eyewall*

No one was aware of the storm's sudden force. Not the Hurricane Hunter crew trapped in its center. Not the family marooned on a resort island while searching for their missing teen. A deadly Category Five hurricane has never hit the Georgia coast in modern times. Until now.

"Buzz Bernard bursts on the scene with EYEWALL, a compelling and suspenseful tale told with the insight and authenticity of one who has walked in the world of the famed Hurricane Hunters and endured the harsh realities of a major, devastating storm. Great characters combine with razor-sharp suspense and leave you breathless. A one-sitting, white-knuckle read."
—Vicki Hinze, award-winning author of *Deadly Ties*

"A well-crafted tale you can't put down; characters you care about; a spot-on insiders look at hurricane forecasting and flying."
—Jack Williams, author and founding USA TODAY Weather Editor

"A dramatic and frenzied story of how an angry hurricane collides with the frailty and heroism of human nature. After reading the exciting and emotional EYEWALL, I admire even more those who work to protect us from the next category five."
—Michael Buchanan, co-author and screenwriter, *The Fat Boy Chronicles* and *Micah's Child.*

"Riveting . . . Intrigue, power struggles . . . Frightening reality from several perspectives . . . EYEWALL will keep you more than interested. Having been on location interviewing survivors of a Cat 4/5 hurricane that hit Charleston SC in 1989 (Hugo) and witnessing the destruction left in its wake I fully understand how a Cat 5 might impact a barrier island along the southeast coast of the United States. The author takes us there and describes in frightening detail the impact of this scary scenario."
—Marshall Seese, retired anchorman and meteorologist, The Weather Channel

Plague

by

H.W. "Buzz" Bernard

Bell Bridge Books

Bell Bridge Books
PO BOX 300921
Memphis, TN 38130
Print ISBN: 978-1-61194-176-0

Bell Bridge Books is an Imprint of BelleBooks, Inc.

We at BelleBooks enjoy hearing from readers.
Visit our websites – www.BelleBooks.com and www.BellBridgeBooks.com.

10 9 8 7 6 5 4 3 2 1

Cover design: Debra Dixon
Interior design: Hank Smith
Photo credits:
Biohazard symbol (manipulated) © Deformer | Dreamstime.com
Cityscape (manipulated) © Ekaterina Novikova | Dreamstime.com
Background texture (manipulated) © Kheng Ho Toh | Dreamstime.com

:Lpx:01:

For my wife, Christina,

whom I'm blessed to have

In 2008, a congressional commission warned, ". . . given the high-level of know-how needed to use disease as a weapon to cause mass casualties, the United States should be less concerned that terrorists will become biologists and far more concerned that biologists will become terrorists."

Chapter One

NORTH METRO ATLANTA, GEORGIA
SUNDAY, AUGUST 18

David Gullison stared into the bathroom mirror, terrified by what he saw. Someone he didn't know, someone he'd never known. There was something almost demonic about his image. His eyes swam in crimson. Dead rubies. His face, flushed and splotched with tiny scarlet blooms, gave the appearance of Edelweiss gone bad. He looked the caricature of an aged, hard-drinking Irishman. But he knew it wasn't age or booze. It was much worse than that.

The pain came again, squeezing his gut, wrapping around his chest. It had started suddenly a couple of days ago. At first it was just his back. "Too much golf," his wife said.

"Maybe."

"No maybe. I warned you. Take it easy. You're retired now."

Then the fever had come, boiling up inside him like a pyroclastic flow. His throat felt as though a cheese grater had been dragged through it.

"The flu," his wife said. "Go lie down for a while. I'll get some aspirin."

"Yes," he said. He'd flopped down on his bed and didn't move for twelve hours. It was unlike any flu he'd ever had. He felt as if he were on fire, burning up from the inside out. He struggled to take deep breaths; his lungs suffused with fluid. He coughed, deep hacking wheezes that expelled fine sprays of mucus tinged in pink.

The pain spread, invading his stomach and bowels, locking them in vise grips of agony. Vomiting and diarrhea followed. Nonstop.

Now the cramping hit again, sharp, wrenching. He leaned over the sink and vomited once more, long after there shouldn't have been anything left to bring up. A tarry mixture, black and red, flooded into the basin. It was as if his insides were liquefying, turning to jelly. He gripped the edge of the sink, but had no strength left. The room spun in a dizzying spiral.

He knew he'd waited too long; knew he needed to get to an emergency room. He tried to call for his wife, but before he could, the searing effluent rose in his throat again. He sank to his knees and crawled toward the toilet, but failed to make it in time. A rush of burbling flatulence shot from his bowels. A vile, malodorous slime of blood and dark, stringy tissue ran down his thighs and splattered onto the floor. It oozed over the bathroom tile, staining it with a harbinger of something far worse to come.

He lost consciousness and collapsed into the repulsive emulsion.

SUNRIVER, OREGON
SUNDAY, AUGUST 18

Richard Wainwright stood alone on the first tee of a golf course in Sunriver, just south of Bend, as the rising sun lifted into a pristine cerulean sky. The slanting rays lit the Cascade Mountains in a manner that exaggerated the contrast between their snow-capped peaks and the verdant darkness of the forests cloaking their slopes. Overhead, a golden eagle orbited, perhaps waiting to catch a ride on the first thermal of the day. The deserted fairways, notched among corrugated lava buttes and bubbly knobs of pumice, sported a fringe of sagebrush and juniper beneath open stands of ponderosa pines. The air, brisk and tinged with just a hint of dust, was redolent with the essence of evergreens. He could have been in the Garden of Eden. Yet he found no joy in the setting, for he was lost in memories, wrapped in melancholia, and clinging to a ghost that would never return. Karen.

He stepped up to the ball, eight-iron in hand, and took his stance, committed to hitting the perfect shot. He began his backswing, but was interrupted by the ringing of his cell phone. He plucked the phone from his golf bag.

"Wainwright," he said.

"Rich, I was hoping I didn't wake you. I know it's early out there." The soft, deep rumble of a familiar voice.

"Ned. Good lord, it's been awhile. What on earth are you doing these days? I'd heard you'd retired."

Ned laughed, a sardonic chuckle. "And the answer is: two ex-wives, five kids in college and a huge mortgage in Greenwich."

"Ah, then you're still billing yourself as the nation's top executive headhunter?"

"Business has never been better. There's actually increasing demand for competent executives these days. Ones with integrity anyhow. Like you. And, well, I've got this company that's in a real bind."

Richard drew a deep breath. He probably shouldn't encourage Ned. But what the hell, it couldn't hurt to listen. "Okay, lay it on me."

"Actually, it's an easy assignment. Three months, six months. An Atlanta biotech firm, BioDawn, needs someone to step in and stabilize it while they find a new CEO. It's a solid operation, well respected, in good financial shape. All you have to do is come in and look pretty. Hobnob with the investors and tell them everything's going to be okay. And it is. Nothing nefarious here. The money people and board of directors just want a firm hand on the tiller while they ferret out new leadership. And there's no firmer hand than yours."

Wainwright waited for Ned to elaborate. When he didn't, Wainwright challenged him. "Don't give the mushroom treatment, partner. I know damn well there's more to the story than what you're telling me. I can hear it in your voice." Richard sat on a bench adjacent to the tee box and gazed out at a nearby pond. A sub-surface wake knifed through the water. A beaver performing homeland defense.

Ned didn't respond immediately.

"Ned, talk to me. Why is the CEO being replaced?"

"He's dead."

"That hardly seems like a situation that would, as you said, put a company 'in a real bind.'"

"So are the COO, CFO, executive vice president and chairman of the board."

"Whoa, whoa, whoa. What happened to 'easy assignment'? Jesus, what happened to the corporate hierarchy?"

"Plane crash. The corporate Gulfstream was on its way to Munich from Atlanta when it disappeared over the Atlantic somewhere between Bermuda and the Azores. Only bits and pieces of wreckage were found. It may have been an explosion of some sort. But we'll never know for sure."

"Why were all those guys on the same plane?"

"Not too smart, I know, but they were young and inexperienced in the travel safeguards that bigger corporations use. They had their own plane and were excited to be going to Germany to open a new office. They probably viewed it as more of a field trip than a business trip."

"Still . . ."

"Yeah, I know. They're all dead."

"I'm sorry to hear that, Ned. But you know I'm out of the game."

"Yeah, but I want you back in. You were a legend."

"No, a myth."

"Not the way I heard it."

"That was twenty years ago."

"Whatever it was, it launched your career. Stepping out a window onto the ledge of a New York City office building; threatening to jump unless a group of Wall Street investment bankers agreed to back a federal bailout loan for Brighton-Reames Aerospace."

"It was a joke, a youthful shenanigan by a wet-behind-the-ears CFO. I only stuck one foot out the window. I had no intention of going any farther."

"Joke or not, it worked. You became a star."

"I was lucky." Richard stood and walked back toward the tee.

"No. You were the epitome of competence and integrity. You went on to raise more companies from the dead than Jesus Christ could have. And, on top of everything else, you oozed charisma. Even people you intimidated or fired respected you."

"Yeah. But I pissed off a lot of folks. Too hands-on, they said."

"Bull shit. That was your style, your strength. You could smell out deadwood like a hog after truffles. You knew how to read employees and understand their motives, their goals, their integrity, their competency . . . or lack thereof. You couldn't have done that with your butt anchored in a corner office someplace."

"Ned, read my lips—well, you can't. So I'll speak slowly. I. Am. Retired. It's a beautiful day in Oregon. The sun is out. An eagle is soaring overhead. I'm on a golf course. And I've got it almost to myself." A slow ripple fanned out over the pond as the beaver approached the shore.

"Spare me. You don't know a Callaway RAZR from a Gillette razor. Don't light me up."

"I'm not available. And I know what a Callaway RAZR is. You have to know that before you can retire."

"You're too goddamned young to be retired. Look, I heard what happened; I know you had some heavy duty shit laid on you. And I know you've heard all the platitudes, but . . ." He paused.

Richard sensed he probably didn't want to hear what Ned would say next, but then again, maybe he did.

Ned spoke softly, his words threaded with compassion. "You can put down the cross, Rich. Nobody will blame you. It's been over two years. It's okay. Get back in the game, move on with your life."

The beaver surfaced and fixed its gaze on Richard and his eight-iron. Richard dropped the club and covered the mouthpiece of his phone. "Relax," he yelled at the animal, "I'm hitting in the other direction."

"Who are you talking to?" Ned asked. "I thought you said the course was deserted."

"A beaver."

There was a long pause on the other end of the line. Then, "You're bored, aren't you?"

"Shitless."

"I win."

"Yeah, I was good. But you were always better."

"There'll be a ticket waiting for you at the Redmond airport early this afternoon. Quick hop to Salt Lake, then Delta—first class, of course—to Atlanta. You'll get in late this evening. There'll be a driver at Hartsfield-Jackson waiting to pick you up. And bring your clubs. Lots of great courses in Atlanta. You'll have plenty of time to hone your game."

Though he didn't believe in sixth sense, something gnawing at Richard told him that wouldn't be the case.

DOWNTOWN ATLANTA, GEORGIA
SUNDAY, AUGUST 18

Alnour Barashi stared down from the window of the Sun Dial Restaurant, 73 floors up in the Westin Peachtree Plaza, at the weekend throngs below. At the crowds strolling through Atlanta's Centennial Olympic Park, people perhaps headed for the CNN Center, the massive Georgia Aquarium or the World of Coca-Cola. *Americans, a nation of infidels.* He imagined all of them—men, women, children—writhing in agony. Dying.

He gazed at the structures that towered skyward around him: the Bank of America Plaza, One Atlantic Center, 191 Peachtree Tower. Great steel and glass icons that symbolized everything he despised about American culture: its ill-gotten wealth, its excesses, its arrogance. "Faah," he mumbled to himself. He finished his lunch, paid the bill in cash, and left.

Back in his apartment, he reclined in a chair and lit a cigarette. He inhaled deeply, tilted his head back and blew a plume of smoke toward the ceiling. He repeated the action several times until a thin, hazy stratus blanketed his small quarters. Relaxed, he reflected on the fact there was one thing he liked about America, Atlanta in particular: its mild climate, a welcome counterpoint to the ice-bound years he'd spent working at the Koltsovo Institute of Molecular Biology in Siberia.

But that was far in the past. Now it was time to breathe life into the legacy of Koltsovo. He placed his cigarette in an ashtray and rummaged through a desk drawer. He pulled out a well-worn roadmap of metropolitan Atlanta, opened it and spread it over the top of his desk. He studied the red circles he'd made earlier on the map. With a ruler calibrated in millimeters, he measured the distance between the circles. He retrieved a calculator and tapped in some numbers. Time, speed, distance. He'd done this before, but wanted to make certain. No margin for error. Thousands, perhaps tens of thousands, would die. He didn't want to be one of them. He wanted his escape to be clean, and for that his choreography—attack, move; attack, move; attack, flee—had to be perfect.

He smiled, or at least imagined he did. His face, he knew, rarely betrayed emotion. Perhaps the world would never be aware of his genius, his accomplishment, his lethal bioengineered virus, but Allah would, and Allah would be pleased. Allah understood the scientific acumen, the years of labor, the dedication that had been invested in the effort.

Satisfaction washed over Barashi. His determination and patience had been rewarded. The prize: a recombinant Ebola virus as easily transmittable as the common cold. It was something known in the field of microbiology as a chimera virus, named after the mythological fire-breathing creature with the head of a lion, body of a goat and tail of a snake.

The virus had only one more trial to pass, a field test he'd initiated Thursday. He already was convinced the pestilence would prove its lethality, but wanted to be one hundred percent positive. Tomorrow or the next day he'd call area hospitals to see if either, or both, of his targets had been admitted. He expected they had. And was certain there'd be others.

From his briefcase, he pulled a journal. He scribbled some notes in it, then snapped it shut. It made a sharp but tiny sound—a note of confidence, of celebration, of victory. He reached for his cigarette. Too late. It had burned out, leaving only a skeletal cylinder of ash. He brushed it into the center of the ashtray.

He leaned back in his chair, closed his eyes and considered what he was about to unleash. In the 14th century, bubonic plague, the Black Death, swept through Europe claiming more the 25 million lives. Death was excruciating. Victims often endured a week of continuous, bloody vomiting and decomposing skin before gasping their final agonizing breaths.

Now, Barashi mused, it would be America's turn. Payment had come due. *For its arrogance, for its imperialism, for its brutality. For its dismissal and humiliation of us. For its crusade to project its values onto our culture and our religion.*

But no more. Of that he was certain. He held the power: the Black Death of the 21st century.

Chapter Two

NORTH METRO ATLANTA
SUNDAY, AUGUST 18

David Gullison awoke into a confused, Kafkaesque world. He had no sense of what time it was. Day or night? He didn't know. He wasn't even sure where he was. In a bed, he was certain, but . . . Images and voices swam through his mind as if in an abstractionist dream. He wondered if this was Thursday, his day to play golf with Alan. They always got an early start. He shifted his head to look for his alarm clock. There. But the numbers didn't make sense. They constantly changed, blinking on and off, pulsating. And why were there so many of them?

He endeavored to sit up, but was too weak. Warm liquid dribbled down his chin. He labored to breathe, but there was something covering his mouth. He raised his hand to remove it, but his arm seemed constrained by wires or tiny cables. *Smothered. I'm being smothered.* He twisted and turned in a brief, futile attempt to free himself, but again his strength abandoned him.

He tried to scream, but only gagged and coughed. Searing pain lanced through his throat and wrapped itself around his tongue. He inhaled repeatedly, rapidly, but couldn't gather enough oxygen. It was as though his lungs had turned to moth-eaten lace. Each breath produced no more than a hollow rattle.

Dr. Arthur Willand concluded he should stop looking at pictures of himself. These days he was mildly put off by what he saw: a middle-aged man who looked much older than he really was. His close-cropped blond hair was prematurely flecked with gray, and a nascent double chin—too much time in emergency rooms, not enough time in exercise rooms—hung underneath his freckled, Charlie Brown face. And it was days like today that made him a viable candidate for Grecian Formula.

Because North Georgia Regional Hospital was a Level II Adult Trauma Center, one of four in metro Atlanta, Willand had seen his share of severed limbs and gaping wounds and been splattered by more geysering arterial blood and projectile vomiting than he cared to remember. But what he was dealing with today in the patient by the name of David Gullison was something beyond his ken. Far beyond.

Gullison seemed to be leaking blood from every orifice in his body, eyes and ears included. Dark, bloody emesis and diarrhea speckled the treatment room, filling it with the fetid stench of putrefaction. The patient's stare was vacant and distant; his body, puffy and swollen. His testicles had ballooned to the size of a grapefruit and turned black and blue. His blood pressure had plunged.

Attempts to stabilize him, to give him IV fluids and medicines, proved futile. A needle inserted into his skin would launch additional hemorrhaging. He was a human colander, unable to retain his own blood. Transfusions were attempted, but blood seeped out as fast as it went in. Dabs of gel foam, used by surgeons to stanch bleeding in severed capillaries, were useless. His blood had lost its clotting capability.

Dr. Willand shook his head in disgust, not at what he was seeing, but at his inability to do anything. He turned to the head ER nurse, a middle-aged slip of a woman with soft, brown eyes who could bark orders like a Marine drill sergeant or soothe a patient with the compassion of Mother Theresa.

"Doris, are we sure Mr. Gullison doesn't have a clotting disorder?"

"Positive."

Well, he does now. "Where'd he come from? What's his background? Who brought him in?"

"His wife. They live just a few miles from the hospital. She said he'd been sick for a couple of days—vomiting, diarrhea—but that he got a little better yesterday. They thought he might be getting over it. Then he began hemorrhaging this morning. She's wondering if it isn't just a bad case of the flu or food poisoning. Like that stuff folks get on cruise ships."

"A Norwalk-like virus? Were they on a cruise recently?"

Doris shook her head. "Mrs. Gullison said they haven't traveled outside the U.S. in over a year."

"Well, I don't think it's the cruise-ship shits anyhow. This guy is a lot sicker than that. Let's get a blood sample down to the CDC. They should be able to tell us for sure. In the meantime, get Mr. Gullison started on whole-body type-O blood transfusions. At least we can fight a holding action until we figure out what we're dealing with and how to treat it. Oh, and have a respirator standing by, too. This stuff is attacking his lungs."

"It's attacking everything."

Willand nodded. A small shudder ran through him. "Let's err on the side of caution. Have people suit up around Mr. Gullison. Masks, gloves, eye protection. No visitors. Isolate him. And Doris?"

"Yes?"

"Be really careful."

David's insides felt as if they were being gnawed away, chewed into chunks of raw meat. A hot sword of terror knifed into him. *Oh, God, I'm being eaten from the inside out. Something is eating me. Please, God, no.* He tried to scream again, but no sound came, only a thin dribble of fluid from his mouth.

His heart quivered, a sack of blubber struggling for life in a dead environment. Shadows hovered over him, a piercing squeal filled his head. He jerked erect, seizing, retching uncontrollably, spewing grainy, coffee-ground-like vomit into whatever covered his mouth. Abruptly, something narcotic surged through his being, and he sank into a netherworld of nightmares.

It didn't last. He awoke once more into a world devoid of time and place. A world where only pain existed—excruciating, unending, relentless. Excruciating? Too weak of a word to describe it. The mere touch of something resting on him—a bed sheet, perhaps?—sent waves of agony through his skin. Now, just one thought, one hope, consumed him: death. *Merciful God. Let me die. I ask in your Son's name.*

He thought someone called his name, but wasn't sure. His brain, suddenly infused with bright yellow and red light, seemed to explode. Then nothing. Only blackness. His sense of being slid into an infinite, limitless void. And the pain ceased.

"I'm sorry, Mrs. Gullison, I'm truly sorry. We did everything we could, but he was just too far gone. We tried to defibrillate him, but there was zero response, absolutely nothing. It was as if his heart had disintegrated. All his other organs had failed, too, kidneys, liver, lungs, everything." Dr. Willand shook his head, partly in sympathy, partly in disbelief. He didn't like this part of his job; didn't like telling spouses or parents or children they had lost someone they loved. Someone who had loved them. He didn't like failing. He especially didn't like not knowing what he was dealing with.

Mrs. Gullison, seated next to him in an anteroom near the ICU, sobbed in great, gasping bursts, her head buried in her hands, her body shaking with the trauma of sudden grief. Dr. Willand rested his hand on her shoulder, cold comfort in her agony.

"What was it?" she choked out between sobs. "What killed him? He always . . ." the words wouldn't come. Dr. Willand waited while she composed herself. She did finally, but kept her head bowed. She held her hands together, but they were in constant motion, writhing like a tiny, knotted ball of snakes.

"He was always so healthy," she said at last, finishing her statement. "He exercised. He didn't smoke. He ate right. He had a checkup every year. There was nothing wrong with him, doctor, nothing. How could he have died like that? It was so . . . ugly." The tears came again.

He patted her shoulder. Ugly wasn't the word for it. Agonizing. Cruel. Excruciating. Calamitous. Ugly didn't begin to describe it. It was as if AIDS had ransacked Gullison's body in a matter of days. From a standing start to the speed of sound in metaphorical seconds.

"I'll be honest with you, Mrs. Gullison. We don't know. Sometimes we come up against that. A rare illness. An emerging disease. A new virus or bacterium. But we'll find out. I promise you. We've notified the state health department, and we've sent a sample to the CDC, the Centers for Disease Control. They'll find out what this was."

Mrs. Gullison nodded, then began sobbing again, this time silently, softly. She appeared to be an attractive, middle-aged woman, but the ordeal with her husband had taken its toll. Her short, henna-hued hair was disheveled, and her clothes, wrinkled—casualties of long hours of vigilance at the hospital; hours without sleep.

"Is there somebody I can call for you?" Dr. Willand asked. "Family? Friend?"

She shrugged.

"I could have the hospital chaplain come sit with you for a while. Would you like that?"

"That would be nice."

He rose. "I'll have him paged."

She lifted her head and said, "Thank you for trying, doctor. I know it wasn't your fault."

He took an involuntary step back. She stared at him with bloodshot eyes. Not merely bloodshot, but bathed in crimson as though all the tiny veins in her eyeballs had shattered.

"Mrs. Gullison, perhaps we should have a look at you, just to make sure—"

She raised her hand in protest. "I'm fine," she said. "I just need some rest." As if to punctuate her lie, she broke into a spasm of coughing, watery hacking coming from deep within her lungs.

"No," he said. "You're sick." *My God, what is this?*

DRUID HILLS, ATLANTA
SUNDAY, AUGUST 18

Dwight Butler, a virologist in the Viral Special Pathogens Branch of the CDC sat sequestered in his office. He'd been called in on an emergency. Now he remained there late in the day because he was—he could think of no other way of putting it—scared shitless.

Outside, lightning illuminated the darkness in almost continuous high-voltage brilliance. An artillery barrage of thunder rumbled steadily. "It's the angels bowling," his grandmother used to tell him as a child. Adjacent to the cluster of tightly-packed brick and concrete structures that comprised the CDC, a dark river of rainwater streamed down Clifton Road.

"No angels tonight," he muttered as he stared out at the storm without really seeing it. His thoughts were elsewhere, wrestling with something far less visible: metastasizing fear. He realized he didn't look like a man who should be frightened of anything. Truth be told, there were people frightened of him. In the parking lot at night, he'd witnessed coworkers who didn't know him take the Great Circle Route of avoidance if he approached them.

By any conventional standards, he certainly didn't look like a doctor, which he was, courtesy of Johns Hopkins University. With a polished ebony head, bulging muscles and a gold earring dangling from his right earlobe, he came across as an African-American Mr. Clean. But unlike Mr. Clean, he sported a bushy, black mustache that drooped over the corners his mouth like the horns of a Cape Buffalo.

His boss, J. W. Zambit, Chief of Special Pathogens, had been appalled by Dwight's appearance the first time they'd met. Not by his mustache or earring, but by his casual manner of dress: khaki shorts, a flowered Caribbean shirt and gnarly leather sandals. "You can't come to work looking like you're going to a Jimmy Buffet concert," Zambit snapped. "People will think I've hired a Parrot Head."

"What you've hired," Dwight fired back, "is the best damned virologist on the East Coast. Bugs don't care what I wear."

He had backed up his boast, and Zambit never raised the issue again. Still, a low level of tension festered between the two. Zambit from time to time would mumble under his breath about decorum in the pathogens branch "going to hell in a hand basket," words clearly directed at Dwight. Dwight, for his part, never passed up a chance to poke a stick in Zambit's eye, usually by arriving late for meetings and then walking in humming "Margaritaville" to the beat of his clip-clopping sandals.

Once, they'd almost reached a level of détente. Several of the staff had been in a Buckhead bar kicking back on a Friday evening after a particularly arduous week, and Zambit, after a couple of belts, had asked Dwight in a non-adversarial manner, "So why flip-flops and not hip-hop?"

Dwight crushed a tiny orange drink-umbrella between his thumb and forefinger. "I grew up in Newark. My father was killed in the riots there in the late 1960s, and my mother wasn't really interested in being a mother. I was raised by my grandmother, bless her soul, but I survived by being a street punk. I discovered my appearance helped; it intimidated people." He tossed the crumpled paper umbrella onto the table.

"Still does, I hear." Zambit took a swig of his Dewars.

"Yeah. Well, that's part of the reason I've gone Key West." He spread his arms in a insouciant gesture. "What you see here is the kinder, gentler 'Dee Butt.'"

"Dee what?"

"Dee Butt. Street name. Long ago. A life I escaped. It never was me. Give me a pair of cheap sandals, a sunset, and a rum and Coke, and I'm a happy man." A grin on his face, he leaned toward Zambit. "How about you, boss. What makes you happy? Anything? Or are you always going to be a stiff with pipette up his ass?"

Dwight regretted almost immediately saying the words, but he knew you couldn't un-ring a bell. The opportunity for peaceful coexistence spiraled into history.

This evening, Dwight had no thought of peaceful coexistence with anything. His laid-back nature and professionalism had been pushed to limits he'd never imagined. He recalled only once before being this terrified: in an SCCA sports car race. He'd lost the brakes on a Porsche Carrera screaming into a sharp right-hander at Watkins Glen and could only hang on and try to grip the seat with his butt cheeks as the car ripped through a fence and hurtled into heavy underbrush at over 100 mph. He still loved fine cars, but his high-speed excursion into the Upstate New York woods had ended his career as an amateur competition driver.

When he picked up the phone to call Zambit, he discovered he was back in the Porsche on an out-of-control ride. "Calm down," he said out loud. He punched in the number of his boss's home phone.

"Dr. Zambit," a voice on the other end of the line said.

"Zamby, this is Dwight."

"The hell you calling in the middle of a storm for? You'll get us both electrocuted. Or was that your plan?"

"Actually it wasn't. But you may feel like you've been electrocuted after this call is over."

The phone line popped and crackled as a lightning bolt lanced onto the roof of an adjacent building. Zambit yelled for his wife to bring him a portable handset. There was a pause, then Zambit said, "I gather you're about to lay some serious shit on me."

"Think of it as an elephant dump."

"You'd never pass up an opportunity like that, would you?"

"We've got Ebola in Atlanta."

Chapter Three

DRUID HILLS, ATLANTA
SUNDAY, AUGUST 18

Brief silence ensued on Zambit's end of the line before he said, "I think lightning fried our connection for a moment. What did you say?"

"The samples that came in from North Georgia Regional Hospital earlier today, they tested positive for Ebola."

Again silence. Then, "Are you shitting me, Dwight? This isn't one of your 'let's yank the boss's chain' little antics, is it?"

"I wish it were. I ran an ELISA on the blood sample. It came back positive for Ebola antigens—"

"It's a nonspecific test, you know that. Ebola antibodies have shown up in the blood sera of Native Americans in Alaska, for Christ's sake, people who've never been anywhere near Ebola or vice versa."

"I did a PCR, too."

"And?"

"That's what scared the crap out of me. The genetic structure looks a lot like Ebola-Zaire and a lot like Ebola-Reston. Zaire, as lethal as hell to humans; Reston, lethal only to monkeys."

"The guy that's sick, the guy the samples came from, he isn't a monkey, is he?"

"Obviously not. What's your point?"

"That if he's sick, it's Zaire, not Reston."

"I know that. That's scary enough. But here's what's even scarier; that if he's got—actually had, he died this evening—Ebola, it could be an airborne form. Yeah, Reston doesn't make humans sick, but it sure as hell does a job on monkeys and is probably transmitted through the air."

The lightning relented slightly, dwindling to occasional flickers somewhere over Stone Mountain. The thunder morphed to distant grumbles. Zambit's breathing into the phone became arrhythmic, almost spastic. Finally he drew a deep breath and said, "Dear God. You're telling me we're dealing with Ebola that's mutated, become transmittable through the air, like the flu or a common cold?"

"Could be. But I haven't looked at it yet. I haven't done the electron microscopy to confirm it's a filovirus."

"Let's do that before we go running in circles, waving our arms and screaming."

"Okay. But if we discover it's a filovirus, then can we go running in circles, waving our arms and screaming?"

"Wait for me, and we'll do this Kodak Moment thing together. I'll be there in about 20 minutes. At least the friggin' storm is letting up."

"*Au contraire*, bossman. It may be just starting."

"That's what I like about you, Dwight. Happy, happy, joy, joy."

An hour after Dwight phoned Zambit, the two men, clad in full-body positive pressure protective suits, sat in a Biosafety Level-4 lab at the CDC. The suits, tethered to an external air supply, were topped by large, boxy, transparent hoods. Though not unaccustomed to Level-4 labs, Dwight's heart rate soared. The reason, he understood, was simple. Level-4 labs were reserved for work with organisms lethal to human beings. For the most part, there were neither treatments nor vaccines for diseases triggered by BSL-4 agents.

Dwight peered through the protective hood and manipulated the dials and switches controlling an electron microscope. A greenish glow radiating from the microscope's viewing screen in the darkened lab, together with the men's bulky protective gear and breathing hoses, lent them the appearance of deep-sea divers. And like deep-sea divers, they were in an alien environment. Dwight well knew they had entered a world where the tiniest mistake—a leak in a hose, a rip in a suit, a tear in a glove—could kill them. Not instantly like it would a diver, but slowly, agonizingly, efficiently. No one needed to remind him that the margin for error in a BSL-4 lab is absolute zero.

The virologist moved the scanning microscope slowly across a landscape—a cellscape, really—looking into a world magnified 150,000 times, far beyond what most people could ever imagine. It was like viewing the earth's surface using satellite imagery, searching for unique structures that signaled trouble, such as burgeoning cumulonimbi—precursors to hurricane formation—in a disturbance over a tropical ocean. Neither man spoke, their hoods suffused with the noisy rush of piped-in air.

To clearly converse under such circumstances sometimes required turning off the air supply, not a popular procedure. The fluorescent image of the viewing screen reflected off Zambit's faceplate as Dwight slid the focus of the microscope from one cell to the next, searching for what he did not want to find but knew he inevitably would.

Then it was there. A cell destroyed, appearing riddled with worms or microscopic snakes. Dwight twisted a dial, and the image grew larger. The cell was dead, "eaten" alive not by a horde of worms or snakes, but by a virus.

"Don't let this be," he muttered. He turned to Zambit who nodded, confirming what they saw: a filovirus, Ebola, unique in appearance in the universe of human viruses—narrow and stringy. It reminded Dwight of emaciated spaghetti, albeit spaghetti invisible to the naked eye. Spaghetti lethal to human beings.

Despite the air hissing into his helmet, he heard the pounding of his pulse, a steady, staccato reverberation. There's no way Ebola-Zaire or Ebola-Zaire-Reston, or whatever the hell this was, could be loose in the U.S., he thought. No way. The only confirmed deaths from Ebola until now had occurred in Africa, its natural reservoir.

He turned to Zambit. "What the hell is going on?" he yelled. "How the fuck did Ebola get into America? Into Atlanta, for God's sake?" His respiration became choppy. He struggled to catch his breath. He yanked at his air hose.

Zambit jumped toward him, put a restraining hand on his arm. "Come on. Out now," he said loudly. He inclined his head toward the exit and guided Dwight ahead of him, careful not to rush, careful not to tear his suit.

Minutes later, after passing through a Lysol shower in their suits and then through a body shower, the two men sat naked in a dressing room.

"Sorry about that," Dwight said.

Zambit ignored him, staring dead-eyed at a row of lockers in front of him. He finally looked at Dwight, as though the sound waves had been delayed in reaching him. "What?"

"Never mind."

Zambit stood and stepped into his boxers. "All right," he said, "what's first?"

"I'd like to find out where this stuff came from, but I don't think that's our priority at the moment."

Zambit nodded and pulled on his pants.

"First," Dwight continued, "we need to call North Georgia Regional, tell them they're hot as hell, tell them to nuke the place, everyplace the victim was. And isolate everyone who worked with him, everyone who handled samples, clothing, bedding; everyone who got near him. Then we need to find out if they've admitted anyone else with the same symptoms. We'd better contact other hospitals in the area, too." He was standing and pacing now, forgetting he was naked as a maple in winter. "And we need to notify the state health department. Probably the FBI, too."

Zambit pulled on his shirt and raised an eyebrow at Dwight. "You don't think—"

"I'm like a goddamned virus right now. I don't think, I just react. I'd like to believe this is some kind of bizarre, point-off-the-curve, explainable anomaly. But right now we don't know. We don't know jack shit, in fact. Yeah, I think we at least need to give the FBI a heads-up. Just in case."

Zambit stepped into his loafers. "Okay. Agreed. Lord, I hope we can keep this away from the media until we get a handle on it. Anything else?"

"Better beef-up the emergency operations center."

"I'll call the director. Oh, and Dwight?"

Dwight stopped pacing and looked at Zambit.

"It's okay if you're a little scared."

"It wasn't for myself . . . what happened in there," Dwight said, annoyed Zambit had brought it up.

"I know. It's for what it might mean for everyone. Let me say it again, it's okay if you're a little scared, because I'm petrified."

Dwight nodded, then in a whisper said, "And there before me was a pale horse."

Chapter Four

NORTH METRO ATLANTA
MONDAY, AUGUST 19

Richard Wainwright pulled his rented Mini Cooper S into a reserved parking slot at BioDawn International early on his first day on the job as the company's interim CEO. He shut off the engine, set the parking brake and gazed into the hazy dawn. Intellectually, he acknowledged it was time to end his self-imposed exile from the corporate world and pitch himself back into the workforce. Emotionally, he remained ambivalent. He had lost so much.

But he knew Ned and his other friends were right. He had to press forward. He exited the car, placed his briefcase on top of it and took a moment to survey his new domain. The corporate headquarters resided in a tree-studded office park, a bucolic campus surrounded by a sprawl of unchecked growth and business development. Dogwoods and azaleas, long since past their spring glory, lined a well-manicured walk leading to the headquarters building, a gleaming five-story glass and steel structure. Two similar but smaller buildings, each two stories, flanked the larger one on either side. Adjacent to the building on the right, a compact blockhouse-like structure squatted behind a Cyclone fence topped with razor wire. Unlike the other BioDawn facilities, the blockhouse was windowless except for several tall, narrow slits near its entrance. The building seemed out of place.

Richard grabbed his briefcase and headed toward the main entrance. Heat and humidity hugged him in a steambath-like embrace, a palpable change from the semiarid freshness of Oregon's high desert. He ran the back of his hand across his brow, sweeping away beads of perspiration, unexpected for so early in the day. He knew, however, they were the result of more than the weather. The image of an exploding Gulfstream jet filled his mind.

He entered the building, checked the directory for the executive offices—fifth floor—then walked up the stairs to his new, albeit temporary, job as CEO of the fourth largest biotechnology company in the world.

He discovered he needed a key card to enter the executive suite, so he rapped on its double glass doors to gain the attention of someone inside. He caught his breath as a woman approached. It was as though he were back on the Brickyard at North Carolina State University. Back in a moment years ago when he'd initially glimpsed his first love, Martha De la Serna. Though their relationship hadn't endured beyond college, the residue of its awkward passion had, lodging itself permanently in his subconscious, then slithering out at unexpected times, like now, to remind him of youth gone by. Of guilty pleasures.

Although the woman walking toward him was uncommonly attractive, she looked nothing like Marty. She opened the door. "I'm Anneliese Mierczak," she said, introducing herself, "and since your credentials and reputation precede you, I have no doubt you're our CEO pro tem. Welcome to BioDawn." A touch of smokiness, drizzled in syrup, permeated her voice.

"Richard Wainwright," he said as they shook hands. "Rich will do."

She laughed lightly. "No, Mr. Wainwright will do. I'm your executive assistant, not your lover."

She smiled, and her dark eyes flashed something at him, just the hint of a tease perhaps, the essence of a challenge. But probably he had read too much into a fleeting glance. Still, he was no stranger to the advances of women, however subtle and understated they might be—a glance, a word, a touch. At six-foot-four with obsidian hair swept back into a tight pony tail and a face that remained tanned and taut even after four decades, he realized he was not unattractive.

Of course, the fact he made a great deal of money and held positions of significant power made him even more desirable to a certain subset of females: lionesses on the prowl. Sexual temptation, at least until recently, had stalked him constantly. Despite being lured—well, to be honest, allowing himself to be lured—to the brink more than once, he had remained monogamous and resolutely faithful to Karen. Even now. Even after she was gone.

Though Marty had been attractive and, to a point, uninhibited when it came to dealing with his male urges, it was Karen who'd captured his soul. Karen Howerton. Wild and reserved; demanding and selfless; silly and wise. A girl/woman, the daughter of a Marine Corps colonel; a young lady not afraid to put a young lieutenant at Camp Pendleton in his place. Not afraid to surrender her life and unconditional love to a man leaving the Corps and embarking on a journey in the corporate jungle, armed only with a Harvard Business School degree. He could have asked for no better gun-bearer.

A wave of nascent guilt surged through him as Anneliese led him into the interior of the suite. Her form-fitting black skirt and white blouse left little to the imagination and little room to doubt that what one saw was real. Her face could have sold cosmetics or graced the cover of *Town and Country*. But he sensed something contradictory about her, something both alluring and forbidden. Maybe even dangerous. One of his strengths as a CEO was in evaluating people, and he instantly judged he should tread carefully around this woman.

He shook off his contemplations as she ushered him into his office. A wide, tinted window in the far wall overlooked a small pond backed by a stand of pines and oaks at the rear of the building. The pond, about an acre in size, was encircled by a gravel walkway along which several wooden park benches resided.

A polished mahogany desk and matching conference table the size of a small airfield dominated the office. The table was rigged for videoconferencing and topped by an electronic topography of computer terminals and telephones. Leather chairs stood at attention along the table's periphery while something akin to a rollaway throne towered behind the desk.

Color photographs of BioDawn facilities around the world lined the paneled walls of the office. Above each, a digital clock indicated the local time: Tokyo, Munich, Stockholm, London, Kuala Lumpur, Zurich. Slick, colored posters touting the benefits of BioDawn products and research also adorned the walls.

In contrast to the ordered symmetry of the photos and posters, the huge desk presented a cluttered landscape of paper and binders. Corporate literature. Project summaries. Annual reports. Balance sheets. Resumes.

"Well," Richard said, "I see I've got my homework cut out for me."

"If it would help," Anneliese said, "I could schedule project managers and key people from accounting and finance to brief you."

"The sooner the better, Ms. Mierczak—"

"Anneliese. You don't work for me. Other way around, remember?" A hint of a smile snuck across her exquisitely chiseled features.

"All right, Anneliese. Set up the briefings for my office." He looked at his wristwatch, forgetting he was surrounded by clocks detailing global time. "Let's start right away, say ten o'clock. Project managers only. I'll go over the financial stuff myself."

DRUID HILLS, ATLANTA
MONDAY, AUGUST 19

Mid-morning. Doctors Butler and Zambit sat in a small anteroom, a team room, adjacent to the CDC's EOC, the Emergency Operations Center. Dwight surveyed the facility, noting that nearly half its 85 workstations were occupied. In order to avoid leaks to the media and thus preclude panic, employees had been told they were working a no-notice exercise; a sort of operational readiness inspection. It was a subterfuge that likely had a short shelf life.

Dwight, fighting fatigue, stared at a stack of hand-scribbled notes on the table in front of him. He reached for a pen that lay nearby and in the process bowled over a paper cup full of fresh coffee. Dark liquid flooded across the table, splattering his notes and dribbling onto his shirt.

"Shall we take that as an omen?" Zambit asked.

"I think we've had enough friggin' omens already," Dwight muttered as he dabbed at his stained shirt and soggy notes with paper towels.

Zambit waited.

Dwight continued his mop up.

"North Georgia Regional is scrubbing down everything in its ER with bleach, Lysol, whatever they've got," he said. "They've isolated the doctors and nurses who had contact with Mr. Gullison and are monitoring them 24/7. Mr. Gullison's body will be cremated today."

"Additional cases?"

"'Fraid so. Mrs. Gullison was admitted to North Georgia last evening. Same symptoms as her husband."

"Shit. Any more?"

"Yeah." Dwight examined his blotchy notes. "A Mr. Alan McCarthy delivered himself to St. Joe's late last night. HF-like symptoms."

"St. Joseph's knows what to look for?"

"Yeah," Dwight said, "they do."

"Hopefully there's a commonality between McCarthy and Gullison. Hopefully we aren't dealing with diverse sources." Zambit's voice resonated with a strange timbre. A violin string about to snap.

"They were best friends, in fact. Golfing partners. They lived in the same subdivision."

Zambit sipped his own coffee and grimaced. "Good thing you spilled yours," he said. "How much social contact did Gullison and McCarthy have the past few weeks?"

"Not much, apparently. According to McCarthy's wife, just once a week on the golf course."

"I assume that neither worked in a bioresearch lab, handled monkeys or traveled to Africa recently."

"Nope. Gullison was retired. McCarthy is an investment advisor."

Zambit expelled a long breath and pushed his coffee away. "I take it there's no other common point of intersection? Like a theater, a restaurant, a sporting event?"

"We'll have to delve more deeply into that. In the meantime, I'd like to dispatch a field team to the subdivision. Have it prowl around homes, yards, the golf course, maybe the country club. Gather some samples, ask questions."

"What's the cover?"

"State health inspectors checking on the source of a possible salmonella outbreak."

"Flimsy. And the country club isn't going to like it." Zambit rested his elbows on the table and steepled his hands underneath his chin.

"Well, we could go running in circles—"

"Yelling Ebola, Ebola?"

"Yeah."

"Salmonella it is." Zambit paused, then added, his voice still strained, "Let's do it quickly and quietly. I have a feeling we've just heard the starting gun fired in a 100-yard dash."

Dwight sat silently for a moment. With his forefinger he moved a wad of coffee-saturated paper towels in a slow circle on the table in front of him. A soft babble of voices from the EOC drifted into the room.

"What?" Zambit said.

"Well, if this stuff is spread through the air, then we've got a lot bigger problem than just doctors, nurses and immediate family. Like this guy McCarthy. As an investment advisor, he probably saw clients. And he had contact with co-workers in his office. A good hack or sneeze, and he's an Ebola bomb. Somebody inhales a half-dozen virions—"

"Hold it, hold it," Zambit barked. "Time out. Let's keep our imaginations under control. All we've got at this point is a hypothesis based on something you saw in the virus's genetic structure. We don't really know how it's transmitted. Let's just go with what we're certain of, namely that we've got Ebola-Zaire, with a capital E and a capital Z, right here in River City, and that Gullison's probably the index case. We'll keep an open mind on airborne transmission, but for the time being, let's get a cordon around the sick people and those they were in close contact with. And let's try to figure out where the hell this stuff came from."

"Yes, but what if—"

"No 'what ifs,' Dwight. We go with what we know. Let's not run off the rails again."

Run off the rails again. A reference to Dwight's moment of panic in the Level-4 lab the previous night. Dwight ground his teeth together, biting down on his ire, pissed that Zambit had raised the issue once more.

"You're right," Dwight said. "Sorry. Better get me a paper bag to breathe into." He stood and stalked out of the room.

Chapter Five

NORTH METRO ATLANTA
MONDAY, AUGUST 19

By four p.m., the last of the project managers at BioDawn had finished briefing their new CEO. Though he didn't understand a lot of the technology employed by the corporation, Richard did understand he was at the helm of an eminently successful and innovative firm. Its operations focused on discovering recombinant biopharmaceutical products, products that had the potential to be developed as therapeutic and diagnostic tools for the treatment of cancer, HIV/AIDS, multiple sclerosis, hepatitis, diabetes and various infectious diseases. A noble and, he quickly came to realize, extremely profitable calling.

The project balance sheets suggested the multimillion-dollar company was on solid financial footing. A couple of efforts were leaking a bit of red ink, but overall BioDawn appeared to be in a strong position to attract and retain investors.

He pushed his chair back from his desk, stood and stretched. He walked to the window and looked out. The pond below him lay in late-afternoon shade. Its dark and unrippled waters reflected towering white cumulus cauliflowering into a blue-gray haze. A chipmunk, its tail on Viagra, sprinted across the gravel path and startled a squirrel constructing a small earthen cache.

A lone stroller, a man idly puffing a cigarette, moved along the path. He turned his head to follow the excited dash of the chipmunk. He flipped his cigarette in its direction, not maliciously, just casually, then glanced up in the direction of Richard's office. Richard, knowing he could not be seen through the heavy tint of the windows, watched the man until he turned and disappeared in the direction of the fenced-in blockhouse.

The blockhouse. Richard had forgotten about it. It hadn't come up during the course of the briefings. All of the projects he'd been brought up to speed on were being carried out in the labs flanking the administration building. There had been nothing about any efforts being pursued in the odd, windowless structure.

Perhaps Anneliese could shed some light on what went on there. He stepped to his desk to call her. But before he could punch the intercom button, Anneliese's voice came through the speaker.

"Sir, you have a call from a Mrs. Anthony Scarelli. Do you want me to take a message?"

"Should I know her?"

"Tony Scarelli's wife."

Richard decided he should know her and did his best to process the name, running it quickly through the overloaded Rolodex in his brain. He pictured BioDawn's executive roster and scrolled down to Scarelli, Anthony. Executive vice president. *Sometimes I scare myself.*

"Tony Scarelli," he said with satisfaction. "Executive vice president. Killed in the plane crash."

"Yes, sir."

"I'll take the call."

"Line two."

He picked up the phone. "Mrs. Scarelli," he said, "this is Rich Wainwright. I want you to know I'm truly sorry for the loss you and your family suffered. I obviously didn't know Tony, but from all I've read he sounded like a fine man. He certainly displayed exemplary leadership at BioDawn. He seemed to be on top of everything."

"Yes—" She paused and breathed steadily in and out, as if pondering what to say next.

Finally she said, "Maybe too much so."

He waited, not wanting to prompt, not wanting to disrupt whatever she was struggling with. It apparently was something other than, "How's the life insurance claim coming?"

After several moments, she expelled a long breath and said, "I'm not sure the plane crash was an accident. Tony said there were some things going on at BioDawn . . ." Her words trailed off abruptly, but just as quickly she resumed speaking, moving the conversation in a different direction. "Could we meet for lunch, Mr. Wainwright? I'm uncomfortable talking about this on the phone. Maybe a little frightened, too. Look, when I tell you what I know, which may not be much, but probably enough to raise some eyebrows, I want you to see me, look me in the eye. So you'll know you're not dealing with some grief-stricken, whacko conspiracy theorist. Would that be okay?"

Richard realized his left hand was aching. He had a death grip on the telephone receiver. He attempted to relax. "Mrs. Scarelli, I'd be more than willing to look you in the eye and listen to what you have to say. I'll have my assistant, Ms. Mierczak, set up a reservation for us tomorrow and get back in touch with you."

"Thank you, Mr. Wainwright, thank you so much. I know I maybe should have taken this to the police. But I really wanted to discuss what I know, what Tony told me, with someone in the company first. Someone who could be very objective. I need my concerns validated."

Richard said he understood and hung up. He spun his chair around and stared out the window. He flexed his left hand. It continued to throb.

He sensed Anneliese's presence, Carolina jasmine in a soft afternoon, even before she spoke.

"Sir," she said.

He swiveled to face her. "Yes, Anneliese?"

In the mottled late-day sunlight filtering through his office, her face appeared flushed, a rosy tint beneath a flawless Mediterranean complexion. She brushed a tumble of dark brown hair out of her eyes as she approached his desk.

"Is there anything else I can do for you before I go?" she said.

"Just a couple of things." He asked her to make lunch reservations and contact Mrs. Scarelli. Then he said, "The building behind the Cyclone fence—nobody briefed me on what goes on in there. Is there any paperwork on it? Project reports? Financials?"

She shrugged. "I'll check. I really don't know anything about it. 'Close-hold,' I think, was the term used to describe it. Only the senior executives in the company were involved."

"And they're all . . . deceased."

"Yes."

Deceased. Accidentally or deliberately? He wasn't sure. The rational part of his brain, the part he knew he should pay attention to, told him to back off, let this go, stop playing detective. But he couldn't. It wasn't in his genes to be a spectator or an uninvolved bystander.

If he could probe just a bit more deeply, learn a smidgen more, garner a piece of evidence, he might be able to enlist help: the FBI, police, a private investigator, whatever seemed appropriate. But first he needed to talk to Mrs. Scarelli to find out what she knew, and he needed to uncover some documentation on the mysterious blockhouse project.

"See what you can dig up," he said to Anneliese.

"I think there are some locked file cabinets that were taken out of your office—your predecessor's office—after the accident and put in a storage room. I'll see if I have a key for them."

Richard checked his wristwatch. "It's late," he said. "Go home. Tackle it tomorrow."

She nodded.

"Thanks for your help today."

She winked at him, turned and walked toward the door. Over her shoulder she said, "It's my job to help; to keep you out of trouble."

Really? He smiled at her.

Richard switched on his desk lamp. He'd decided to stay late, going over the financials of BioDawn one more time. His first pass through them had indicated a fiscally healthy company, solidly in the black, but something hadn't seemed quite right. He hadn't had time to make a more detailed examination, but now, in the solitude that descends on most office buildings after hours, he'd be able to analyze the balance sheets more closely.

The keys on his calculator clicked softly as he totaled up the profits project by project. *There it is. Jumps right out.* The total came out to far less than the profit listed as the corporate bottom line. By about 10 million dollars. Somebody cooking the books? He didn't think so. In terms of risk-reward, something that small and that obvious probably wouldn't be worth it. Ten million. Small potatoes in the garden of corporate greed. Had he missed something? He went back over his work. The figures checked out. An accounting error? Again, he doubted it. A professional accountant would never let something like that slip by.

A soft rap on his door broke his concentration. He looked up. Anneliese stepped into the office. She had several file folders tucked under her arm.

"What happened to 'it's late, go home'?" Richard asked.

"Work to be done," she said. "Besides, I don't leave until the boss does."

"Then I'm afraid you'll have to write off prime-time television for the next six or seven months." He looked at the folders she carried. "What have you got?"

With the practiced walk of a model, one foot placed gracefully in front of the other, she glided around the desk and stood next to him. He looked up as she bent to place the folders on his desk. He felt the warmth of her body. Her breast brushed his face. The touch seemed to linger just an instant too long. His pulse quickened, a frisson of craving sweeping through him. She stepped back without acknowledging the encounter. But her eyes suggested she was very much aware of it. He looked away.

"A contract, project reports and cash flow data," she said, "I think for whatever kind of work is being carried out behind the fence. You asked, remember?"

He nodded. "Thank you. Where were they?"

"Stuck in the back of a file cabinet. I had to paw through quite a few drawers before I found them."

He stood and faced her. "Anneliese, go home. That's an order. I'm going to be here quite awhile longer going over this stuff. You've gone above and beyond already. Home." He pointed at the door.

"You sound like a soldier."

"Four years in the Marines."

"You can take a man out of the Marines, but you can't . . . well, you know the rest. Can I get anything else for you before I go?"

"No. Oh . . . do you need to be escorted out?"

"A security guard will walk me to my car." She reached out and touched his arm. "I don't want to find you asleep at your desk when I come in tomorrow morning."

"You won't. Good night, Anneliese."

After she left, he thumbed idly through the folders she'd delivered. He still sensed her touch on his cheek. Again, a ripple of guilt darted through his psyche, as though his reaction to another woman's sexuality somehow shattered the bond of trust he and Karen had had. Yes, Karen was dead. But their bond, even now, seemed transcendental, inviolate, eternal.

He wasn't immune to erotic arousal, but after seventeen years of loving—deeply loving—the same woman, to be attracted to another, no matter how superficial or transient, felt essentially, adulterous.

Lightning flickered outside. Large raindrops splattered against the window. A long, rolling peal of thunder shook the building. He opened the top folder of the stack.

He finished his work sometime after nine o'clock. He sat quietly for a while, thinking about Karen, about Anneliese and the reaction she had ignited, and about where that reaction had led: back to Marty De la Serna. Strange. *How'd that happen?*

He'd lost track of Marty, but had read, perhaps in an alumni magazine, or heard, maybe through a mutual acquaintance, that she was a minister—a minister, of all things—in Atlanta. *Well* . . . He found a phone book in the credenza. Yes, she was listed. Senior Minister, Community United Methodist Church. Somewhere nearby, he judged. *Perhaps if I have time* . . .

He left the building and stepped into the clutching humidity of the night. The rain had ceased, leaving only a diaphanous mist hanging over the office park, giving it the look of a damp Scottish moor. Sporadic lightning illuminated a distant horizon, though Richard wasn't sure which one. He hadn't yet established his sense of direction here.

A cacophonous chorus—pianissimo—of chirps, hums and croaks filled his ears. The hidden choir fascinated Richard. It was hard to believe so many tiny creatures sustained their existence in a burgeoning urban environment. He stepped in a puddle, and a startled frog long-jumped out of harm's way.

He reached his car and placed his briefcase on the ground beside it. He stood listening to the night music while he reviewed what he'd learned the past few hours. Whatever work was going on in the blockhouse was off the books, yet generating millions of dollars per year in income. It apparently was a military contract let by the United States Army, but there was a singular lack of details. No work descriptions, no schedules, no contacts. Curious. Not even a phone number.

And the payments were coming from a bank in the Cayman Islands. Since when does the U.S. military make payments to a contractor from an offshore bank? Some sort of classified project? Off the books not only for BioDawn, but perhaps for certain oversight elements of the federal government? Richard decided he'd turned up more questions than answers. Well, he'd get to the bottom of it tomorrow. He'd pay the windowless building a visit and find out for himself what was going on. BioDawn was his command, his responsibility, and he sure as hell was going to know what he was captaining.

He picked up his briefcase and unlocked his car. He glanced at the blockhouse. Lit by floodlights reflecting off a thin layer of fog, it appeared to be almost floating. Away from the building, along the fence line, a flash of motion caught his eye, and he shifted his gaze. In the shadows between the bright smudges of light, and partially obscured by the mist, he barely made out a figure. At first he couldn't tell which way it was facing, but as he watched, the faint red glow of a cigarette traced an upward arc. Whoever it was was facing outward. *Watching me? The same person I saw from my office this afternoon?* He shrugged it off and climbed into his car.

Sudden movement adjacent to the Mini startled him. Someone yanked open the passenger-side door. A lithe, attractive woman slid into the seat next to him. The Mini's interior light illuminated her impeccable attire: a short-sleeved, Ralph Lauren blouse; dark slacks; bronze sandals. With spiky blond hair bearing frosted highlights, dangly earrings, and a gold safety pin piercing her right eyebrow, she could have been a rock star. But the well-toned muscles of her tanned arms suggested she was something else. Richard's left hand dropped to the door handle. Picking up on his reflexive reaction, the woman smiled at him, an attempt at reassurance, perhaps; but her smile was devoid of warmth. Cold. Dead.

He fought to recover from the start she'd given him and forced himself to return her smile. "Good evening," he said, struggling to conceal his confusion and gain control of the situation. Being on the defense was not a role he played well or even accepted.

Without responding to his greeting, the woman reached into her purse and withdrew a small object. Before his brain could register what it was, she pressed a button on the side of it, and a black, spear-pointed blade sprang out. A knife. She lowered it into her lap and looked at it admiringly, as other women might a string of Tahitian pearls. "In case you're wondering," she said, "it's a Microtech Combat Talon. I'm very good with it."

Chapter Six

NORTH METRO ATLANTA
MONDAY, AUGUST 19

Richard stared at the knife, knowing from his time in the Marine Corps exactly what it was—a killer's weapon. Its slightly curved blade, short and serrated, enhanced its slicing ability. "You want the car?" he asked.

"This little shit box? A strange choice for a man of your stature."

"My stature?"

"A high-profile CEO."

My first day on the job; what does she know about my profile? "Maybe you shouldn't stereotype CEOs," he said. His gaze remained fixed on the knife. His heart rate ratcheted up ever so slightly.

"I would have thought a Maybach, perhaps, not a Mini," she said.

"Okay, not my car then. My wallet? My briefcase?" He reached toward the rear seat.

"Hands on the steering wheel, Herr Wainwright," she snapped, her words wrapped in a guttural German accent. She lifted the Combat Talon from her lap.

He placed his hands where she told him. Quickly.

"How do you know my name?" he asked.

"I know a lot about you," she said. "Perhaps more than you do." She flashed her icy smile again.

He moved his gaze to her face, attempting to gauge her intentions, decipher the reason for her presence. But there was nothing to be read, nothing being offered but her arctic beauty and an implicit threat. His experience in the boardroom had taught him that humor can often disarm a tense situation. It seemed worth a try.

"I suppose you're not here to ask me to dinner and a movie," he said. The interior lighting of the Mini dimmed.

"My, you're a quick study, aren't you?" Her hand moved so rapidly he didn't see the blade. He merely heard it plunge into the seat between his legs, inches from his crotch. He froze, stunned by the speed of her action. He was even more dumbfounded by what she did next. She leaned over and kissed him lightly on the cheek.

"You're a handsome man," she said, surprisingly softly. "Under different circumstances dinner and a movie and maybe something else—" with her free hand she stroked the inside of his thigh "—might have been, shall we say, enjoyable. But that's not why I'm here. I came only to deliver a message. And a warning. One that will keep you alive." She withdrew the knife. "You brought your golf clubs?"

He nodded, afraid to speak, afraid his voice would betray the fear festering in his gut.

"Use them. Often. Don't get overly curious about what goes on at BioDawn. Your reputation precedes you. You're known as a highly competent, hands-on executive. Your integrity is unquestioned. If you have a fault, it's to micromanage, to get too involved in corporate operations. That won't serve you well here. Quite the opposite. It will get you killed."

A pickup truck with roof-mounted flashing orange lights paused behind the Mini.

"Corporate security," the woman said. "Why don't you just give them a friendly wave, let them know everything is okay." A command, not a suggestion.

Richard turned and lifted his hand, a friendly gesture. The driver of the pickup flashed its headlights and departed.

The woman raised the knife and swept it slowly back and forth in front of Richard's face. A metronome of menace.

"All you have to do for the next few months is smile, back slap, nod wisely. Grip and grin, in the American vernacular. Let things run as they are. Let the board of directors do its work selecting a permanent chief. Before you know it, your job as temporary CEO will be over, and you'll be back in Oregon hunting and fishing."

"I don't hunt," he said, relieved his voice didn't squeak.

She retracted the blade of her knife. "I'll bet you could learn."

"Who are you?"

"The who isn't necessary. The what is." Her eyes, their green depths bottomless and vacant, focused on his.

"Then what are you?"

Again the smile. It spread across her face slowly, as if being painted on.

"An intimidator," she answered. "I make sure things get done." She patted his cheek lightly, almost sisterly, then once more let her hand drop to his crotch. "Remember what I told you. If I come calling again, I won't kiss you, I'll kill you." She brought her face close to his, her warm breath an antithesis to her demeanor. There was no odor of cigarettes, so she wasn't the person he'd seen behind the fence.

"No. Strike that," she continued. "I won't kill you. I'll merely—how should I say it?—'customize' your manhood. For men, I find that a much more potent deterrent."

He tried to speak, but his throat had constricted into a paralyzed knot.

The woman waited, then tapped him on the nose with the blade of her knife. "What?" she said. "You wanted to say something?"

He composed himself. "How about I just go home, back to Oregon?"

She shook her head. "Won't work. You're needed here; at least the illusion of your competence and integrity is. If you decide to say *Auf Wiedersehen*, I'll make certain it's the last time you do. Humor me, follow orders. Keep yourself out of Eunuchs Anonymous." She laughed lightly.

She put the knife back into her purse, then, maintaining her gaze on Richard, withdrew a small photograph and rested it against her chest. "One more thing," she said. "Don't contact the police or FBI. Don't seek help. Because if things become, shall we say, too difficult for me, they'll become unbearable for you, even if you're beyond my reach." She showed him the photograph, holding it near the windshield so the parking lot lighting illuminated it. "There are other targets, you see."

A cryogenic shock wave almost stopped his heart. The photo was of Jason, his younger brother. Wheat-colored hair tumbling over his round, blue eyes; his lips curled into an almost perpetual smile. Carefree and compassionate, always acting the big brother, not the little brother. Richard could still feel Jason's arms around him at Karen's funeral comforting him as he shook in uncontrollable waves of grief. "Don't worry, Dickie," he'd said, "I'll take care of you. I love you, bro'."

Richard struggled to breathe, to catch his breath. He glared at the woman, but knew it was an effete rebuke.

"Your hands are on a dead man's switch," she said. "If I disappear, so does your brother. I'm not operating alone." She slipped from the car, slammed the door and strode toward a double-parked SUV.

Richard remained with his hands locked on the steering wheel of the Mini for a full minute after she departed, too rattled to even register the color of her vehicle, let alone its make or license plate. Finally, he released his grip on the wheel, leaned back, calmed himself and attempted to analyze what had just happened.

He'd been warned off, under penalty of death or disfigurement, or a similar fate for his brother, of doing anything at BioDawn other than being a figurehead CEO. A corporate Buddha squatting behind a desk. He didn't have the option of leaving, didn't have the option of seeking help. He recalled the lyrics to a song he'd once heard someplace: You can't win, you can't break even, you can't even quit the game.

What the hell have I walked into?

He considered the possibility the assault was a practical joke commissioned by Ned, but Ned had never done anything like that before and had no reason to now. The incident certainly wasn't a case of mistaken identity. The woman had addressed him by name, had his brother's picture.

But assuming the threat was for real, why alert him to the fact there was something for him to be suspicious of at BioDawn in the first place? Why not just let him have free rein until he stumbled onto whatever he wasn't supposed to discover, if indeed he did, and then go into the saber-rattling routine? It seemed as if his lady intimidator, as she called herself, had gotten her cart before the horse.

Well, no matter. He was not by nature a passive spectator. He hadn't made a professional name for himself by being detached, aloof and hands-off. There apparently was something dark festering within the walls of BioDawn, and the lady's warning had served only to ignite his intrinsic curiosity. His response, he understood, was preordained. He knew full well he was hard-wired to do exactly what he had been warned not to: Immerse himself in company business. But—memo to self—very, very carefully.

He started the Mini and, on constant alert for other intruders—silly, now that the horse was out of the barn—returned to his apartment. He considered calling the police, but decided against it, for he wasn't the only one who had been threatened. His brother Jason, in faraway Oregon, had been thrown into the mix, too.

Richard retrieved his cell phone and called Jason. When his brother answered, they exchanged small talk briefly about the weather, University of Oregon football and the price of gas. Then Richard explained why he was in Atlanta, but left out any mention of blondes with knives and airplane crashes.

"Hey, Jason," Richard said, trying to sound casual, "you haven't had any strange phone calls recently, have you?"

"Strange?"

"Well, like from people you didn't know, or maybe hang-ups, like someone checking to see if you're home but not wanting to identify themselves?"

Jason answered with a raspy chuckle. "You mean other than from some guy in Nigeria wanting $600 so he can free up a million-dollar trust fund a long-lost great uncle left me?"

"Yeah. Other than that."

"No. Why?"

"And no one hanging around your apartment or office that looked, well, suspicious or out of place?"

"No, just the usual guys in overcoats and no pants. You're starting to weird me out, bro'. What's up?"

"Nothing, really. I had some concerns that government investigators doing a background check on me might be looking a little too hard at other members of my family. None of their business."

"Background check?"

"I'm taking over a corporation that does some work for the Department of Defense."

"Oh. Well . . . if it's about that pedophilia charge—"

"Jason, cut it out." His brother obviously wasn't taking this seriously, which was fine. That suggested he hadn't been alarmed by anything or anyone, which in turn indicated he probably wasn't being watched or monitored. On the other hand, if he were under surveillance by pros, he most likely wouldn't be aware of it.

"Hey, Dickie, if anyone contacts me, I'll let you know. Okay?"

"Don't worry, kid. Everything is fine," Richard lied. "I'll be in touch."

He hung up, stood and swiveled his head from side to side in a futile attempt to relieve the band of pain tightening around his neck and shoulders.

Sure, everything is fine.

NORTH METRO ATLANTA
TUESDAY, AUGUST 20

Richard wheeled his Mini into the BioDawn parking lot the following morning shortly after sunrise. Only a half-dozen cars populated the lot. None looked similar to the vehicle his blonde assailant had driven. A green pickup truck, white block lettering, SECURITY, on its door, patrolled the far end of the parking area.

Richard parked his car in its designated slot and stepped out into the already-stifling dawn. Instead of going directly to his office, however, he walked along a winding concrete path toward the blockhouse. He reached a gate in the surrounding fence. A sign warned that no visitors or unauthorized personnel were allowed entry. Richard decided he was neither and withdrew the ID/key card he had been given the previous day and ran it through the electronic reader. Nothing happened. No beeps, no clicks, no green light. He tried again. Still nothing. He heard footsteps behind him.

"Sir?"

Richard turned quickly, tensing. A slender black man with a lean, borzoi-like face and wearing a white shirt with a badge, approached him. He was unarmed. The green pickup idled in the lot behind him.

"Sir, only a few people have access to this facility. Dr. Gonzales and maybe a couple of dozen others."

"I'm the new CEO here, Richard Wainwright." Richard extended his ID card toward the guard.

The man ignored it. "Yes, sir, I recognize you, I've been briefed. I'm Ralph Pepperill, the overnight security supervisor."

Richard nodded his acknowledgement. *Big help you were last night.* The two men shook hands.

"You'll need to see the corporate security manager about getting a clearance so you can be granted access here," Pepperill said.

"A security clearance?"

"Yes, sir. This is a military-sponsored project, and only people with the proper clearance are allowed inside the fence."

"I see. Well, I'll look into it." But he had no intention of waiting for the government to grind through a background check and grant him a clearance. He knew that could take months.

"Let me know if I can help," Pepperill said.

"I will. Oh, by the way, who is Dr. Gonzales?"

"Alano Gonzales. He's the head honcho. I really don't know much about him. A brilliant man, I understand. He keeps pretty much to himself. Scurries in and out most of the time without so much as a wave or nod. Kind of like those big ol' rats you sometimes see near the tracks in MARTA stations." He chuckled at his own simile.

"MARTA?"

"Sorry. The Metropolitan Atlanta Rapid Transit Authority."

Richard nodded. "But Dr. Gonzales doesn't *look* like a rat, does he?"

"Oh, no, sir. I didn't mean to say that, it's just that he kind of behaves that way, kind of . . ." He searched for the right word.

"Furtively?"

Pepperill shrugged.

Not the right word, or not sure of the word? "Okay, Mr. Pepperill, thanks for the information. And one more question, does Dr. Gonzales often work late at night?"

"He's usually here until well after dark, sir."

Chapter Seven

NORTH METRO ATLANTA
TUESDAY, AUGUST 20

Dr. Arthur Willand awoke with a start. *No, no, don't let it be, dear Jesus, please don't let it be.* He had broken his own ad hoc rule and slipped out of the close-monitoring environment of the hospital to come home and catch a few hours rest. But now he was wide awake, writhing in agony. It was as though someone had twisted an auger into the top of his skull; as if his head, neck and shoulders had been compressed in a hydraulic vise.

After the call from the CDC warning of a serious problem, he'd quickly read up on Ebola hemorrhagic fever. He knew the early symptoms. Severe frontal and temporal headache, generalized aches and pains, maybe a fever. He'd learned the virus was transmitted through the blood or bodily fluids of an infected person. He tried to remember if any blood, vomit or diarrhea from Mr. Gullison or his wife had splattered into his eyes, mouth or nose. No, he was certain. He hadn't pricked himself with an infected needle or nicked himself with a scalpel. And he didn't recall that the virus could be spread through the air. But . . .

He pushed himself out of bed and stumbled into the bathroom. From the floor below, he heard his wife puttering in the kitchen. She had strict orders to keep her distance. He stared into the mirror, into crimson looking-glass eyes. His heart fluttered, and he took a step back, drew a deep breath. No. Not right. Too early for bleeding under the conjunctivae. That, he knew, should come later, not at the onset of the disease. *I'm okay.* It was just that he hadn't had more than three hours sleep in the last twenty-four. *No wonder my eyes look like Bloody Marys.* And the headache—probably just tension induced. *God knows, I'm under enough pressure.*

He walked back to the bedroom and sat on the edge of the bed. His heart raced, betraying his reasoned conclusions, re-igniting his terror. Sometimes you can know too much, he thought, just too damned much.

Dr. Willand stood. "I won't die that way," he whispered. Clinging to the edge of his bed and then his dresser for support, he shuffled to his closet. He extracted a lockbox from the rear of a shelf above the hangar rack. He punched a simple combination into a numerical lock. The lid of the box sprang open. He withdrew a Smith & Wesson .38-caliber handgun. He popped the cylinder open. Empty. A container of shells was tucked into the corner of the box. He picked it up. It felt almost full. He replaced it. He put the gun back into the box, locked it and stuffed it back on the shelf.

He forced himself to return to his earlier deduction, though mired in denial it might be: *It's just a tension headache.* He re-entered the bathroom and washed down a couple of Tylenol with a handful of water from the faucet. After rinsing his face with a damp washcloth he walked unsteadily downstairs, called goodbye to his wife and left for the hospital.

With the air conditioning in his car on full blast and the Tylenol doing its thing, he felt better by the time he reached North Georgia Regional. He entered the ER and spotted Doris, the head nurse. She smiled when she saw him, but her expression changed as he approached her.

"You look awful, sir. Are you sure you're all right?"

"I'm just tired. Too much going on, too little sleep."

She took a half step back from him. "I don't know, doctor. I think you should—"

". . . see a doctor? Doris, I'm fine. I'll catch up on my sleep tonight, and I'll be as fresh and eager as a new intern tomorrow." He almost believed the words himself. "Get me up to speed here. Have there been any other admissions showing signs of hemorrhagic fever?"

"No, but . . ." She lowered her gaze to the floor.

"But what?"

"Marie Coughlin and Lizzy DiNero called in sick this morning. Their symptoms sounded like HF."

Dr. Willand closed his eyes and tipped his head back. "No," he muttered, "no." Marie and Lizzy were two of the nurses who had attended David Gullison when he was first admitted. "Get 'em back into the ER as soon as you can. As patients."

Doris nodded.

"And how about Mrs. Gullison? What's her status?"

Doris kept her distance as she answered. "Not good." She shook her head. "We've been unable to control her vomiting and diarrhea. And she's showing signs of renal and liver failure. The saddest part is there isn't much we can do for her."

"I know. I know," Dr. Willand said softly.

"Can you think of anything? Anything at all?" Doris's entreaty seemed edged in fear.

"Say a prayer, I guess." *For me, too.* He brushed a patina of perspiration from his forehead.

In his office, Richard buzzed Anneliese on the intercom. Even through the tinny system, her voice seemed infused with a musical lilt when she answered. He still sensed her breast brushing his cheek the previous night and struggled to fend off his prurient reaction to it. "Get in touch with Dr. Gonzales, please," he said. "Tell him I'd like to meet with him this morning."

"Yes, sir. Oh, and sir, I've set up a lunch reservation for you and Mrs. Scarelli at a place called Cortez's. Noon. I'll give you directions when you're ready."

A few minutes later Anneliese rapped softly on his door and stuck her head into the office. "Sorry, sir. Dr. Gonzales is out of town until next Monday or Tuesday."

"Do you have his itinerary?"

"No, sir. He typically operates on his own."

"So I've gathered." Richard leaned back in his chair and studied Anneliese's face for a moment, looking for some sign that last night's encounter had been something other than incidental. There was none. He motioned for her to take a seat at the conference table that abutted his desk.

"I understand you don't know anything about Dr. Gonzales' work," he said, "but do you know anything about Dr. Gonzales himself? Have you overheard any stories? Picked up any rumors?"

"Not much," she said. She crossed her legs, allowing her skirt to edge up. "I've met him once or twice. Friendly enough, but he's an odd duck, a loner. I think he might be from South America, but I'm not sure. He speaks excellent English. I heard he already had a top secret clearance when he arrived here."

Richard raised his eyebrows. "It's kind of unusual for a foreigner to be running a classified military project, isn't it?"

Anneliese shrugged. "He's a naturalized citizen. And I would think he's been thoroughly vetted. I guess the project he's working on is pretty important. I assume it was set up to piggyback on BioDawn's capabilities."

"That's probably not the only reason." Richard recalled the large sums of money flowing in from the Caymans.

"I'm sorry I couldn't be of more help, sir."

"Every little piece of info I can pick up helps. Thanks. And if you have the directions to Cortez's, I'll take a look at them now."

Richard arrived at Cortez's, an upscale Caribbean-Mexican-themed restaurant, about fifteen minutes before noon. He judged it would be easier for Mrs. Scarelli to spot him rather than vice versa. He peeked into the restaurant's interior. Broad fans made of woven palm fronds and attached to long rods swept back and forth just below the ceiling. The usual buzz and muted clatter of a busy luncheon establishment was augmented by soft background music. A good environment for a private conversation.

He returned to the restaurant's alcove and seated himself, watching the lunchtime crowd stream in: business people from professional offices, and clerks and shoppers from a nearby mall. He eyed the women in particular, looking for a "plumpish middle-aged brunette"—Mrs. Scarelli's words.

In a way, he dreaded meeting her, having to look into the face of someone who'd lost a spouse, see the pain in her eyes, hear the despair in her voice, sense the hollowness of her soul. He never knew what to say, how to reach out to such people. Much as his friends had not known how to comfort him after Karen died. For many of them, he knew, it was easier just to stay away.

As he sat, he remembered waiting for Karen one afternoon, maybe a decade ago, maybe a hundred years ago, in a shabby little seafood restaurant on the Oregon coast. Shabby, but given to superb food—grilled Chinook salmon, stuffed Dungeness crab, steamed razor clams—and prices to match. They were in Cannon Beach, once nothing more than a few weather-beaten buildings, now a crowded town of overpriced galleries, gift shops and craft stores.

They'd spent the morning prowling the main street, admiring paintings of frothing oceans and rocky capes; decorations crafted of seashells, bone and driftwood; and handmade furniture hewn from indigenous spruce and fir. They'd laughed at the T-shirts and baseball hats available from the Bite Me Bait Company. And decided they didn't have a clue how they might assemble a three-tailed kite that looked like a Spanish galleon.

They had separated for awhile, each exploring stores of their own interest after agreeing to meet at the seafood place. Karen arrived late, clutching several shopping bags. There was a crowd of people waiting to be seated, but Richard already had claimed a small table. He waved at Karen.

Karen, still turning heads in her forties. Tall, tan, fit. She took care of herself, not the bank account of a plastic surgeon. Her blond hair, French-braided, framed a face yet to be visited by the dreaded crow's feet. Blue sunglasses hid big, brown eyes. A handsome young man in his twenties wearing a University of Washington sweatshirt and cut-off jeans walked over to her. Karen and the young man engaged in an earnest conversation; she laughing, he clutching his chest as though having a heart attack. Together, they walked over to Richard.

"I apologize for hitting on your wife," the man said. "But I thought maybe if I shook hands with the luckiest guy in the world, some of his luck might rub off on me." They shook hands.

Karen smiled and said, "It's more than luck, junior. He's good. That's why I love him."

After her sudden suitor departed, Karen pulled a baseball hat from one of her bags. "Here," she said, "entirely inappropriate for a CEO." BITE ME in big letters on the front of it, BAIT COMPANY in tiny letters underneath.

"Entirely," he said. "I love it." He slapped it on.

It remained there the rest of the day. It was the only thing he wore that evening as he dived under the covers of their bed, the slider of their condo wide open to the thundering Pacific surf and chilly, drifting mist. They made love to the rhythm of the swells, a slow wash of passion building to a crescendo, exploding like breakers crashing on a beach, then sliding peacefully away, a receding sheen of sea foam, to return again.

He looked at his watch. A quarter after. Mrs. Scarelli was late. He stood and paced the alcove, thoughts of Karen trailing after him as though tethered to his soul like a numinous anchor.

By 12:30, he grew apprehensive. Had he shown up at the wrong restaurant? Had there been a mix-up on the time? He called Anneliese on his cell phone. Yes, he had the location and time right. No, Mrs. Scarelli hadn't contacted the office.

He asked for her phone number and called it. An answering machine with a man's voice—her late husband's?—informed him he'd reached the Scarelli residence, please leave a message. He didn't. At 12:45 he called Anneliese again. She still hadn't heard from Mrs. Scarelli.

"Get her address for me, please, Anneliese. I'm going to drive over there and make sure everything is okay."

Twenty minutes later, Richard, following the directions Anneliese had given him over the phone, turned his Mini into Mrs. Scarelli's subdivision, Appalachian Chase. It was an upscale community, not the peak of the register, but very well-to-do. Homes in the half-million-to million-dollar range, he judged. Large, neo-Southern traditional. Stone and stucco, huge decks, three-car garages. Nice, but lacking the architectural imagination and diversity found in the Northwest. A number of the houses abutted a golf course, others overlooked a lake that appeared to be of substantial size.

He wound his way along the twisting main road, one intersected by lanes, cul-de-sacs and courts. Magnolias, sweet gums and Bradford pears draped over the road, providing a verdant, sheltering canopy. Thick layers of Bermuda grass and Emerald Zoysia carpeted sprawling front yards.

Traffic along the road was sparse. Just a few kids home from school for the summer borrowing dad's BMW, one or two moms herding the family SUVs to the grocery store, a handful of repairmen and yard workers clattering along in scarred pickups and vans.

Turning left on Fox Run, he pulled up to 345, the Scarelli address, and paused at the foot of a modestly sloped driveway. He looked for signs of activity around the home. There appeared to be none. He wondered if Mrs. Scarelli had perhaps forgotten their appointment, lured instead to the mall by lady friends for lunchtime gossip over soup and sandwiches. Not likely, it seemed, considering she herself had suggested their meeting.

He drove to the top of the driveway, stopped the car and got out. The muted cries and laughter of children filled the air, probably emanating from a backyard pool farther down the street. The desultory rasp of a cicada floated by on a humid zephyr. Richard waited a moment, then strode to the beveled-glass front door and rang the doorbell. From inside came soft chiming in response. But nothing else. No sounds of movement, music or voices.

Stepping back from the door, out of the alcove that sheltered it, he examined the house. It boasted two stories and a meticulously-rendered gray flagstone exterior. Three huge picture windows, accentuated by white plantation blinds, dominated the front. Well-manicured crape myrtles, Japanese hollies, azaleas and rhododendrons stood guard along the perimeter of the home. Small, solar-powered lanterns lined the walkway from the driveway to the front door.

Richard continued listening, but heard only the frolicking children and lonely cicada. He walked back into the alcove and rang the bell again. Next door, a gasoline-engined lawnmower sputtered to life, its mechanical growl drowning out everything else. A dense growth of bushes and trees partitioned the homesites, so Richard was unable to see who might be operating the mower. Maybe a neighbor who knew something. He'd check later, if necessary.

He pressed his face against a small pane of octagonal glass in the front door, placed his hands on either side of his head, making blinders for his eyes, and tried to peer in. But the glass was too thick to allow him to see anything clearly. He stepped away and moved to what looked like a living room or family room window. To reach the window, he ducked under a crape myrtle heavy with red blossoms. In doing so, he startled a party of honey bees into hyperactivity. He sprang backward. But the bees made only diplomatic protests before buzzing off to more tranquil flora. He moved forward and once again formed blinders with his hands and pressed his nose to the window. The blinds on the interior were tilted up to ward off the afternoon sun; he couldn't see in.

Backing out from underneath the crape myrtle, he walked to the side of the house. The lot on which the home sat sloped down toward its rear, so the only windows in view were too high to reach except by ladder. He unlatched a gate in a waist-high picket fence and entered a heavily-wooded back yard. The ground was spongy and moist, and the vague odor of decaying leaves and pine needles hung in the air. At the rear of the house, a concrete patio sat underneath a wooden deck that ran half the length of the home. Sliding glass doors gave access from the house to the patio. Curtains were drawn across the sliders, so he couldn't see in. He rapped sharply on the glass and listened, but the only thing he heard was the raucous lawnmower next door. Cautiously, he tried to open the slider. Much to his relief, it didn't move.

He walked up onto the deck. Wicker furniture, two large sun umbrellas and a gas grill with more gadgets and dials than his car sat on the structure. Two sets of sliders opened onto the deck from the house. Since there were no curtains or blinds to contend with, Richard worked his way along the porch, stopping every few feet to plaster his face against the glass and stare into the interior of the home like some mid-afternoon voyeur. He could see the headlines now: Biotech CEO Arrested as Peeping Tom. But the inside of the house was dark and still. Uninhabited. He knocked on the glass and attempted to open the sliders. Neither brought results.

As he descended the steps of the deck and approached the rear of the garage, the grating roar of the lawnmower grew louder. It never seemed to fade. You'd think the guy would be pushing it around, not letting the damn thing stand in one spot. There was a door leading into the garage, and Richard tried that, too. Locked. He spotted a window and wriggled behind a holly tree to reach it. The holly's leaves bit into his face and hands. His suit jacket protected his upper body, but he was paying a price for wearing it, sweating profusely. He stood on his tiptoes and looked through the window. There didn't seem to be a car missing. He could see a Lexus, a Mercedes and a new Volkswagen Beetle.

Oh, shit. He realized suddenly why the mower hadn't moved. Too late. He whirled.

Chapter Eight

NORTH METRO ATLANTA
TUESDAY, AUGUST 20

Richard's spiky-haired parking lot greeter from his first day on the job stood only five feet away. Using the noise of the lawnmower as cover, she had crept up behind him. She held the black-bladed Microtech knife low, near her right hip, ready to slash. Her left arm was cocked in a defensive position across her abdomen. Crouched slightly, she glared at Richard with the intensity of a tigress about to charge.

Richard eased himself out from behind the holly. He fixed his gaze on the knife, ready to spin and dodge if the weapon were thrust at him.

"The intimidation business a little slow?" he asked. "A few extra bucks helping Hispanics cut grass?"

The woman managed a thin smile. "Other way around. I give them a few extra bucks, and they're off like the Road Runner for a long lunch at Taco Bell." She retreated a step or two and motioned for Richard to follow. "I take back what I said yesterday morning."

"Which part of what you said?"

Richard attempted to run through a mental checklist of the military hand-to-hand combat moves he once knew, but it was a futile effort. The list was tattered and incoherent, a victim of time and disuse. Besides, he realized he was no match for a professional killer, which this woman obviously was.

"The part about you being a quick study. I tell you not to get too curious, to head for the golf course, lay low, and here you are peeking through windows in broad daylight. Looking for a little afternoon delight?"

"Looking for Mrs. Scarelli."

"A married woman. Shame on you, Herr Wainwright. You could have done better with me." She brought her left arm up and casually unbuttoned the top of her blouse, exposing a deep, tanned cleavage. She stepped closer to Richard. "See what you missed." She moved the knife back and forth in a slow, threatening motion. "Too bad. Next thing you know, your voice is three octaves higher. And nookie will be something you only dream about. Men can be such slow learners."

Richard decided he had one chance. One moment. The woman had moved her defensive arm out of position. Overmatched or not, he would not go gently. He launched a furious kick at the knife. The weapon flipped into the air, and the woman staggered backward, cursing. He propelled himself forward; a defensive end sacking a quarterback. An explosion of breath burst from her lungs as they both went down. He ended up on top of her, his knee in her gut. He drew his fist back for a *coup de grâce* to her face but wasn't quick enough. In an overwhelming blur of motion, she was on top of him, straddling his prone body.

The roar of the mower abruptly ceased, and the ambient cadence of a quiet afternoon in suburbia returned. "Well," the woman panted, "Mexicans back from lunch. Your lucky day. A little awkward for slicing and dicing now. Too many witnesses."

She ground her pelvis slowly against his. "And maybe you *wouldn't* have done better with me than Mrs. Scarelli." She leaned forward until her mouth was inches from his face. "I have a weakness for sex. I have a penchant for killing. It makes for a strange combination. More than one of my . . . acquaintances, shall we say . . . was coming and going at the same time."

He stared at her, her words not quite registering.

"Think about it," she said.

"Jesus."

She stood, brushed herself off, retrieved her knife. "Your lucky day," she said again. She extended her hand, offering to help Richard up.

He knew the battle was in abeyance, but refused to accept her assistance. He scrambled to his feet on his own. "Mrs. Scarelli," he demanded, now more angry than intimidated, "what happened to Mrs. Scarelli?" He took a step toward his attacker.

She backed off slightly, raised the knife. "You really are *ein Dummkopf*, aren't you? Why won't you give it up? Stop poking around?" She locked her gaze on his, the victor staring down the vanquished. "If I'm forced to, shall we say, reiterate my position, you won't have a fighting chance. Next time you'll never see me coming."

She lowered the knife, retracted the blade and slipped the weapon into a pocket of her slacks. She started to walk away, but turned and answered the question he'd asked originally. "I know you won't believe me, but I have no idea what happened to Mrs. Scarelli. Like you, I'm just a hired hand."

"And still no business card?"

"Veronica von Stade," she said. "Interpol has files on me. But don't believe everything you read. Just believe in me. I do what I'm contracted to do, and I do it very well. Remember that if nothing else."

"Emergency room, please. This is Dr. Adams at the CDC." Alnour Barashi waited for his call to North Georgia Regional Hospital to be forwarded.

"E. R.," a voice responded.

"Yes, hello," Barashi said. "This is Dr. Isaiah Adams at the CDC. I'm following up on some earlier contacts we had regarding a patient who was admitted to North Georgia a day or two ago, a Mr. David Gullison." Barashi tried to sound confident and convincing. He was only assuming that North Georgia and the CDC had had contact by now. Isaiah Adams was a name he'd selected at random off a CDC roster.

"A moment, Dr. Adams. Let me get Dr. Wells, I believe he talked with the CDC earlier."

Dr. Wells came on the line.

"I hate to bother you again," Barashi said, "but there's been some confusion here at the CDC regarding the status of Mr. Gullison. You know how it is in government bureaucracies, one hand doesn't know what the other—"

"No problem, my friend, no problem. I know what you're talking about. Spent six years in the Air Force. It's a goddamned wonder we ever won any wars. Yeah, poor Gullison, passed away yesterday." He lowered his voice. "So you guys think it might be Ebola. Jesus, talk about gettin' our floppers caught in the ringer. How on earth do you think Gullison got Ebola? Or vice versa."

"That's what we're working on. Unfortunately, there may have been others. An Alan McCarthy. Did you have an Alan McCarthy admitted there?"

"I'll check, hold on."

Barashi drummed his fingers idly on his desk. So Gullison was dead. Good news. The virus hadn't lost any of its virulence in the test attack, a clever effort if he did say so himself. Knowing that Gullison and McCarthy would be the first golfers on their course last Thursday as they always were, Barashi had tethered a balloon filled with the viral pathogen to a bush near the third tee, driven off a short distance in a golf cart, then burst the balloon with a pellet gun as the two golfers approached.

The airborne virus had worked to lethal perfection. *"Allahu Akbar,"* Barashi said softly. Allah is Most Great.

Wells came back on the line. "No McCarthy here," he said, "but you knew about Gullison's wife?"

"His wife?"

"She's been admitted with HF symptoms. Looks like she might have been infected by her husband."

A wave of euphoria washed over Barashi. "I'm sorry to hear that," he said. "What's her status?"

"Terminal, I'm afraid. Oh, and I understand there may have been a gentleman admitted to St. Joseph's with HF symptoms. Maybe that's your McCarthy guy."

"Yes, could be. I'll check. Thanks."

Barashi hung up. *"Allahu Akbar,"* he repeated. In only a matter of days, 9/11 and the destruction of the Twin Towers would be rivaled by a new terrorist attack.

"My," Anneliese said, "did you and Mrs. Scarelli get into a little tiff ?" A bemused look graced her face as she stood close to Richard and brushed the scratches on his face with her fingers. Her touch seemed more suggestive than healing.

"I didn't find Mrs. Scarelli," he said. He peeled off his suit jacket and strode into his office. He sat heavily in the chair behind his desk. Anneliese disappeared briefly, then entered the office and walked around behind him.

"Here," she said, "this will make you feel better." She tilted his head back and, using a moist washcloth, rubbed the red marks on his face in soft, easy motions.

She eased the back of his head into her cleavage, resting it between the firmness of her breasts. Her perfume, sweet and narcotic, beckoned him with a primitive call, a siren song of Lorelei. He sensed in her rhythmic breathing something urgent yet suppressed. Something waiting to be discovered, ignited. A combustible secret. It excited him, but at the same time concerned him, though he couldn't articulate the reason. He merely knew it was there.

Anneliese leaned forward, drawing his head deeper into the alluring valley of her body. "You need someone to take care of you," she whispered.

Her warm breath caressed the side of his face, and he sensed in her voice the resonance of something ancient and foreign, the echo, perhaps, of a long-lost culture. *Who are you?*

She stepped back, yet continued to stroke his face with the wash cloth.

"What happened?" she asked. "You went to Mrs. Scarelli's house, and she wasn't there?"

He gently removed her hand and washcloth from his face. "Thank you, Anneliese," he said. "You're a good nurse. But before I answer your questions, I need to sort out a few things. Give me some time. We can talk later."

Anneliese looked puzzled, perhaps a little hurt, but accepted her dismissal. "I'll be at my desk," she said.

He nodded. After she left, he did a Google search on his computer: Veronica von Stade. Several entries popped up, the most recent being a year-old newspaper article from *Die Welt*. He struggled to translate the piece—his college German was rusty—but managed to get the gist of it. In Europe, von Stade was part legend, part myth, but no one knew how much of each. She was wanted by Interpol for questioning in a number of murders and assassinations, but had managed to elude authorities for over a decade. A female Jackal.

It was surmised that on several occasions she had used sex to lure her victims and may actually have killed at least one while having intercourse with him. *Coming and going at the same time.* Richard's chest tightened. He continued reading.

She basically was apolitical, a killer for hire. But her handiwork hadn't surfaced recently, and there was speculation she might have "retired" or been killed. *Do I have news for you.* Not much was known about her background, but investigators were fairly certain her parents had been members of the Bader-Meinhof Gang, the German terrorist organization that rose to prominence during the early 1970s.

The only photograph of her was grainy and slightly out of focus, apparently shot through a telephoto lens. It didn't look much like the blonde with spiky hair who had assaulted him, but it was hard to judge. It was an old picture. Besides, it didn't make any difference—he knew what she looked like *now.*

Richard clicked off the computer and drew a deep breath. Nothing made sense. A plane load of executives, dead. An off-the-books corporate project no one seems to know anything about. A frightened lady who schedules a meeting and disappears. A German hit woman who threatens my manhood, my life. *Jesus, Mary and Joseph.*

A soft tap on his door. Anneliese peeked in. "Did you get the phone number I texted you?"

"I haven't checked my messages lately."

"I found a telephone number in one of Mr. Arguello's files."

"Arguello, the CEO . . . former CEO?"

She nodded. "It's a number for a Colonel Landry. I don't know if it has anything to do with the project you're interested in, but . . . well, I'll let you decide."

He pulled up the message. The number carried a 678 area code, a local exchange. He thanked Anneliese and, after she left, considered his options. They were, quite simply, back off or press on. If he went for the latter, he knew he would be getting into dirty business. *Who am I kidding? Dangerous business.* The image of von Stade and her pet knife floated through his head, like detritus on the waters of an oily harbor.

And then there was Anneliese. Was she somehow part of all this, too? Or was her subtle sexual aggression genuine? He doubted it was genuine. He'd wandered into a looking-glass world shrouded in darkness, and she was somehow part of it. He didn't believe in coincidences, that this woman had become infatuated with him the minute he'd set foot in BioDawn. So, what to do? Play the smitten male, he decided; he just might find an illuminated crack in the labyrinth.

The bottom line was this: He had built a career on attacking his challenges, not letting them assault him. The stakes, to be sure, were higher now, higher than just losing his job. But with Karen gone . . .

He punched the number. The phone rang a dozen times before it was answered. "Yousamrid. Colonel Landry," a voice said.

"I'm sorry. Yousamrid?"

"USAMRIID. The U.S. Army Medical Research Institutes of Infectious Diseases. This is a branch office at Dobbins Air Reserve Base in Atlanta. Can I help you?"

"I hope so," Richard said, and explained the situation.

When he had finished, Landry said, "Yes. I heard about the plane crash. Tragic. I'm very sorry, Mr. Wainwright. And yes, BioDawn is doing work under contract to USAMRIID. But the effort is top secret. I understand that as acting CEO you'd like to have a handle on what's going on, but if you don't have a security clearance—"

"You can talk around the classified stuff. I know how it works. Look, I don't want to be a hard ass about this, Colonel, but I'm not a hands-off CEO. I want to know what's going on under my command. As a senior military officer, you can understand that. And if you can't help me, I'd consider making some phone calls to senators or representatives and voicing my concerns. But that's not the route I want to go."

Landry sighed. "No, that's not the route you want to go. I'm a busy man, Mr. Wainwright, but I'd be glad to meet with you briefly tomorrow and at least try to give you a feel for the project. Talk around the classified details, as you say. How about 1300?"

"One o'clock? Sounds fine. Where are you located?"

"It's probably easier if I come to BioDawn, Mr. Wainwright. Less of a hassle, really. By the time you got through security at the main gate here, then wandered around looking for my office, we probably could have completed our meeting. So, to save time, I'll grab a sandwich and eat in my car on the way there. Okay?"

"1300 tomorrow then, Colonel. Thank you."

DRUID HILLS, ATLANTA
TUESDAY, AUGUST 20

In the team room at the CDC, Doctors Butler and Zambit reviewed recent events.

"Anything from the field team yet?" Zambit asked. Rumpled and bleary-eyed, he brushed at a dab of dried mustard—residue, perhaps, from a quick lunchtime hot dog—that clung to the corner of his mouth.

"Nothing," Dwight said. "No clues. No leads. No ideas. But we do have more bad news from North Georgia Regional."

"What?" Zambit said, his voice husky, tired.

"Two of the nurses who attended Gullison are displaying HF symptoms. And another individual, a Mr. Jamie Deland from Gullison's subdivision, was admitted around noon today with something that sounds frighteningly similar."

Zambit rolled his eyes. "Any connection to Gullison or McCarthy?"

Dwight tapped his finger on a sheet of paper resting on the table in front of him. "Yeah. This is interesting. The only link between Deland and Gullison and McCarthy is that Deland was in the twosome immediately behind Gullison and McCarthy last Thursday on the golf course. Gullison and McCarthy were the first ones out that morning."

Zambit jerked upright. "Jesus, you know what that suggests."

"That our Ebola visitor might not have got here by accident. It's sure as shit not indigenous to the U.S. So if these guys picked it up on a *golf course*, somebody had to have planted it."

Zambit stood. "I think you just rang the bell for full FBI involvement."

"Maybe. But as you like to remind me, all we have so far are suspicions and coincidences. No hard evidence."

"The field team combed the golf course?"

"It did. But even if something had been planted or released there, there wouldn't be any trace of it now. Rain, wind and sunlight would have seen to that. Washed it away, dispersed it, destroyed it."

"But if it's airborne—"

Dwight waved his hand dismissively. "Wouldn't matter. It still would have had only a short lifespan. Exposure to oxygen alone would have doomed it fairly quickly."

Zambit began pacing. "Did the team find *anything* that raised the hair on the back of their necks?"

"Nothing. Just the usual golf course litter. Beer and soft drink cans, Styrofoam food containers, cardboard golf ball boxes. All empty."

"No exploding golf balls?"

"Clever. No, we would have heard about that."

"Any reports of suspicious activity, people? Anything out of place?"

"These guys aren't crime investigators, Zamby."

"Yeah, I know. That's the FBI's job. Let's get them going." He reached for a nearby phone, then withdrew his hand. "What do we tell people in the meantime? I mean, do we tell Atlanta to stop playing golf?"

Dwight smiled weakly, sardonically. "To stop playing tennis, going to malls, public swimming pools, baseball games?"

"Stop going outdoors?" Zambit said, in effect, answering his own question.

Dwight pursed his lips and stared into the distance. A dark, amorphous image—a scenario, really—plodded through his mind. He didn't want to acknowledge it, didn't want to articulate it, but it already had grabbed him by the shoulders and was shaking him violently.

Zambit read it. "Say it," he said.

"What if," Dwight said, his voice strained, "this was a deliberate act—."

"A terrorist act?"

"Yes. A terrorist act, but only a test. A sort of Spanish Civil War. Like the Nazis in the '30s prior to World War II, trying out their new weapons and tactics in support of General Franco's insurgents?"

"And then comes the hammer," Zambit said, picking up the thread of Dwight's analogy, "the Blitzkrieg. The invasion of Poland. Of the Low Countries. Of France." He punched in the number of the FBI.

Dwight closed his eyes and sucked in a deep breath, trying to steady himself, trying not to think of what might be coming. "Please let me be wrong," he whispered to no one in particular. Yet he sensed the presence of something apocalyptic.

Chapter Nine

NORTH METRO ATLANTA
TUESDAY, AUGUST 20

Alnour Barashi checked the hose fittings on the jury-rigged mechanism he'd designed and built, then tested an electronically activated pump that was an integral part of the device. A mist of spray erupted from a nozzle fitted to the end of a slender pipe. The cone formed by the spray appeared a bit too broad. He adjusted the setting of the nozzle to narrow the cone and at the same time give it greater range. When the spray contained Ebola—today it was only water—he wanted it to shoot as far away from him as possible. He knew he was playing Russian roulette with his planned attack, that he might not survive it himself, but it was a risk he was willing to accept. This was his calling, his purpose in life, and he wished to make certain of its efficacy. He sought maximum stealth, maximum dispersal, maximum terror.

Russian roulette, he reflected. An ironic term, for that's where all this had begun so many years ago. Russia . . .

NEAR THE SOUTHWESTERN SIBERIAN CITY OF
NOVOSIBIRSK
LATE DECEMBER 1991, THE END OF THE SOVIET ERA

Paralyzing cold. Thirty degrees below zero, maybe forty or fifty. It didn't matter. Despite wearing thermal underwear, three flannel shirts, a sweater, two pairs of wool pants and a heavy arctic parka, Sami Alnour Barashi shivered uncontrollably as he walked toward the main building in a complex of over two dozen drab structures: The Koltsovo Institute of Molecular Biology. A factory of death.

Nine o'clock in the morning, and the sun still hugged the southeastern horizon. Ridiculous. Barashi's breath, in the dead calm of the tardy dawn, trailed out behind him in a crystalline contrail. He'd expected more snow, but the bleak taiga landscape was blanketed by only a few inches. How could people live here? An electrified fence surrounded the sprawling facility. Tracked vehicles of an elite Russian guard patrolled its perimeter.

He'd stopped shaking by the time he was seated in the office of Uri Sherbokov, his designated escort, minder, keeper—he wasn't quite sure of the proper title. Sherbokov, a lean man with thinning hair, a pockmarked face and nicotine-stained fingers, looked up from his desk where he'd been studying an official-looking dossier. "You speak English?" he asked.

"I studied at Emory University in America." *As if you didn't know.*

"So. We have a common language then. I am Uri Sherbokov. Welcome to Vector."

"Vector?" Barashi asked. He leaned across the desk and shook hands with Sherbokov.

"The Russian State Research Center of Virology and Biotechnology. We call it Vector." Sherbokov studied the paperwork in front of him. "You have been vetted by the army?"

"Thoroughly. Or I wouldn't be here."

"Yes, of course. So. Vector. It was founded by Biopreparat in the early 1970s." He stopped. "You know Biopreparat?"

Barashi nodded. He knew it well. It had been created in 1973 to provide civilian cover for advanced military research into biological weapons. It currently was under the titular control of the Minister of Medical and Microbiological Industries, but the majority of its personnel came from the army, keeping it effectively under military authority. In a phrase, Biopreparat was the Soviet equivalent of America's World War II Manhattan Project. There was one huge difference, however: Biopreparat was dedicated to developing biological "bombs," not nuclear ones.

But as the Soviet Union had begun to crumble, so had financial support for the massive Biopreparat war machine. At its peak, it had employed tens of thousands of people at forty sites dispersed throughout Russia and Kazakhstan. Now, Barashi knew, the Russians were desperate for money, desperate to keep at least a portion of Biopreparat alive. Especially the apparatus known as Vector.

For that, they had been able to set aside their inherent xenophobia and allow him into Koltsovo. It was a win-win-win situation. He could contribute to their effort, they could add to his learning, and most importantly, his presence would allow large sums of cash to flow into

Koltsovo. The money, Barashi was well aware, came from several Middle Eastern radical Islamic organizations.

"Vector," Sherbokov continued, "was founded to concentrate on one of the most difficult challenges of bioweaponeering: making viruses into weapons. Here we work with smallpox, Venezuelan equine encephalitis, Russian spring-summer encephalitis, and hemorrhagic fevers such as Ebola and Marburg. We are also developing techniques to make smallpox and Marburg into bioweapons." He paused and stared at Barashi. "You are appalled?"

"Hardly." Barashi looked at the window behind Sherbokov. He couldn't see out. A thick layer of frost on its exterior had rendered it translucent. The only thing appalling here was the weather. He shifted his gaze to Sherbokov. "I see what you're involved with as being important. Very important. Certainly it presents daunting intellectual and technological challenges. But it also promises fruit for the oppressed and the weak. I think now there is only one preeminent military power left in the world: America. And I'm convinced this is not good for any of us, Russians, Arabs or Muslims. There may come a day when we—you, me—will need to defend ourselves against its imperialism: Its export of capitalism, religion, liberal democracy; its support of Israel; its hunger for oil."

Sherbokov shrugged, and Barashi stopped talking. Perhaps the Russian was more concerned with the threat to his job than any threat, real or imagined, from America. But then again, he wasn't an Arab.

Sherbokov took out a pack of cigarettes and offered one to Barashi. "You smoke?" he asked.

Barashi reached for the offering. "Bad for your health," he said.

Sherbokov let loose a deep, rumbling laugh that ended in a cough. "So. You are worried about your health?" he said when the coughing subsided. He extracted a cigarette for himself, lit it, then Barashi's. "Perhaps you should not be working here."

"Is it that dangerous?"

"Everything we work with here will kill you. You make a mistake, you have an accident, you are dead."

"Researchers have died?"

Sherbokov held his cigarette in his hand, his elbow resting on his desk. "1988. Nikolai Ustinov was injecting the Marburg virus, a slightly less deadly relative of Ebola, into guinea pigs. He was working through a glove box and wearing only two thin layers of rubber gloves instead of the thick mitts he was supposed to. The gloves gave him more flexibility to control the little animals, but he was not following standard procedure. The rules stated guinea pigs must be strapped to a board before injecting them. Ustinov perhaps thought the guinea pigs would be quieter if he held them.

Or perhaps he was just in a hurry."

The Russian inhaled deeply from his cigarette, blew the smoke back into the stale air of the office, then continued. "A technician assisting Ustinov became distracted and bumped him accidentally. Ustinov's hand slipped just as he was pressing down on the syringe. The needle went through the animal and punctured his thumb. Only a half centimeter in. But the virus was highly concentrated. There was, and is, no effective antiserum. He was dead in less than three weeks."

Sherbokov paused. A sad smile crept across his face. "All the time Ustinov was dying, his colleagues were not allowed to stop working. After he was dead, they cultured the virus that had killed him. They discovered it had mutated. The new variant turned out to be particularly virulent. It was weaponized as a replacement for the original. We named it 'Variant U.'"

"After Ustinov?"

"Yes."

"Probably not the legacy he wished."

"No." Sherbokov studied the paperwork in front of him and took another drag on his cigarette. A long, glowing ash dangled precariously from the end of it, then broke off and tumbled onto the papers. He swatted distractedly at the nuisance. "So. You earned a Ph. D. at Emory. An excellent school."

"Yes, it is. I studied in their microbiology and molecular genetics program."

"America is not all bad then?"

"In terms of technological innovation and application it perhaps has no peer." He took a puff on his own cigarette and tapped the end of it into a ceramic ashtray molded into the shape of a double helix. "It's the export of their religion and culture, often by blunt force, that my part of the world is fearful and suspicious of."

"You are a Saudi?"

"No. I attended King Abdul Aziz University in Jeddah, but I was born into a family of Marsh Arabs in southern Iraq."

"Marsh Arabs?" Sherbokov leaned forward, his cigarette dangling from his lips. A layer of acrid tobacco smoke, bitterly pungent, formed a gray overcast near the ceiling of his office.

"Near the confluence of the Tigris and Euphrates Rivers," Barashi said, "the Ma'dan people, Marsh Arabs, have spent the last 5000 years subsisting on farming, fishing and hunting. They dammed the rivers, built irrigation canals and erected cathedral-like homes made of reeds. The marshlands they developed were the Middle East's largest wetland ecosystem."

"Yet you left."

"My parents saw no future for me in a country dominated politically by

Sunni Muslims—the Marsh Arabs are Shiite—and Saddam Hussein's Baath Party. They persuaded an uncle to smuggle me into Saudi Arabia. That's where I was raised."

"Perhaps you will go back now, now that the Americans have liberated Kuwait and destroyed Saddam's army?"

Barashi waved his hand in dismissal. "Faah!" He spit the word out. "The Americans didn't finish the job, they didn't get Saddam. Instead, they encouraged the Kurds and Shiites to do it, then betrayed them. Now, in retribution against the Marsh Arabs, Saddam has begun a systematic effort to drain the marshes, to drive out all remaining residents and allow his military greater access. Soon there will be nothing left but salt desert. Dead. Useless. Like my family. Like so much of the Arab world." He thrust his cigarette into the double helix dish, creating a small explosion of ashes, and ground it out with fierce effort.

"I understand," Sherbokov said, almost softly. He paused, then stood. "Come, I wish to show you something." He reached for his parka that hung by its fur-rimmed hood on a plain, wooden coat tree. "Just so you don't think the Americans cannot be challenged in science and technology."

"We have to go out?"

Sherbokov chuckled. "You prefer to hibernate in my office until spring?"

"When is that?" Barashi wasn't sure that such a season even existed here.

"May, sometimes June."

"Faah," Barashi said again. He donned his own parka and followed Sherbokov out the door.

They crossed the Vector campus toward what appeared to be a relatively new, yet singularly unattractive—as only the Soviets seemed capable of producing—multi-storied building in a far corner of the complex. The wind had come up, and the snow on the concrete-like earth drifted over the sidewalk in long, white streamers, like sand blowing in a desert. The sun had struggled a bit higher into the sky, but not much. Barashi held up his gloved hand. Only three fingers separated the horizon from the sun's disc. He mumbled a curse wreathed in condensation from his breath. The brittle cold bore into him even more deeply than before.

They reached the building, number fifteen, surrounded by yet another fence, and entered through a checkpoint guarded by a Kalashnikov-toting soldier and an emaciated German shepherd. Inside, they climbed several flights of stairs, then walked along a dingy yellow hallway festooned in what Barashi assumed were propaganda banners. He couldn't translate the Cyrillic writing, but Sherbokov saw him eyeing the standards.

The Russian pointed at one and said, "'Fulfill our Five-Year Plan in four years!' Well, we'd better. Russia may not survive another five." He gestured at an adjacent banner. "'Long Live the Communist Party of the Soviet Union.' Out of date already." He shook his head in disgust, or disappointment, Barashi wasn't sure which.

Traffic in the corridor was not heavy, but steady; mostly men and women in white lab coats and pants. All had picture ID cards clipped to their smocks. "In Russia," Sherbokov said, as he returned a nod one of the workers gave him, "we divide our biocontaminant areas into three levels or zones. The U.S. and most of the rest of the world use four. We're in Zone One. It's mostly administrative and security offices, and laboratories that prepare nutrient media."

Sherbokov turned left at an unmarked corridor. "We're going to be entering a 'hot' zone now, Zone Two. We won't be going into Three, so don't worry. Three is where we work with the really nasty stuff; filoviruses like Marburg and Ebola, for instance. No vaccines, no cures."

At the end of the corridor they came to a steel door. The door was marked with a symbol familiar to Barashi, the four intersecting rings used as the international warning for biohazard. Sherbokov punched in a code on a keypad. The metallic click of a heavy-duty latch releasing followed. There was a slight hiss of air as he pulled open the door. Barashi felt a tiny breeze following them as they stepped into a connecting hallway.

"We keep Zones Two and Three under negative air pressure," Sherbokov said. "If something bad happens inside, if there's an accident, if a hot agent is released, we don't want it getting out of the containment area."

He turned to look at Barashi, who was behind him. "So. This is a sanitary passageway. We'll strip, get examined by a nurse, then put on 'antiplague' suits."

"Strip? Examined? You mean naked, by a woman?" Barashi felt more uncomfortable over that eventuality than entering a biohazard zone.

Sherbokov laughed. "She's seen it all before, my friend. Your equipment is no different than any other man's. She'll stick a thermometer under your armpit, then examine you for cuts or bruises. Any kind of a little nick, any blood at all, and you go no farther."

They moved into a small, white-tiled room lined with lockers. They undressed, then Sherbokov pointed to another door. "Time to meet nurse Hammersickle," he said. Barashi hesitated, and Sherbokov laughed again. "Don't worry, she won't hurt you. But don't make any sudden moves." He chortled softly as he opened the door.

Nurse 'Hammersickle'—Svetlana turned out to be her real name—was a Russian bear of a woman with tiny, pig-like eyes and a wispy, gray mustache. She said nothing to the two men as she took their temperature and examined their skin thoroughly, even checking their mouth and gums.

Finished, Svetlana flicked her head toward an adjacent door, and the men moved on.

In the next room, the hum of a heavy-duty ventilating system became apparent, and an unusual odor permeated the air. Barashi wrinkled his nose. It was something he had smelled before but couldn't readily identify.

"It's a disinfectant, hydrogen peroxide," Sherbokov said. "It's sprayed into Zones Two and Three from those nozzles." He pointed to an overhead latticework of exposed pipes, valves and vents.

The journey to see whatever Sherbokov wanted to show him was becoming a bit surreal for Barashi. Here he was, standing naked in a bioweapon hot zone in the middle of a Siberian winter, being showered by hydrogen peroxide after getting groped by a hulking Russian woman.

Sherbokov seemed to sense the Iraqi's discomfort. "You'll get used to it," he said. "It'll become routine within a few weeks. So. Time to don our battle dress."

He gestured toward a series of stalls that contained the requisite attire for Zone Two. "Watch me. Then I'll step you through the procedure."

Barashi looked on, shivering slightly—perhaps a bit from the chill in the air, perhaps a bit from apprehension—as Sherbokov pulled on a pair of long-johns and white socks, followed by a surgeon's smock that reached to his ankles. Next came a cloth hood with openings for his eyes and nose. It made him look akin to the KKK clowns Barashi had seen pictures of in America. Next, Sherbokov pulled on high rubber boots, then a pair of thin rubber gloves. Finally, he picked up a sealed respirator mask and set of goggles and slung them over his shoulder. "Let's get you suited up now," he said, "then I'll show you how to use the respirator."

It took another twenty minutes to get Barashi properly attired and comfortable using the breathing apparatus. "Breathe normally," Sherbokov urged. "Relax. We aren't going deep-sea diving. The respirator is more a precaution than a necessity."

Once Barashi's breathing had settled into a controlled rhythm, they stepped into a dimly lit lab filled with the muted sound of something churning or mixing. In the middle of the room stood a metal vat. About five feet high, it had a convex top and was enclosed within thick, stainless steel walls. A plethora of pipes sprouted from the container and disappeared into the ceiling.

"The first of its kind in the world," Sherbokov announced, gesturing at the vat. His voice sounded distant and distorted because of the respirator mask.

Barashi looked at him.

Sherbokov continued. "It's a 630-liter viral reactor for manufacturing weaponized smallpox."

Barashi's heart rate accelerated.

"Mikhail Gorbachev signed off on this as part of the Soviet Union's last five-year plan. Overall, the equivalent of one billion U.S. dollars was funneled into Soviet biological weapons development over the past decade. It allowed us to catch up with and surpass Western technology. Come. Look."

They moved to the opposite side of the reactor and a small, thick window on its domed roof. Barashi peered in, struggling to get a clear line of sight through his goggles. An agitator at the bottom of the vat churned an innocuous-looking liquefied mixture.

"The pipes coming out of the reactor," Sherbokov said, "are for disposing of waste and extracting weapons-ready material. We produce about 100 metric tons per year of weaponized variola virus. Smallpox."

Barashi tried to whistle softly, a habit he'd picked up in America, but it didn't work well with a sealed mask over his mouth and nose.

Sherbokov seemed to think he was gagging and stepped toward him.

Barashi held up his hands. "I'm fine," he said. "And impressed. One hundred tons!"

"Yes. You are perhaps interested in weaponized smallpox?"

"Not necessarily," Barashi said, recalling what Sherbokov had told him about Nikolai Ustinov. "You say the Marburg virus became more virulent after it killed your colleague?"

Sherbokov nodded. "A virus grown in laboratory conditions often becomes more potent after it passes through a live incubator: an animal or a human. In Ustinov's case, the Marburg virus morphed into a much more powerful and stable pathogen."

"What about Ebola?"

"Ah, my young friend, you must like poking your finger in the eye of the Grim Reaper."

Barashi smiled. "Maybe. At least at a distance. Tell me about Vector's work with Ebola."

Sherbokov seemed to think about his response, or whether to respond at all, but after a short silence said, "Then let us continue our conversation in Zone One, without respirator masks." He beckoned Barashi away from the reactor, and they walked toward the exit.

A half-hour later they were dressed again, walking through a hallway in Zone One.

Sherbokov picked up the conversation they had aborted in the lab. "We have found it much more difficult to cultivate Ebola than Marburg. For a long time we had difficulty achieving effective concentrations of Ebola, but think now we have overcome that."

"What about its virulence?"

Sherbokov laughed, a bleak chuckle devoid of humor and edged in darkness. "Ebola is the most deadly virus in the world. It probably couldn't mutate into anything worse than what it is already. In 1976, an outbreak of Ebola in the Republic of Zaire killed 280 people of 318 infected. That's a death rate of almost 90 percent. That's pretty damn virulent. And a God-awful way to die."

"Have you weaponized it yet?" Barashi asked.

"We haven't been able to cultivate enough of it to integrate it into a weapons system. And of course, as with any hemorrhagic fever, there's the problem of developing a truly effective delivery system."

Barashi nodded.

Sherbokov continued. "Hemorrhagic fevers, at least those deadly to humans, can be transmitted only by direct contact with the secretions—blood, vomit, feces, urine, even saliva—of infected people. Syringes can be dangerous, too, as poor Ustinov found out. Usually the disease is spread among caregivers: family, friends and healthcare workers." Sherbokov fumbled in his shirt pocket for his cigarettes but couldn't find them. He cut loose with a string of invectives in Russian.

"Sorry," he said. "Left my cigarettes on my desk. So. Ebola can replicate—in effect, live—only within the cells of a host, that is, an animal or human being. The trouble is, at least in terms of the virus, it devastates its host. Kills it. It needs to find a new host, a new home, as quickly as possible. Or it dies. Fortunately, for humans, it can't be transmitted through the air. At least that's never been observed outside of a laboratory setting."

"But if it could be?"

"You mean like the common cold?"

"Yes."

"Then the world wouldn't have to worry about overpopulation any longer."

The men walked on in silence, their boots clicking on the hard linoleum floor, echoing off the cold walls of Koltsovo's Building Fifteen. Barashi thought he could hear the moan of the frigid Siberian wind outside. Or maybe it was just the icy breath of death.

But there would be no icy breath of death in Atlanta. Death, yes. But riding the warm breezes of a gentle Southern summer, not the icy gales of Siberia.

Satisfied his dispersal mechanism worked and would be reliable, Barashi dried it, disassembled it and stored it. He checked again to make sure he had the proper inventory of mounting brackets and hardware, then marked and stored them, also.

Though it was possible his venture might fail, that seemed a low probability outcome. He'd planned meticulously, run the scenario over and over in his mind, rehearsed the actual attack at least a dozen times: timing it, looking for pitfalls, developing contingency actions. Still, he was a realist. Shit happens, as Americans liked to say, so he had prepared for that eventuality.

From a commercial-quality freezer he withdrew two heavily wrapped, tightly sealed boxes, each about the size of a desktop computer printer. Each container held a seed stock of his chimera Ebola. The Ebola was packed in a glass jar secured within an aluminum canister. The canister, in turn, was suspended in a sea of dry ice inside a Styrofoam box. For all anyone knew, the box could have contained Omaha Steaks. But the box would never have been recognized as such, for it was so heavily layered in duct tape the Styrofoam was hidden.

Given the nearness of his attack, it was time to transport the seed stock, the backup virus for his weapon, to a place of safekeeping. Only he and one or two others knew where. In case he didn't survive his mission, someone else would be able to start over. In truth, the thought appalled him, for he realized there were few people, maybe no one, who could accomplish what he had.

That concern aside, he'd rented a small unit at Castle Vault Public Storage near the airport and bribed the owner to allow him to wire for and hook up a small freezer within the unit. In addition to the bribe, which was substantial, he paid two years advance rent. The weaponized Ebola would be there waiting. For him, if needed. For someone else, if Allah so willed.

The time had come to find out.

Chapter Ten

DRUID HILLS, ATLANTA
WEDNESDAY, AUGUST 21

Two FBI Special Agents, Jeremy Babb and Al Merriwether, sat with Dwight and Zambit in the CDC team room. The door of the room was shut, dampening the chatter from the adjacent EOC. Dwight knew rumors were circulating among the employees manning the EOC workstations that something other than an exercise was afoot. He assumed it would be only a matter of time—hours? a day or two?—before the media caught wind of the possibility that Ebola might be involved. He and Zambit had already concocted a cover story. A lab monkey infected with a deadly virus had escaped from a secret research facility and found its way to Gullison's golf course. The escapee was captured and destroyed. Too late, however, for the first two twosomes out last Thursday morning. But everything was under control now. *If only.*

"So what should we be looking for?" agent Babb asked. Middle-aged and pudgy, a friar's hairdo fringed his bald head. With his pen poised over a notepad, he looked more like an accountant than a federal law enforcement officer.

Dwight shrugged. "Like we explained to you, we have only suspicions this might be a terrorist attack. As far as we know, there's been no communication from any group or individual claiming responsibility for it." He paused to see if this would elicit a response from the agents.

Agent Merriwether shook his head. "Nothing on our end. Any chance this could be just some kind of accident or weird circumstance?" Merriwether, young and lanky, sported tiny, round eyeglasses and wore his dark hair close-cropped. Dwight guessed he couldn't be more than a few years out of college.

"Sure," Zambit said, "but there's just too much circumstantial evidence pointing the other direction. Something happened on that golf course. A deliberate release. Ebola, at least in America, doesn't just pop up. It's not endemic to this country. Especially a mutated or bioengineered version of it. In fact, there are only about a dozen Level-4 labs in the country that could even handle the virus. And there aren't any terrorists working in them."

"So you think," Babb said. "But back to my question." He nodded at the notepad in front of him and tapped his pen on it impatiently.

"Okay. 'What should you be looking for?'" Dwight said. "I suppose any kind of unusual activity on the golf course that morning. Somebody who didn't belong. Somebody acting strangely, suspiciously. Somebody spraying something. Maybe an aerosol bomb of some sort. I don't know, you guys are the detectives."

"Yeah, like there aren't dozens of people out walking and running on golf courses every morning before play starts. Like the front and back nines aren't swarming with Hispanic workers by sunrise. But you're right, we're the gumshoes." Babb, looking a bit exasperated and probably deciding he wasn't going to get any useful input, put down his pen.

"What would happen," he said, after a short pause, "if some sort of full scale attack with this Ebola stuff really took place? Just assuming, that is."

Zambit looked away. Dwight fiddled with his earring and waited for Zambit to answer, but he didn't. Finally, Dwight drew a deep breath and said, "Just assuming. Look what SARS, a severe form of pneumonia, did to Hong Kong for a few weeks in 2003. Virtually shut it down. And SARS had a mortality rate of just under 10 percent, mostly in the elderly and already-sick. Ebola? You could be looking at a death rate of up to 90 percent. No way to treat it. No way to prevent it. An overwhelmed health care system. An attack in Atlanta, like on MARTA or at a ball game . . ." He stopped talking, fearing his voice would betray him, give away the terror gnawing at his gut. His small audience waited in silence.

He drew another deep breath, steadied himself and went on. "Hundreds of thousands," he said, "hundreds of thousands of people would die. The populace would live in absolute fear, cowering in their homes. Barricaded. Or maybe just the opposite, maybe everyone would flee. Or try. A mass exodus. Anarchy. Who knows. Commerce would cease. Hartsfield-Jackson, the busiest airport in the world, would close its doors. Air traffic around the country would be paralyzed. Terror? We can't image. Remember the kind of death we're talking about here. Not a gentle passing in the night.

A descent into the Ninth Circle of Hell. 'Abandon all hope, you who enter here.'"

"Dante," Merriwether said softly.

Babb cleared his throat and spoke to the virologists. "You sound as if you believe, if this *is* bioengineered Ebola, that it was developed outside the U.S. and smuggled in."

Zambit nodded.

"Then why would the terrorists wait to test it here, not where it was developed?"

Zambit and Dwight stared at each other. Then Dwight said, "I think you've just suggested a totally new dimension for your investigation."

"Like a covert Level-4 lab, you mean? Here in the U.S.?"

"Something like that," Dwight said.

Babb picked up his pen, examined it, clicked the retractable ball point in and out a couple of times. Then he looked at Dwight. "How in the hell would someone get Ebola into this country in the first place?" he asked, looking like a high school principal wondering how a kid got a gun into class. "I mean, if this is a weaponized virus, the terrorists had to start with something, right?"

Dwight snorted derisively. "Smuggling Ebola in would be the easy part. We've had scientists stuff vials of plague bacteria into their suit jacket pockets and carry them back to research facilities in the U.S. from overseas. Another example: A number of years ago, a former director of South Africa's biowarfare program, a guy by the name of Daan Goosen, freeze-dried some weaponized bacteria, crammed it into a toothpaste tube and slipped it to a retired CIA agent. The agent carried it back to the U.S. and dropped it into the laps of the FBI. Turned out it was something that carried the genes of a common intestinal bug fused with the DNA of a deadly pathogen that causes gas gangrene. In a toothpaste tube."

Dwight leaned toward the FBI agents as he continued to speak. "So getting Ebola into America would not be a challenge. During the height of the Cold War the Russians certainly were playing around with the stuff. And the security around their former biowarfare facilities is so shitty now it would make Disneyworld look like a maximum security prison. Someone could buy the virus on the black market—I'll bet there's a farmers' market for virologists someplace—package it cleverly, poke it in a little jar, label it beluga caviar and fly it to America."

"And we're worried about bombings and airline hijackings," Babb said.

"Yeah. Well, looks like that's changed," Dwight said.

"And how much time, would you guess, do we have?"

"A week maybe. Less. Hell, I don't know. Assuming the worst, assuming our suspicions are founded, the bad guys know their stuff works;

they know by now it's probably been identified; and they know by now a red flag probably has been run up. Why would they wait before delivering their kill shot?"

Babb stood, preparing to leave. "I don't know," he said, "but we'd damn well better hope they do."

NORTH METRO ATLANTA
WEDNESDAY, AUGUST 21

Colonel Landry arrived at Richard's office promptly at 1300 hours, military time. He appeared the archetype of a field grade officer: tall and lean with a hard, weather-beaten face and the searching eyes of a predator. His hair, brown flecked with gray, was sawed into a buzz cut. His uniform blouse bore five full rows of ribbons and devices in addition to a Master Parachutist Badge, a Combat Infantryman Badge, a Combat Medical Badge and a Ranger Tab.

"You've been around the block a few times I see," Richard said, extending his hand to the colonel.

Landry accepted the proffered greeting. "Too many blocks, too many times."

"It's a bit unusual for an officer to have a Combat Medical Badge, isn't it?"

"I came up through the ranks. Earned the badge in Iraq in '91 when I was just a Snuffy. OCS after that."

"So, you're not a doctor?" Richard gestured at a chair. Landry sat.

The colonel gave a halfhearted chuckle. "I learned how to patch up holes, jab guys in the butt with needles and set broken bones, but that was the extent of my medical training. I guess the Army figured that qualified me for project officer on the BioDawn effort."

Richard smiled and studied Landry more closely. He liked the man, yet there was something vaguely disconcerting about him. Like a plumb bob slightly off-center, but maybe not enough to worry about. "Well," he said, "what can you tell me about that effort?"

Landry sat back in his chair and stared out the window for a moment. "Probably not as much as you'd like," he said, turning his gaze back to Richard. "It's pretty damn sensitive stuff."

"Which, I gather, is why our money comes from a bank in the Cayman Islands."

Landry nodded. "Yeah. This project is so far off the books you won't even find a torn page. There are some things you just don't want civilians poking around in. Quite frankly, we've gone to great lengths to make absolutely certain there are no records, documents or orders that some eager-beaver senator or hot shot GAO investigator can glom on to. Even more to the point, the kind of 'stuff' we're playing around with needs to stay well below the public's radar horizon. There are watchdog organizations out there that would go into lunar orbit if they knew what was going on here."

"I'm not your enemy, Colonel. I'm just a guy who wants to know what's happening in my house."

Landry squirmed in his chair, but stopped abruptly, apparently aware of what he was doing. Ever so briefly his eyes reflected something hard and remote, but just as quickly whatever it was disappeared, replaced by a practiced tractability.

"I know," he said. "My problem is your security clearance, or lack of it. Without it, I can't go into the detail I was able to with your predecessors."

"Let's try broad generalities then. Why BioDawn?" Richard began doodling on a sheet of paper. Badges, ribbons, insignia. Something continued to bother him about Landry, but he couldn't get his arms around it.

"That's easy, Mr. Wainwright. BioDawn has been involved in several pioneering efforts. The company is recognized and well-respected for its accomplishments. It has precisely the kind of expertise and experience that lend themselves to the military applications the army is attempting to develop."

"The lead researcher, I gather, is Dr. Gonzales?"

"Yes. He's not BioDawn, though. He's an army contractor. Brilliant, driven, reclusive. I'll bet you haven't met him yet."

"He's about as approachable as Sasquatch."

Landry started to grin, but aborted it. "I don't know too much about his background, but I do know he earned his Ph.D. at Emory. He excelled, I'm told, in DNA recombination, and transcription in bacteria and viruses." He emphasized the words "recombination" and "transcription."

Richard nodded, realizing the colonel was talking around something, but he didn't have the faintest idea what. DNA recombination? Transcription? *What the hell is that all about?* "How does that fit the army's interests?" he asked, hoping the answer would put Landry's words into some sort of usable context.

Landry stood and walked to the window behind Richard's desk and looked out. "I should turn my resume in here," he said. "Half the buildings I've worked in the last 25 years date from World War II. Most of them were condemned, but the army didn't have any place else to put us." He turned and paced back to his chair but remained standing.

"All of the stuff I'm about to tell you is unclassified. It's public record, not that a lot of people worry about it or pay attention to it. But I suspect you'll be able to cobble the information together and come up with a pretty good idea of what goes on behind closed doors." He inclined his head in the direction of the windowless blockhouse. "And I hope what I say will allay any fears you might have; that you'll realize the work going on here is vital to our national interests, to the defense of our country."

Richard looked down at his doodle pad, then back up at Landry. "Talk to me."

"Are you aware the Soviets once had a huge biowarfare program? Biopreparat. From the early 1970s to the early 1990s it cranked out thousands of tons of the most deadly germ agents in the world. Smallpox. Plague. Anthrax. And a lot of other lethal shit whose names I can't even pronounce." Landry paced back and forth in front of Richard's desk.

"At the peak of the Biopreparat program, the Russians had the capacity to produce 4500 metric tons of anthrax per year. 4500 tons. What on earth were the goddamn Russkies going to do with 4500 tons? Bubonic plague: 1500 tons. Smallpox: 100 tons. We hadn't even weaponized the stuff, and they could spew out 100 tons a year if they wanted. During the 1970s they maintained a stockpile of 20 tons of smallpox at an army depot in a place called Zagorsk. 'Didn't want to be caught short,' they said. Jesus."

Richard scribbled some figures on his pad. "Were the Russians the only ones who had the capacity to wage germ warfare?"

"No. The South Africans, believe it or not, had a secret bioweapon program called Project Coast."

Richard's eyebrows arched up.

"Yes. They built quite an arsenal of anthrax, botulinum toxin, Ebola, Marburg and human immunodeficiency virus—HIV. Wonderful folks that they were they shared their treats with opponents of apartheid. Handed out chocolates laced with anthrax, beer mixed with botulinum, and sugar spiced with salmonella. They even considered going after Nelson Mandela when he was in jail." Landry stopped pacing and shook his head in apparent disapproval.

"And the U.S.?" Richard asked.

"We're never nasty enough, are we?" Landry sat. "Yeah. We had the capacity to manufacture small amounts of debilitating but not necessarily fatal bugs. Stuff called tularemia, Q-fever, Venezuelan equine encephalitis, staphylococcal enterotoxin B"—he stumbled over the pronunciation—"and of course anthrax. But not much. Less than 100 tons."

Richard drummed his pen on the desk. He was surprised by what Landry had told him, but didn't see a connection to BioDawn.

"So what am I missing here, Colonel? How does BioDawn fit into the germ warfare program?"

Landry leaned forward, as if to share something conspiratorial with Richard. He lowered his voice to a gravely stage whisper.

"The Russkies didn't stop at just stockpiling this shit, they made it more deadly. They created antibiotic-resistant strains of it: anthrax, plague, tularemia. Scientists at a facility called Obolensk went even further. They took the gene that makes diphtheria toxin and spliced it into plague bacteria. Superplague with diphtheria. Nice, huh? Not only that, they were investigating the feasibility of introducing Ebola into smallpox. Who needs things that blow up, right? Old fashioned. Our enemies can come after us with crap we can't even see now."

"But the Russian and South African programs are—"

Landry held up his hand. "Dead, yes. But what happened to all those unemployed bioweapon scientists? You think they're growing grain for vodka on the Russian steppe? Selling souvenir T-shirts in Moscow? Driving busloads of tourists through Kruger National Park? You think their knowledge isn't for sale to the highest bidder? You think there aren't enemies of America out there ready to turn a few of these guys into instant capitalists?" His voice got louder with each interrogative.

Richard waited for a direct answer to his question, but Landry hadn't finished his mini-tirade.

His face had turned the shade of a scarlet maple in October. "There's a place called Koltsovo in Siberia. It was one of the Soviet's largest and most sophisticated bioweapons facilities in the early '90s. Top secret. Highly secure. The researchers there worked on really lethal stuff, smallpox and all kinds of hemorrhagic fever viruses: Ebola, Marburg, Machupo, Crimean-Congo. You name it, they were dicking around with it somewhere in a biosafety lab. After the Soviet Union collapsed, a group of western scientists visited Koltsovo in 1997. They found the facility half empty and protected, and I use the term loosely, by only a handful of guards; guards who hadn't been paid in months. You think they gave a flying fuck if any of the smallpox or hemorrhagic fever viruses got legs?" Landry stopped and drew a deep breath. The intensity of the color in his face diminished.

Richard decided to take a stab at BioDawn's role. "So the U.S. Army thinks it's time to bioengineer some weapons of its own?"

"No, nothing offensive. No weapons. But we need to develop more effective defenses. There are currently no useful vaccines against many viral diseases, including the hemorrhagic fevers. Not that BioDawn has the facilities to deal with something like that. But there're plenty of other areas that need research and development. Without getting specific, or classified, let me toss out a few things. In animal studies, the plague vaccine was found to be ineffective against airborne dissemination of the disease. And guess what? The Soviets were rumored to be working on airborne plague."

Landry took a handkerchief from his pants pocket and wiped a sheen of perspiration off his forehead. Then he continued speaking. "So, there would appear to be ample opportunity to develop more effective vaccines against some pretty nasty bugs. But there are other routes that need exploration. We should be looking not just at vaccines, but antiviral drugs, too. Such as for smallpox, since right now we have only enough vaccine for lab workers and the military. So you see, we need help." Landry sat back in his chair, clasped his hands behind his neck and waited for a response.

Richard studied the notes he'd made. He'd circled several to separate them from his doodles.

"So, you're telling me BioDawn could be doing a Lewis and Clark routine, putzing around with plague or smallpox, searching for safe, effective vaccines? Shouldn't an army lab be doing this?"

Landry looked at his watch and stood. "Well, I need to be on my way," he said. "I want to assure you there's nothing nefarious about this project, Mr. Wainwright, but it's nothing that needs to be talked about, either. Loose lips . . ." He held his forefinger to his mouth and flashed a cold, reptilian smile, something akin to an alligator clacking its teeth in warning.

Richard hated to admit defeat, especially on home ground, but he knew he'd learned as much from Landry as he ever would. Virtually nothing. "Ms. Mierczak will see you out," he said. "Thanks for your time."

He reached across his desk and shook Landry's hand. As he did so, his gaze fell again on his rank insignia. Silver eagles, wings spread, gripping a sheath of arrows. A full colonel. Richard's breath caught in his throat.

Landry nodded, turned and strode out of the office.

Richard, his head swimming in a flash flood of confusion, watched him go, then stared at his doodle pad. He'd crudely sketched the insignia of an oh-six, a full colonel, sketched it the way he remembered it from a young lieutenant's perspective: The eagle's head looking forward, the clutched arrows pointing to the rear.

Landry had worn his backward, on the wrong shoulders so that the birds' beaks pointed to the rear, the arrows, forward. It was a mistake newly-minted colonels and movie colonels sometimes made. "Just remember," a crusty old oh-six had once told him, "the head looks forward; great expectations. The arrows point the other way; ready to be jammed up your ass when something goes wrong."

Richard slammed his fist onto the desk. He'd been reeled in. Landry obviously was no rookie colonel. Which meant he wasn't a colonel, period.

Somewhat tentatively, Anneliese poked her head through the door. "Everything okay?" she asked.

"Fine," Richard said. "It's just a damn good thing I wasn't born a fish."

"A fish?"

"Too easy to reel in."

"Oh. Well." She appeared puzzled and apprehensive at the same time. "Is there anything else I can do?"

"Bring me a phone book, please."

"Do you want me to make some calls?"

"No. This is something I need to follow up on myself."

A short time later he punched in the main number for Dobbins ARB and asked to be connected to Colonel Landry's office.

"I'm sorry," the female voice on the other end of the line said, "we've no listing for a Colonel Landry. What unit is he with?"

"USAMRIID."

"Say again."

He spelled it out.

"I'm sorry, sir, no listing for that either. Maybe the colonel is somebody who's here TDY." Temporary duty.

"Maybe. Thank you." He hung up.

Using an Internet search, he learned USAMRIID was headquartered at Fort Detrick, Maryland. He punched the number for the post and asked for the organization. He was connected immediately. A gruff sergeant answered. Richard identified himself and asked for Colonel Landry.

"Colonel who?"

"Landry. Full bird. He's a project officer."

"Project officer! What project?"

"BioDawn. In Atlanta, Georgia."

"Hold on." A lengthy pause followed. Eventually, the sergeant returned. "Sorry, sir, there's no Colonel Landry assigned to USAMRIID. And nobody here has heard of a project called BioDawn."

"It's a corporation."

"That either."

"The colonel is assigned to your branch office at Dobbins Air Reserve Base in Atlanta."

"I think you got some bum information, sir, we don't have an office at Dobbins."

But Richard already had realized as much. He thanked the sergeant and thumped the receiver down in anger. Or perhaps fear, though he wouldn't yet admit that to himself. The only thing the meeting with Landry, or whoever he was, had accomplished was to add another blind passageway to the warren of non-information, disinformation and threats.

Anneliese, seeming to sense his frustration, poked her head into the office. She smiled, a sweet school-kid smile. "I'm sorry things aren't going better," she said. Her soothing tone reminded him of Karen, the way her maternal instincts would kick in after he'd had a hard day.

"Some days you get the bear, some days the bear gets you," he said.

"Bear, one; Mr. Wainwright, zero?"

"Worse than that, I think."

"I'm sorry. Is there anything I can do, anything I can get you?" She stepped into the office.

Richard held up his hand. "No," he said. "Look, why don't you take off a little early and enjoy what's left of the afternoon."

She hesitated, then said, "I do have some errands to run."

He shooed her away with a dismissive flick of his hand.

He spent the remainder of the afternoon replaying in his mind the bizarre events of the past few days, trying to freeze-frame clues and splice scenes that would suggest his next step, but it was a fruitless effort. He found no diaphanous genie, arms folded, smiling benignly, arising from the swirling crosscurrents of deception and menace to grant his wish of enlightenment.

He considered, momentarily, bailing out. Returning to Sunriver. Back to bucolic beaver ponds and food-bearing widows. But even if he could, even if von Stade hadn't threatened his kid brother, Sunriver would provide no escape, no haven. Karen's specter would smother him, wrapping itself around his memories and thoughts, squeezing the joy from them like a hungry python.

No, better to deal with the poltergeists of the present, not that he had a choice. A faux colonel. A will-o'-the-wisp scientist. A vanished informant. A quasi-mythical assassin. And Anneliese. He shook his head. No answers, only questions.

And questions, too, about the risk to Jason. Richard wondered if the threat levied against his brother had been for real or only a straw man. Time for another bed check by big brother. He phoned Jason.

"Hey, bro'," Jason answered. "Twice in one week! To what do I owe the honor? You still worried about over-zealous investigators stalking me?"

Richard forced a chuckle. "Nah. Nothing like that. Just lonely, I guess. New job. Far from home. It's good to hear a familiar voice."

"You sure you're okay, Dickie? Sometimes I don't hear from you for weeks on end."

"Look, kid, I'm fine. How about you, any new women in your life?"

They lapsed into banal chatter for fifteen minutes. After they said their goodbyes, Richard felt better but still somewhat circumspect about Jason's situation.

Richard stood and retrieved his briefcase. *Time to call it a day.* As he left the office, he scanned the latest news headlines on his iPhone. While waiting for the elevator to whine its way from the lobby to the fifth floor, he read the introductory paragraphs of the lead stories. He noted with only idle curiosity a piece headlined: "Three die from virulent flu-like disease in metro Atlanta." The elevator arrived. He slipped the phone into his pocket and stepped into the lift.

Outside, evening was devouring the waning daylight, and the setting sun had turned thin mares' tails of cirrus into pinkish-orange filaments miles above the earth's surface. Richard surveyed the parking lot carefully before exiting the building. At the far end of the lot, the flashing amber lights of the patrolling security vehicle cut through the dusk. He walked toward his car. Like an old mackinaw, the sultry embrace of the growing darkness wrapped itself around him—but couldn't prevent the chill that shot up his spine.

A figure sat in the passenger seat of his Mini.

Chapter Eleven

NORTH METRO ATLANTA
WEDNESDAY, AUGUST 21

Richard pivoted and headed back toward the building.

"You really should lock your doors," Anneliese called after him.

Richard stopped and turned. "I thought you'd gone home," he said, his heart rate decelerating from its sudden foray into double time.

"I did. I had to prepare supper. You're invited."

"Not much notice." He walked to the Mini.

"Your meeting didn't go well this afternoon, I could tell. You need to unwind a bit. Relax." She flung open the driver's-side door. "Get in. Take me home." A velvety command.

He hesitated, then, recalling his decision to play the smitten male, he threw his briefcase onto the rear seat, got in and started the car. As he backed out, he glanced at Anneliese. Headlights from vehicles on the main road reflected from her eyes, illuminating a sexual fierceness he hadn't seen, only sensed, before. On one level, he knew he should refuse her invitation in order to evade her jasmine-scented fantasy world and, if nothing else, dodge temptation. On another level, he needed to learn how she fit into—for she surely must—the web of mystery and threats that had descended upon him.

They reached the exit to the lot. "Left," she said.

The Mini yowled onto the main road. Anneliese fed him a constant stream of terse directions—lefts, rights, straight aheads—and within ten minutes they pulled into a gated apartment complex, Tara Bluffs. A sign at the entrance boasted the community overlooked the Chattahoochee River. He parked the car. She took him by the hand and led him up a flight of stairs to a second floor apartment. She unlocked the door and pulled him gently inside. "Jacket," she said.

He removed his suit coat and handed it to her.

"Tie." She held out her hand.

He slipped off his tie.

"Good start," she said. "Now tell me what you drink."

"Jack Daniels. On the rocks."

"I wouldn't have guessed. Scotch or a martini, maybe. Not whiskey. Have a seat while I hang these up and get our drinks." She gestured toward the living room.

Soft, indirect lighting revealed a room tastefully, and not inexpensively, decorated. A cream-colored leather couch and chairs. Teakwood end tables. A coffee table inlaid with Italian tile. Persian rugs protecting an ash-blond hardwood floor. He seated himself on the couch.

Several pieces of framed modern art—he didn't know what else to call them: swirls and blotches of color slapped onto white backgrounds—interspersed with Ansel Adams photography and Georgia O'Keeffe paintings, hung on the walls. A bouquet of sunflowers sprouted from a terra-cotta vase. Yet the apartment seemed somehow cold, devoid of emotion and character, devoid of Anneliese. There were no pictures of her, no pictures of family members, nothing that reflected her presence. It could have been a hotel suite.

The clink of bottles and glasses reached his ears as she prepared the drinks. He stood and walked to the kitchen.

"Smells good," he said.

"Me, the Jack Daniels or the chateaubriand?"

"Booze never smells good."

"Two choices left."

"In rank order then: You, dinner. Can I help?"

"Everything's ready. But if you'd like, the plates are up there." She pointed to a glass-faced cabinet next to the sink. "Silverware in there." She indicated a drawer snugged beneath a black granite countertop. "And you might as well grab the carving knife and put it next to the carving board." She gestured at a drawer adjacent to the one holding the utensils.

He completed his tasks, and she shooed him back to the living room. The plaintive, almost bluesy voice of a female vocalist, drifting from a hidden sound system, trailed him into the room. Anneliese, bearing drinks, followed.

"Who is that?" he asked. "The music."

"Adele. You don't know her?"

"I know Janis Joplin. Madonna."

She shrugged.

He held his drink up to the light, as if inspecting it. "Why wouldn't you have guessed whiskey?" he said.

She sat next to him on the couch, kicked off her shoes and tucked her legs underneath her. She wore a short, black, evening-style dress that migrated north along her thighs. Not quite to the pole, Richard observed, but pretty damn close. Two thin shoulder straps supported the top of her dress, and he wondered if they were up to the job. Anneliese was not over-endowed, but her blessings probably put most of her clothes to a severe tensile-strength test. She clearly had not provided them any extra help tonight. She was a woman not embarrassed by what nature had given her.

A crease of a smile unfolded across her lips. "You just don't seem like the whiskey type."

He sipped his drink. "Why not?" He looked directly into her eyes and softly chanted, "Whiskey, raw whiskey and wild, wild women . . ."

"Do you think I'm a wild woman?" Her tone was playful. She shifted slightly, and her dress rode toward the arctic circle.

Richard forced himself to stay focused on her eyes. "I don't know what to think about you, Anneliese. Who are you?" He set his glass on the coffee table. "Tell me about Anneliese Mierczak."

She tugged her dress down, just slightly, and turned her head away for a moment as if studying Ansel Adams' *Yosemite*, then said, "My mother was Cuban, my father, eastern European."

Richard let his gaze drift over her again. "A mix of East and West," he noted. "It turned out well."

She smiled and laughed softly, a complement to the muted background music that permeated the room with sexual moodiness. "Thank you."

"How did your parents meet?"

"Daddy was born in the Ukrainian SSR. He met Mother during the time he was working for the Russians in Cuba in the 1980s."

Richard reached for his drink. The Jack Daniels burned as it went down. He wasn't much of a drinker and could feel a mellow buzz vibrating in his head.

"But you were born in the U.S.?"

"Boston. And it was there I met a nice Italian kid from the North End who won my heart and hand, and I married when I was 20." She raised her glass to her lips, sipped and set it down. "Vodka," she said, "maybe I'm more Russian than Cuban."

He took another swallow of whiskey. He felt a bee racing around in his head as though it had discovered a clover farm. "If I may ask, what happened to the marriage? Obviously you're not—"

She reached out and touched his sleeve. "You may ask. It didn't last long. Italians, I discovered, traditional Italians like my husband anyhow, wanted their wives to stay at home and raise kids. Preferably, lots of kids. Well," she paused and looked into her vodka, "I wasn't able to get pregnant—whether my problem or his, I don't know—and I wasn't about to stay at home, anyhow. It wasn't a marriage made in heaven. So we parted ways, amicably, thankfully, after a few years. But I walked away with nothing. No money. No marketable skills. No job."

"You needed a better lawyer."

"I couldn't afford one." She paused and eyed his drink. "If you're interested, I've got something we could smoke . . . a little more kick than Jack Daniels."

He declined and pulled the conversation back to the track it had been on. "So it's been tough then, making it on your own?"

"I kicked around doing secretarial and menial clerical work for awhile, living in YWCAs and cheap apartments and discovering most of my bosses were more interested in raising my skirt than my status."

"I'm sorry," he said. *A warning or a titillation?*

She wriggled closer; their legs touched. She reached out again, this time stroking his cheek lightly with her hand. "Thank you," she whispered. "You're a good man, decent. You've treated me like a lady. And since you won't ask, I'll tell you, because you'll wonder like any man would. I got ahead, became an executive assistant, because I discovered I had a unique talent for managing and overseeing the minutia of corporate business, the sorts of things that can overwhelm busy executives. I didn't have to compromise my morals. And yes, I like men." With the hand that had brushed his face, she tipped his chin up and leaned into him, kissing him on the lips. Softly but firmly. She pulled back. "But I pick my own."

Richard knew he'd been picked; the question was why? But it was a question quickly becoming lost in a world lit by the fire in Anneliese's eyes, spiced with her perfume, warmed by her nearness, shared in the rhythm of her breathing.

She fitted her legs more firmly underneath her and squirmed into him. Her dress hiked northward again, this time past the point of no return, revealing ebony panties. The straps of her dress tumbled from her shoulders, and her breasts seemed only a single inhalation away from total freedom. She kissed him again and guided his hand to her breast, sliding his fingers over the corrugation of its areola until they reached the erectness at its center. With her other hand, she explored his lap until she found his own erectness.

She released her exploratory grasp and pulled back. "Bedroom," she said. It came out hoarse, barely audible. A gasp. She stood, pulling him up by his arm. The top of her dress crumpled gracefully around her waist. He stood, and they embraced, locked together, each feeling the other's firmness, sharing the other's excitement and anticipation. Their lips feathered one another's, lightly at first, then more resolutely and rapidly.

Again Anneliese stepped back, this time turning and in a quick, smooth motion pulling her dress over her head and dropping it to the floor. She stepped out of her panties and pivoted to face Richard. Nothing left to the imagination. A gift of grace. Naturally airbrushed. She beckoned him toward a hallway. "This way," she whispered and backed into the dimness of the hall, her gaze fixed on him, her eyes aflame.

He followed her. "A minute," he said, and inclined his head toward the restroom as he passed it.

"Less than a minute," she answered.

He stepped into the bathroom, turned on the light and shut the door. He fought to control his breathing. He placed both hands on the sink, leaned forward and studied the image in the mirror. Be careful, he told it. He shook his head rapidly from side to side, as if trying dispose of its fuzziness by centrifugal force. Bad combination, Jack Daniels and testosterone. It didn't take a genius to figure out the Achilles Heel of most fallen CEOs: sex or money. He was one step from the edge.

Anneliese's passion was set in an unnerving context of too many mysteries and too many unanswered questions. He wasn't going to unravel them in her bed.

But overlaying all was the numinous presence of Karen. He knew it was foolish; foolish to be faithful to a memory, foolish to feel as if he were about to cheat on his wife. Yet the feeling was there, as palpable as if he had kissed Karen goodbye before he left for work this morning. For better or worse, he was still married.

He realized he could be banished from the ranks of manhood for what he was about do. But he also understood if he didn't do it, he would be making a monumental error of judgment. There were just way too many pieces of a puzzle on the table, and none of them was fitting into place.

Anneliese's voice floated down the hallway, intermingling with the music. "Dessert is early," she said. Teasing. Luring.

He turned off the bathroom light and stepped into the hall, halting at the door of the bedroom. In the semidarkness he could make out Anneliese's form in bed, draped by a flowery sheet. She raised herself on her elbows and looked at him. The sheet clung momentarily to her breasts, then slid away. Richard closed his eyes.

Anneliese giggled, the soft laugh of a woman, not the titter of a young girl. It was more suggestive than pejorative. "It's impolite to keep a lady waiting," she whispered.

He opened his eyes. "I don't mean to be impolite . . ." A battle raged within him—lust versus common sense—and he fought to get his words out. "I . . . we need more time for this, Anneliese. I didn't come here with this in mind. I—"

"I know you didn't. I didn't either. It just happened."

Did it? "Then let's let it evolve from here. You're an incredibly beautiful, desirable woman. This isn't rejection. I'm just saying, let's find out if we truly feel something for one another, give our passions a chance to simmer down and our emotions an opportunity to mature." *And give me a little more time to find out what the hell is really going on here.*

She sat all the way up. The sheet crumpled to her thighs. "No," she said, "it's not that, is it? You're concerned with propriety, aren't you? CEO and his assistant. Scandal. Decadence. That sort of thing? It's okay. This is between us. Two discreet adults. Not adulterers."

Subdued light played over her exquisite topography, shading it in tones of pearl and peach. His resolve wavered. But countering that was a certain rigidness in her voice that hadn't been there earlier, a hard edge to her words, as though they'd been touched by sleet. A warning light glowed brightly within his subconscious.

He backed away from the bedroom. "It's not right, not yet." He knew he had to get out of the apartment quickly or succumb to certain basic male instincts that were about to overwhelm him. In a physical sense, he really wasn't a good candidate for sainthood or monkdom. He turned and walked toward the front door, grabbed his coat and tie, then paused. He faced back toward the bedroom. "Dinner tomorrow night, Ms. Mierczak?"

She didn't answer, but appeared in the hallway, swathed in a terry cloth robe. "Don't go," she said. She hugged the robe around herself and padded toward him. "Don't go."

A tinge of desperation nuanced her voice, darkened her eyes, but Richard had no idea why. He opened the door and stepped out. "Sneak into my office in the morning and give me a kiss . . . if you feel so compelled."

"Rich—"

He shut the door and walked quickly down the steps to his car. He leaned on the top of the Mini and drew a deep breath. Several. A thin smile of a moon hung in a muddy sky, and the cicadas sounded as if they were involved in raucous, symphonic warfare.

Richard couldn't shed the feeling he'd just triggered a tripwire. But connected to what?

Chapter Twelve

NORTH METRO ATLANTA
THURSDAY, AUGUST 22

Richard arrived at work early the next morning. Except for a couple of cars, one of which he assumed was Anneliese's left from the previous night, the parking lot was empty.

He remained disturbed by the events of the previous day, both his encounter with "Colonel" Landry and his rendezvous with Anneliese. A strange afternoon and a strange evening. He climbed the stairs and checked his watch. It would be another hour before Anneliese arrived, by taxi or with a friend perhaps, and he was glad for a period of quiet in which to plan his day. It was time to orchestrate some bold moves, and he welcomed a chance to analyze the possibilities.

He hadn't gotten very far before a sharp knock rattled the office door.

Anneliese? Early? Richard stood and stepped from behind his desk, not knowing what to expect from her, not even knowing what he was hoping for. "Yes?" he said.

The door opened. Not Anneliese. A balding, middle-aged black man with the build of a gone-to-seed NFL tight end—his paunch more prominent than his chest—lumbered into the room. Dressed casually in jeans and a sagging white polo shirt, an unlit cigar in his mouth flopped up and down like a doll's broken arm. He held out a wallet ID: a picture and a badge.

"Detective Lieutenant Jackson, Fulton County police," he said. "The guard patrolling the parking lot escorted me up here."

Richard examined the ID. It appeared legit. "Come in, Lieutenant," Richard said. What now? Had the incident with von Stade at Mrs. Scarelli's house caught someone's attention?

The detective, with a surprisingly quick gait for his bulk, strode toward Richard and extended his hand. "Stoney Jackson," he said. He didn't crack a smile, but the oscillating cigar clamped between his lips probably made that impossible.

"Richard Wainwright. What can I do for you, Lieutenant Jackson?"

"Coffee?" The detective flopped into a chair without being asked and removed the cigar from his lips.

Richard returned to his chair.

"Normally I could offer you something freshly brewed, but my assistant is late this morning, and she's usually the one that gets things going."

Jackson surveyed the office, not paying attention to Richard's response.

"Nice digs," he said. "I could fit my entire squad in here. Guess I sure as shit chose the wrong profession. You been with BioDawn long, Mr. Wainwright?"

"Hardly. Think of me as a temp. I just started this week."

"But you're from around here? The Southeast, I mean."

"No. In fact, I was called out of retirement from Oregon."

"Long way from home then. Wife with you?"

What does this guy want? "I'm a widower."

"Oh. You're here by yourself then?"

"Not to be rude, Lieutenant, but I'm guessing you didn't bypass half a dozen Starbucks and Dunkin Donuts because you heard BioDawn had the best coffee in town."

Jackson placed his cigar on the conference table. "Sorry. I'm being a little too in-your-face. I'm told I get that way when I'm on a murder case." He looked Wainwright in the eye.

Richard sensed something dark pass in the space between him and Jackson. *Murder?* "Murder?" It came out more an exclamation than a question.

Jackson reached into the back pocket of his jeans and withdrew a notepad. "Anneliese Mierczak, thirty-three, found deceased in her apartment at three o'clock this morning. Neighbors said she worked at BioDawn." He paused, again fixing Richard in his gaze.

The words fell on Richard like a thunderstorm downburst. He felt himself blanch. His chest tightened, and he struggled to breathe. Without warning, the room became a whirling kaleidoscope of colors and hues. He closed his eyes, leaned back in his chair and tipped his head toward the ceiling.

Jackson waited.

Richard fought off the shock and opened his eyes. "She worked here, yes." His voice was barely above a whisper.

"Ah," Jackson said and waited again.

"She was my executive assistant."

"So you'd known her only a few days?"

"Yes."

"When did you see her last?"

"Yesterday."

Jackson, his face creased, but something short of weathered, held his gaze on Richard. "A little more precise, if you could, please. Yesterday morning? Yesterday afternoon? Yesterday evening?"

Richard drew a deep breath. *This is crazy. Over the top. A corporate jet crashes. The BioDawn welcome wagon is a German with a knife. Mrs. Scarelli disappears. A phony colonel defends a bogus project. My executive assistant tries to seduce me—and ends up murdered.*

"You're sure she was murdered?"

"You first. Yesterday morning? Yesterday afternoon? Yesterday evening?"

"Yesterday evening."

"What time?"

"Your turn."

"Don't try to play hardball with me, Mr. Wainwright. You'll lose. What time?"

Richard reached for his phone. "Time for my attorney, I think."

"In Oregon?"

"He'll know somebody here."

Jackson put the dead cigar back in his mouth and rotated the stogie in uneven circles with his lips. He stopped after a few seconds and removed it.

"Put the phone down," he said. "Ms. Mierczak's throat was slit. Carving knife from the kitchen. No sign of forced entry. She knew whoever killed her. Let them into her apartment." He tapped the cigar on the table in a staccato rhythm. "What time, Mr. Wainwright?"

"How do you know it wasn't a suicide?"

"People who kill themselves slit their wrists, not their throats. Or they shoot themselves. Or take pills. What time?"

"Cutting a person's throat. Sounds almost professional."

"Let me be the detective. What time?"

"You know I was there, don't you?"

"Witnesses reported seeing a man about your height driving a small, red and white boxy car leaving the apartments about ten p.m. When I arrived here this morning there was a red and white Mini Cooper parked in the CEO's spot. Your spot, your car, I assume."

"I had drinks with Ms. Mierczak last evening. I left about ten. She was very much alive when I left her." *Now there's an understatement.*

"Tell me about your visit." He jammed the chewed-on cigar back into his mouth.

"You want me to light that for you? It's okay if you smoke in here."

"I don't smoke. Tell me about you and Ms. Mierczak."

Richard related to Jackson as much as he felt comfortable telling, omitting any reference to the attempted seduction, which he knew the detective wouldn't believe anyhow. The attempt or his response to it.

After he'd finished, Jackson said, "There was a dinner ready to be warmed up and eaten, but it was untouched. Something Ms. Mierczak prepared for the two of you?"

"We talked, we drank, it got late. I excused myself."

"Ah." Jackson's gaze flitted around the room again. "This place is like a furniture store showroom," he said. "High-end stuff. I assume you do well as a CEO. Do you mind if I ask how much you make?"

"I do. But I'm well off."

"Yes. I'd figured that out on my own." Jackson chewed hard on his cigar and it almost tumbled from his mouth as he talked.

"Ms. Mierczak was wearing only a robe when we found her. A beautiful woman, yes? You're telling me nothing else happened between you two? Just a little private happy hour?"

"Nothing sexual went on, if that's what you're intimating."

"You guys are used to getting your own way—"

"'You guys'?" The response was a bit more snappish than Richard intended.

"My bad. CEOs. CEOs are used to getting their way. Money. Power. Prestige. Heady stuff. Women are attracted to it. Maybe you misread Ms. Mierczak, tried to take things a bit further than she intended. Met with some rejection—"

"So I slashed her to death?" Anger replaced Richard's shock.

"Don't get bent out of shape, Mr. Wainwright. I'm just doing my job." The cigar jumped up and down in his mouth like a tachometer needle on a Formula 1 racer. "Sorry if I come across as overbearing, but to be honest, I guess I do have a bit of a hard-on for guys who sit behind desks all day raking in multimillion dollar salaries, lucrative stock options and guaranteed pensions, while the peons, the people who keep the corporations afloat, bust their butts just to make ends meet. And then half the CEOs turn out to be crooks."

"So, do I live down to your standards?"

Jackson stood. "We'll see. Nice chatting with you. Stick around."

Richard rose from his chair. "Am I a suspect?"

"For the time being, you're just Mr. Wainwright. Let's see what the crime lab guys come up with." He moved toward the door. "Maybe we'll get lucky. Find some prints on the knife. Some blood under the victim's fingernails."

Jesus. The carving knife. My prints. An easy match with my military record. "How long?" he asked. He had to force the words out.

"How long what?"

"To check on . . . never mind."

Jackson removed the cigar from his mouth. A slow, purposeful move. "Something you need to get off your chest, Mr. Wainwright? Something you want to tell me? It might go easier in the long run."

"I didn't kill her."

"Well." Jackson fit the cigar back between his lips. "Maybe you'd better call your lawyer after all." He stared at Richard's face. "Nasty looking scratches."

"Holly bush," Richard said.

"Yeah," Jackson answered. He turned and left.

Richard sank into his chair, a convoluted amalgam of emotions swarming over him: shock, anger, sadness, fear, confusion. For once in his life he didn't know what to do next. As a CEO he had always had Plans B, C and D in his back pocket, always understood if he needed to apply more yin or more yang, always could adjust to new circumstances. But now he was just the driver of an automobile in an uncontrolled spin on black ice, along for the ride, in control of nothing, waiting for a crash.

Intuitively, the bizarre events of the past few days seemed intercomnected, but he had no idea how. He recalled the words of a classmate at North Carolina State, a Cherokee Indian, who once told him, "The raindrops from where we stand seem random. If we could stand somewhere else, we would see order in them." But Richard had no idea where to stand, could see order in nothing. He was Alice in Wonderland, lost in a looking-glass world.

He attempted to sort through the confusion, structure it, fit it together in a way that made sense. By noon, he gave up. Only Picasso-like, Cubist images of von Stade, Anneliese, Colonel Landry, Detective Jackson and the block house behind the razor wire fence bounced around in his head. He had to get away from the office to clear his mind, settle his feelings, focus his thinking. He needed someone to talk to, someone he knew, someone he could trust.

He made a quick phone call.

Then, sunroof open, air conditioning off, he lit out in the Mini, hurling it with abandon through dense lunchtime traffic. The sharp bark of the car's exhaust spurred him on. He envisioned Karen seated beside him, hair flying, her melodic laughter challenging the wind. But the specter of his late wife morphed into that of Anneliese, and he winced at the indelible image of an exquisitely beautiful woman, gone. *What did you get yourself mixed up in, Anneliese?*

He approached a sharp right-hand turn onto a quiet looking two-lane road and downshifted hard, sliding the car through the corner. He up shifted and accelerated into a leafy, green tunnel of kudzu-draped sweet gums and oak. He slammed the car into high gear. Then he saw the sign:

NORTH FULTON UNITED METHODIST CHURCH
MARTY DE LA SERNA, SENIOR MINISTER.

Chapter Thirteen

**NORTH METRO ATLANTA
THURSDAY, AUGUST 22**

Richard pulled the Mini into the church's main parking lot. He remained in the car with the engine idling while he debated entering the church. He wasn't a religious man, at least not deeply so, but after Karen died he'd often found peace in conversations with the minister of a small Congregational church in Bend. Pastor Tommy Offenbach had been simultaneously comforting, nonjudgmental and intellectually challenging.

The stifling midday heat seeped into the Mini and Richard closed the sunroof and turned on the air conditioning. He reviewed, for perhaps the hundredth time, the events of the past twenty-four hours. He couldn't accept the position he was in. He'd always attempted to live his life in a manner above moral reproach, a cut above the diminishing ethical standards now accepted by an increasing number of high-profile CEOs and political figures.

He believed strongly that his education, his accomplishments and his accolades entitled him to nothing except responsibility, and demanded that in all actions he remain above suspicion. And yet, here he was, if not a full-fledged murder suspect, at least a man who'd been in the wrong place at the wrong time and probably under the wrong circumstances. He needed to talk with someone about that face to face. Someone like Tommy Offenbach.

But here in Georgia, Tommy wasn't an option. So Richard had chosen a woman with whom, as they say on the soaps, he had a history. Not a sexual history in the narrow, Clintonian definition of the phrase, but certainly a history of intimacy: youthful, uninhibited physical exploration.

Coming here seemed the right choice. It felt natural to reach out to someone he'd known, someone who'd known him. A minister. And yet, now that he had time to decelerate and reflect, was there some other motive driving his choice? Something recondite, something he wasn't willing to acknowledge? An unarticulated desire, perhaps, to blow on the embers of an old flame? Foolish. She'd be married, have children, be living her own life.

Perhaps he was propelled by mere curiosity to see how she'd weathered the years, what her journey had been like, what kind of woman she'd turned out to be. Or maybe—and now he had to admit he was cutting closer to the marrow—he was simply trying to escape the specter of what had been his greatest love and greatest failure: Karen.

He shut off the engine and got out of the car.

Ambivalence about entering the church suddenly swarmed over him. Could he be putting Marty at risk? Could von Stade be following him? Would it be better for him to leave? One woman, Mrs. Scarelli, had already disappeared. And another, Anneliese, had been murdered. Von Stade claimed no part in Mrs. Scarelli's disappearance, but what about Anneliese's demise? On the other hand, what did it matter, why believe anything von Stade said?

While he mulled the possibilities, he leaned against the top of his Mini, scanning the parking lot and adjacent road for any threats, for any vehicles that seemed to be tracking him. The parking lot contained only a handful of cars, and they'd been there when he'd arrived. Traffic on the road was sparse. None of it turned into the church lot.

Richard maintained his vigil for a full fifteen minutes, listening to the lazy concert of the cicadas and allowing the humid Georgia heat to soak into his body. He made a slow 360-degree pivot and surveyed the area around him. No human movement appeared.

He got back into his car and circled the church, making a careful reconnaissance of the other parking lots. Empty. Satisfied he was alone, he returned to the front lot, parked and exited the Mini.

He entered the church. Cool quietness filled its interior. Light filtered through elevated stained glass windows into a spacious vestibule and danced across its floor in a patchwork of soft hues. Signs at an information desk directed visitors to the sanctuary, choir room, library, offices, classrooms, meeting rooms and a prayer room. Another sign, hand lettered, sat on the desk. *Gone to lunch. Be back at 1. Darcy.* Darcy, Richard assumed, was the receptionist.

He walked down a hallway toward the offices. He came to a plaque with Marty's name on it. An arrow underneath her name pointed to a connecting hallway. At the far end of that hallway, a cleaning lady, her back to him and on her hands and knees, scrubbed the floor. She wore a stained, gray sweat suit, raggedy walking shoes and a tattered baseball hat that looked as if it might have tangled with a document shredder. He tried to make his footfalls audible so as not to startle the woman.

She turned and looked up as he approached. He wondered if she spoke English. "Is Minister De la Serna in?" he asked, clearly enunciating his words.

"Yes." Her face, dark brown and round, suggested a Mexican or Central American heritage. Strands of black hair snaked out from beneath the baseball hat and clung to her damp forehead.

"It's nothing important, and I'm not a church member, but I thought . . . well, I'd just like to talk with her for a bit if she has time."

The cleaning lady stood and gestured toward the minister's office. "Have a seat, please. I'll go get her." With her foot she pushed a bucket of dirty water against the wall and tossed a cleaning rag into it. She turned into a nearby doorway and disappeared.

Richard entered the office and lowered himself into a comfortable but well-used leather chair. Cracks and abrasions, like the skin of an old dueling *meister*, crisscrossed its arms and cushions. Richard's fingers feathered the roughness of the leather as he surveyed the dimly-lit room. A slow eddy of dust motes drifted through a single shaft of sunlight that brightened the office's interior. Ramparts of cluttered bookcases stood against its walls. What limited wall space there was was obscured by photographs, framed documents and religious paintings. One photo in particular caught his eye. He stood and walked over to it. It appeared to have been shot along a fishing stream somewhere in the Mountain West; the background suggested Montana or Wyoming. A group of young men, a young woman and an older woman, all wearing broad smiles and lots of L. L. Bean, held up a string of rainbow trout. He was sure the younger woman was Marty. He leaned closer to the picture, trying to see her face more clearly.

"So now I'm a fisher of men," a voice behind him said. A voice that years ago had whispered things in his ear a minister might rather forget; words of passion within the confines of an old Chevy whose windows became translucent with the condensation of heavy breathing on winter nights. He turned.

"The picture was shot on the Madison in Montana . . . quite a few years ago," the owner of the voice said, her words becoming hesitant as she stared at Richard. "Mom, me and my brothers—do I know you?" She squinted at him over the top of half-glasses perched on her nose.

"Yes," he said, "you know me."

She smiled at him, though more with her eyes—soft, blue, large—than with her mouth. They were eyes that had once gazed at him with adolescent adoration. Now though, they were searching and a bit circumspect. And certainly more mature.

"I'm sorry," she said.

"No," he said, "I am. I'm being unfair. Richard. Richard Wainwright."

"Oh, my goodness. Rich." She gasped and raised her hand to her mouth. "The pony tail, the glasses . . ."

He removed the tiny rectangular spectacles he always wore, more for effect than necessity, and slipped them into the pocket of his suit jacket. He extended his hand toward her.

She ignored the proffered greeting and instead stepped forward to hug him. "Out of the blue," she said. "I'm speechless."

"You never were before."

She stepped back and looked him up and down. "Over twenty years. You look great. Some sort of an executive, I gather?" She fingered his jacket.

"Retired. Well, un-retired. That's why I'm in Atlanta."

"I suwanee," she said, fanning herself with her hand as though she were about to faint, a playful gesture. She stopped and pointed at the leather chair. "Please," she said.

As she seated herself behind her desk, Richard examined her more closely. Shoulder-length wheat-colored hair laced with silver framed a face unblemished and amber, a complexion suggesting unbridled vibrancy. Tiny wrinkles, signs of character more than age, crinkled the edges of her eyes. Attractive, he thought, not drop-dead beautiful, but good looking. She obviously had taken care of herself. Then again, maybe it was just good genes or good luck.

"I apologize," he said, "I should have called. It was kind of a spur-of-the-moment thing."

"It doesn't matter. It's just good to see you. I'm thrilled, really. Life can be dull without surprises."

Yea, verily, he thought. He pointed at a framed certificate on the wall. "Speaking of surprises. A minister?"

"Wake Forest Divinity School. 1989. I guess after we drifted apart my life became meaningless and hollow. I found fulfillment in religion. I considered becoming a nun for awhile."

He stared at her, stunned, unwilling to believe their relationship had been that powerful, their split that traumatic.

She giggled. "Had ya there for a moment, didn't I?"

He expelled a long breath.

"It was a calling, a true calling. I love my work. And you? Has life been good?"

He hesitated before answering. "Ups and downs," he said.

She picked up on the delayed response. She leaned forward, elbows on her desk and hands folded together beneath her chin, and studied him. It was an easy, natural appraisal, not so much an examination as an attempt to make a connection.

"You didn't come here on a whim," she said, and waited.

"No . . ." He wanted to excuse himself, to leave; what he wished to discuss suddenly seemed too private, too . . . male.

"You can talk to me," she said, "I'm a good listener, a willing listener. What you say in here, stays in here. Like a lawyer-client, doctor-patient relationship." She sat back in her chair, a swivel model that squeaked in protest.

"I don't know."

She nodded toward the photograph he'd studied earlier. "I can do guy talk, if that's what you're worried about. Five brothers. I thought I was one of them for my first seven years. And I had a boyfriend at North Carolina State . . ." A rosy tint colored her neck, then rose to her cheeks, a tide, perhaps, of guilty recollections.

He remembered, too. Breathless explorations of each other's body. *Maybe not the sort of thing to be recalled in a church.* He smiled, hoping it didn't register as a leer.

She smiled back, a disarming offering of bronze lips and aquamarine eyes. "So, my point is, you aren't going to say anything that will shock me. I think I've heard it all, or at least most of it. And besides, I won't be sitting in judgment of you. I'll be offering a friendly ear." Her chair squealed again, a piercing little cry, as she shifted slightly. "Give me a chance."

"Your chair needs some oil."

"Yes. I was hoping it wasn't me." She laughed softly, easily.

"You're a ways from that, I think."

"You're evading." She flicked her head to one side, a gesture he remembered from college. "Look, if you want, I can get one of our other ministers for you. You know, wears pants, spits, watches football."

He laughed. He'd been finessed, he realized, put at ease. But her technique had worked. "No," he said. "As I remember, you were into football. Didn't spit, but football . . . yeah."

"Go Wolfpack," she said. "In case you've forgotten, we held hands at the games. And you're wrong about spitting. My oldest brother taught me how to do that. Probably why I had trouble getting dates in high school. Tell me why you're here."

"Starts on a golf course in Sunriver, Oregon," he said.

Thirty minutes later he finished. Marty sat with her eyes closed and hands locked behind her head. Contemplating his story, Richard hoped, and not catching a power nap. He waited for her to speak.

She opened her eyes after a minute or two and placed her hands on the desk. "I can't help you with the mystery aspect of what you've told me," she said, "but I can reaffirm the morality of your actions. And I'm deeply sorry about Ms. Mierczak. Maybe, as you said, you suffered a lapse in good judgment when you accepted her invitation, but I think that was just a natural male reaction on your part. I do remember a little about that." She colored slightly again, then continued. "Reflexively, you delivered yourself into temptation. Then, against all odds, walked away from it. Most men wouldn't have. I commend your decision."

"You seem willing to accept my story at face value," he said, "accept that I'm not a killer." He studied her face for a reaction that might suggest otherwise.

"Someone who just committed murder isn't going to walk into a church and volunteer that he didn't, then support it with a detailed story about a sexual dalliance, chateaubriand and a carving knife. More importantly, I know you."

"What bothers me," he said, "is that there's an obverse side to this moral coin. If I'd stayed with Anneliese, she might still be alive."

"Or you both might be dead. You made the right choices. What happened after you left was none of your doing. Someone else made that decision. I know what you're feeling, what the irony of the situation is. Hindsight is always 20/20. But the real world, the one in which we live and make choices, is distorted by astigmatism. So we do our best. And that's what you did." A soft rapping on the door frame interrupted their discussion. Marty looked up.

A dark-haired woman with over-sized glasses and a small, pouty mouth stuck her head in the door. "I'm back from lunch, Reverend. Can I get you anything?"

"No, Darcy, thank you," Marty said. She looked at Richard. "May I offer you something? A Coke? Iced tea? Glass of water?"

"Nothing. I've got to be going."

Marty held up her hand, a signal for him to remain. "I think we're all set, Darcy. Thanks."

"Reverend?" Darcy said.

"Yes?"

"The cleaning lady left a bucket in the hallway. Do you want me to put it away?"

"I'll take care of it."

"Yes, ma'am."

After Darcy left, Marty said, "She's afraid I'll start scrubbing floors if I find a bucket and rag out there. I've been known to pitch in when the cleaning crew gets behind. Some people don't like seeing me on my hands and knees. They say it's not befitting a church leader."

"Is it?"

"Jesus washed His disciples' feet. The least I can do is wash a few floors."

"Well then, I don't want to keep you any longer," Richard said, "I'm sure you've got floors to clean or sermons to write." He started to rise.

"No," she said, "we aren't finished."

"What do you mean?"

"I mean there's something you haven't told me. I'm good at reading people. I see something in your eyes. Sorrow, loss, hollowness. Tell me."

He looked away, then at the picture of Marty and her family on the Madison. It reminded him of the Deschutes. He turned back to Marty. "We built a home in Sunriver—"

"We?"

"Karen and me. Karen, my wife. We were going to retire there, our high-desert mecca. But while I was still working she was diagnosed with breast cancer, an aggressive, unstoppable strain. She fought, and fought, and fought . . ." His voice trailed off. His eyes welled. "I quit work to be with her, but all I could do was stand by and watch. Hold her hand. Utter meaningless words like some village idiot. When it came to the most important thing in my life, I was powerless. Impotent. Helpless. A clown in big floppy shoes and a rubber-ball nose. I betrayed her." He snapped the words out in an eruption of frustration and anger.

Marty stood and walked to him. She hugged him, then kissed him on the cheek. "I'm so very sorry," she whispered. She knelt beside him and took his hand. "Don't beat yourself up," she said. "You gave her the most important thing your ever could: your presence when she needed it most. All she wanted was your love and comfort, to ease her transition. She didn't expect you to save her, only to be with her when she walked through the Valley." She gave his hand a firm squeeze and stood up.

He stared straight ahead. "I went back to work after she died, but my heart wasn't in it any longer. After about a year, I bailed out and moved to Sunriver. But it was a hollow pilgrimage. Stupid. The place became more of a hermitage than a home." He turned to look at Marty. "I can't let go of her."

"I won't tell you time heals. It doesn't. But it does soothe the pain. And you don't have to let go of her, not ever. But you do have to let go of your guilt. That's what's shackling you. Not Karen."

"I know. But it's . . . hard."

"Of course it is. You invested your life in her. You don't easily give up something like that. And you don't have to. But you do have to back off from it. Acknowledge it, but don't embrace it. Don't let your love for Karen crush you to death. I didn't know her, but I do know she wouldn't want that."

He nodded. "Thank you," he said. "I need to be going." He stood and walked toward the door.

"I'll walk with you."

They reached the vestibule. At the front door, Marty stopped and stared out into the parking lot. "Will you be back?" she asked.

"I don't want to intrude."

"You're not. It was nice to see you again. Besides, I want to make sure you're okay. This business you're mixed up in, it sounds dangerous." She turned to look at him. "Are you sure you shouldn't go to the police?"

"They came to me, remember? I'm a potential murder suspect, not a citizen in trouble."

"Well, my door's always open."

"You've got a church to run and a family to take care of—" He stopped abruptly and spread his hands, as if seeking forgiveness. "I didn't even ask about that, did I? So focused on my own damn problems."

"Married to the church, I guess," she said, dismissing his tacit apology. Their gazes met.

He couldn't be sure, but he felt she'd answered a question both asked and unasked.

She opened the door for him. "Be careful," she said and rested her hand on his shoulder.

He allowed the touch to linger for a moment, then stepped into the incandescent afternoon. A blast-front of heat washed over him as he scanned the parking lot again for any sign of von Stade or anyone else who didn't appear to belong. Nothing.

He entered his car, turned on the engine and hiked the air conditioning to maximum cool. He waited for awhile, surveying the parking lot through the hot, glassine shimmer rising from its surface. Finally, convinced he'd not placed Marty in any danger, he left.

Chapter Fourteen

DRUID HILLS, ATLANTA
THURSDAY, AUGUST 22

"Not a damn thing, not a goddamn thing. You'd think after forty-eight hours we would've turned up something. We've got a dozen agents assigned to a task force. But we haven't been able to ferret out an eyewitness who saw anything unusual last Thursday, haven't found any physical evidence how Ebola might have been let loose, haven't even been able to come up with an informant."

Special Agent Babb clenched his fist and hammered the table in front of him. A pen resting by his notepad hopped into the air like a startled frog. The other men in the CDC anteroom—Dwight, Zambit and agent Merriwether—twitched reflexively at the explosion of frustration.

The group remained silent until Merriwether spoke. "We've set up surveillance on all individuals with suspected terrorist links, no matter how vague, in the Atlanta area. We've even dragged in a few for questioning. We've talked with residents of the Arab and Islamic communities, even with a handful of mullahs. Nothing. If we're dealing with a terrorist cell, it's certainly been able to maintain a subterranean profile."

"What if we're not dealing with a cell?" Dwight asked. Unconsciously, he tapped out a soft rhythmic beat on the floor with his right sandal. Zambit glared at him, and he stopped.

"You mean, what if we're dealing with an independent operator? A lone wolf?" Babb said.

Dwight nodded. "A lone wolf or maybe just two or three guys on their own."

"Could be. Or maybe it's a sleeper outfit. Like those Russian agents we ran out of the country in 2010."

"You think it might be Russians?" Zambit asked.

"No. I'm not saying that. I'm saying it could be a group that's integrated itself into our culture and been living here for years, running under the radar. Seemingly ordinary folks."

"Okay, not Russians then," Zambit said, "but how about some of those right-wing, American militia whackos, like blew up the Oklahoma City federal building?" He looked around the table, apparently seeking support.

Babb shook his head. "Doubt it. You may have answered your own question. They like to *blow up* stuff. Weaponized Ebola is a little too sophisticated for them."

"I agree," Dwight said. "Whoever bioengineered this virus is brilliant. He may be bent on mass murder, but he's an exceptionally gifted individual. I'd guess we aren't dealing with a run-of-the-mill terrorist—sorry, I'm afraid that's an oxymoron."

Babb steepled his hands beneath his chin. He remained silent for awhile, apparently churning something over in his mind, then said, "Let me toss this out. If we consider motive, it pretty much points the finger at an Islamist or Islamist group—"

"Islamist," Dwight said. "Someone who adheres to radical Islam?"

"Yes. I suppose it's religious profiling, but those are the guys who've been trying to snuff us out for the last three decades. I'm thinking the motivation, whether it's hatred or ideology, has been nurtured for a long, long time. Probably whoever we're looking for, and let's assume it's a he, isn't driven by simplistic, traditional notions of martyrdom. He's not anticipating a romp in eternity with a harem of virgins, and he's not after post-attack financial support for his family. He very well could be operating independently. He may be getting his money from an anti-U.S. organization or even a government, but I have a feeling he's calling the shots, not the other way around."

Dwight drummed his sandal again. "In other words," he said, "we might not hear from this guy again until he's ready to attack?"

Zambit stretched his left leg underneath the table and stepped hard on Dwight's tapping foot "Cut it out," he mouthed.

Dwight stopped, but glowered at Zambit in return.

"Just for the record," Merriwether interjected, looking at Babb, "what makes you think it's a he?"

"Male chauvinism, maybe. But assuming this individual is from an Arab or Islamic culture, it's males, much more likely than females, who would have had access to the education and training necessary to pull off a feat like this. And to answer Dr. Butler's question, yeah, this guy may not surface again until he's ready for the big show."

"What about a lab?" Merriwether asked. "He's got to have a lab someplace, doesn't he? Maybe we should be looking at that angle."

"I suppose he could have jury-rigged something in a basement or attic someplace," Zambit said. "It might not meet any viable safety standards, but it would be damn hard to find."

"I disagree," Dwight said, his words curt. He welcomed the chance to tread on his boss's toes, if only metaphorically. "If you're messing around with Ebola, you'd want a highly sophisticated facility. Given that our terrorist buddy probably isn't operating out of a government lab, we might want to look at university-affiliated or privately run facilities that have Level-4 capabilities."

Zambit fixed Dwight in an icy gaze.

"Shit. Why didn't you mention this sooner?" Babb snapped. "Talk to me."

"Don't get your hopes up," Dwight said. "Those labs have pretty tight security. If there were some hanky-panky going on, we probably would've caught a whiff of it by now."

"Names and places, please." Babb sat with his pen poised over a notepad.

After writing down the information, he handed the pad to Merriwether. "Get on it," he said.

"Yes, sir." Merriwether excused himself and left the room.

"So where are we?" Zambit asked.

"On a 100-foot bungee drop with a 101-foot cord, I think," Babb answered. "We've got somebody running around out there with weaponized Ebola, and we don't have a clue who he is or where he is, and it's sudden-death overtime. He's launched one little pinprick attack, so limited we can't even find evidence of it, and killed how many?"

"Seven. Five remain hospitalized," Dwight answered.

"And a major attack?"

"Multiply that number by a thousand. Ten thousand. Hell, I don't know," Dwight said, "millions." An atavistic dread stirred within him again. "Remember, this stuff spreads like the flu, through the air, person to person. It's not just the initial attack that would kill people, but the exponential spread of the virus afterward."

"Has Homeland Security been notified?" Zambit asked.

Babb nodded. "Yeah. But I don't know what they're going to do, if they're going to raise the alert level or not. They're between a rock and a hard spot. If they jack up the level and don't give specifics, then the alert probably gets ignored, you know, 'There they go, crying wolf again.' If they offer details, that there's suspicion a deadly virus is about to be unleashed in

Atlanta—and we're not even sure of that—does that help or hurt the situation?

"Would people know what to do or how to behave? My guess is, they wouldn't. Chances are, all such a warning would accomplish would be to throw the city into a panic. Yet, if a warning isn't issued and an attack occurs . . . well, I'd hate to be in Homeland Security's shoes."

Babb stood and gathered his paperwork. "Gentlemen, I don't know about you, but I'm going out and get drunk. Care to join me?"

Dwight stared at Zambit. Neither responded.

"It's a joke, gentlemen, a joke," Babb said. "But it's the only humor I can find in this."

"Actually," Dwight said, "I thought it was a pretty good idea."

NORTH METRO ATLANTA
THURSDAY, AUGUST 22

Alnour Barashi retained one notebook, one chronicle of his work, and slipped it into a desk drawer in his office. The remainder of his notes and records he'd shredded. One journal would be enough, one record of his legacy; a legacy that began in Koltsovo and would end in Atlanta. He understood what he was about to do could easily cost him his life, but it was a potential sacrifice willingly accepted. His name, he had no doubt, would live in legend through centuries to come as the one who at last brought America to its knees; as the one who triggered the re-ascendancy of Arab and Islamic cultures. No longer would his people suffer death, depravation and humiliation at the hands of the U.S. and Israel. America would be so mired in its own tragedy, one that would relegate 9/11 to the background of history, that it would cease being a significant player on the world stage. An invisible death was about to blanket the imperialist nation, unfurling over it like a burial shroud.

Barashi policed his lab and office, making certain no critical evidence remained. He was confident the facility would not be discovered before he launched his assault, but just in case, he'd removed the viral cultures and thoroughly sterilized the lab equipment. The lab eventually would be unearthed, of course, but investigators, while suspecting what it might have been used for, would never be able to prove it. Not that it would make any difference after the fact.

He sat behind his desk and lit a cigarette. He dropped the match into a ceramic ashtray shaped like a double helix, a gift from Uri Sherbokov at Vector. Barashi inhaled deeply, then leaned back and blew a spiraling column of smoke toward the ceiling. He thought about his trusted agents,

Ebraheem Khassem and Mahmoud Al-Harbi.

Al-Harbi, an Arab-American and convert to Islam, knew nothing about the true nature of the Ebola project. His job had been essentially administrative: ordering supplies, handling correspondence and meeting with other scientists in the facility to coordinate their "supporting" research. He additionally was tasked with keeping other researchers at arm's length from the "classified" work being carried out in the building's bioengineering laboratory. Al-Harbi was safely removed from the stage now, however, dispatched on a trip to California to shop for a new electron microscope.

Khassem, however, worried Barashi. Khassem was the only other person who knew what was going to happen. The potential weak link. Yet Barashi was reluctant to eliminate him, for he was a friend as well as a brother Arab and Muslim. Still . . . He inhaled again and tapped a glowing ash into the double helix. *I shall have to watch him. Just in case, for he has seemed distracted and distant as of late.*

He spun lazily in his chair and surveyed the office, its walls, bookcases and table tops. He would come back tonight, his final visit, and remove the remaining items, his journal, a few text books and a collection of electron micrographs. Then he would begin his countdown.

He had known Anneliese less than a week, so it seemed strange he should miss her. Perhaps it was her efficiency, her concern for him, the lilt in her voice, the sweetness of her perfume. But Richard knew that wasn't it. *Be honest.* It was her sexuality, her passion, her directness that had almost consumed him. In the end, though, it was Anneliese who had been consumed. And the answer to whatever had ignited her pyre, and the key to the threats and mysteries that permeated his life, lay in the blockhouse. That much he was sure of.

He knew now what he was going to do next. In the wake of his visit with Marty and her verbal absolution for his sins, real or imagined, he finally was able to concentrate, to define a course of action, to plan a counterattack. Threats from Veronica von Stade notwithstanding.

He called up an employee roster on BioDawn's intranet and obtained the office location of Trey Robinson, the corporate security manager. Second floor. It was late evening now, and Richard assumed most employees had departed the building. He descended the stairway to the second level, stopping and listening on each landing for footfalls or voices. Nothing.

He reached the second floor and paused after he stepped into the hallway. No one talking. No elevator whine. No sound of doors being opened or shut. He walked to Robinson's office and tried the knob on the solid wood door. Locked. Not that he would have expected otherwise. It was a simple lock that required a key inserted into the center of the knob. The kind a movie hero can always pick. But Richard didn't know how. *Old fashioned way then.*

He knocked softly on the door. No one home. He stepped back and listened again for telltale sounds of late-working employees. All that reached his ears was the white-noise silence of an office after-hours. He judged the distance from his hip to the door, shuffled back a half step, drew his right knee up and launched a kick. His heel hammered home just below the knob. The door sprang open, ripping away part of the frame and splintering the wood around the knob. *Low bidder, a wonderful thing.*

He stopped and listened one more time. There seemed to be no reaction to his forceful entry. He slipped into the office, shut the damaged door, switched on a light and seated himself behind the security manager's desk. He surveyed the room. To his left, standing shoulder to shoulder, were several four-drawer file cabinets. To his right, resting against the wall, was a long oak credenza topped by several bowling trophies and pictures of, presumably, Robinson's family.

Richard, deciding what he was looking for would be kept within easy reach, ignored the cabinets and credenza and started with the desk. A vertical row of drawers lined either side of the desk with the top drawer in each row secured by a small key lock. Richard had guessed that would be the case, and withdrew a sturdy screwdriver from his suit jacket pocket. He went to work on the right-hand drawer, sliding the blade of the screwdriver into the drawer, then leveraging it against a broad steel pin that secured the drawer into its frame. A loud pop announced success. The drawer and all those beneath it sprang free. In the bottom drawer he found what he was looking for: several sets of key cards. He pocketed the cards, shut the drawer, flipped off the light and stepped into the hallway. He froze. The electromechanical groan of the elevator assaulted his ears.

He moved back into the office and listened. The elevator stopped. He heard its doors slide open—*damn it, this floor*—then the determined gait of someone heading in his direction. He calculated whether he had enough time to dash for the stairwell at the far end of the hallway. Not a chance. The thud of heavy shoes drew closer to the office.

Chapter Fifteen

NORTH METRO ATLANTA
THURSDAY, AUGUST 22

Richard guessed the approaching footfalls belonged to a security guard. *Must have triggered a silent alarm.* Plan B, then. He stepped into the hall just as Ralph Pepperill, the night security supervisor he'd met earlier in the week, drew abeam of the shattered door.

"Sir?" Pepperill exclaimed, his lean face unable to hide his surprise at seeing Richard.

"Someone broke into Trey Robinson's office," Richard exclaimed. "I was just leaving work, taking the stairs, when I heard a loud crash come from this floor. Decided I'd better investigate. I found Robinson's door like this. Thought I heard someone running away, but I'm not sure."

"It set off an alarm," Pepperill said. He leaned around Richard, trying to peer into the darkened office. "I'd better call the cops." His breath reeked of hard salami and cheap mustard.

Richard dropped his hand to his coat pocket, attempting to conceal the bulge of the pilfered key cards. "No," he said. "This is a DOD matter. Contact Robinson first, then we'll see where we go from there."

"I'd better have a look," Pepperill said, not responding to the suggestion and reaching for the light switch in Robinson's office.

Richard laid a restraining hand on him, gently. "Don't touch anything in there, Mr. Pepperill. It's a crime scene now. Slap some yellow tape across the door and leave someone up here tonight. Call Robinson first thing in the morning."

"SOP is to call him immediately, sir. I can't wait 'til tomorrow."

Richard started to protest, but realized he probably was treading on dangerous ground, that his reticence would sound suspicious. "Fine," he said, "follow procedure." He knew the time frame for what he wanted to do tonight was about to be compressed. He hadn't counted on this. Well, maybe Robinson lived a long way away. Maybe he'd gone out to dinner. Or a movie. Or a ball game.

"What about the police, sir?" Pepperill picked at his teeth.

Richard shook his head. "No. I'll be the spear catcher for that decision, Mr. Pepperill. Get Robinson out here first."

"You'll be around, sir?" Pepperill asked as he walked toward the elevator.

"In the area," Richard said. A premonition slithered into his thoughts and flicked its tongue. He sensed he'd initiated something he was going to regret.

What the hell. He patted his pocketful of key cards and waited until Pepperill had departed before descending in the elevator.

Outside, the peeps, squeals and rasps of night creatures competed with the low throb of traffic noise off a nearby freeway. Richard stood in the shadows of BioDawn's main building and watched the patrolling security truck. A young man was behind the wheel. Pepperill, he assumed, was occupied trying to get in touch with Robinson. Richard waited until the truck reached the far end of the parking lot, then walked briskly toward the fence surrounding the blockhouse. He'd picked two of the stolen key cards as the most likely candidates to open the gate and held them at the ready.

Sweating profusely, perhaps as much from apprehension as the stifling humidity, he reached the gate. He jammed the first of the cards into the reader. Nothing happened. The red light on the mechanism continued to wink insolently at him. He withdrew the card and tried again, this time inserting it more slowly. Still nothing. He slid the second card into the reader. This time there was a metallic click, and the light flashed green. The gate, mounted on rollers, trundled open, pulling back parallel to the fence. Richard stepped inside. He glanced into the parking lot to see if the security patrol was returning. He couldn't spot it and decided it was somewhere behind the buildings that comprised the corporate complex.

As the gate rolled shut, Richard moved toward the main entrance of the blockhouse. For this door, he'd selected only one card, one conveniently marked *bldg 4*. He inserted it into the reader. The indicator light blinked green, and the door clicked. He pushed it open and stepped into the building. He checked his watch. He'd allow himself fifteen minutes, twenty at the most.

He stared down a long, brightly lit corridor. Except for the hum of the air conditioning, there was no noise, no sign of activity in the blockhouse.

He walked down the hallway—it appeared to be the main one—inspecting the layout of the interior and listening for any sounds that suggested the presence of someone else. The heels of his leather shoes echoed off the hard tile of the floor. The walls of the hall, painted a drab green, stood in stark contrast to the mahogany-paneled opulence of the building in which he worked. He felt as if he were strolling through the corridor of a deserted hospital.

A series of laboratories, according to identifiers on the doors, lined the left-hand side of the hallway. On the right, spaced evenly, were several intersecting corridors. He walked to the end of the main corridor where he encountered a small break room.

He turned and retraced his steps. Now that he was in the blockhouse, he didn't know what the hell he was looking for, what he'd expected to find. To him, the building looked like a run-of-the-mill research facility. But he was certain something off kilter was going on in here.

He walked to where he'd entered the building and turned into the first connecting hallway. Offices lined both sides of the hall. The doors to the offices were solid with no windows, so it was impossible to tell if anyone was in them, working late. At the end of the hallway, he turned into a short connecting passageway that led to a parallel corridor identical to the one he'd just left. He moved along the hallway inspecting the names on the office doors. Dr. Donald Archway. Dr. Ruth Ires-Barnwell. Dr. Cegeon Yee. Mr. Rafael Cordova. Meaningless to him. He reached the main hallway again and paused, considering his next move. He decided the labs and offices needed to be checked individually, but knew that idea was equivalent to spitting into the wind. He hadn't enough time. Besides, he'd noted the locks on the offices; not electronic ones, but old-fashioned pin-and-tumbler ones, the kind that required keys. And he didn't have any. "Shit," he said softly. He wasn't qualified as a spy.

The subdued sound of a door opening and closing came from behind him, from the hallway he'd just scouted. He spun around. A wraith of a woman, small and mousy with a disheveled tumble of brown hair, walked toward him. Head down, fumbling with her briefcase, she didn't notice Richard until she was almost upon him.

"Oh," she said, jerking to a stop, her walking shoes making a sharp, rubbery squeal on the tile, like a basketball player in a gym.

"I'm sorry, miss, I didn't mean to startle you," Richard said. He made a quick decision; he'd found a target of opportunity. "I'm Richard Wainwright." He pulled out his ID. "I'm the CEO *pro tem* at BioDawn. I was supposed to meet Dr. Gonzales here this evening, but I'm afraid I don't know where his office is."

The woman, with a pinched fox-like face, looked closely at the ID, then him. Apparently satisfied they matched, she set her briefcase on the floor and extended her hand. "I'm Dr. Rathke," she said. "Cynthia Rathke. I heard we had a new boss, but I guess I don't pay much attention to administrative goings-on. Buried in my work, I'm afraid." She forced a smile without revealing her teeth. They shook hands, her grip, limp and irresolute.

"What is your work, Ms. Rathke? I'd like to know more about the products and processes BioDawn is developing."

She shrugged. "Most of it's classified. But in general terms, I do research in recombinant DNA. Hoping ultimately to develop more effective vaccines and antidotes for some really nasty bacteria and viruses."

"Such as?"

"Smallpox, various forms of plague and viral encephalitis, tularemia, Ebola."

Pretty much the same stuff the bogus colonel had mentioned. Except for Ebola. He'd heard the name before and knew it was deadly, but didn't know exactly what it was. "Anything specific?" he asked.

"That's about all I can tell you," she answered.

"I understand. Perhaps then you could direct me to Dr. Gonzales' office."

"Well, I'm not sure he's around. He seems to travel a lot, and even when he's here, he's pretty elusive. But, I guess if he told you to meet him here . . ." She cast an uncertain gaze up and down the hall, as if thinking Gonzales might materialize.

"Do others work as late as you?" Richard asked, wanting to learn if he would be alone after she left.

"Not normally. I'm usually the last one out." She picked up her briefcase. "I'll show you where Dr. Gonzales works." She moved down the main corridor in the direction of the break room and stopped at one of hallways running perpendicularly to the right. She pointed down the hall. "Dr. Gonzales' office is behind that door." The hall was much shorter than the others and terminated at a door through which entry could be gained only with a key card. "It's a restricted area," she said. "I'm sorry, but I don't have access to it."

That's all right," Richard said, "I'll get in." His hand rested casually on his coat pocket.

"There's a phone on the wall beside the door," she said. "You can probably call his office, and he'll let you in."

"Thank you, I'll do that. Good night."

He walked down the hall toward the door. She followed.

"I'll be fine," he said. *How do I get rid of her?*

"I'll just make sure you're able to get in."

Great. Now she decides to be Miss Responsible. He reached for the phone's handset, stood in front of the key pad to mask it from Rathke's view and punched in his own extension. He let the phone ring several times, then began a monologue. "Ah, Dr. Gonzales! Richard Wainwright. I was worried you might not be in." He paused, keeping the handset jammed hard against his ear so Rathke wouldn't hear the continuing ring-backs.

"No, no," Richard said, pressing on with his charade. "No problem at all. Your colleague, Dr. Rathke, was kind enough to show me the way." He paused again. "Yes, I understand. Tell you what, I'll see Dr. Rathke out while you wrap up what you're doing." Another pause. "Great. I'll meet you here in about five minutes." He turned to Rathke and flashed a thumbs up. He replaced the handset on the phone, quickly between ring-backs.

"Thank you so much," he said to her. "Dr. Gonzales will be out shortly. I certainly appreciate your help." He swept his arm toward the main hallway. "I'll walk with you to the door." Rathke hesitated, then smiled wanly and began walking, Richard at her side.

After making certain she'd left the building, Richard returned to the entrance of the restricted area. He hadn't the slightest idea which of the key cards, if any, would allow him entry. He had no choice but to try them all. He thumbed through the cards, checking to see if any had markings that suggested it would open the door. None did. One by one, he slipped them into the reader. The red light indicator was relentless in its response. Richard's hope waned. He had only three cards left when the light blinked green, and the electronic lock clicked.

He pushed on the door, a heavy steel barrier, and it groaned open. He stepped into a nearly-dark alcove. It took his eyes a moment to adjust to the artificial dusk. There appeared to be an office or laboratory to his right. But it was what lay straight ahead that sent a chill whispering across his neck and shoulders. Another steel door, broader than the one he'd just opened, blocked his way. Subdued, deep blue light streamed out through a thick window in the door. But it wasn't the door or the light that drew his attention, it was what was on the door: a symbol—four intersecting red rings; and lettering—**BIOHAZARD**. Underneath that was printed:

AIR-LOCK/DECON. PROTECTIVE
SUIT/BREATHING APPARATUS REQUIRED.

Richard's stomach did a half gainer, and his breathing quickened. *Biohazard?* He stepped to the window and peered in. Several, what looked like space suits, hung suspended in a tiny room suffused with ultraviolet light. Switches and digital readouts filled the right wall of the room. In the back wall, another door sported a tiny red "4." The vague odor of disinfectant, diluted but potent, filled his nostrils. He retreated from the window and drew a deep breath. He looked to the side of the door. A keypad indicated that knowing the proper numeric code was the only way in. Not that that made any difference. He had no intention of going any farther. But he knew he'd stumbled onto something that shouldn't be here. Something dangerous. Something deadly.

He took another step back, then felt cold metal against his neck.

"Nine millimeter. Don't turn around," a voice said.

At North Georgia Regional Hospital, Dr. Willand, bathed in sweat and doubled over, his arms clenched around his midsection, sat on a chair in an otherwise empty patient room. The vomiting and diarrhea he so desperately feared had finally begun, flushing away the self-deception he'd clung to for the last two days. He wasn't over-tired. He didn't have a tension headache. He knew all too well the symptoms of Ebola. He was dying.

The virus was already at work, billions upon billions of them, swimming through his bloodstream like swarms of rapacious moray eels. He pictured it. The virus exploding in his body, replicating itself over and over the only way it could, by latching onto living cells and taking over their reproductive machinery.

There was no malevolence in this "intent" he understood, the virus was merely doing what it was designed to do: make copies of itself to ensure its survival. In the process, it destroys its hosts, growing crystalloids or "bricks" of virus within the cells. The bricks continue to expand until they touch the walls of the cells. Then they explode into hundreds of individual viruses, or virions. They burst through the cell walls and sprout from their surfaces like Medusa's hair, microscopic snakes ready to slither into the bloodstream in search of their next host. It's a process that multiplies with frightening rapidity, exponentially. A single Ebola virion reproduces itself in about eight hours. As few as half a dozen Ebola virions can infect a human; the incubation period is as little as two days.

Ebola attacks platelets and endothelial cells in blood vessels with particular ferocity. Platelets allow blood to clot; endothelial cells keep it and other fluids from leaking out. With Ebola in full cry, blood ceases to clot, and capillaries can no longer contain it. Pinpoint hemorrhages and oozing plasma blossom on the surface of major organs as their tissue begins to rot and die. The functions of the kidney, liver and spleen begin to fail. The initial symptoms of crushing fatigue, searing pain and burning fever hammer the victim with frightening suddenness.

The attack within the body intensifies. Fragile blood vessels around the gums and along the soft mucosal surfaces of the gastrointestinal tract begin to rupture with the slightest provocation. The conjunctiva, the membrane covering the cornea of the eye and the inner surface of the eyelid, may bleed profusely, making the eyeball appear infused with blood. Red spots, petechiae, appear on the skin; underneath are tiny hemorrhages. The lining of the throat becomes a mush of destroyed tissue with the consistency of raw hamburger. A pus-like substance drains from the tonsils. The throat becomes swollen and acutely painful. The victim cannot even swallow his or her own saliva.

The destruction of the gastrointestinal tissues accelerates. Severe cramping lances through the victim's abdomen. Watery diarrhea and non-stop vomiting set in. The vomiting becomes excruciating as the lining at the back of the throat begins to peel away.

The microvascular bleeding intensifies. The intestinal lining sloughs off and is defecated, along with copious amounts of tarry blood, in ripping bouts of diarrhea. Explosions of vomit infused with blood and dead tissue shoot from the victim. The emesis has the appearance of liquified coffee grounds.

Internally, the destruction mounts. The kidneys, deprived of oxygen and nutrients by ceaseless hemorrhaging, stop functioning, and the blood becomes toxic with waste normally excreted in urine. The virus goes after the heart and brain. The underlayers of the skin grow pulpy; white blisters intermingle with the petechiae producing a maculopapular rash. The skin of the victim becomes so flushed and sensitive that even the touch of a bed sheet triggers agony. But the victim perhaps no longer cares. He or she is probably comatose or delirious now, or maybe thrashing violently as grand mal seizures wrack the body. The virus has invaded the brain, clogging it with dead blood cells, squeezing off its blood supply.

Even the heart fights a losing battle, leaking blood, hemorrhaging into the ventricles and atria. Finally, the victim's blood pressure tumbles precipitously. The skin blanches and turns clammy. The victim slips into shock from loss of blood and fluid into surrounding tissues. If there are attending physicians, they become desperate. They attempt transfusions and force IV fluids into their patient, but the devastated vessels are like sieves. They merely leak the fluids back into the tissues and sometimes the lungs. Mercifully, death is imminent. Ebola has won. Its conquest has taken a little as eight days.

Dr. Willand wished with all his soul he were home, in his bedroom, next to his closet and the Smith & Wesson .38 in the lockbox. He breathed heavily in and out for a few moments, calculating whether he could make it back to his subdivision. No, he decided. Besides, what he contemplated would be the act of a coward, a man thinking only of himself. It was about other people, too; people who would have to attend to him, or whatever was left of him: his wife, EMTs, firemen and policemen who wouldn't realize the blood splattered throughout the bedroom would be more deadly than anything they'd ever encountered.

No, he wouldn't do that. *Besides, maybe there's still a chance . . .*

A wave a nausea surged through his esophagus, and acidic vomit slashed at the back of his throat. He raced for the restroom across the hall. He fell to his knees in front of the toilet and leaned his head over the bowl.

Chapter Sixteen

NORTH METRO ATLANTA
THURSDAY, AUGUST 22

A heavy-smoker's breath tinged with garlic whispered into Richard's ear. "Why didn't you just take her to bed, Mr. Wainwright? She'd be alive, you'd be alive, everything would be fine."

"I *am* alive."

"Not for long."

The trip-hammer thud of Richard's heart reverberated through his head, the pounding so deafening he could scarcely make out the words of the man behind him. He drew a deep breath, then another, willing himself to quash the panic welling up within him. Willing himself to think. He understood that for the next few moments, time would be his most valuable ally. With time he could analyze, plan, act. *Talk, ask questions, stall. Buy time.*

"Who are you?" he said.

There was no response, only a slow, world-weary expulsion of sour breath.

"Dr. Gonzales? Dr. Alano Gonzales?"

"Walk toward the door. Please."

Richard detected a hint of an accent, but couldn't place it. It wasn't Hispanic.

The gun prodded him toward the steel door labeled BIOHAZARD.

"Stop. Extend your arms and lean forward on the door. Spread your legs."

He followed the commands of his captor. Then nodded at the door. "What goes on in there? Why the biohazard warnings?" *Keep talking.* He needed every second he could get.

"You're much too inquisitive. Much too hands-on, Mr. Wainwright. Why couldn't you have just sat on your Armani-trousered ass and counted your money like most other CEOs? All you had to do was babysit this operation for a few months. Shake hands. Slap backs. Not go sniffing around like some goddamn coon dog trying to root out a wild boar."

"Did I?"

"Did you what?"

"Root out a wild boar?"

"Faah!" the man snorted, almost as if offended.

"Are you Dr. Gonzales? If I don't have long to live, why not tell me?"

The notion of his death unsettled Richard. His mind dug at his suppressed terror, attempting to unearth it, grab it, run in hysterical circles through the fields of his imagination.

"Dr. Gonzales doesn't exist."

The words yanked Richard's focus back to the man holding the 9mm on his neck. "No?" he said. "Then who are you?"

Silence.

"Better I should know my executioner than not."

"Yes."

"So?"

"I am Sami Alnour Barashi. Iraqi, but a naturalized U.S. citizen."

"But not a doctor?"

"Oh, yes, my friend. I studied in Saudi, Russia and America. Right here in Atlanta, at Emory University, as a matter of fact."

He was loosening up, talking. *Keep buying time.*

"A learned man, then?"

"Some would say."

"What is your area of expertise?"

Barashi chuckled, but it ended in a hacking cough. "America will know soon enough."

An icicle of terror rammed itself into Richard's gut. "Know what?"

"Too many questions, Mr. Wainwright. You never know when to stop."

"Not much point in stopping now, is there?"

Richard closed his eyes, scrolling back through Barashi's words. What was it he had first said? *Why didn't you just take her to bed?* Delayed, the impact of the words slammed into him. Barashi knew! He knew about Anneliese. He knew what went on, what almost went on, in her apartment. Had he . . .? "Did you kill her?" Richard half turned his head. The gun bored into his neck with even more force.

"Who?"

"Anneliese."

"You know, Mr. Wainwright, you're a maddening man. If you'd been less diligent about your job, displayed less integrity, walked on the same feet of clay as so many other executives, we wouldn't be standing here tonight. You about to die. Me with yet another complication."

"A complication? Is that what Anneliese was?"

A long sigh. "No. You were the complication. From the moment you arrived. Too much interest in what went on behind these doors. Too eager to meet with distraught widows—"

"Mrs. Scarelli? You—"

"Me? Oh, I don't know. The Western obsession with 'closure,' I think. Americans are hung up on closure; so certain a measure of peace can be found in understanding who or what killed their loved ones that they cling to threads of hope so frayed they wouldn't support a prayer. When I learned Mrs. Scarelli had contacted you—"

"Anneliese? Anneliese told you?" Richard caught his breath. He was well aware he'd been poking at the edges of something dark and dangerous, but had no idea until this moment of the full depth and breadth of the conspiratorial swamp into which he'd waded.

"Pay attention, Mr. Wainwright, we're talking about Mrs. Scarelli. An anonymous call to her was all it took. A promise of stunning revelations about her husband's plane crash, and she loses all caution; gets into a car with a complete stranger and ends up at the bottom of the Chattahoochee River. Hope, Mr. Wainwright, the undying hope for closure." He clucked his tongue, a father saying Shame, shame. "But there is no real closure, is there? Only ongoing despair, ever-present sorrow." He coughed, a smoker's wheeze. "And maybe, if we're lucky, revenge."

The pressure of the gun on Richard's neck relaxed slightly as Barashi shifted his weight.

"You killed her?"

"I made her disappear. I thought that would be enough, that when you didn't hear from her again, you'd brush her off as a flighty, confused widow. Instead, you just kept coming."

"Why wouldn't I? You lit a firecracker under my ass before I even stepped through the front door of BioDawn."

"Lit a firecracker under your ass?"

"Not you specifically. Your lady intimidator, Veronica von Stade, waving a knife in my face and telling me not to get curious."

"You're making stuff up, sir."

"She knew—"

"She knew nothing. Because there is no such person."

The statement hammered Richard like a baseball bat to his forehead. It didn't make any sense. Yet why would Barashi lie?

"What about Anneliese?" Richard's heart beat at an uncontrolled gallop.

"What about her?"

"Was she part of this? Was she working with you?" Somehow the question seemed more important than any of the others he'd asked.

Barashi seemed to sense its gravity, too, for he delayed several moments before answering. When he finally did, it was with measured words. "She worked for me, not with me. And only for money, not ideology. She had no knowledge of my work. When she told me you were asking questions about what went on in the blockhouse, I knew I had to do something to slow you down—" He pressed the gun more forcefully into Richard's neck. "—for all the good it did."

"But why kill her?"

"Because she failed. All she had to do was get you into a compromising situation; you dip your wick, she cries rape. As blatantly trumped up as the charge would've been, it would've been enough to send you packing and get you out of the way. You'd have been disgraced, discredited and dismissed. Out the door with your tail between your legs. An anathema to the board of directors.

"That didn't work, but I realized your dalliance presented me with another opportunity: to frame you for murder. *That* would get you off my trail. But no, here you are, the relentless hunter." Barashi snorted softly. Frustration.

"Why did Anneliese think you wanted me out of the way?"

Richard's brain worked on two levels now: continuing to coax Barashi's story into the open while at the same time trying to develop a lifesaving plan. One thing he knew, he had to get turned around. He could do nothing with his back to the man and a gun in his neck.

"I told her I had reliable information that you were going to steal BioDawn's proprietary technology, spirit it off to some other pharmaceutical corporation, the highest bidder. She bought it. The rush of a little danger, a little sex—"

"And a lot of money."

"Ah, yes, there was that."

Richard's thoughts spun through his mind like tumblers in the Cirque du Soleil. He had to keep the questions coming, keep stalling, check his burgeoning anger, hatch a plan however half-assed and futile it might prove.

"But murder, why?" Richard asked. "Weren't you concerned that would only shine a floodlight on BioDawn and your so-called research?" He spit the words out, struggling to hold his rage in check, wanting to spin around and pummel the piece of human trash behind him. But he knew Barashi would shoot him before he could turn even halfway.

"My work here has been off the books, not directly connected to BioDawn," Barashi answered. "No one knew what I was doing, and no one seemed to care as long as the money kept coming." Barashi paused and sighed. "No one until you came along."

"The plane? Your work, too?" Richard asked.

"Enough, Mr. Wainwright. I'm going to give you a code for the keypad. After I give it to you, move your hand slowly to the pad and enter it."

"And Colonel Landry? On your team?"

"Eight. Five. Zero. Seven. Seven. Three. Punch it in. Please."

He doesn't want to kill me out here, Richard realized. *Too open to discovery. He wants me in that lab, in the lion's den, his lair. No fucking way I'm going through that door.*

"Come on, the colonel? I know he's a phony."

"An actor. A paid actor. Another effort to slow you down. Now punch in the goddamn code. I won't ask again." Barashi's voice rang with anger.

"No."

The gun moved to his spine, pressed more firmly. "No?"

"No." Time to call his bluff. "I'm turning around. I'll do it slowly."

The biggest gamble of my life. Maybe my last. He moved his feet together, dropped his arms and stood erect, his back still to Barashi. He decided if Barashi pulled the trigger, if his life ended here, he would never feel it. Thus he dismissed his terror. He began to pivot. A degree at a time. The pressure of the gun relented.

He completed his turn and looked into the eyes of Alnour Barashi. Wolfish. Dark. Cold. Yet burning with the intensity of lasers. They seemed to radiate something primitive, carefully cultured, nurtured from generation to generation—if not genetically, then certainly socially: unrelenting, unapologetic hatred.

Richard returned Barashi's gaze, knowing it was no match for the Arab's sociopathic stare. The small, olive-skinned man watched him without speaking, his pistol leveled at Richard's nose.

"Fool," Barashi said finally.

"Me, a fool? I don't think so. I'm not the one who slits the throats of women, preys on the losses of widows, brings down the airplanes of innocent men. The acts of a coward. A fool."

Barashi's eyes flickered.

"Then you make a fool's mistake." Richard paused.

Barashi cocked his head slightly, a quick movement. His eyes on fire. Lips dry.

"A fool's mistake," Richard went on, "thinking I came here alone."

"You did."

"You forget BioDawn has a corporate security manager."

"He left at five o'clock."

"Of course he did." Richard smiled. Condescendingly. A seed of doubt planted, he hoped.

A bead of sweat traced a trail of uncertainty across the bridge of Barashi's nose.

"You surely didn't think you'd get away with this?" Richard inclined his head in the direction of the lab. Whatever "this" was.

Barashi's mouth curved into a thin-lipped grin. "You don't know, do you? You don't know anything."

His eyes narrowed to pinpricks of darkness as he continued to speak. "What it's like to live your life in degradation, humiliation, hopelessness. What it's like to coexist with terror in your own home, trembling under the constant threat of American or Zionist bombs plunging through your roof." His words came out clipped and sharp, like jabs of a spear. "Well, America will know. Know the despair of realizing not even their homes are safe. Terrified to step from their doors. To draw a breath." His chest heaved, his gun-hand trembled.

Now, Richard thought, now. He looked directly behind Barashi, as though spotting someone, then let his gaze drop quickly, as if trying to hide a mistake.

Barashi caught the look, uncertain what to do, what it meant. A bluff? Or someone behind him? He jerked his head around in a snap movement to glance to his rear.

Richard launched himself, aiming his head at Barashi's chest, just below the upraised pistol. Barashi already was turning back, saw Richard coming, squeezed the trigger. The blast from the gun deafened Richard, and he felt rather than heard the air erupt from Barashi's lungs as he nailed the Arab dead-center in his sternum.

Both men crashed to the floor, Richard on top, his arms wrapped around Barashi in a bear hug. But Barashi's gun arm was unencumbered. He wielded the 9mm like a club, slamming it against the side of Richard's head.

Red and white arcs of lightning, manifest agony, exploded through Richard's skull. Instinctively, he rolled off Barashi, away from the threat of another crushing blow. As he did, Barashi, still fighting for breath, twisted his body, struggled to bring the pistol to bear on his attacker.

In Richard's pain-infused vision, Barashi shimmied and wobbled like a summer mirage, yet the larger man sensed an advantage: his greater reach. He shot his right hand in the direction of Barashi's gun arm and found it just as Barashi yanked the trigger. Richard's flailing swat altered the trajectory of the bullet just enough. A rush of compressed air, the bow-wave of the shell, swept across his forehead.

Richard's ears rang in a cacophony of deafening thunder as Barashi screamed unheard curses. The two men, still prone, faced each other, Richard's hand grasping Barashi's wrist with the force of a steel-jawed bear trap. Barashi, unable to aim his gun at Richard, contorted his body violently, trying to extricate himself from Richard's grip. Richard jammed a knee into Barashi's midsection, hoping to catch his crotch. He missed, smashing it into his abdomen instead.

Barashi's mouth sprang open, an "O" of surprise, as the force of Richard's attack propelled him backward. Richard flung his body across Barashi's, smashing the Arab's gun arm down hard, onto the tile. The 9mm tumbled from his hand, skittered across the floor toward the far wall.

Richard, dizzy, temporarily deaf, half blinded, struggled to stand, eyes on the gun. He rose unsteadily, but Barashi lashed out with his legs, knocking Richard's out from under him. He toppled. Barashi turned away, scrambled toward the pistol on his hands and knees.

Richard tried to focus, spot the gun, judge the distance. It was a race he couldn't win. Barashi would reach it first. There was only one option. Get out. He staggered to his feet, searched for the exit. There. It swam distorted in his vision, as if under water. He forced his feet to move toward it. He thought he was running, but wasn't sure. He reached the door.

An indistinct explosion registered in his brain. Something smacked into his shoulder, stinging, bruising. He reached the door, extended both hands and hit its crossbar release. He stumbled into the hallway and kept going. Waves of pain radiated from his shoulder. He reached the main corridor, turned, kept running. He was surprised he was moving so fast, no longer young, no longer in the best of shape. But fear and pain are great motivators, superb adrenaline producers. He didn't turn to see if Barashi were pursuing. He didn't have to. He knew he was.

He saw the building's exit ahead and sprinted even harder, zigzagging as he approached it. A spray of wood erupted from one of the laboratory doors. Plaster geysered from a wall. The only way Barashi could get a clean shot, Richard realized, would be if he stopped his pursuit and fired from a static position. But if he stopped, that would give Richard the few seconds he needed to escape. Either way, Richard figured he had the edge now. The wild firing ceased, and Richard assumed Barashi had opted to stop and steady himself for a final shot.

Richard hit the door at full velocity. His hearing had partially returned; something cracked past his head, the near miss of a bullet, a sound he hadn't heard since live-fire training in the Marines. He hurled himself into the floodlight-lit yard. His only impediment now was the sliding gate in the fence. He dashed toward it, saw a green-glowing button adjacent to it, hammered it with his fist. With agonizing slowness, the gate yawned open. He looked back. Barashi appeared at the door of the blockhouse. As soon as the gate had pulled back mere inches, Richard squeezed through, ripping his suit jacket on a metal prong.

He bolted toward his Mini, saw the headlights of a vehicle approaching him, flagged it down.

The driver, Trey Robinson, stuck his head out the window. "What the hell's going on here? Pepperill phoned, said—"

"Call the police," Richard panted. "Barashi has a gun." He pointed toward the blockhouse as Barashi charged through the gate.

"Who?"

"Dr. Gonzales. He's armed. Shooting. Gone nuts. The police, call the police." Richard hoped to hell Robinson had a cell phone with him.

Robinson's eyes widened to the size of tennis balls. He became a bobble-head doll, his gaze jerking from Richard to Barashi and back again.

Richard realized Robinson's ambivalence could cost him his life. "Get out of here," he yelled, "go, go." He resumed his sprint and looked over his shoulder. Barashi, gun shielded behind his back, strolled casually toward Robinson, waving a greeting. Robinson opened the door of his car. Richard stopped, wheeled. "Don't get out," he screamed. "Stay in the car."

Robinson hesitated, one foot out the door, did his bobble-head routine again. Barashi approached, raised the gun, fired two rounds into the security manager's head. Robinson toppled back into the car, then slid out, feet first, crumpling onto the pavement. Barashi stepped over him, reached into the car, turned off the lights and ignition.

Richard turned and ran. He reached the Mini, fumbled for his keys, thumbed the remote unlock, scrambled into the car. He cranked the engine and rammed the gearshift lever into reverse, screaming in pain as he did so. A lava flow of agony knifed through his shoulder. The tires squealed in shock as the Mini leapt backward, then forward. Richard accelerated out of the lot, wincing in pain and yelling as catharsis each time he shifted. In his rearview mirror, he spotted a volley of muzzle flashes. A blizzard of glass and plastic blew through the car.

Richard reached the exit onto the main road, the Mini still sounding healthy, but probably not looking that way. The searing in his shoulder bordered on excruciating. Sweat poured off him in thick rivulets, whether because of the pain, shock or fear—or all three—he didn't know. He forced himself to focus on his escape and bulled the Mini into traffic, incurring the wrath of at least half-a-dozen drivers, all of whom laid on their horns. Oncoming cars flashed their headlights at him, and he realized his were off. He switched them on, glanced in his side mirror, saw headlights coming out of BioDawn. Barashi.

Chapter Seventeen

NORTH METRO ATLANTA
THURSDAY, AUGUST 22

A distorted storm of color—sodium lights, traffic signals, neon signs—whirled in Richard's vision. Using his rearview mirror, he tracked Barashi's headlights through the swarm of traffic that buzzed along the busy multi-laned road. The boulevard, lined with strip malls, car dealerships and gas stations, offered no escape routes. He had no idea where he was running to; didn't know where the police station or hospital was; knew there was nothing to be gained by dashing for his apartment. He fumbled for the cell phone in his suit jacket, thinking 911. But it was too dark, and he was too rushed to operate it. He left it where it was.

Up ahead, a red traffic light. He slammed on the Mini's brakes. The traffic behind him compressed, Barashi four or five vehicles back. Richard saw an opportunity. To avoid using his right arm, he reached across his body with his left and slipped the gearshift lever into first. The Mini was the lead car in its lane. Before the traffic signal changed back to green, there would be a green arrow for left turning vehicles in both directions. That would be his opening, his chance.

He revved the engine. Cross-traffic cleared, but not before three cars ran the red. He popped the clutch, peeled straight through the intersection, darting directly in front of a dual-lane phalanx of turning vehicles. He searched for flashing blue lights. Nothing. *Of course not, not when I really need a cop.* He shifted into second gear, winced, nailed the accelerator to the floor and wove through traffic with Go-Kart aplomb. Albeit sloppily. He wasn't a skilled driver to begin with and now was hurting badly. At least the Mini was forgiving.

The pain in his arm spread, metastasizing throughout his body. His vision tunneled. His thoughts narrowed. His mind focused solely on survival, on fleeing to a place of safety, a familiar haven. Here, where he was an outlander, he knew of only one.

A minute or two later he blew into an intersection he was certain he had come through earlier in the day. He snapped the steering wheel to the right and accelerated down a dark lane shrouded in drooping trees. Thankfully, not much traffic. A good thing, for the yellow center line on the road blurred and wiggled in his sight. Waves of pain rippled through his body.

Perhaps a quarter mile behind him, headlights appeared, moving fast. He rounded a bend in the road, saw the entrance to the parking lot of Marty's church. Think, he told himself, Think. *Must lose Barashi.* He switched off the Mini's lights. He depressed the clutch, coasted into the lot and, not wanting his brake lights to be seen, pulled gently on the parking brake to slow the car. The pursuing headlights raced past the church. But Richard knew they'd be back. Still, there'd be enough time to warn Marty, keep her safe . . . if he could.

He staggered from the car.

Barashi slowed his vehicle. He'd lost his quarry. No traffic appeared ahead of him on the sparsely-traveled road. Not even the moving shadow of a fleeing car without headlights. There was only one place Wainwright could have turned off. Barashi spun his steering wheel, threw his vehicle into a lurching 180-degree turn and raced back toward the church.

Once there, he circled the main building slowly, carefully, and found the shot-up Mini parked in back. He pulled in behind it, keeping his headlights on high beam. He slapped a fresh 17-round clip into his Glock and stepped from his vehicle. He approached the Mini from the rear, pistol extended in front of him. An empty car greeted him, but a smear of blood stained the driver's seat. He checked his watch, cursed. Wainwright had gained a good five or six minutes on him.

Barashi drove to the front of the church, parked and—holding the gun behind his back—entered the darkened vestibule. Several hallways fanned out from there. Down one corridor, a scrubwoman on her hands and knees, wielding a large brush, swiped it over the floor in broad, lazy circles. A ratty-looking baseball cap perched sideways on her head, and a tattered sweat suit hung on her like peeling wallpaper. She looked up as he approached. A bored stare.

"Did a man just come in here?" Barashi asked. "A hurt man, maybe bleeding?" He kept the gun behind his back.

She shrugged, went back to her scrubbing.

Barashi stepped closer, put his foot on the brush.

She stopped her work, looked up again. "Are you the police?" she said. A hesitant, tired voice. Maybe a little frightened.

"Just tell me. Did a wounded man come into the church during the last five minutes or so?"

She nodded, her eyes more alert, wider now. "He was shot in the shoulder. Reverend De la Serna called the police, then took him to the hospital. North Georgia Regional, I think."

"When?"

"Maybe a couple of minutes ago."

"You're sure?"

"I saw the man come in, he was hurt. I paged the reverend. I watched them leave."

"Where is the reverend's office?"

She inclined her head toward the far end of the hall. "Down there. Next left."

Barashi stuck the 9mm into the back of his trousers, covered it with his shirt and walked in the direction of her nod. The scrubwoman stood. "The reverend left. She's not in." Her voice seemed edged in panic.

Barashi turned. "Her? A female?" He wasn't a devout Muslim, but the idea of a female cleric was repugnant.

The woman nodded.

"Faah," he snorted and stalked toward the office.

Marty sensed her flimsy charade coming apart at the seams. Barashi was not going to take her word. "I told you they left," she yelled after him, raising her voice to warn Richard who lay wounded in her office.

Barashi wheeled, glared at her, raised a finger to his lips. He reached the door of her office, turned the knob, nudged the door partially open with his foot. He reached under the back of his shirt with his right hand and brought out a handgun. With his left, he switched on the office light. He took a two-handed grip on the pistol, crouched and kicked the door wide open. Still in a crouch, he burst into the office.

Terrified, Marty found herself frozen in place, an impotent stalagmite in her own church, waiting for the explosion of Barashi's gun.

But then, nothing. Slowly, Barashi backed out of the office. Head down, pistol up, he appeared to be tracking something on the floor. He turned away from Marty and continued down the hallway, the 9mm extended in front of him.

Marty trailed at a discreet distance, seeing the drops of blood on the carpet that Barashi followed. He reached a rear exit, pushed open the door and peered out into the darkness.

He muttered an obscenity and yanked the door shut, sending a metallic reverberation careening through the empty corridors of the church. Wainwright had escaped. There was no point in pursuing him further. The lab was exposed, yes, but it made no difference now. Even though the authorities would be able to figure out what the facility had been used for—the pathogens handled in a Level-4 lab narrow the possibilities markedly—they still would be clueless regarding the time and targets of his attack.

He tucked the gun back into his waistband and strode past the petrified charwoman. "Back to work," he said, pointing at her brush.

While at Emory, he'd made a cursory study of the Christian religion and its strange abstract notions of love, tolerance and forgiveness. Yet the only verses of the Bible he'd bothered to memorize were two from Revelation, passages rife with images of horror and despair. He recalled them now, in this place of Christian worship, Christian hypocrisy: "The fifth angel poured out his bowl on the throne of the beast, and his kingdom was plunged into darkness. Men gnawed their tongues in agony and cursed the God of heaven . . ."

He reached the front exit and paused, listening for the scrape and grate of the scrub brush to resume.

Marty continued moving the brush in uneven circles long after she'd heard Barashi's footfalls fade. Her arm trembled so badly she could barely control the motion of the brush. Her fear had subsumed her instinct to pray. *Well, too late now.* She stood on wobbly legs and dunked the brush into a bucket of gray water. She picked up the pail and walked to the vestibule. She stopped and listened. Nothing. Quiet. She moved to the exit. No one around. She opened the door and walked halfway down the sprawling stairs that fronted the church.

Only a few cars remained in the parking lot, and she recognized all of them—hers and those of the few employees who normally worked late. She walked back to her office.

She entered cautiously, not knowing what to expect. Certainly not what she found—Richard, his face pale, sitting on the floor behind her desk, looking up at her with dull eyes. She came around the desk and knelt by him. "Don't tell me you were hiding under the rug," she said.

He shook his head.

"Where then?"

"Kitchen."

"The blood?"

"Nail polish. I found some in your desk drawer. Left a trail to the exit. Hid in the kitchen 'til I heard Barashi leave."

"Lucky for you I don't use pink."

"Barashi might have thought I was anemic." It seemed a struggle for him to get the words out.

She didn't laugh. "This scared the hell out of me, you know."

"Are ministers supposed to say that?"

"What?"

"That they've had the hell scared out of them?"

"Only when they have."

"I'm sorry, I shouldn't have dragged you into this."

"Oh, fine, now you get a conscience." She tried to make her words sound light, but wasn't sure she succeeded. "Well," she said, "let's have a look at you."

She peeled off his jacket, then his bloodied shirt. It appeared as though the bullet had passed through his shoulder without hitting anything critical. There was a moderate amount of blood and bruising, but nothing that hinted at shattered bones or arterial bleeding. Tissue and muscle damage, yes, but nothing serious. Her biggest concern was that he seemed on the verge of shock.

"Lie down," she commanded. She grabbed a cushion off a nearby chair. "Here, put your feet on this." She tucked the cushion under his heels.

She probed his wound lightly with her fingers, her heart fluttering. She felt strangely, even guiltily, exhilarated. Perhaps from the sudden change of pace in her life, perhaps from having stared evil in the face and called its bluff, or maybe—and she tried to prevent herself from articulating the thought—from remembrances of winter nights in a steamed-up Chevy. Her fingers traced the firmness of his shoulders and back; something stirred deep within her, something that had lain dormant, suppressed for years. *No.* She withdrew her hand as though it had been singed and ordered her thoughts back to the Biblical straight and narrow.

"Let me get a washcloth and some bandages," she said, "and I'll patch you up. But maybe you should go to a hospital after that."

He shook his head. "I'm feeling a little less cobwebby now, nurse." He attempted a grin, but failed. He winced in pain instead.

She reached out and touched the side of his face. "Looks like the guy took a Louisville Slugger to you, too."

"Nine millimeter, actually."

"You ever think of going into a different line of work?"

"Like CEOs run into this all the time."

"I'll be right back," she said, "I need to get a first-aid kit."

She returned shortly and began working on his shoulder, cleaning the wound and applying antiseptic. "You seem to have kept a pretty cool head through all of this," she said. "Military? I seem to recall you were ROTC."

"Ouch," he said, squirming. "I was commissioned by the Marines. Four years."

"Hold still." She grasped his shoulder more firmly, swabbing its shredded flesh with determination. "Were you ever in combat? Ever shot at before?"

"I was never under fire for real. Lots of live-fire exercises though." He flinched as she sprayed antiseptic onto his wound.

"I was terrified tonight, you know," she said.

"Join the crowd."

"But you did something, you reacted. I was paralyzed, a total wimp."

"No, you did just fine. I didn't expect you to leap on his back and hammer him with a scrub brush."

"Ministers aren't supposed to do that." She placed the antiseptic back into the first-aid kit.

"That's my point. Under the constraints of your calling, you did just fine. You held your poise."

"I lied."

"I think God will forgive you."

"I know. But what . . . what if I'd had to shoot him or something?" She swallowed hard, unsettled by the thought. "I don't think I could have done that."

"Oh, I'm not so sure. If someone were threatening to kill you, it might come pretty naturally."

She shook her head. "No. I'm afraid I'm strictly a Matthew 5:39 gal." She examined his wound closely, dabbing at it with a piece of gauze.

"A what kind of gal?"

"Matthew 5:39. 'If someone strikes you on the right cheek, turn to him the other also.'"

"Our modern world is way beyond cheek-slapping. Think bullets and bombs."

"Even so. I don't know. Long before I had a calling to enter the ministry I couldn't kill anything. Sort of inherent, I guess. My brothers used to take me rabbit hunting in the North Carolina mountains. I always aimed high if I saw a bunny. My brothers thought I was just a lousy shot." She began swathing his shoulder in a bandage. "I'm not sure I know how to do this."

"Here, help me sit up." He extended his uninjured arm to her. "It'll make it easier for you."

She pulled him into a sitting position, then continued to wrap his shoulder. Still, she struggled with the task. "Good thing I'm into saving souls, not bodies," she muttered.

He attempted to raise his arm to make her work less of a challenge, but was unable lift it. "That's pretty sore," he said, "I don't know how in the hell—heck—I'm going to be able to drive. Can't shift."

"Don't worry. I can chauffeur you around for awhile."

"Not a chance. I need to get out of here. I've already put you in danger."

"'Yea though I walk through the Valley . . .' I'll be fine. I've got a .38 in my desk."

"That doesn't track very well with Matthew."

"I have an alter ego: a hit woman." She instantly regretted her flippancy. "Sorry, not funny. I forgot you actually encountered one."

"That's okay. She's apparently more of a slicer than a shooter."

"Nice you can find humor in that."

"Well, I know turning the other cheek wouldn't have worked."

"You're positive?"

"With all due respect, Marty, most ministers never come face-to-face with someone who wants to relieve them of body parts or put holes in them."

She finished binding Richard's shoulder, then sat next to him. "You're probably right," she said. "Ministers, priests, rabbis, most of us live lives that are largely insular and isolated. But maybe we have to. Maybe that's what keeps us in touch with God."

"And the rest of us? We aren't?"

She dismissed his question with a flick of her head. "Your contact with Him can be as close or distant as you want. My colleagues and I just have different job requirements, that's all." She stood up and looked down at Richard. "How's the shoulder?"

"Hurts. But at least the rest of me is feeling better." He put his left hand on the carpet, preparing to push himself up, then stopped. He looked up at her. "Do your job requirements parallel your personal beliefs?"

She sucked in a sharp breath. She'd always thought of her response as being polished and subtle. No one before had ever picked up on the personal evasiveness embedded in it. "Why do you ask?" she said, her words hesitant.

"You made a point of separating the two: job requirements and personal choices regarding God."

She bent to help him up. "It was just an academic distinction."

He stood and stared directly at her with the same intelligent, compassionate gaze that had made her tremble with infatuation over twenty years ago.

"Bullshit," he said softly. "You said earlier you know me. Well, I know you, too. There's something you're hiding from me. Maybe from everyone. Something that happened—"

"I'm the minister," she interrupted, "you confess to me, not vice versa."

"Don't hide behind your ecclesiastical skirts, Marty."

"Don't overstep your bounds," she snapped.

He held up his good arm and backed off. "I'm sorry."

"Me, too." She bowed her head. She'd overreacted when someone had been only trying to reach out to her.

"Truce?" he asked.

"Of course." She shifted her thoughts back to the matter at hand. "Let me call the cops. Get some EMTs here. My nurse work was pretty sloppy."

"Just help me on with my shirt," he said. "I need to get out of here."

"Read my lips: You. Are. Not. Leaving. You just told me you can't drive." She stepped to her desk and picked up her phone.

"No," he ordered. "No police. I . . . let me gather my thoughts."

"About what? Someone tried to kill you."

"I know, but law enforcement agencies will have flooded BioDawn by now. Security will have told them I was there. This guy Barashi they may not even know about. Then there's the matter of me being a 'person of interest' in the murder of my executive assistant. I'm thinking I may want to talk to a lawyer before I talk to the cops again."

A phone rang, the soft chime of a cell.

Richard looked at Marty.

"I don't have one," she said.

He reached for his jacket, extracted his iPhone.

"Wainwright," he barked, answering the call.

Marty watched the color, what little was left, drain from his face as he listened to whomever was on the other end.

Chapter Eighteen

NORTH METRO ATLANTA
THURSDAY, AUGUST 22

The BioDawn parking lot shimmered in baseball-stadium brilliance as floodlights pierced the night, illuminating static herds of law enforcement vehicles. Cavorting moths and darting night birds performed an ageless ballet in the incandescent glow. Half-a-dozen TV satellite trucks, like electronic gargoyles, squatted along a perimeter defined by yellow crime-scene tape, a boundary beyond which the media were not to venture. Police stood in small groups carrying on animated conversations. They stopped and watched as Dwight Butler, dressed as if he were arriving in Margaritaville, not at a killing ground, strode past, heading for the blockhouse. His sandals clip-clopped in counterpoint rhythm to a timpani of crickets.

Within the restricted zone, a sheet covered the body of what the virologist presumed was the murdered security manager. A dark pool of liquid exuding a slight coppery odor oozed from beneath the sheet. Next to the victim's automobile, a handful of investigators plied their trade, searching for the minutiae of physical evidence.

Near the blockhouse, bomb-sniffing dogs and FBI experts using electronic probes scoured the exterior of the illegal lab, searching for booby traps, he guessed. After they finished, Dwight, not trusting the Chemturion gear left behind by Dr. Gonzales, donned a CDC protective suit with self-contained breathing apparatus. He drew a number of deep breaths to slow his respiration rate, then entered the terrorist's lair. As he pushed through the airlock door, he caught his reflection in the door's window. He thought he looked slightly ridiculous, something akin to the Pillsbury Doughboy wearing a bee keeper's hood. He didn't laugh.

The door hissed shut behind him, and he waddled slowly, carefully into the bowels of the Level-4 containment facility. It was obvious it had been used for bioengineering. Two electron microscopes and their ancillary computer equipment dominated the lab. Stainless steel counters, sinks and storage racks lined the walls. A proliferation of wires and hoses, like high-tech jungle vines, dangled from the ceiling. Specimen slides, clean, sat next to the microscopes. Small cages, empty, rested in a dark corner; they obviously had housed test animals of some sort. Probably very unfortunate test animals.

A chill slithered up the back of Dwight's neck. He intuitively sensed what had gone on in here; he'd seen it at the CDC—magnified 150,000 times. He didn't touch anything for he knew FBI and CDC investigators still needed to gather evidence. It probably would be a wasted effort, for he was virtually certain they would find a sterile lab, devoid of any trace of Ebola. CDC's Special Pathogens Branch would have to confirm that, but whether it found anything or not would be academic. There was not an iota of doubt in his mind he was standing at ground zero of the 21st century equivalent of Trinity in the New Mexico desert, 1945. He thought of what J. Robert Oppenheimer had said then, recalling a line from a Hindu poem: "I am become Death, the shatterer of worlds."

But now it was a microscopic virus, not a megaton bomb.

"What's that?" Agent Babb asked, pointing to something that looked like a tiny horizontal bar graph. He peered over Dwight's shoulder as the virologist leafed through a journal he had found in Dr. Gonzales' office.

"It looks like the genome of Gonzales' bioengineered virus. Remarkable. Remarkable." Dwight ran his finger along the diagram. "There. Ebola-Zaire. And here, Ebola-Reston. See?"

Babb shook his head. "Not really. You mean there are different kinds of Ebola?" Dwight had explained earlier the basics of the virus and how it kills, but not much else.

Dwight looked up. His eyes, heavy and tired, felt as if they were responding to the weight of what had been discovered. He snapped the journal shut and leaned back in his chair. "The first recorded outbreak of Ebola," he said, "was noted in Zaire, now the Democratic Republic of the Congo, in 1976 near the Ebola River. Over 300 people were infected, and almost all of them died. Later that year, another outbreak swept through a small area of Sudan killing about 150 people. Thus we had Ebola-Zaire and Ebola-Sudan."

"Named for the geographical location of the outbreak?"

Dwight nodded. "And their unique genomes. There's also a subtype known as Ivory Coast, but only one case of that has been recorded. A new strain popped up in 2007, Ebola-Bundibugyo. But Zaire and Sudan are the main ones, and they seem to recur sporadically. Zaire mainly in the DRC and Gabon; Sudan primarily in Sudan and Uganda. The last big explosion was in 2007 in the DRC. 264 people got sick, over 70 percent died."

"So the outbreaks are confined to Africa?" Babb plopped heavily into a chair across from Dwight.

"Of the type fatal to humans, yes. In 1989, there was an outbreak of Ebola in monkeys in a quarantine facility in Reston, Virginia. That's what the book *The Hot Zone* was about. Four people developed antibodies to the virus, but none became ill. The monkeys didn't fare as well."

"The monkeys were from Africa?"

"No. The Philippines. And there's been several outbreaks of Ebola-Reston since then. In Texas, again in Virginia, and also in Italy and the Philippines. Bad news for monkeys, but not for humans . . . fortunately."

"So where does it come from, where does it live, Ebola?"

Dwight stood to stretch his legs, to force himself to remain alert. The adrenaline rush from earlier, from entering the lab, had worn off.

"The virus is what we call zoonotic, animal-borne," he said and began pacing, his sandals slapping the floor. "It needs an animal host to maintain itself. But so far we've been unable to identify its natural reservoir. All we know is it lives in the rain forests of Africa and Asia. Bats were a prime suspect for a long time, but researchers screened over 3000 vertebrates, including 500 bats and 30,000 arthropods, and came up with nothing. Zip. Zero. It's damn discouraging."

An FBI agent stuck his head in the door and spoke to Babb. "Sir, just wanted to let you know the County Police Mobile Command Center is setting up operations in the parking lot. We've also asked the Army's Technical Escort Unit to send a couple of companies. They might be able to help with rapid sampling and decontamination, if it comes to that. We've also got two Marine FAST companies on the way, one from Norfolk, the other from Yorktown."

Babb gave a thumbs-up, and the agent departed.

"A FAST company?" Dwight said.

"Fleet Antiterrorism Security Team. They have a variety of skills, including counter-surveillance, security ops, urban combat and close combat. They won't necessarily go hunting for our terrorist, but they can help defend and set traps around potential targets."

"If only we knew what his targets were," Dwight said, then added, "You know, if he lets this shit loose at the airport—"

"It's a major international crisis within hours," Babb interrupted. "Yeah, I know." He paused, appearing to be lost in thought for a moment, then said, "I'm puzzled over something you said earlier. The numbers on the Ebola outbreaks you cited don't sound that large. A few hundred victims at most. That doesn't exactly smack of disaster."

"Ebola-Zaire and-Sudan outbreaks tend to be self-limiting since the virus can't survive without a live host. Once the host, the victim, dies, the virus stops replicating. Even before that happens, though, Ebola is spread only through close contact with victims, by way of their blood primarily. But now, with Gonzales' bioengineered contagion . . ."

He picked up Gonzales' journal and waved it. "This guy's taken Reston, harmless to humans, but capable of airborne transmission, and married it to Zaire, highly lethal to humans. Even if it survives only a few hours outside a host, we've got a bug that can infect from a sneeze or puff of wind; good God, from a deep breath while you're out jogging or playing tennis. You'd never know it was there." He slammed the journal back onto the desk. "And now we don't have a clue where this sonofabitch is, let alone when or where he's going to attack. If we're lucky, we've got maybe a day or two to figure it out."

"Hell," Babb said, "not only don't we know where this bastard is, we don't even know for sure who he is. I'm betting not Dr. Alano Gonzales."

"And Richard Wainwright, the CEO? How's he mixed up in all this?"

Babb shrugged. "Don't know. Maybe he isn't. Maybe he's just a walk-on. Or maybe he and Gonzales had some sort of alliance that fell apart. All I know is he's wanted for questioning in the murder of his executive assistant and in the shooting of the security manager here."

Richard pressed the phone firmly to his ear, wanting to make certain of what he was hearing.

"So," the voice on the other end said, "you have met Dr. Sami Alnour Barashi."

"Who is this?"

"Someone who knows him. Someone who has worked with him." The voice, soft, well-modulated, heavily accented, Middle Eastern, paused, then said, "Someone who knows what he is going to do."

Richard, stunned by the words, stared wide-eyed at Marty who flashed him a what's-going-on look. He shook his head in puzzlement, then said to his caller, "Say that again."

"I know what Barashi is going to do."

"And that is?"

"Oh, yes, like I am just going to blurt that out, Mr. Wainwright."

"Why are you calling then?" Richard, his head fuzzing, plopped into a chair, the one he'd sat in during his first visit to Marty's office.

"To arrange a meeting," the voice on the phone continued.

"Ah, let me guess. I'm the prey, you're the bait."

"As you Americans say, 'the cat is out of the sack.' It would not make much sense to kill you now."

"Revenge?"

"Barashi will have his revenge. But he does not care about *you* any longer. Ironically, I am probably at greater risk now."

"Money. You want money then." Richard pointed at a notepad on Marty's desk. She handed it to him along with a pen.

"I do want money, Mr. Wainwright. But only enough to get me out of the country and established elsewhere. This is not an information-for-money offer. I am not interested in getting rich. I am interested in staying alive."

"Explain."

"I have no love for Americans, Mr. Wainwright. To me, the martyrs who destroyed the Twin Towers are heroes. But Dr. Barashi has become blinded by his hatred, enamored of his scientific achievement. He is planning to unleash a plague on America that cannot be contained. Cannot be held within sovereign borders, cannot discriminate among Christian, Jew or Muslim. He lets it loose in Atlanta, twenty-four hours later it is in London, Jerusalem, Cairo and Melbourne. I want out. Away. As fast as I can. I want America to stop him. But if you fail, or even if you foil the attack and he escapes, he will hunt me down to the ends of the earth. Two hundred thousand dollars. In cash."

"Not going to happen, my friend. I can't get that kind of cash on short notice."

There was no response.

"You still there?" Richard said.

The voice responded in tight, angry tones. "This is not a bloody intelligence souk, Mr. Wainwright. I am not bartering. Two hundred thousand. Cash. Pocket money to a company like BioDawn. Take it or leave it. Either way, I am on a plane out of Atlanta by midday tomorrow."

Richard had been involved in tough negotiations before, but this, he realized, would be his toughest. And one he couldn't afford to botch. "Listen to me," he said, keeping his tone firm but non-confrontational, "corporations, large or small, just don't have that kind of currency lying around. And neither do banks, believe it not. I know. I've been involved in big transactions before. It takes several days lead time to set up large cash withdrawals."

"Then you're shit out of luck, Mr. Wainwright."

"And so are you. You'll be on the run with empty pockets. How far do you think you'll get? How long do you think you'll be able to hide?"

Silence ensued from Richard's caller.

"Look," Richard said, knowing he had the advantage now, "we both want something here. You want money, I want information. I have a proposal."

"Tell me."

"I can get a cashier's check—"

"No check. Cash, damn you." The words came out almost in a shout.

"Listen to me, my friend. We can make this work. The cashier's check will be drawn on a Wells Fargo Bank. Once it's cut, I can't stop payment on it. I'll bring you the check plus a couple of thousand in cash to get you started. I have no interest in stopping you or deceiving you. I merely want what you have. Your price is fair."

"I don't trust you."

"Yes? And I should trust you?"

A long pause, then: "Okay. We have a deal, Mr. Wainwright."

"Time and place?" Richard picked up the pen, but discovered he couldn't grip it. It slipped from his fingers and cartwheeled onto the carpet.

"Ten o'clock. A place on South Atlanta Parkway called Diamond Cutters. Near the airport."

"What's that?"

"What is what?"

"Diamond Cutters."

"It is what Americans call a gentlemen's club," Richard's caller said. "A titty bar, I believe I have heard it referred to as."

"A good Muslim would know these things, of course."

Again, a clipped, outraged voice on the phone. "I know you wish to believe all Muslims are unfaithful and weak before Western temptations, Mr. Wainwright, but it is not so. I have never been in such a place. I have chosen it precisely for that reason and because it is open twenty-four hours a day. Also, it is a public place which will afford both of us an opportunity to scout for traps."

"How will I know you?"

"You will not; not until I sit beside you. Take a seat at the bar and wait. You are not a hard man to recognize. And if I even think you have brought the police or FBI—even *think*, not know—you will never see me. Understood?"

"Perfectly. But there's one more thing."

"Yes?"

"Your name."

"My name?"

"Yes, if you want a cashier's check."

"Ebraheem Khassem."

"Spell it, please."

Khassem did. Then said, "Ten o'clock," and hung up.

"What was that all about?" Marty said. She hovered next to Richard.

"Ever been to a strip club?" Richard asked.

"Been to one! I used to work in one. Before I came to Jesus."

"This is another hit woman bit, isn't it?"

"You don't think I could have been a stripper?"

"I think you could've been. I don't think you were." Richard sensed there was something glowing, a fire in a peat bog, deep in the persona of this curious woman he thought he knew but wasn't so sure now. Flippant and fanciful on one hand; thoughtful and learned on the other. A minister harboring the soaring imagination of a screen writer.

"So what's the deal?" she asked.

Richard paused before responding. He didn't wish to drag Marty any deeper into this. He'd already put her in harm's way. And her whimsical attitude was, well, disconcerting. Could she be relied upon? Was she really taking this seriously?

Yet, for transportation, what options did he have? A taxi? He wouldn't exactly be a forgettable fare: six-foot-four, pony-tailed, wounded in the arm and probably being promoted on TV as a "person of interest" in two shootings. The same drawbacks would apply to mass transit. Not only that, he was totally unfamiliar with Atlanta's train and bus system.

If Marty were just going to provide a vehicle and maintain a low profile, then she'd probably be okay, not in jeopardy. Still . . .

Against his better judgment he answered her by saying, "I'm going to need a driver."

Chapter Nineteen

NORTH METRO ATLANTA
FRIDAY, AUGUST 23

Richard slept fitfully on a cot Marty set up for him in the church's choir room. Shortly after sunrise, as he drifted in and out of a semiconscious slumber, the ringing of his cell phone jerked him fully awake. Khassem again? Enough daylight filtered into the room to signal it was morning, but the illumination wasn't bright enough to help him spot his cell. Instead, he stood and stumbled toward the source of the ringing.

He found the phone resting on a stack of hymnals and answered the call. "Richard," he said.

"Where the hell are you?" A commanding, cranky voice. American. Not his caller from the previous evening.

"Who is this?"

"A detective with a warrant for your arrest."

"Ah, Lieutenant Jackson. Good to hear from you again."

"Look, Mr. Wainwright, let's make this easy for both of us. Two hours. Turn yourself in in two hours at the nearest police station."

Richard, in his underwear, perched on the edge of the cot. "Charges?"

"The murder of Anneliese Mierczak. We're also very interested in talking to you about the shooting of Mr. Trey Robinson, BioDawn's security manager. You broke into his office. Oh, and our friends at the FBI and Homeland Security would like to chat with you, too. Seems as though they've got you scoped out as some sort of Osama bin Wainwright." Jackson chuckled at his play on words.

"Let's start with Mierczak," Richard snapped. "What's the evidence?"

"For one thing, your fingerprints all over the murder weapon."

"That's it, fingerprints? The Three Little Pigs were on firmer ground than that. Look, I took the knife out of a drawer at Ms. Mierczak's request before dinner. We were having chateaubriand."

"Well, I'm just one little pig, hot shot. All I want is your ass off the street. To pick up on your fairy tale schtick, you seem to be leaving a trail of bodies like Hansel and Gretel left bread crumbs."

"All you have to do is check the parking lot surveillance cameras to see who shot Robinson."

"Fried by lightning in the storm the other night."

"How convenient."

"For you or me?"

Richard sensed the temperature of his core rising, about ready to blow the containment dome. "So how do you know I was even there last night? No pictures, no witnesses."

"You probably should have shot Dr. Rathke, too. And maybe the night security supervisor for good measure. Seems as though he found you loitering near the kicked-in door of Robinson's office."

"Yeah, I guess I'm a total fuckup as a criminal. Next time around I'll go into police work. The standards seem a bit more relaxed."

"Two hours, Mr. Wainwright, two hours. We'll find out who has relaxed standards."

"Tell you what, lieutenant, let's forget about the two hours. You're obviously not competent enough to know where I am, or you wouldn't be issuing some limp dick ultimatum for me to turn myself in. But I'll do you a favor—get out your magic decoder ring so you can take this down—the guy you want is Sami Alnour Barashi, alias Dr. Alano Gonzales. I met him, face to face; struggled with him. He chased me out of the lab. Shot at me. Killed Robinson. I don't know what he's planning, but I damn well remember his words: that Americans will know the despair of realizing not even their homes are safe; that they'll be terrified to step from their doors, to draw a breath. Tell your federal friends that. Tell them those words. Then do some real police work."

A long silence ensued on the other end of the line. Richard pictured Jackson self-immolating. Finally the detective spoke. "I'll do that, Mr. Wainwright. I'll do some real police work. Think of that when I slap the cuffs on you by the end of the day. Maybe you'll have a whole new arsenal of snappy remarks by then." He hung up.

"Asshole," Richard yelled. He stood and flung the phone onto the cot.

"Please, Lord, don't let that word be in one of the hymns we're singing Sunday." Marty stood in the doorway, left hand over her eyes. "Tell me when you're decent." In her right hand, she held a fresh shirt.

Richard pulled on his pants, an awkward, one-handed effort. "Sorry," he said. "But I guess you having a basketball-team-worth of brothers won't absolve me from—"

"I never peeked into their bedrooms," she interrupted. "And if they said a foo-foo word, they got their mouth washed out with Dial." She removed her hand from her eyes and stepped forward to give Richard the shirt. "I found this in our clothing stockpile. I think it will fit."

She helped him struggle into the shirt. Their gazes locked briefly, the convergence transient and tentative. Yet in that fleeting glance, he glimpsed the suggestion of some sort of nascent mischief. It puzzled him. "You're ready for today?" he asked. "I apologize for imposing."

"You're not imposing. I volunteered. What's the plan?"

"As soon as the nearest Wells Fargo branch opens, we go there. I need to get a cashier's check and some cash." Then he told her about his conversation with the detective.

She nodded, seemingly unfazed that she might be harboring a murderer. "You certainly know how to sweet-talk people," she said.

"I used to be good at it."

"You're out of practice," she said. "You'll get your groove back." She pointed at his cell phone. "Speaking of being out of practice, I don't know much about technology, but I thought people could be located through those things. GPS or triangulation or something."

"Oh, shit," Richard said.

"There you go again."

"Sorry. Let's get out of here."

"Meet me out front in ten minutes."

Richard stood in the church parking lot waiting for Marty. The minister's car appeared from around a corner and pulled up to Richard. He opened the passenger door, but stepped back quickly, jerking upright.

"It's okay," Marty said, "it's me." She smiled at him from behind large, amber sunglasses. Her hair was pulled up neatly and tightly beneath a fashionable, broad-brimmed straw hat. A lightweight white blouse, unbuttoned at the top, didn't reveal cleavage, but did fit in such a manner that no one would doubt she possessed secular blessings as well as divine. A sliver of a smooth, tanned thigh peeked from behind a calf-length skirt slit up the side. Black, to offset the blouse. Strappy red leather sandals completed her image transformation. Richard's eyes lingered a bit too long on the thigh.

"That's the idea," she said, as Richard dropped into the passenger seat.

"What's the idea?"

"I don't want people looking at my face, just in case there's somebody in Diamond Cutters who might recognize—"

"Oh, no, no, no." He reached out and gripped her forearm. "You're just dropping me off. No way you're coming in."

"Like I'm going to sit out in a parking lot and wait for you in that sleazy part of town." She pressed the accelerator and exited the parking lot; her skirt shifted; more material fell away from the slit, providing an enticing panorama.

Richard's gaze dropped to her thigh again.

"See. Works pretty well," she said, tugging the skirt back into place.

She turned to look at him, her dark glasses and straw hat enhancing an aura of youthfulness, hinting at a latent sexiness. But also suggesting something else. Something that heightened Richard's worry. Impetuousness, perhaps? Impulsiveness?

"All I want you to do is drive around the block a few times," he said. "I shouldn't be in there very long. And remember, I'm supposed to come alone."

"You need backup."

"You've been watching too many cop shows. Besides, neither one of us is armed. That kind of rules out effective backup."

"I moonlight as a hit woman, remember."

"And stripper."

"That, too."

Once again Richard's misgivings about dragging Marty deeper into this hastily conceived and quite possibly dangerous operation bubbled to the surface. But now he was committed. Too late to change horses—or drivers—in the middle of a stream.

She pulled into a Wells Fargo Bank. It took Richard only twenty minutes to secure the cashier's check and $2500 in cash, $500 for himself—reserve money—and $2000 for Khassem.

Minutes later, Marty drove down an entrance ramp onto a multi-laned high-speed freeway that would carry them south to Atlanta. A knot of confused thoughts twisted through Richard's mind, mostly centered on whether he was doing the right thing, whether he was walking into a trap set by Barashi, whether he was putting Marty into a situation more perilous than he could imagine.

But he wondered about Marty herself, a point off the curve as ministers went, probably even as most women went. A gnawing fear that he was putting a loose cannon into a canoe gripped him. He studied her as she focused on driving, intent on maneuvering in heavy traffic careening along at over 70 mph.

"Tell me more about what happened after NC State," he said, "after we . . . after I left."

She shrugged. "Not much to tell. Seminary at Wake Forest, worked my way up through small churches in Tennessee and Alabama, was offered the job as senior minister here about five—"

"Not what I was asking about. You've changed since I knew you. Not surprising, I guess. I've changed, too. But there's something else, something you're hiding, something you're camouflaging with your light-heartedness and flippancy. What happened to the Marty I knew in college? Who am I working with here to save the world? Or at least Atlanta."

She laughed softly. "Is that what we're doing?"

"I don't know what we're doing. And I'm certainly not sure what you're doing."

"I'm the wheel man."

"Wheel woman. Come on, talk to me. We're sort of partners in crime now."

She glanced at him. "It's good for ministers to walk on the other side of the tracks every once in a while. You know, experience the netherworld of lost souls. Hobnob with the opposition. Understand why we do what we do."

"No. It's not that; you already know that." He'd sat at enough negotiating tables with corporate and legal jive talkers to recognize bull shit. He debated saying what he said next, but decided if he were going to draw Marty out, it would have to be with a frontal assault. He turned and ran his eyes up and down her, making sure she was aware of his appraisal. She tensed.

"You're an intelligent and very attractive woman," he said, "and not unaware of it. I can't help but be curious—"

"About why I'm not married?" She leaned on the horn as a wallowing SUV cut in front of her. "Dork!" she yelled.

"Me or the driver?"

"Maybe both," she muttered.

"Yes, about why you're not married," he said, completing his sentence, though Mary already had.

"You think my sexual orientation might be . . . skewed?"

"Hardly. I know better."

A red tide rise slowly from her neck to her jaws, finally to the tips of her ears. She remained silent for several moments, and Richard knew he'd touched an exposed nerve.

Chapter Twenty

ATLANTA
FRIDAY, AUGUST 23

Marty's thoughts drifted back to a place she rarely went, to a private reliquary where she stored remembrances better left interred. Remembrances of her own shortcomings, her own sins, her own brokenness. Memories, almost, of another life. At least of another time. Ancient events rarely exposed to light and reflection, and certainly never discussed with staff or congregation.

Yet she needed to talk about them, wanted to talk about them, wanted to blow the dust off her emotions and reveal that she was, after all, only ordinary. Only a woman.

A minister, yes. But still a woman, one who needed the social salve that words and interaction with others bring. Interaction with people who understood, who accepted her as a human being, not someone anointed to a higher order. Daring to take her eyes off the road again she looked over at Richard and saw in him someone she could trust. Objective, fair, nonjudgmental. Her confessor. Once, her almost-lover.

"It wasn't easy being a female divinity student at Wake," she said, turning her head forward, "especially one who, I guess, looked more like a cheerleader than a candidate for a convent. When it came to dating, I was either the target of a conquest—you know, 'Hey, I got in the preacher-lady's knickers'—or viewed as a virginal ice queen."

"You weren't, were you?"

"Weren't what? Virginal?"

"No. An ice queen."

"You know better than that." She colored slightly again, then concentrated on merging into traffic where two Interstates came together just north of downtown Atlanta. The task completed, she continued talking. "No, if anything, I was afraid I'd melt polar ice when it came to sex. From certain experiences I'd had at NC State I knew how much heat and heavy breathing could be generated by, shall we say, pseudosex." She reached over and patted his leg. This time she didn't blush. "I was eager to reach the sexual promised land, but at the same time I knew and respected the constraints of my calling. Then I met Paul, let there be irony, a fellow divinity student, and knew I'd found true love."

"We all did, at that age."

"Looking back, of course it was nothing more than hormones and infatuation. But it didn't seem like it then, not with Paul, he was the one and only. I knew it would last forever. We moved in together, covertly, of course, off campus, and became inseparable. Eternal lovers. It couldn't be wrong, not between two people who had committed their lives to one another and their souls to Christ." She maneuvered her car into the diamond lane.

"But it went wrong?"

"Way wrong. Morons that we were, we didn't bother with protection. I suppose we figured if God could ordain divine birth he could do the same for birth control. Anyhow, He didn't. I got pregnant, and Paul hit the road to Damascus or wherever the heck he came from originally. He didn't receive a revelation, and I never saw him again."

She gripped the steering wheel hard, her earlier insouciance DOA in her memories. "I prayed a lot," she continued. "Prayed for forgiveness and that the love of my life, the father of my baby would come back. Prayed and prayed and prayed. I think God forgave me, but that was the extent of His intervention. I offered the baby up for adoption and got on with life."

Richard placed his hand on her forearm again, softly this time. "I'm sorry," he said, "I probed a little too deeply."

"No," she said, "I needed to talk about it." She lifted her glasses and looked directly at him. "Do you think I'm a trollop?"

"Watch the road, we branch off to the airport here someplace. No, I don't think you're a trollop. What I do think is that I shouldn't be psychoanalyzing you. I only got a 'C' in psych 101."

They moved slowly along a clogged stretch of Interstate through central Atlanta, the Downtown Connector, where I-75 and I-85 shared common ground, cutting through a cubist landscape of tall buildings and brown haze.

"I'm not asking for a session on the couch," Marty said. "I'm just curious. You're good at reading people."

She braked the car as it entered a tight, sweeping curve, and the material of her skirt parted company at the slit again. This time she didn't readjust it.

"You're a tease," he said.

"I'm too old."

"You're wondering."

"Well?"

"The equipment's in fine shape."

"And?"

"And . . . you're sure you want me to go there?"

She nodded.

"If you're okay with pop psychology then, this is Dr. Wainwright's analysis: I think you still have a healthy interest in sex and a lingering fear of romantic commitment. But as a church leader and Christian you reject promiscuity, and as an individual abandoned by a lover, you're apprehensive about involvement with men. That makes it difficult, I would guess, to harbor anything but fantasies about sex."

"What kind of fantasies?"

"I don't know anything about your fantasies. But I think you're playing one out right now, in the guise of a disguise. You've seized an opportunity to at least play a role. Just a walk-on part. What would it be like, you wonder, to dress like a high-priced call girl, a thousand-dollar a night hooker. To walk into Diamond Cutters—and by the way, you aren't—and feel like a stripper punching the clock in a classy club."

"Maybe that's *your* fantasy."

He laughed, but only briefly. It was good to be back with Marty. Good to be back with an old friend. Yet he still felt the presence of Karen. Amorphous and ethereal, but palpable.

"You know," Marty said, "you need to stop punishing yourself."

"Punishing myself?" His surprise was genuine.

"She glanced at him, her eyes liquescent, filled with compassion. "Karen is still with you. I can tell. The way you fall silent every once in a while. I understand. You stood on the sidelines and watched the life being sucked from her. You told me how you felt: helpless, impotent, useless. There was nothing you could do to ease her suffering, assuage her fear. Nothing you could do to save her. I wasn't there, but I know how you reacted, how anybody would have. You cried out to a deaf God, wrung your hands, cursed. But still it was Karen who bore the cross, not you. You were just a spectator."

The exit to Southern Pines Avenue came up. "Off here," Richard said.

Then added, "Go on."

"So, after Karen passed, you shouldered the cross. You manufactured guilt for your perceived failures as a husband. I believe you're a truly moral man, Rich, but I also believe you imprison yourself by denying your needs, both emotional and sexual." She turned and studied him briefly. "Blunt talk from a lady, yes?" She waited for a reaction.

"A lady minister. An old girl friend."

"Am I right?"

He gave a one-shoulder shrug. "I've never really thought about it in that light."

"Then do it," she responded. "Live your life."

Funny she should choose those words—he wondered just how much of his life he might have left. He turned and looked out the rear window. Three cars followed them off the exit. Two went into the left-hand turn lane. The third, a black Lincoln Town Car, followed them to the right.

"South Atlanta Parkway should be on the left in a few blocks," he said, monitoring the GPS on her dash. He asked her to adjust the side view mirror so he could track the Lincoln. It trailed them at a discrete distance.

They reached South Atlanta Parkway and turned. The Town Car turned behind them. If wisdom came with age or office, it certainly had blown by him. Here he was, unarmed, being tailed and toting around several thousand dollars in cash in a neighborhood where they probably shot first and asked for your money second.

"There's a black Lincoln following us," Marty said.

"I know." Richard kept watch on the large, black automobile.

After another 30 seconds, he said, "Pull over. Stop. If the Lincoln comes up behind us and somebody gets out, stomp the gas and go like a bat out of hell."

"Cool. I've always wanted to do that."

"What?"

"Go like a bat out of hell."

"I'm not sure you're taking this very seriously."

"Sorry," she said, "just whistling past the grave yard."

The Town Car cruised on by, and Marty pulled away from the curb. "Rats," she said, "I was ready for the big chase scene."

"Still whistling?"

She shrugged. "I don't know."

"There it is up there, on the right." Diamond Cutters loomed several blocks ahead, a large two-story concrete structure that dominated a neighborhood of boarded up, burned out businesses; a liquor store with steel grating laced across the windows; and a pawn shop squatting in a lot littered with trash and surrounded by a razor-wire fence. Inside the fence, three dogs that looked like dingoes lounged in the shade of a sick-looking oak.

Marty approached Diamond Cutters. A neon sign big enough to have lit a runway at Hartsfield-Jackson crowned the club. A fenced-in parking lot, with few vehicles, sprawled adjacent to the building.

"Drive on past, then go around the block. A couple of times. Slowly, so I can check it out."

"You really know what you're doing?"

"I don't have a clue."

She cruised around the block and came toward the club again. Across the street, a man in shabby jeans and a soiled, torn T-shirt pushed a shopping cart containing his estate—three cardboard boxes—along the sidewalk. Near the corner of the club, a man in a business suit appeared to be in serious negotiation with a lady of the night who'd decided to work overtime.

"Think she's earning her way through college?" Marty asked.

"She's not old enough to be in college. Go around again."

They came up on the club a third time. The homeless person, some distance away now, continued to push his baby Bekins along. The negotiation on the corner had apparently concluded, for the man and woman were nowhere to be seen. Behind Marty's car, a white Dodge Ram pickup eased to the curb and stopped. Richard turned to watch it. A man wearing a tan duster, sunglasses and a gray porkpie hat got out, locked the door and walked down the street, away from the club. Richard couldn't tell if he was black or white, but pegged him as a pimp.

"Let me out here," Richard said. "Wait in the lot."

"We went over this already."

"Then keep driving around the block. Or around the neighborhood."

"Okay."

"Enough with the fantasies. Understood?"

She nodded.

He got out and shut the door. He made a motion for her to roll down her window. He stooped. "Remember, around and around and around. Keep moving. No games."

She smiled at him and leaned toward the door. Her breasts fell against the constraints of her blouse, and it was only then he realized she wasn't even wearing a bra. "Be careful," she said.

He stood up. "Go," he responded. He felt control of the situation slipping away from him. The loose cannon had broken from her moorings and was rolling unchecked, a lit fuse ready to ignite her fantasies.

He waved her away and stepped into Diamond Cutters.

Chapter Twenty-One

SOUTH METRO ATLANTA
FRIDAY, AUGUST 23

Inside Diamond Cutters, a dusky world of throbbing music and shimmering mirrors threaded with a vague essence of hopelessness greeted Richard. The bleak atmosphere suggested that here anything and everything was for sale. He checked to make sure the back pocket of his pants, the one containing his wallet, was securely buttoned, and waited for his eyes to adjust to the dimness.

"Hi," a voice said.

It came from a woman at his side. He hadn't seen her approach. Her eyes, dilated—whether from the interior darkness or something else, he couldn't judge—flickered in a sort of Brownian motion as her gaze darted around the room. Her pale, freckled face, heavily made up, was framed in a tangle of hair the color of a bad sunburn. A green evening dress encased a body just beginning to surrender to the challenges of being thirty-something. The low-cut top of the gown exposed a cleavage that was on par with the Columbia River Gorge where it parted the Cascade Mountains.

"I'm Wendy. If you'd like to sit awhile, I've got some time." An expensive cologne couldn't mask a breath embalmed in a chain-smoker's fetor.

"Wendy, I'm sorry. I'm meeting someone. Perhaps another time."

She forced her face into a pout. "I might be busy next time."

"I'll take a number."

"I can't give that out," she answered, missing Richard's little joke.

"I'm sorry," he said, "we probably could have had a scintillating conversation."

She frowned at him, puzzled.

"We could've had fun," he explained, not wanting to dig the needle any deeper. "You seem like a nice lady, Wendy. I'll look for you next time. Is that the only bar in here?" He nodded to his left, toward a long mahogany-railed structure, backed by a mirror, that ran the full length of the club.

"That's the only one," Wendy said.

At the rear of the establishment, several dozen TVs, the set-pieces of a sports viewing section, festooned three walls. To Richard's right, a vast lounge area revealed a clutter of tables and secluded booths, empty at this hour. Soft, indirect lighting, a low ceiling and walls draped in dark fabric fell short in their attempt to portray something classy.

Separating the lounge and bar was an elevated runway with several vertical poles and overhead speakers the size of commercial air conditioning units that shook the nearly-deserted club with Richter-scale enthusiasm.

"Thanks," Richard said. "Next time." He nodded to her and walked to the bar. He climbed into a high, wooden chair, making certain there was no one seated near him on either side.

The bartender, a wiry little man with thin, brown hair and Ben Franklin spectacles approached Richard, leaned across the bar and cocked his head so he could hear.

"Irish coffee. No whipped cream," Richard said. He knew he didn't have to say easy on the whiskey. That would be automatic.

"You got it, buddy. Give me a minute or two to make sure the coffee's fresh."

Richard turned to survey the club. A leggy, raven-haired girl wearing nothing more than a Revlon smile and red high heels came onto the runway and began a suggestively choreographed dance with one of the poles. She twisted into contortions that firemen never dreamed of, that in fact probably would have turned their faces scarlet. She shimmied the lower part of her body in mock ecstasy against the pole while at the same time leaning her head and shoulders back, allowing an overhead spotlight to illuminate breasts the size of—and probably the same consistency as—south Georgia watermelons.

Richard found the performance strangely repulsive and turned his attention to the few patrons in the club, all of whom sat along the perimeter of the runway. One man apparently had found the show less than stimulating. Cheek resting on the narrow flat railing edging the runway, his snores provided an almost inaudible counterpoint to the thudding beat of the music.

Another visitor appeared more interested in the sports section of the *Atlanta Journal-Constitution* than the girl feigning an orgasm with a brass pole. Not everyone seemed put off by the show, however. Across from the snorer, a young man, probably barely old enough to be in the place, nursed a beer and watched in rapt attention as the girl begin to focus what little interest she could muster on him. The kid fidgeted self-consciously; Richard guessed a certain part of his anatomy had begun to outgrow its allotted space.

Next to the youth, two men seemed to be discussing some sort of business deal. At least one of them was, the older of the two. The other, a moon-faced kid in an ill-fitting business suit, seemed to be having a difficult time attempting to follow what the older guy was saying while at same time making certain he didn't miss a single bump or grind of Miss Melons. Periodically he'd nod his head, but it appeared to be more in time with the music than in response to what he was being told.

Richard figured that was the point of this distracting venue: The kid would agree to whatever his opposite was proposing or selling, and only in the light of day, and absence of liquor and sexual suggestion, would he realize he'd signed off on a pig in a poke.

Richard scanned the establishment carefully. Nothing seemed threatening or out of place, though he doubted he would have known if something were. He had no frame of reference.

"Eight bucks, buddy." The bartender slid a steaming mug of coffee toward Richard.

"Must be a lot of Tullamore Dew in there."

"I don't price 'em, I just pour 'em, partner."

Richard laid a ten on the bar. In the mirror he watched the dancer wrap herself around the pole, a Boa Constrictor squeezing its prey. The man reading the newspaper peeked over the top of it in the direction of the bar. He made brief eye contact with Richard, then lifted the paper and went back to reading. The booming music suddenly ceased, and the girl fell away from the pole, laying out on her back, arching her body and fixing a vacant gaze on the kid with the beer. The kid stood, tugging at the crotch of his jeans, leaned across the runway and placed a bill between her monolithic breasts. Richard wondered if she'd been raised near Stone Mountain.

A flash of sunlight filled the club's entrance. Richard turned his head. A figure silhouetted against the exterior brilliance paused for a moment, then walked toward the lounge. But even before the new arrival was clearly visible, Richard recognized the broad-brimmed straw hat. "Ah, shit," he said. He turned away, grabbed his coffee and took a long swig.

"Everything okay, buddy?" the bartender asked.

"Why can't women ever do what they're told?"

The bartender shrugged. "Do I look like Dr. Phil?"

Richard watched Marty in the CinemaScope mirror behind the bar. Wendy was watching her, too, ready to pounce like a lioness defending her territory. Marty seated herself at a table on the far side of the runway. She removed a compact from her purse and powdered her face, then took a hard look in the direction of the bar. The bartender put two and two together. "You know that lady? Not many just stroll in here by themselves at 10 o'clock in the morning."

Richard wondered if she'd just blown the deal, scared off whomever he was supposed to meet. "Casually," he said.

"Trouble?"

"No. No trouble." *I can only hope.* He took another draft from his coffee mug.

The snoring man jerked awake, apparently startled by the abrupt silence in the club. He looked around and spotted Marty. He took a comb from his shirt pocket and ran it through his hair. He tucked the comb away, produced a small container of breath freshener and sprayed a shot into his mouth.

The man with the newspaper looked at Marty, too, then Richard. He seemed to be trying to make a connection, but couldn't quite fit the pieces together. He tossed the paper onto the runway and stood up. Short and dark with a thin thread of a mustache and thick, wavy hair, he remained in place for a moment, surveying the club. Then he moved toward Richard. Richard tracked him in the mirror, but the man walked past, toward the restrooms in back.

The music started up again, and another young woman wearing nothing more than what she was born with plus platform shoes strutted onto the runway. She actually was more realistically proportioned than her predecessor, somewhat more restrained in her movements, her sexuality more implicit than explicit. Still, Richard saw Marty's eyes widen as the dancer embraced the pole, sliding her pelvis up and down the brass shaft.

Another flash of light near the door drew Richard's attention. As the transient illumination faded he made out the form of the pimp he'd seen outside earlier, the guy in the duster and porkpie hat. A strange outfit for mid-summer. Dressing for effect, Richard decided.

The guy still had his sunglasses on. He remained near the door momentarily, then moved off toward the rear of the club, heading for the sports viewing area. He stayed on the far side of the runway, passing close to where Marty sat. As he continued walking, Marty's gaze followed him. She looked toward the bar briefly, then back at the pimp. It was almost as if she recognized him, but wasn't sure. Somebody from her congregation? Not likely. But who? A tiny warning light glowed amber somewhere near the base of Richard's brain. Coming from the other direction, Mr. Sleepyhead made his way toward Marty. Richard's intuition told him it was time to bail out, that there were suddenly way too many players, and no way of identifying who was in the game and who wasn't.

He stood to go, but felt a restraining hand on his shoulder.

"Do you have the money, Mr. Wainwright?" asked the same voice he'd heard on the phone the previous evening. The voice's owner, the newspaper reader, seated himself next to Richard.

"You are Ebraheem Khassem, I assume?" Richard held his gaze on the man's eyes.

"Yes." The man leaned in close, placing his mouth next to Richard's ear and whispered, "I worked with Alnour Barashi. You know him as Dr. Alano Gonzales."

"I know him as Barashi, too." Richard patted his damaged shoulder.

"Of course. Last night. Then you understand the danger. Let us make this quick then." Khassem kept his mouth near Richard's ear, his words competing with the pulsing throb of the music. His breath suggested he'd had a cheese omelet for breakfast.

Richard glanced in the mirror, saw Mr. Sleepyhead standing at Marty's table, bending over, making his pitch, and getting a good view down the front of her blouse. She seemed taken aback by something he said, and in shock covered her mouth with her hand, then said something back. He laughed and she did, too. She smiled sweetly at him, tugged him by his collar down to her face and spoke into his ear. He jerked backward, sputtering and cursing. The only words that reached Richard's ears were "dyke pervert." The man stumbled back to his seat by the runway. Richard returned his attention to Khassem.

"Yes," Richard agreed, "we can make it quick." The sooner he and Marty were out of this modern-day den of iniquity, the better.

"You have the check and the cash?" Khassem asked.

Richard made certain no one was watching, then withdrew twenty one-hundred-dollar bills from his wallet. Covering the currency with his hand, he slid the money along the bar to Khassem.

The informant snatched the bills, placed them surreptitiously in his lap and riffled through them. Satisfied the amount was correct, he nodded and stuffed the money into his pants pocket. "The check," he demanded.

Richard opened his wallet again. From it he plucked the Wells Fargo check and laid it on the bar. He allowed Khassem to view it, then just as the Arab reached for it, picked it up and replaced it in his wallet. "As soon as the deal's completed," Richard chided.

The bartender approached, probably hoping for another eight-dollar coffee order. From the back of the club, the pimp strode in their direction. "Tell me what Barashi's planning," Richard said, his gaze following the pimp. *Why such a determined gait?*

"This will help," Khassem said. He extended a small piece of paper toward Richard.

Richard took the scrap and glanced at it. A hand-written list of some sort. He jammed it into his pocket. He was more interested in the approaching figure. Something was wrong. The pimp and his ankle-length duster. The hat. Shades. Way out of place. A disguise. Hands not visible. Something beneath his coat. Fully exposed, Richard tensed. The pimp, just a half-dozen paces away, kept his head down.

Khassem leaned toward Richard, focusing on him, nothing else. "He's going after the tent—" He stopped, seeing something in Richard's eyes.

Four strides. The pimp lifted his head. Even behind the sunglasses the face was unmistakable.

"Barashi!" Richard yelled, his warning challenging the thudding music. Khassem turned.

Two strides.

Richard stood. Something hit the floor, bounced, stopped. Barashi broke into a sprint. Without calculating or counting, Richard knew he had five seconds. "Over the bar!" he screamed at Khassem.

Four seconds. Khassem froze. Richard threw himself across the top of the bar.

Three seconds. Richard plunged onto a hard, corrugated rubber mat behind the bar, dragging the befuddled bartender down with him. Someone cursed loudly.

Two seconds. Richard scrambled along the mat, trying to distance himself from the grenade on the other side.

One second. He curled into a ball.

Thunder and lightning erupted simultaneously. A shock wave of compressed air and heat swept over Richard, the dense mahogany of the bar deflecting much of the blast upward. Liquor bottles disintegrated like punctured balloons, showering him in a squall of booze and multi-colored glass shards. The panoramic mirror fractured into crystalline lacework, then spilled from its frame in a slow-motion waterfall. The bitter after-taste of chemical ignition hung in the air, mixing with a roiling cloud of gray-black smoke that filled the club with an acrid haze.

Part of the ceiling fell away, and tiny rivers of flame darted from the gaping hole. An alarm clattered, although Richard had trouble differentiating it from the residual ringing in his ears. Someone screamed. Someone else shouted. Overhead, the automatic sprinklers opened up, and cascades of water showered down.

Richard struggled to his knees and peeked over the shattered escarpment of the bar. Khassem's body, its trunk at least, lodged in the broken superstructure of the counter. A bloodied arm and leg lay on the smoldering floor nearby. A rolling moan from behind Richard drew his attention. The barkeep, bleeding profusely from a head wound, crawled on his hands and knees through the coarse carpet of broken glass lining the floor.

"Stop crawling," Richard commanded. "Sit up. Press this against your scalp." He tossed the bartender a towel he found next to a stainless steel sink that hung limply from broken supports.

The bartender stared at him, through him. "What happened?" he said.

"Hand grenade. Put the towel on your head, it'll stop the bleeding. Cops will be here in a minute." Richard stood. The sprinklers soaked him, but at least had cleared the smoke. He wiped the water from his eyes and searched for Marty. He couldn't spot her. She'd been beyond the radius of the damage, so shouldn't be injured. Frightened and stunned, maybe, but . . . *Where the hell is she?*

He clambered over the bar and staggered toward where she'd been seated. Water continued flooding into his eyes and, half-blinded, he stumbled through the smoldering debris. He fell over the legs of an inverted chair. He tried to stand, but the room spun in centrifugal anarchy, and he went down.

A hand under his armpit lifted him up. "Come on, buddy, let's get out of here." It was the young kid who'd been nursing a beer near the runway.

"Wait," Richard said. He scanned the area where Marty had been seated. Deliberately. Slowly. Carefully. She wasn't there.

"Come on, mister, this place is on fire," the kid said, his voice threaded in urgency. He steered Richard outside, and they staggered into piercing sunlight. Richard squeezed his eyes shut against the brightness, then slowly opened one, searching for the white pickup. Nowhere to be seen. Across the street, several people who'd been in the club, both patrons and entertainers, stood together, gesturing wildly to each other. No Marty.

"You okay?" the kid asked.

"Yeah," Richard said, "things have stopped spinning and ringing." He drew a deep breath. "Thanks for yanking me out of there." Sirens wailed in the distance. He knew he couldn't afford to wait around. The last thing he needed was for the police to identify and arrest him. The first order of business was to find Marty. The second, to stop Barashi. And undoubtedly the two were linked. "You got a car?" he asked the kid.

"Around the corner." The kid looked at him uncertainly. "You should stay here. Get some medical attention."

"I'm fine. Just got the wind knocked out of me." Probably a slight concussion, too. He remembered a down-at-the-heels motel he'd seen in the distance as he and Marty reconnoitered the area earlier. "My motel is about five blocks from here. I'd really appreciate it if you could drop me there."

The kid hesitated.

Richard fished a $50 bill out of his wallet. "For your trouble," he said, handing it to the young man.

"This way," the kid said.

Thick, black smoke shot from the roof of Diamond Cutters. Apparently the sprinklers had been less than totally effective. A police car and fire truck rolled up as Richard and the young man departed.

As they walked, Richard tried to sort out what had happened. Barashi obviously had tailed Khassem to the club and discovered a providential chance to eliminate not only the informant but the man who had exposed his lab. Revenge. Two for one. Marty must have been a target of opportunity. *But why? If Barashi thought he'd eliminated me, then why grab Marty?* Unless he'd recognized her from the church and decided to seek retribution for her deception there.

The thought shot a mailed fist into Richard's gut. He doubled over, wobbled toward the curb, leaned over and retched. Nothing came up.

Chapter Twenty-Two

SOUTH METRO ATLANTA
FRIDAY, AUGUST 23

Richard pushed open the door of room 29, second floor, James Street Motor Hotel. He'd registered as Eddie Beauchamp, slipped a big bill underneath the bulletproof glass separating him from a disinterested clerk, and didn't wait for change. No questions asked; no credit card required; no ID needed.

He stepped into the room. The reek of cleaning solvent and insecticide assaulted him. But there was something else that pervaded the room, something transcendental: a vague odor of despair, deceit, defeat. He flipped on the overhead light. It flickered and failed. He found a lamp by the bed. It struggled to life, illuminating a carpet with enough spots to make a leopard feel at home, furniture from the Eisenhower era, and a bedspread so threadbare it could have served as a juice strainer. He looked at the covering more closely and recoiled. The stains on it suggested directions he didn't wish his imagination to follow.

A scuttling sound emanating from a corner of the hovel distracted him. The noise seemed to be coming from a Mr. Coffee perched on top of a scratched and maimed dresser. He stepped over to the little machine and peered into its water reservoir. A cockroach the size of his thumb had managed to squeeze through the plastic grating covering the top of the reservoir, but now was trapped on the bottom, unable to scramble up its slick walls to freedom.

"Yeah, me too," Richard said. He covered the Mr. Coffee with a towel from the bathroom. The scuttling ceased.

Richard collapsed into a chair that creaked in protest and listed starboard. He stared out the room's single, grimy window. Drifting smoke rendered a warehouse across the street a colorless monochrome. Sirens intermingled with the ambient industrial and automotive sounds that penetrated the motel's flimsy walls.

He considered his situation. What the hell else could go wrong? *A whacked out Arab—running around with some kind of virus that can kill half of America—murders Anneliese, shoots me, blows up a strip joint and snatches Marty. And I can't even go to the police for help. Then there's the female Jackal. If she isn't working with Barashi, how does she fit into any of this?*

He turned his head toward the trapped roach and said, "We're both fucked, you know."

In truth, he refused to believe that. He'd built his career on attacking his challenges, not letting them assault him. But he needed a starting place, a point to launch from, and he needed it quickly. Whatever Barashi was planning on attacking, he wouldn't wait long to do it. And he wouldn't wait long to take his revenge on Marty.

"He's going after the tent—" Khassem had said. Tent. Richard remembered the piece of paper Khassem had slipped him just before Diamond Cutters erupted in a fireball. He pulled the scrap from his pocket and looked at the names printed on it. Elysian Fields. King's Landing. Magnolia Heights. Crystal Corners. Nightingale Meadows. Willow Springs. Horseshoe Bend. Brookfield. Towns? Streets? Venues? He didn't know. There certainly seemed to be no obvious connection to a tent.

But first things first. He needed to get cleaned up and change his appearance, to whatever extent he could, if he had any hope of operating with some degree of impunity in his pursuit of Barashi. He needed a weapon, too. Brains and fists weren't going to cut it any longer, not in this looking-glass world of deception and terror.

As a young marine he'd taken an oath to protect and defend his country. Just because he no longer wore the uniform didn't absolve him of that duty. But his determination to wade even deeper into a swamp rife with the stench of death went far beyond idealism. With Marty's disappearance, the confrontation with Barashi had become personal.

He felt drawn to and responsible for Marty in ways he had no woman since Karen. But was there a genuine emotional connection between him and Marty? There seemed to be. Or were they only trying to recapture something more vivid and sensual in recall than reality? Lost youth? Lost opportunities? Could he be merely speaking for himself? It didn't make any difference. He had to find Marty. And that meant finding Barashi.

An hour later, Richard walked along the sidewalk of a derelict, half-abandoned strip mall just west of the airport. He wore several new purchases: casual khaki slacks; a light blue, short-sleeved polo shirt; and a pair of overpriced tan and brown deck shoes. An Atlanta Braves baseball hat and cheap sunglasses hid much of his head and face. A disposable cell phone jounced in his pants pocket. He entered a gun shop, Bubba and Chuck's.

The store sported a proliferation of glassed-in display cases containing shotguns, rifles and handguns. Richard had no idea what the laws were regulating handgun purchases in Georgia, but figured he'd find out soon enough.

A black man looking somewhat akin to a Volkswagen Beetle on harbor pylons waddled out of a side room to a position behind a sales counter. "He'p ya?" he said.

"I'd like to buy a handgun," Richard responded, "but I have no idea if there's a permit required, a waiting period, background check or what."

The man grunted in response and spat something brown into a bucket underneath the counter. "Gotta crim'nal record?" he said.

"No." *Not yet, anyhow.*

"Gotta driver's license?"

"Yes."

"Money?"

"Of course."

"Ya gotta gun, then."

"That's it?"

The clerk nodded, wiped his arm across his mouth. "I run a fed'ral and state background check on ya through the so-called National Instant Check System, but, yeah, that's it."

Richard examined the selection in the display case. "Let me see the Glock, the 9mm."

He felt comfortable with a 9mm. He'd qualified as expert with one in the Marines. But that was a long time ago and with his right hand. His skills now would be in question, and if he had to shoot, it would be with his left hand. His right shoulder remained sore and immobile.

The man lumbered over to the case, pulled a key from somewhere deep within the folds of his pants and unlocked the display. He withdrew the gun and slid it across the glass top to Richard.

"Superb weapon. One-piece polymer frame. Double action. Seventeen-round box. Parabellum ammo."

Richard hefted it. "Nice," he said. "I'll take it. Box of ammo, too."

"Driver's license." The man held out his hand.

Richard gave him his license.

The man looked at it, then Richard. "Mind takin' off the hat and shades." More of a demand than a request.

Richard removed them. The man looked again at the license. "Don't look like ya."

Richard's stomach knotted. "I shaved my head."

"Shitty job. Looks like Looseana cane field stubble." The man hawked up a small tidal wave of something and jettisoned another chunky blob into the bucket. "Anyhow, cain't he'p ya."

"What's the problem?" Surely this guy couldn't know the police were looking for him.

"Cain't sell to outta-state residents. Y'all need a Georgia ID."

"I don't have any alternatives, then?"

The clerk shrugged, which in and of itself seemed an effort. "I could sell ya a piece, but I'd have to ship it to a licensed dealer in . . ." He looked at the license again. ". . . Ory-gone."

Richard took back the license. "I know you've probably heard this before, but I need protection today. Someone's trying to kill me." He felt foolish saying it.

"Go to the cops."

Richard put the license back in his billfold. "They won't help." He withdrew a $50 bill. "Where would a man from out of state go if he needed a handgun immediately?" He laid the bill on the counter.

The man cleared his throat. It sounded like something sloshing around at the bottom of a deep well. "Cain't take no bribes, man. I'd lose my license, get thrown in the pen." He ran his eyes up and down Richard as if assessing the possibility he was something other than what he said.

Richard laid another $50 on the countertop. "I'm not asking you to do anything illegal. All I'm asking for is a little help, a little information."

"Ya think just cuz I'm black, I prob'ly hang with crim'nals and shit?" The clerk made no move to pick up the bills.

"I think because you run a gun shop you probably have your ear to the ground; know what goes on around here. Legal and illegal." Richard plopped another bill on the glass. "It's my ass that's hanging out in the wind right now, not yours."

The man eyed the bills, obviously weighing whatever pros and cons needed to be balanced. Without saying anything, he tapped the bills with his index finger. Richard added $50. The man tapped again. Another $50. The clerk forced a jowly smile and smothered the bills with a hand the size of a small ham. "I heard there might be a guy," he said.

"Tell me," Richard said. Negotiations were over. He stuffed the wallet back into his pocket.

"Street out front here? Turn right, go two blocks. Then left, three blocks. Ollie's Bar. It's on the right. Ask for a dude called Leatherhead." The clerk slid the bills off the counter.

"Leatherhead?"

"Like ya said, it's your ass hangin' in the wind, not mine."

"Thanks for your help." Richard turned and strode toward the door.

The clerk wheezed and called after him. "Hey, man, don't be walkin' into Ollie's with that wad on your butt." He pointed at Richard's wallet. "Y'all'd be safer trollin' for sharks with your Johnson."

Richard found Ollie's after a fifteen-minute walk. The neighborhood surrounding it bore a vague resemblance to Baghdad at the height of the Iraqi war. A dead rat on the curb in front of the bar lacked crowd control for the flies swarming over it. A semi-functioning neon sign in the iron-barred window of the establishment advertised Bud_eis__ _eer. And the steel door marking the entrance to the facility looked as though it had lost an argument with an assault rifle.

The afternoon sun, naked and intense, burned down from a cloudless sky. Sweating profusely, Richard yanked open the door. A wash of chilled air laden with the essence of stale beer and dried urine rushed past him, fleeing the confines of the darkness within. He stood for a moment near the entrance, letting his eyes adjust to the dimly lit interior.

"Shut the goddamn door," someone yelled.

Chapter Twenty-Three

SOUTH METRO ATLANTA
FRIDAY, AUGUST 23

In response to the crude demand to shut the door, Richard held up a hand in supplication, closed the door and stepped into Ollie's. Once his pupils had dilated, he threaded his way through a maze of chairs and tables toward the bar. Most of the tables were empty, stained by food and liquor and scarred with cigarette burns. A couple of men at one end of the bar followed his progress. He moved away from them and plopped down on a bar stool with an eviscerated cushion.

The bartender, a middle-aged black man with an afro, gold incisors, and a patch over his left eye, stepped quickly toward him. "Hot one, huh?" he said.

"Too hot. How about a Coors?"

"Comin' up. Call me Cozy, by the way."

"Cozy? Like the old jazz drummer?"

"Yeah. Cozy Cole. You know him, man? One of the great ones."

Richard nodded. "Played with Cab Calloway and Louis Armstrong."

"Among others."

Richard, sensing an opportunity to connect with the bartender, asked, "Who else? My knowledge of the swing era is, well, kind of limited—a few dozen LPs inherited from my old man."

"That's okay. Most people don't have a clue who Cozy Cole was. Yeah, he played with Jelly Roll Morton and Benny Carter, too."

"Big names back in the day," Richard said. He glanced in the direction of the two men who had watched him enter Ollie's. One of them continued to fix him and Cozy in an intense stare.

Cozy retrieved a Coors from a cooler behind the bar.

"Say, maybe you can help me with something else," Richard said, returning his attention to the bartender.

"Maybe. Always willing to help a brother, even if he ain't my color." He flipped an Atlanta Falcons coaster onto the bar, set the Coors on top of it.

"I was told I might find a man called Leatherhead here."

Cozy stood with his hands on his hips and shook his head. "Don't know no Leatherhead, man. 'Fraid you gotta bum steer."

Richard made an act of fishing in his pocket. He pulled out another of the $50 bills from the cash he'd withdrawn earlier from Wells Fargo. "This is all I've got, Cozy. It's yours if you can set me up with Leatherhead. Look, I'm not a cop, not a PI, not a bounty hunter. I just need to talk with this guy. I need his, well . . . assistance. How about it?" He put the bill on the bar but kept it covered with his hand.

"You don't look like the kinda guy needs to be dickin' around with someone named Leatherhead."

"We've all got different needs." Richard took his hand off the bill. "Whaddaya say?"

Cozy slid the money off the bar. "Hang around for awhile. I'll ask some questions. No guarantees."

Richard nursed his beer and waited. Cozy disappeared for a brief time, then reappeared and carried on a whispered conversation with the two men at the far end of the bar. One of them—sleepy eyes, stringy, bleached hair, and dark sinewy arms so heavily tattooed they looked like the sleeves of a patterned sweater—got up and sauntered toward Richard.

He didn't smile and seated himself next to Richard. "Got a smoke?" he said. He kept his gaze forward, staring at the liquor bottles on the wall behind the bar.

"Don't smoke," Richard answered. "How about a beer?"

"Make it a shot."

Richard signaled Cozy. "Black Jack for my friend here."

"Ain't your fuckin' friend. Who the hell are you?"

"Call me Craig," Richard said.

"Yeah. Well, okay, Craig. Why you lookin' for someone called Leatherhead?" Cozy poured the shot. The man downed it in a swift gulp.

"I understand he might have something I'm looking for."

"Like?"

"A gun."

The man snorted. "Try a gun shop."

"Didn't work. I'm from out of state."

"Yeah. Well, you're shit out of luck, too." The man got up to go.

But Richard knew negotiations were on. He signaled Cozy. "Another hit for my bar mate."

The man sat back down. "My friends call me Halfcock," he said, apparently failing to see the irony in his name.

"What should I call you?"

"Not that." He tossed back the second shot. "Who told you you could find someone called Leatherhead here?"

"Street talk."

"Bull shit. You wouldn't know street talk from Shakespeare."

"You're right. But I'm here. I'm ready to buy. You know a vendor ready to do business or not?"

Halfcock, his eyes semi-glazed and struggling to focus, turned and looked directly at Richard. He inclined his head toward the restrooms at the rear of the tavern. "Step into my office," he said, his breath foul with liquor and cigarettes.

"I may not know street talk from Shakespeare, buddy, but I've managed to stay on the turnip truck for quite a few years. We got business to transact, we do it right here."

A vein pulsed in Halfcock's forehead, and Richard hoped he hadn't nudged the guy's detonator.

"Gotta know if you're carrying or wired, numb nuts," Halfcock said.

Richard stood, placed his left hand on the bar, let his right dangle, and spread his legs. "Do your thing," he said.

Halfcock did, probing for a weapon or hidden microphone. All he found was the motel key, cell phone and five fifty-dollar bills. He slapped the money onto the bar and counted it out loud. "Two-fifty," he said. "Two hundred and fifty stinkin' bucks. I thought you said you were ready to deal. This . . ." He picked up the bills, then let them flutter back down onto the bar. ". . . might work at Toys 'R' Us. Not here."

Cozy looked at the money, too. "All you had, you told me. A Grant was all you had." He helped himself to another $100. "Gratuity," he snapped.

Halfcock's eyes moved like goldfish darting around in an aquarium. Richard wondered if the guy was about to live up, or down, to his name, and decided he'd better try to gain control of the situation. He pushed off from the bar and spun to face his inquisitor.

"I've got the money," he said. "You get me the seller." He stuffed two of the remaining bills into Halfcock's shirt pocket. "Finder's fee," he said.

Halfcock looked at his pocket, then at Richard. He started to say something, but had trouble forming words. His dancing eyes suggested chaos in his brain. He shuffled back to his friend at the end of the bar. The two talked in hushed, earnest tones, then Halfcock pulled out a cell phone and made a call.

Richard sipped his beer, his heart thumping like a woofer in a low rider. He hoped these guys didn't realize how far out of his element he was. Halfcock certainly wouldn't, he was in low orbit over Mars or someplace. But Cozy . . . As if reading his thoughts, the bartender plopped a jigger of whiskey down next to the coaster.

"Y'all gonna need something stronger than a Coors," he said. He smiled, his gold teeth suggesting caution lights at a dangerous intersection. He leaned across the bar and whispered, "You do have the money, don't you?" A warning cloaked as a question.

Richard fingered the shot glass, tried to meet Cozy's one-eyed gaze with an unblinking stare of his own, and shrugged. "What do you think?" He downed the shot. He hoped there was a Wells Fargo branch nearby. He was out of cash. He hadn't counted on having to buy an illegal handgun.

"I think y'all are a little ol' pigeon that's fluttered into a falcon's nest," Cozy said. He pointed at the empty jigger. "'Nother? Like to keep my big tippers happy."

Richard declined. Halfcock stumbled by, mumbled for him to sit tight, and went out the front door. His companion disappeared in the opposite direction. Presumably they had instructions to pull sentry duty.

After fifteen minutes, a man built like Popeye on steroids loomed through the front door, his bulk eclipsing any sunlight that tried to sneak in behind him. He stood in place for a moment, a penumbra of menace outlining his massive frame. No one shouted at him to "shut the goddamn door."

"See ya," said Cozy, as the silhouette lumbered in Richard's direction. There was no doubt who it was. The man's head, the size of a prize-winning pumpkin, was topped by hair the hue of rust and bound into neat dreadlocks. The leathery folds of skin that enclosed his freckled face lent him the appearance of a Shar-Pei puppy with five o'clock shadow. He heaved his body onto a stool next to Richard. "Hear you been asking about a man called Leatherhead," he said.

"I'm guessing I don't have to anymore," Richard responded.

He studied the new arrival. The man's large green eyes shimmered with an ironic hint of merriment, although it probably was something else; perhaps the reflected assurance of someone who knew he had the upper hand, thought he'd found an easy mark. A falcon with a pigeon in his nest.

"So, shall we get down to business?" Leatherhead said. "I understand you wish to conduct, shall we say, an *unsanctioned* transaction?"

Richard nodded.

"My compatriots were worried about your, uh, capitalization." Leatherhead's voice, soft and controlled, carried the undertones of something hidden and malignant.

"They needn't be, and you needn't be." *But I am.*

"Ah. Well then, what might you be looking for? High end? Serviceable? Economy?" Leatherhead signaled Cozy, who arrived promptly with a Coke.

"High end would encompass what?"

Leatherhead sipped his beverage. "Inventory liberated from municipal and federal law enforcement agencies. Top quality. Guaranteed. Untraceable, of course."

"Of course."

"We can talk S & W, Beretta, SIG. Any preference?"

"You're the expert. I defer."

"I'm honored by your confidence."

Leatherhead turned on his stool to survey the handful of customers in the dingy tavern. His scan completed, he nodded, as if certifying to himself the identity of the clientele. "A businessman can't be too careful," he said. "It's a shame. So many white-collar crooks around these days."

He swirled the Coke in his glass, then watched the resultant cyclonic vortex. "Well, what would I recommend? I suppose as a solid citizen I should urge you to buy American. Smith & Wesson, for instance. But for more bang for the buck—pun intended—I think you should consider a SIG-Sauer P228. Swiss-German craftsmanship. Weapon of choice for the British SAS, U. S. Navy SEALs and FBI. Exceptionally reliable. Very safe. You can carry it with a round chambered and bring it into action as fast as any revolver."

Richard smiled. Leatherhead had just cast the first line, fishing for big bucks. "You said you guarantee your merchandise?"

"Certainly. Nothing in writing, you understand. But then, I've never had a dissatisfied customer."

"Any dead ones?"

The pupils in Leatherhead's eyes narrowed to microdots. The flesh near his ears turned crimson. He slammed the bar with an open palm, a slap that reverberated throughout the room. Heads turned. Richard cringed. And Leatherhead guffawed, a booming laugh that rimmed his eyes with tears. "Sort of like, if the parachute doesn't work, bring it back for a refund?" he managed to choke out.

Richard finished his Coors in three swallows.

Leatherhead's laughter degenerated into breathless pants. "I should hire you for my customer service department," he said.

"A preferred customer discount would suffice."

"Ah. Yes. Well, you're interested then?"

Richard nodded.

Leatherhead leaned in close. "Three thousand dollars. A brand new

SIG-Sauer P228. Untraceable. Two 13-round magazines. One hundred rounds of ammo."

Richard drummed his fingers on the bar. An act. "What happened to my preferred customer discount?"

"Ten percent. Twenty-seven hundred."

"Twenty-seven hundred? Why not just mug me? You've got the manpower."

"I'm not a thug. I'm a businessman with overhead, risk premiums and profit margins to consider. Twenty-five hundred. Final offer."

"Five hundred."

"Pardon me?" Leatherhead's grip tightened around his Coke. His knuckles went white. "Pardon me," he said again, "did I miss the fucking prefix?"

Time to step out on the ledge, Richard thought. "No, you didn't. And neither did I. Maybe next time, Mr. Leatherhead. Thanks for your time." Richard slipped from his stool, nodded to Cozy and strode toward the exit. He held his breath as he approached the door. Maybe he'd underestimated Leatherhead. Maybe Leatherhead was calling *his* bluff.

He slowed and looked over his shoulder. Leatherhead, ignoring Richard, chatted with Cozy while simultaneously punching in numbers on his cell phone. Richard muttered a soft curse. He'd blown it. Now what? He pushed through the door into the brilliance of the afternoon, fumbled for his sun glasses. Halfcock, standing in front of him, blocked his way.

"Man wants to talk some more," Halfcock said, phone to his ear. "Go back."

A half hour later, Richard and Leatherhead closed the deal at $825. Now all Richard needed was the money.

"Sorry," Leatherhead said, "no credit cards or checks. Just adds to the overhead, you understand."

Richard said he did and stood. "Need to find a bank," he explained, "a Wells Fargo."

Leatherhead closed one eye and cocked his massive head at Richard.

"You don't think I carry around that kind of cash, do you?" Richard said, forcing confidence into his voice. "You're a businessman. You understand."

Leatherhead snorted. "Promptness would be appreciated." He nodded at Halfcock. "My associate will accompany you. Please be so kind as to give him your cell phone. He'll return it when your mission is complete. Like I said, a guy trying to make an honest living can't be too careful these days."

"I fully understand," Richard said. "Your associate, I presume, can direct me to the nearest branch."

"Three blocks," Leatherhead said. "I'll expect you back within half an hour."

Halfcock leading the way, the two men strode through the enervating midday heat to the bank. Richard withdrew $1000 from his personal account, and the men returned to Ollie's.

The exchange, cash for weapon, took place in a rear booth while Halfcock and his buddy stood guard outside. Richard and Leatherhead shook hands and Richard departed, the P228, clips and ammo wrapped in pink tissue paper on the bottom of a Victoria's Secret shopping bag.

Even though he wore dark glasses, the searing afternoon sun forced Richard to squint. Sweat drenched his underarms and threaded down his forehead from beneath his Braves cap. He clutched the shopping bag close to his chest and plodded toward the motel, glancing frequently behind him, more wary now, more cognizant of his surroundings.

He was only mildly surprised when he spotted Halfcock about a block behind him, walking in his direction, trying hard to maintain a steady course, a challenge for his liquor-infused body. Richard increased his pace. Halfcock brought a phone to his ear. Undoubtedly his compatriots were out and about. And undoubtedly they were going to try to repossess Leatherhead's property—former property—and anything else they could find. *No way.*

He reached a traffic light, waited until just before the signal flashed red, then sprinted across the four-lane street. Farther down the avenue, a raucous chorus of horns caught his attention. A dark-colored sedan made an illegal U-turn, bulling its way into oncoming traffic. The driver flashed an upraised middle finger at his detractors. Richard pivoted to look for Halfcock. Leatherhead's lackey stumbled along the curb on the opposite side of the street, looking for an opening in a steady stream of cars and trucks. He interrupted his task to glare at Richard.

Richard jammed his left hand into the shopping bag, feeling for the gun but knowing it was useless. The ammo remained boxed.

Pain—sudden, violent—struck him, shooting through both shoulders, but burning his already-wounded one with particular intensity. "Damn," he yelled. Powerful hands vise-gripped his upper arms and dragged him backward off the sidewalk into a dark foyer.

His heels bumped over a threshold. A door, nothing more than boarded-over shattered glass in a frame, slammed shut behind him. Only two narrow shafts of light from outside knifed through the darkness as he disappeared into an urban crevasse.

Chapter Twenty-Four

SOUTH METRO ATLANTA
FRIDAY, AUGUST 23

Richard guessed he'd been shanghaied by two individuals. Two distinct voices grunted and cursed as he was wrestled into the interior of the building. Hurting badly and disgusted with himself for fixating on Halfcock and failing to watch his rear, Richard put up only a token struggle. Resigned to his defeat, he raised a white flag.

Okay, guys," he said, "take it." He stopped resisting.

"Take what?" one of his captors said.

"The gun." What else would they be after?

The grip on his arms relaxed. "Don't do nuthin' violent, man. We gonna let go your arms now." The voice, rough and rumbly, smacked of something from the projects.

Wallet. They want my wallet. "In my pants," Richard said. He didn't care about the SIG-Sauer, cash or credit cards. All he wanted was to keep his life.

"In your pants what, dude? You ain't gonna take a dump, is you?" A muffled snicker.

"No," Richard said.

"Good. Look through the crack in the door."

"What?" Richard attempted to turn around, but was pushed forward.

"The door."

"Through the crack?"

"You hard a hearin'?"

Richard put his eye next to where a tiny beam of light leaked in. "All I see is traffic. And Halfcock." Standing guard outside.

"The dark blue Caprice? Easin' along next to the curb?"

"Yeah?" The car that had made the illegal U-turn.

"'Lanta plainclothes, man. They real interested in y'all."

"Plainclothes cops?"

"No. Plainclothes transvestites, Whitebread." A second voice, higher pitched, more articulate than the first.

"Who the hell you be, man?" The first voice again. "Whatcho do the cops be eyein' you? Mr. Leatherhead don't want his merchandise fallin' into no wrong hands. You a babe in the woods, you is. You never even spotted those guys."

"Cops?"

"Jeez-us, yes, cops." The other speaker. "They been on you like flies on shit ever since you walked outta Ollie's. Well, turn around. Mr. Leatherhead requested we see you safely back to wherever you be stayin'. Least we can do for a valued customer. Though I doubt we're ever gonna see your pale ass again. Mr. Leatherhead figures you got a short life span."

Well, Mr. Leatherhead may be right. Richard expelled a long, slow breath and turned to face his invisible captors cum saviors. All he could see were white teeth. Two sets. One level with his own, the other, shorter. They were in an abandoned building, that much he knew, probably a crack house. The dead air reeked of rotting food and dried excrement. "So, now what?" he asked.

"So now we get you and your new purchase outta here and lose the cops. Where you stayin' at?"

"James Street Motor Hotel."

A pause, then: "Thought you white boys could do better than that. Okay, bro's out back with some nice wheels. He'll drop you there. Come on."

The two men led him down a black hallway. Something large scurried over his foot and squeaked.

"Don't be steppin' on Mickey." The voice from the projects.

"It was bigger than Mickey."

"Mickey's been snortin'. He just think he big."

They reached the end of the hall. The shorter man cracked open a door and peeked out. Light flooded into the darkness, illuminating a floor littered with empty hypodermics and discarded condoms. The man turned and motioned Richard forward.

"Nothing but the best for our clients." He pointed at a gold 7-series BMW idling in the alley. It sported wheels that probably cost more than Richard's Mini. "Walleye will have you back to the Ritz in a jiff."

"Keep your head down, Homey," the larger man said. Then more softly: "Babe in the woods."

Back in the motel, Richard sequestered the SIG behind a loose air vent grill, then showered until the water ran cold. The grime washed away, he launched a determined effort to connect "tent" to any major ongoing or upcoming events in north Georgia. He leafed page by page through an *Atlanta-Journal Constitution*, but found no obvious matches: no circuses, carnivals, Boy Scout encampments, Civil War reenactments, hip-hop festivals or Oktoberfests (even though it was August). He considered other possibilities. Golf tournaments and automobile races often employ hospitality or VIP tents, but none was being held in or near Atlanta. Oxygen tents: hospitals. *Stupid.* "Shit." He threw the newspaper onto the floor.

He walked to the window and looked out. It was close to four p.m., and the Friday rush home had begun. The street below already had lost a battle to an artery-choking cholesterol of cars and trucks. Vehicles feinted and darted as they fought to gain mere inches of precious pavement. Mostly they sat and idled, spewing a sordid flatulence of exhaust into the pale orange afternoon. A delivery van double-parked next to the warehouse across the street enhanced the congestion.

Humid air laden with gasoline and diesel fumes leaked under the door. Richard switched the air conditioner on high. It clattered in protest and mounted a doomed effort to challenge the miasma—only a portion of it industrial—that permeated the room.

NORTH METRO ATLANTA
FRIDAY, AUGUST 23

Dr. Arthur Willand, the ER physician at North Georgia Regional Hospital, was beyond pain. Finally. Mercifully. In one last, lucid moment he understood the disintegration of his internal organs was virtually complete. The explosions of bloody diarrhea and vomiting had ceased, the nonstop hemorrhaging, ended. Nothing remained for his body to slough off. The virus, he knew, had colonized everything but his soul.

He recognized only dark and light. But he also sensed someone he loved nearby. He drew a shallow breath, knowing it was his last and cursed himself for not having blown his brains out earlier. The agony he'd gone through had been far greater than any man should be forced to endure. If there were a worse way to die, he couldn't imagine it.

He felt a hand grip his, tighten, tremble.

He thought he heard a small cry. His wife's? His?

He exhaled.

SOUTH METRO ATLANTA
FRIDAY, AUGUST 23

Richard switched on the TV to catch the evening news. The image, distorted and vertically stretched, made the reporters look like Coneheads; but the sound was fine. A sense of alarm dominated the broadcast. A wave of palpable concern had broken over Atlanta, a nascent tide of panic. Rumors were rife about a sudden ratcheting up of security at Hartsfield-Jackson Airport, and at Turner Field where the Braves played baseball; about the activation of National Guard units and the movement of active-duty military units into the city.

There seemed to be no answers to a myriad of questions. Was a terrorist attack feared? If so, was the threat-level about to be raised? Was all the activity somehow related to the shooting at BioDawn? To the grenade attack at Diamond Cutters? Why were municipal and state government spokesmen being so vague?

The television scene switched from the anchor desk to BioDawn's parking lot. A man identified as Dr. Dwight Butler from the CDC appeared on-screen. He fielded questions from an aggressive wolf pack of correspondents.

"Dr. Butler, we understand you entered and investigated some sort of illegal laboratory in BioDawn's facilities. Could you tell us what you found?"

"Only that a highly secure lab was in a place where there shouldn't have been a highly secure lab," he answered.

"Meaning what?"

"Meaning that research and development requiring government authorization and oversight, yet having none, was being carried out there."

"Was the work of a biological nature?" The pack of reporters elbowed and jostled one another, closing in for a kill.

The doctor hesitated, seeming to look for guidance from a cadre of officials standing near him. None of them offered to intercede. "We're still attempting to determine that," Dr. Butler finally answered.

"Bullshit," Richard whispered. *You know; you damn well know.*

Another shouted question: "Is there any danger to the public?"

Another man stepped forward to answer. "I'm Special Agent Jeremy Babb of the Atlanta FBI office. I want to assure everyone that all necessary precautions and safeguards are being taken just in case there turns out to be a risk to the general public, although we feel that possibility is extremely remote. We'd be derelict in our duty, however, if we didn't prepare for such a contingency. At the moment—and let me make this clear—we have no evidence of any imminent threat, either accidental or deliberate, to the citizens of Atlanta."

To Richard, the agent's measured cadence and careful choice of words suggested otherwise. He was a man under stress.

The reporters smelled blood. From the din of questions being launched, one landed precisely on target. "Deliberate threat? You mean this could involve terrorist activity?"

Agent Babb ducked, figuratively. "Let me repeat, we have no hard evidence of any immediate threat to Atlantans. As we develop further information, we'll release it in a timely and responsible fashion to the public, and, as necessary, take appropriate actions to ensure the safety of all citizens. Now, if you will excuse us, I'm sure you'll understand we have a great deal of work to do."

He turned and spread his arms, herding Dr. Butler and the others gathered with him away from the phalanx of microphones and cameras. Questions continued to explode around the retreating men like a mortar barrage.

They know, but they don't know. Richard scribbled Butler's name on a notepad. A possible ally. A person who knew what had been developed in that lab. A person who wasn't a law enforcement official, who might be willing to listen to the one man who'd encountered Barashi face-to-face. Butler, he realized, could put into context Barashi's rant that Americans would be terrified to step from their homes. Butler knew. What he didn't know, what no one knew, was Barashi's target.

"Tent. What the hell is the tent?" Richard muttered.

He continued to watch the news broadcast as it segued into a mind-numbing litany of traffic accidents, apartment fires, robberies and gang shootings. But the final story of the hour-long newscast loosed a dagger of lightning through him. It was a feature on something called *Malacosoma americanum.*

Once the story was completed, he yanked a phone book from the drawer of the night stand and flipped to the Butlers, searching for Dwight or D. A long shot, but . . . There appeared to be about four pages of Butlers, including two dozen Butler, Ds, but only one Butler, Dwight.

He punched in the number for Butler, Dwight, on his disposable cell and got a busy signal. He hung up. Then made another attempt. Same result. He tried repeatedly over the next half hour and repeatedly got a busy signal. He realized he probably was competing with the media. Or Butler had taken his phone off the hook.

He decided instead to make another check on his brother, Jason. Jason's cell rang but went through to voicemail. Richard left a message. Jason called back almost immediately.

"Sorry, Dickie," Jason said. "I didn't recognize the number."

"New cell," Richard said.

"Okay. Now tell me what's going on and don't hoorah me this time. You don't call me three times within a few days because everything's copacetic. Let's hear it."

"You're right, kid. I'm in a bit of trouble here—"

"I'm on my way if you need me, bro'. Just say the word."

"No, you can't help. Not on this one. Look, I'll tell you everything tomorrow. At this point, I just need to know you're safe. Tell me that."

"Of course I'm safe. Why wouldn't I be? Damn it. Tell me what's happening."

"Tomorrow. I promise. Look, I gotta go now. I'll be in touch." *At least I hope I will.* He said goodbye over Jason's protestations.

He tried Butler again and hit pay dirt.

"Butler," a curt voice said.

"Dr. Dwight Butler, CDC?"

"As I've explained to everyone who's called this evening, I can't answer any of your questions. You'll have to go through CDC media relations or contact the FBI."

"I'm Richard Wainwright, the interim CEO at BioDawn."

A long silence ensued on Butler's end of the line, then: "Jesus, man, you're wanted for murder. Why the hell are you calling me?"

"I haven't murdered anybody. But I'm aware there's a warrant out for my arrest. That's why I can't approach any law enforcement officials. But I need help. I fought with Barashi—"

"Who?"

"Alnour Barashi. You know him as Dr. Alano Gonzales. I know him as a man who tried to kill me, who shot the security manager in BioDawn's parking lot, who stabbed my executive assistant to death."

"Gonzales is Barashi?"

"Yes."

"Why'd he try to kill you?"

"Because I stumbled onto the lab. I'm the one who discovered it and almost didn't live to tell about it."

"You knew what was going on there, then." More an accusation than a question.

"I didn't, and I don't. But I do know how Barashi is going to disguise his attack, the subterfuge he's going to use." *Malacosoma americanum.* "And I've got some names I think might identify specific targets, but I don't know what they are. I need your help."

"I'm not a detective."

"But you know what Barashi's weapon is, don't you? Despite what you said on TV this evening, you know. I know you know."

Butler didn't respond. Only a faint clicking reached Richard's ears, like Butler tapping his shoe on the floor.

"We can put this together, Dr. Butler, you and me. We both have key parts to the puzzle. But neither one of us can complete it on his own."

"Why should I trust you?"

"Why shouldn't you? What other reason would I call you for? Think about it."

Silence.

"I'll be blunt," Richard said. I'm desperate. You're my last hope. Look, meet with me. If you don't think I'm on the up and up, you can walk away."

"Okay. Against my better judgment. There's a new Cajun bar and grill, Hotmouth Harry's, in Midtown off 14th Street. Meet me there at midnight. It'll be crowded, but I'll be on the patio."

"Good. I'll find you," Richard said.

"Yeah? How will you know me?" Butler asked.

"You're a unique-looking gentleman. I don't think I'll have a problem. And Dr. Butler?"

"Yes."

"You'll come alone, of course?"

"Of course."

Richard hung up, knowing full well that wouldn't happen. If there was one thing he'd learned in the last few days, it was to trust no one.

Chapter Twenty-Five

SOUTH METRO ATLANTA
FRIDAY, AUGUST 23

Richard, mentally and physically exhausted, stripped off his clothes, set the alarm for eleven p.m. and collapsed into the motel room's cheesy bed. The last sound he heard before sinking into a state of narcolepsy was the weak, frantic scratching of the imprisoned cockroach.

Sometime later—he had no idea if minutes or hours had passed—another sound penetrated the depths of his sleep: the soft opening and shutting of his door. Had he not locked it?

"Shhh. It's me. Marty," a voice whispered. "I'm glad I found you."

"Marty?" A dense, swirling fog suffused his slumber.

"Go back to sleep. I know you're exhausted."

He sensed the gentle undulations of the mattress as she sat on the bed and undressed. She slipped under the covers beside him and they embraced, even as he spiraled back into his black, silent world.

He awoke again, this time more fully, with his arm draped over her shoulder, feeling the rise and fall of her body as she breathed softly and steadily, deep in sleep. His hand wandered to her naked breast. A frisson of arousal engulfed him. Had they made love earlier? He wasn't sure. She didn't respond as he shook her gently. From somewhere in the dark, someone laughed. A harsh cackle. Aimed at him? Aimed at them? A rising tide of guilt mixed with lust consumed him.

Marty rolled over to face him. Despite the blackness in the room, he could see her clearly. She smiled with her eyes, seeming to approve of his own gaze fixed on the flowing contours of her rounded hills and smoothed valleys. She reached for his hand. "Don't leave me," she whispered. "Don't leave me again. He'll kill me."

"Who?" he said. He jerked his gaze back to her face. He expelled an audible gasp and snapped upright into a sitting position. It wasn't Marty. Instead, the pleading eyes of Anneliese Mierczak bore into him.

"Be a man," she said. A ring of crimson encircled her neck and rivulets of blood beaded into small pools on the bed sheet.

He yanked himself free of her grasp and dashed for the door. But there was none. And no windows. He beat on the wall, but his fists made no sound. The cackling laughter filled the room now. Caught in an undertow of helplessness, he turned to face Anneliese. "I'm sorry," he said, "I did what I thought was right."

She sat with her face buried in her hands and spoke again, her voice muffled. "What you thought was right? Thought! There are no moral certitudes, you fool. Only what's expedient. Good and evil are relative concepts, viewpoint-dependent."

"No. They're absolute. They're ordained to be."

Anneliese lifted her face from her hands. "Then evil is ordained as the victor."

She arose from the bed and stalked toward him, her blond hair shimmering in the dim light, a short-bladed combat knife held low in her right hand. Not Anneliese. Veronica von Stade.

Frantic, he looked around the room for something to use as a weapon, something with which he could defend himself, but there was nothing.

He flicked his gaze back to von Stade. But it was the blood-infused stare of Alnour Barashi that met him.

Richard backed away.

Barashi, holding a small glass vial in his hands, moved in slow, deliberate steps toward him. "Tell me what this is," Barashi said, "good or evil? Life or death? Ballpark or airport? Suburbs or city? You don't know anything, do you? Nothing." He hurled the vial onto the floor. "Allahu Akbar," he screamed. "I am the fifth angel."

The vial shattered. Richard looked down. The bled-out bodies of newborn babies littered a dirt surface. He screamed into a silent void and flailed his arms, trying to ward off whatever had been in the vial. An alarm sounded. Incessant ringing.

Not an alarm. The telephone. He bolted upright, this time in reality and fully awake. He reached for the phone, yanked the receiver from its cradle.

"Hello."

No response. A brooding silence filled the dark room. Richard, drenched in sweat, sucked shallow breaths in short gasps. He wiped the perspiration from around his eyes and checked the clock on the bedside table. Ten p.m. Too late to go back to sleep. Just as well; at least his nightmares would be held at bay.

Who had called his room? Who knew he was here? And if somebody knew he was here and was after him, they wouldn't have called, they'd have just come. So, a wrong number? Or someone warning him? And if someone warning him, of what?

He walked to the window and cracked open the dust-encrusted venetian blinds. The street below was quiet. Only an occasional car drifted by. The delivery van no longer was double parked, but remained nestled next to the warehouse. Curious. A delivery van left unattended overnight in this neighborhood? Another car drove slowly past. Richard kept watch. Several minutes later, it returned. Scouting the truck? Or scouting the motel? Richard waited. The car came back. A dark-colored Ford Crown Victoria. A law enforcement favorite. He caught a glimpse of a face looking out the vehicle's window toward the motel. Not scouting the truck then.

Richard shut the blinds. The police were on to him. But how? The obvious way, he deduced, was through the kid who'd given him a ride from Diamond Cutters. Perhaps the $50 he'd given the boy had been a red flag. Or maybe the kid had seen something on TV or on the Internet: a picture of a wanted man. Whatever had happened, the cops, probably spearheaded by Detective Jackson, were here now. Richard guessed they were unsure which room he was in. Thank God, he'd registered under an alias.

But nonetheless, he was trapped. The police were merely watching and waiting. The only way out was through the door, along the walkway that fronted the rooms, and down the stairs to the ground floor. Richard dressed, then sat on the bed and wondered how good of an actor he could be. He hoped the people who had him under surveillance were still looking for Richard Wainwright, a pony-tailed, well-postured, sober CEO.

He stood, yanked the grill from the air vent and grabbed the SIG-Sauer. He jammed it into the rear waistband of his pants, covering the weapon with his untucked shirttail. He loaded both clips, then stuffed them along with a couple of dozen extra rounds into his pants pockets. Slapping the baseball hat askew on his head, he made sure the bill obscured the left side of his face. He strode to the dresser, removed the towel from the Mr. Coffee and turned the brewer upside down. The cockroach skittered free. "Run for it," Richard whispered.

He picked up a cardboard ice bucket, made a quick check of the room and opened the door. Weaving slightly, he hesitated for a moment, then turned right, slouching and staggering along the walkway toward the ice machine. He took his time. Just a drunk on his way to get more ice. He didn't look toward the street. At one point he stopped and rested his forehead against the building—a guy who'd indulged way too much in demon rum. He resumed his zigzag course and reached the ice maker sequestered in a 90-degree "L" angle formed by the motel's two wings. The machine, he'd calculated, would be out of sight to anyone watching from below.

A car—truck?—door slammed. Someone shouted. His watchers getting curious? He'd have to move fast now. The end of the walkway opened onto an alley below and was guarded only by a low iron railing. Richard clambered over the railing and, with a one-armed grip on a crossbar near its bottom, dangled his feet toward the first-floor landing. He released his grip and dropped. He hit the concrete floor, flexing his knees to take the impact.

He tensed, still in a half crouch. Voices from the direction of the street drew nearer. And although they seemed to lack urgency, Richard knew he'd elicited the watchers' curiosity and that they were coming to investigate. He turned and vaulted over a low fence into the alley.

He spun and sprinted down the alley, away from the street that fronted the motel. The passageway, dark and cobbled, reeked of decaying trash. He feared sprawling over a passed-out drunk or a scrawny cat searching for a five-star garbage can. A street lamp with a shattered lens marked the end of the alley where it intersected a sparsely-traveled boulevard. Richard reached the intersection, panted to a stop and checked in both directions along the street. He didn't like what he saw. A dark Lincoln Town Car, perhaps the one that had followed him and Marty earlier—he couldn't be sure—idled near the curb about twenty yards to his right. But one thing of which he could be sure, the Lincoln's driver, a female, sported a spiky blond hairdo.

So, he'd blundered into a trap: the police behind him and von Stade ahead of him. How the hell had she gotten here? Working with the police? That seemed unlikely. A better bet was she'd monitored police radio frequencies and picked up chatter regarding a murder suspect at the James Street Motor Hotel.

He computed the odds of making a run for it. Not good. Even though the Town Car faced away from him, von Stade would spot him in her rearview mirror. Could he employ the drunk shtick again? No, at best that would be a delaying action. Von Stade, pro that she was, would get curious and approach him to investigate.

Well, sometimes the best defense . . .

Using his thigh to help him instead of his nearly useless right hand, Richard rammed a loaded clip into the SIG-Sauer, chambered a round and tucked the weapon back into his waistband. A virtually empty city bus buzzed by on the boulevard. After it passed, Richard checked to make certain there was no more traffic, then sauntered up behind the Town Car, his hands dangling at his sides, non-threatening. Von Stade's head turned slightly to the right, checking the passenger-side mirror as he approached.

Richard hoped her hubris allowed her to overlook such mundane tasks as locking car doors in dangerous neighborhoods. If not, there'd be gunfire in the night, probably not unusual in this part of the city.

He ambled along side of the Lincoln. Head down, he coughed into his fist. Then almost in one motion he straightened, wheeled and grabbed the rear door handle. The door opened. He yanked the gun from the rear of his trousers and leveled it at von Stade as her hand dived for something between the seat and center console.

"Don't," he said as he sank into the back seat.

Von Stade obeyed. She locked him in a fierce, predatory glare. Under the glow of the sodium-vapor lamps lining the street, her emerald irises seemed to launch tiny bolts of lightning.

"I'm impressed," she said. "A man not to be dissuaded or intimidated. Gets a gun, slips the police, takes the initiative against me. What next?"

"How about a date?"

"At gunpoint? What kind of woman do you think I am?"

"One who would kill me if I didn't have a 9mm pointed at her head."

"Well, you aren't totally stupid."

A police car turned the corner at the intersection ahead of them and moved slowly in their direction. Richard guessed it contained patrolmen looking for him. He lowered himself behind the seat back, keeping his gun trained on von Stade. "Drive," he said.

"How about instead I just lay on the horn and scream? A damsel in distress."

Chapter Twenty-Six

ATLANTA
FRIDAY, AUGUST 23

"Lay on the horn and scream?" Richard said as the patrol car's spotlight lit up the Lincoln. "An international assassin? I'm not sure you'd want to risk that. But be my guest, give it a shot."

She pulled the Lincoln away from the curb, nodded and smiled at the police as they passed. "Where to, *mein Fuhrer*?"

"Midtown." He sat up. He didn't know where Midtown was, but he wasn't about to let von Stade know that.

"So, we're going on a date after all. I think I might enjoy that."

"Don't get your hopes up."

"Tell me, Herr Wainwright, what do you think you're really going to accomplish? Besides ending up on a coroner's slab?" She looked at him in the rearview mirror, her eyes still low-voltage, angry.

"Stop Barashi. Find Marty."

She turned to look directly at Richard. "Who's Barashi? Who's Marty?" Her hand eased off the steering wheel into her lap.

"Both hands on the wheel." He prodded her shoulder with the gun barrel. "Barashi? You probably know him as Dr. Alano Gonzales. Real name: Sami Alnour Barashi. Marty is a Methodist minister. Barashi snatched her out of Diamond Cutters."

Von Stade laughed lightly, derisively. "And people think *my* bubble is off center. But here *you* are dragging a lady preacher into a strip joint, then losing her. You don't have much luck with women do you? First, Mrs. Scarelli, next your executive assistant, then this Marty . . . what did you say her last name was?"

"I didn't."

"How are we ever going to be lovers if you won't open up to me?"

Richard remained silent.

"Oh, come now. You can't say you've never had—how shall I put it?—a little ache for me?"

"Not after I read an article in *Die Welt*. I think I'll keep my trousers zipped."

"But I'll bet you wondered what it would be like, didn't you? What I would be like? I know you did." She turned to look at him again, the wattage now absent from her eyes.

"I wonder about a lot of things."

Von Stade guided the car onto I-85 and headed north. "And Barashi, how do you plan on stopping Barashi? Assuming I don't stop *you* first. Which, of course, I will."

"Don't count on it. Some days you get the bear, some days the bear gets you. But here's something to chew on: I'll bet you might not want to even try to kill me if you really knew what Barashi was going to do." He watched her face in the rearview mirror and a caught a transient flash of uncertainty. "You don't, do you?"

"And you do?"

"Generally, not specifically." Richard read the overhead signs as the Town Car flashed underneath them on the Downtown Connector. "Get off at 10th Street," he said. A guess. He recalled Butler saying Hotmouth Harry's was off 14th.

"Generalities don't do much good, do they?" von Stade said. The timbre of her voice seemed to change, slipping from flip and assured into words tinged with disquietude. A ploy, perhaps, to put him at ease, draw him out, learn his next move, discover where he was headed.

He didn't respond.

Von Stade inclined her head, ran her fingers through her hair. A pretty woman preening for her date. "I know this will come as a crushing blow to you," she said, "and probably damage my good character, but it doesn't matter to me what Barashi or Gonzales, or whoever the hell he is, is going to do. I've never met the man. You know: cut outs, dead drops, offshore bank accounts. I agree to a contract, my word is gold, and I get my money. Lots of money. That's all that matters." She laughed softly. "Well, that and a swift, clean kill." She paused. "And maybe some good celebratory sex."

"And if you fail?"

"I return the payment and remain celibate. I don't lack for integrity, you know."

Von Stade guided the car onto 10th.

"Pull over, stop," Richard commanded.

She steered the car into a no parking zone.

"Turn off the engine and give me the keys. Move slowly. Keep your left hand on the wheel."

She did as she was told, reaching the keys back to Richard.

"Drop them in the floor well." He didn't want her getting close to him or discovering the limited mobility of his right arm. He waved the SIG at her. "Hands back on the steering wheel." He bent to retrieve the keys with his right hand, a delicate task. As he did so, he glimpsed her jaw go rigid, the muscles in her arm, tense, ready to explode. "I *will* pull the trigger," he snapped. "Don't gamble I won't."

"I don't think so."

"Well, that's my worry. Yours is that you won't have any more."

"Any more what?"

"Worries."

She relaxed. "I must say, Herr Wainwright, you've turned out to be a much more worthy adversary than I would've guessed. All I had to do was dissuade you from nosing around, but you wouldn't quit, wouldn't let go. *Eine Nervensage*," she hissed. She drew a deep breath. "A snap. That's what this job was supposed to be. A snap." She leaned back against the headrest, perhaps in reflection, perhaps in frustration.

"I know the feeling," he said. He spotted a vacant taxi coming up 10th Street behind them. He tucked the gun away and scrambled from the car, flagging the taxi with his left arm. It pulled in behind the Lincoln.

Von Stade opened the door of the Town Car and stepped out. "What's wrong with your arm?" she said, tapping her right shoulder.

"Battle wounds," he answered. He edged toward the taxi.

He should have moved faster. Almost too late he saw her right arm come up, draw back, and in a continuous motion sweep forward letting loose the Combat Talon. "Bastard," she screamed.

The knife cartwheeled through the neon-engraved night. Richard ducked, and the weapon pinged off the taxi's door.

The taxi driver, a little Paki or Indian, babbled incoherently and accelerated away as Richard dove into the rear seat. The forward momentum of the taxi whanged the door shut.

Richard sat up. "Hotmouth Harry's," he said. "You know where it is?"

"Bad woman, vedy bad woman," the driver kept repeating. "We go to police. Okay? Vedy bad woman."

"No police. Hotmouth Harry's."

"Okay. Okay. I know." The driver's gaze remain riveted on the rearview mirror, likely making sure the knife-throwing woman wasn't in pursuit.

Richard asked to be dropped two blocks beyond Hotmouth Harry's. He handed the driver a large tip and admonished, "Stay away from blonde assassins."

"Yes, yes." The driver nodded vigorously and smiled, undoubtedly glad to be rid of a fare who doubled as a dartboard.

Richard ditched his baseball cap in a trash can, then, head down, strolled casually along 14th, a poor soul lost in the night. *And probably a mugging target.*

As he neared Harry's, the urgent, sweaty rhythms of a hard-driving Zydeco band assaulted his ears. Pungent aromas of andouille, etouffee and jambalaya flowed from the restaurant, reminding him of how long it had been since he'd had a decent meal.

He walked past the establishment and swept his gaze over the outdoor patio. It was nearly midnight, but he didn't spot Butler. He needed a better look. He continued up the street a couple of blocks, then crossed and retraced his steps on the opposite side. Once he was in sight of the bar and grill, he paused and leaned against the wall of a building, taking his time to survey Harry's crowded patio and, more importantly, what was going on around it.

It took a minute or two, but he finally picked out Butler, partially screened by the scurrying waiters and milling clientele. He sat alone, near the back of the patio, a mug of beer his only apparent companion.

Richard continued his surveillance. An AT&T van parked about twenty yards to his left contained two repairmen apparently less interested in fixing something than in munching on po' boys and keeping an eye on the shenanigans at Harry's.

Richard watched as a few couples, arm-in-arm and hand-in-hand—not all necessarily male-female—strolled through the night. One duo in particular caught his eye. They seemed to be running a race track pattern in front of Harry's, up and down the street. As far as he could determine, they had no particular destination in mind. Just killing time. *Sure.*

They sauntered toward Richard now, casually chatting with each other. Richard, not wanting them to get a close look at his face despite his altered appearance, bent to tighten his shoe lace. Hard to do with only one functional arm. As he knelt, he felt the SIG working its way up the small of his back, fleeing the constraints of his waistband like a prairie dog ready to pop from its hole.

He rolled backward out of his squat, collapsing against the wall behind him, trapping the gun between his body and the wall before the weapon could tumble free. He let out a barely audible groan as he hit the wall. The couple paused to look at him.

"You okay there, partner?" the man asked.

"Yeah. Too many man-gerillos . . . mergerangoes . . . margaritas," Richard slurred. He kept his head down.

"Help you up?" The man stepped toward Richard and extended his hand.

"Think I'll shtay down here a while," Richard whispered. "Waitin' for my bud."

"Take it easy." The couple continued their stroll.

After they were a block away, Richard stood, keeping his hand on the SIG and jamming the weapon more firmly into the waistband of his khakis. His heart hammered at the same rate as the furious Zydeco beat from across the street. His shirt, saturated with perspiration, clung to him like a wet dishrag. *Not cut out for this.*

He looked again at the patio across the street. A waiter stood at Butler's table, not poised to take an order, but engaged in urgent, close-order conversation. Something you wouldn't expect a waiter to have time to do on a bustling Friday night.

Richard, understanding he was deep in enemy territory, decided to burrow even deeper. Hiding in plain sight.

Barashi, sweat pouring off his body in salty rivulets, had stripped to his undershorts in an un-air-conditioned garage. Using an assumed name, he'd rented an apartment, a "safe house," with an attached garage in Sandy Springs on the northern perimeter of Atlanta months before. Now he used the garage to make final preparations for his attack. He'd wanted more time to ready his mission, but his encounter with Wainwright, and Khassem's betrayal, had forced his hand. If conditions were right, tomorrow would be the day. One America would never forget.

He finished bolting a steel tank and electric pump onto the bed of his Dodge Ram pickup, then carefully checked the pump's wiring. He pressed a hastily-rigged switch in the cab. The pump purred to life with a soft hum. He released the switch and returned to the bed of the truck. Adjacent to the pump sat the tank that would carry the Ebola solution. From the tank, four hoses ran to thin iron pipes mounted vertically on the right side of the truck. At the top of each eight-foot pipe, a nozzle angled outward at 45 degrees. Barashi retightened the fittings between the tank and the hoses and between the hoses and the nozzles. Satisfied, he climbed down from the bed and retrieved two magnetic signs. He slapped one on each door of the cab. The signs would give the presence of the truck at least superficial legitimacy at his targets.

He toweled off and checked his watch. In less than twelve hours, Atlanta would be a very different place in which to live . . . and die. Justice would be served—American justice, so neatly interchangeable with revenge. Not all Western notions were to be discarded.

He thought again of the church lady.

Richard, perpetuating the persona of a down-and-out loner making a Cook's Tour of the local hotspots, crossed the street and shuffled into Hotmouth Harry's. The infectious music and aromas bordered on overwhelming, transporting him into a raucous *fais do do* in the bayous of Louisiana. He elbowed his way to the bar and, because of the din, flashed only a hand signal to the bartender to request a beer.

Mug in hand, he positioned himself so he could watch both patio exits. It was now closer to one a. m. than midnight, so he assumed Butler and his watchers would soon abandon their vigils. But it was almost two before the virologist and his notional waiter pushed their way into the crowd massed in the interior of Harry's and struggled toward the exit. Richard followed at a discrete distance. Once outside, the two men shook hands and parted. Richard tailed Butler, slouching along about a half block behind. The AT&T workers had packed it in, too, and the couple who'd made continuous loops in front of Harry's had abandoned their patrol.

He presumed Butler was heading toward a parking garage, but couldn't be sure. Taxis and MARTA were options, although he thought it was too late for MARTA trains and buses to still be running. A large sign for a parking garage shone brightly several blocks away, and Richard guessed that was Butler's destination. But it wasn't. The virologist paused when he came to a corner, then turned left down a poorly-lit side street. Away from the garage.

Richard reached the corner and stopped. He sensed his plan taking on water and beginning to list. Without looking behind him, he peeled off to the right, crossing the street and moving away from Butler. He didn't want to do that, didn't want to lose the guy, but he had the distinct feeling the jaws of a trap were about to snap shut. When he reached the opposite corner, he turned and glanced back.

His senses hadn't short circuited. He'd slipped a snare. He'd been sandwiched between Butler and yet another pursuer, one obviously working on speculation—or hope, perhaps—sweeping in Butler's wake. The unmistakable bulk of Lieutenant Jackson lumbered up to the corner. The detective took a hard look at Richard, apparently struggling to make a connection between the pony-tailed CEO he'd hassled earlier and the stooped guy with the shaved head. Then Jackson turned to watch Butler, still striding away from him. Richard could tell it was decision time. Would Jackson cross the street and check him out, or continue his rear-guard action on Butler?

Richard didn't allow his gaze to linger on Jackson, didn't want to give the detective any reason to take a closer look. Instead, he turned away, feigning indifference and fixed his vision on the traffic light. He waited for the WALK signal, then lollygagged along the street in the direction of the parking garage, moving slowly, just a little unsteadiness in his gait; a man who'd imbibed in one snort too many but was at peace with the world. He gambled he wouldn't draw any further interest from Jackson; and that Butler would eventually end up at the parking garage. Not that there weren't other car parks around, but this one appeared to be the biggest and nearest.

Jackson apparently decided not to gamble. He turned and paced after Butler, now more than a block ahead of him.

Richard waited almost a half hour in the garage, climbing slowly up and down the stairs of the structure, listening for footfalls, and stepping out of the stairwell periodically to check the elevator.

His patience paid off. The clip-clop of sandals, not shoes—strange—echoed through the stairwell about a quarter to three. The door on the level below him scraped open. He waited a moment and listened, but heard no trailing footfalls. He dashed from the fourth landing to the third and pushed through the door into the garage. Butler. Ambling along in shorts and sandals as if he were coming from a pool party. Richard fell in behind him, not close enough to be threatening, but close enough to make a move. He made a show of searching for his car keys: patting his pants, then jamming his left hand deep into his pocket and fumbling around. The 9mm cartridges made a nice metallic rattle, just like keys.

Butler pivoted.

Richard smiled and nodded. "Always forget where I put 'em," he said.

Butler's Cape Buffalo mustache twitched. "Yeah, me too sometimes. Have a good one, dude." He reached his car, an elderly but pristine Mercedes 500 SEL. He inserted a key into the front door lock and turned it. The vacuum-driven locking system released the locks on all four doors.

Richard approached a Lexus parked to the right of Butler's car and bent over it as if to use a key. He heard the door of the Mercedes open and shut. He spun, yanked open the passenger door, plunged into the car, and snatched the SIG from the back of his pants. He aimed the weapon at Butler. "You don't look like a doctor," he said.

Butler shrugged. "You don't look like a CEO."

Richard settled into the seat beside Butler.

"At least I hope to hell you're Richard Wainwright, CEO, and not some damned car thief," Butler continued, "'cuz I'd sure as shit hate to lose these wheels."

"What about your life?"

"You would have shot me already."

"Come alone, I said."

"I'm a government employee. I can't go around freelancing and setting up secret meetings with wanted murders." Butler started the engine and backed the Mercedes out of its parking slot.

"I'm not a murderer."

"No, I imagine you're not, or you wouldn't have spent the night dodging the local constabulary just to chat with me. Where to?" Butler herded the big car down a twisting ramp toward the garage exit.

"Call it."

"Lots of Waffle Houses open all night."

Richard tucked the gun back into his pants. "I haven't eaten since breakfast."

They approached the exit. "Better scrunch down in the seat after I pay the toll. There still might be a plainclothes guardian angel or two fluttering along the street. By the way, since we're buddies now, call me Dwight."

Richard ducked below the window as they drove out. "Richard here."

Dwight nodded. He steered the car onto Peachtree Street. "Coast clear," he said after a couple of minutes. "So, you think you know how this Gonzales or Barashi or whoever he is, is going to attack?"

"I have an idea." Richard swiveled his head, checking for pursuing headlights. Nothing. "Have you ever heard of *Malacosoma americanum*?"

Dwight thought about it. "No. But as long as we're playing Fictionary, do you know what a filovirus is?"

"No."

"Then I think we're about to have one hell of an enlightening discussion."

Richard stared out the window at the neon landscape flashing by. *Enlightening?* No, it would be much more than that. Terrifying was one word that came to mind.

Chapter Twenty-Seven

ATLANTA
SATURDAY, AUGUST 24

In the dead zone of night—well past midnight, well before dawn—Richard and Dwight sat in a booth at a Waffle House on the northeast side of Atlanta. The usual denizens of the wee hours drifted in and out: cops, drunks, die-hard partiers, workers whose shifts began long before sunrise.

At first glance, the small establishment seemed more a gathering place than a breakfast eatery, but the flood tide of odors—fresh eggs, buttermilk pancakes, pork sausage—greasy but agreeable—that fled from the sizzling grill suggested otherwise. Dwight, his meaty hand twisting a coffee cup in a slow-motion circle, seemed to remain circumspect of Richard, but at least indicated a willingness to partake in discussion.

Richard hadn't eaten since the previous morning and dove with unabated enthusiasm into the scrambled eggs and pancakes delivered by a bubbly waitress with Nicki Minaj eyes.

"Y'all enjoy that now, sir." She watched him attack the food. "There's more where that came from, ya know." She turned to Dwight and patted his arm. "Sure I can't bring ya something, honey, grits or toast maybe?"

Dwight declined. The waitress issued a motherly frown of disapproval and departed.

"Tell me about filoviruses," Richard said.

Dwight did. Everything. He focused on Ebola. No vaccine. No cure. No hope. An excruciating way to die.

"Ebola attacks your body's blood-clotting capabilities with particular ferocity," he said. "It goes after your major organs, devastating your kidneys, liver and spleen. You're racked with crippling fatigue, agonizing pain, boiling fever. Your eyeballs turn blood red. Your throat turns mushy and raw . . . to the point you can't even swallow your own saliva. And there's absolutely nothing that can help you." He paused. "Not even prayer." His words seemed to come from someplace far away. He reached for a glass of water and took a long swallow. He set the glass back on the table.

"Liquefied coffee grounds," he continued. "That's what your vomit looks like. It's filled with blood and dead tissue." He shook his head, as if disturbed by the image. "Things aren't any better at the other end. You're defecating the linings of your intestines in explosions of bloody diarrhea." He voice trailed off to a whisper. "Your shit resembles molten tar."

Richard, whose eating slowed steadily as Dwight's monologue progressed, shoved the last few bites away from him.

"Sorry," Dwight said. "It's not pleasant. It's revolting and nightmarish. But you need to know what we're dealing with. Ebola is a stone-cold killer, and your suffering doesn't end until the virus worms its way into your heart and brain. In the end, your blood pressure tanks, you go into shock from blood and fluid loss . . . and mercifully, you die."

Richard remained silent for a long while before asking, in a quiet voice, "So what did Barashi develop?"

Dwight explained how the terrorist had melded the airborne transmissive qualities of Ebola-Reston with the lethalness of Ebola-Zaire, in effect producing a bioengineered Black Death that floated through the air like microscopic pollen.

The revelation hit Richard with wrecking-ball force. He suddenly understood the full horror of what Barashi was about to unleash. He lifted a glass of water toward his lips, but missed, the liquid dribbling down his chin as his hand shook in a Parkinson's-like tremor. He attempted to draw a deep breath, but struggled against the sensation that a noose had been cinched around his chest and yanked tight. He gasped.

"What is it, man? You okay?" Dwight rose halfway from the booth.

Richard, struggling to compose himself, motioned for the virologist to stay seated. The two men sat in silence for several minutes, Dwight, watching, concerned; Richard, waiting for the noose to loosen.

Finally it did. "Until just now," Richard said, his voice barely audible, even to himself, "I had less than a full appreciation of what Barashi could do. I thought maybe we were dealing with something like anthrax or smallpox, bad enough, but Ebola . . ."

"You know something else, don't you?" Dwight declared, his gaze locked on Richard. "I can see it. Feel it. It's palpable. You're terrified."

"Malacosoma americanum," Richard responded, his voice shaky, "tent caterpillars."

"Tent caterpillars?"

"We don't have tent caterpillars where I live, but there was a feature on TV about them last night."

"I know what they are."

Nasty little black and tan hairy things, Richard had learned; moth larvae that build webs—"tents"—in the crotches of tree limbs and attack its foliage with the ferocity of swarming locusts. They can completely defoliate a tree, strip it bare, within a week.

"They're kind of out of control this year, I gather," Richard said.

"Yes." Dwight said it slowly, as though a dawning awareness of an even greater evil was enveloping him; as if he knew Richard's next words would loose some sort of ineffable dread; something too awful to imagine.

"The only clue I got from the informant at Diamond Cutters before Barashi turned him into kindling was 'tent,'" Richard said. "'He's going after the tent—' And this." Richard slid the slip of paper Khassem had given him to Dwight.

"I understand you control tent caterpillars by spraying them," he added.

Dwight studied the names on the paper. His face tightened into a ligature of concern. He flapped his sandal against the sole of his foot so rapidly it sounded like a mallard taking flight.

"What?" Richard said.

"These are subdivisions." Dwight leaned in close to Richard and pointed at the paper. "Big subdivisions in the northern part of the county. Elysian Fields. King's Landing. Magnolia Heights."

"Oh, God, no," Richard said softly. He closed his eyes. Now it made sense, what Barashi had said earlier about Americans coming to know the terror or despair—he couldn't recall the exact word—of realizing not even their homes were safe. To be afraid to step from their doors, to draw a breath.

Dwight spoke more urgently now, the words tumbling from him in a cascade of disbelief. He saw the same thing Richard did. "So Barashi drives through these neighborhoods in a vehicle that looks like your typical yard care pickup with some kind of pump apparatus mounted on it, and acts like he's spraying for tent caterpillars. He doesn't look out of place. People are used to seeing their trees sprayed when they're infested. So nobody is the wiser for several days until the dying starts. And then it's too late. The virus is loose. Probably all over the world. An airplane trip. A sneeze. A cough. Jesus, Mary and Joseph." He stared at Richard, an empty, despairing look. *What do we do?*

A high-decibel silence settled over the table, though the hammering of Richard's pulse echoed from one side of his head to the other.

Dwight spoke again. "People wouldn't even have to breathe the stuff. Kids and pets walking across yards where the spray had fallen would track the virus into their homes."

"Assuming we're right," Richard said, "when do you think he would do this? Today? Tomorrow? Next week?"

"Why wait? Thanks to you, his lab has been exposed, and he's been ID'd. The fuse has been lit, dude. He ain't waitin'."

A Mixmaster of thoughts swirled through Richard's head, and he struggled to focus on a single issue. He finally found the one that seemed most important. He threaded his fingers together and leaned toward Dwight. "Time of day," he said. "Is there a time of day that would work better than any other for Barashi?"

Dwight drummed his fingers on the table briefly, then said, "Yes, it's best to spray right at sunrise. It's usually calm then. Barashi doesn't want the virus flying all over the place, chasing him around. He wants to be able to control it. So to speak. Also, at this time of year, when it rains around here it's usually in the afternoon, not the morning." Dwight checked his watch, shook his head. "So basically, we're out of time. Sunup's in less than three hours."

"Dawn patrol, then?" Richard surprised himself by saying it.

"Us?" Dwight's droopy mustache rose with his eyebrows.

"Look, it's kind of short notice to convince the cops and FBI that Barashi's going to attack subdivisions. By the time we made our pitch and they muster their forces, the assault could be over. Then there's the little matter of me being wanted for murder, possessing an illegal handgun, and God knows what else."

"Us?" Dwight said again.

"Oh, and did I mention Barashi may have a hostage, a Methodist minister? A female. I'd just as soon not have to explain that, either. Snatched out of Diamond Cutters."

The virologist tilted his head back, stared at the ceiling and expelled a long, slow breath. "Anything else?" he said.

"Well, yeah, there's a professional assassin, one of Barashi's sidekicks I think, who's been trying to filet me with her pet knife."

"Her pet knife?" Dwight stared at Richard.

Richard nodded.

Dwight buried his face in his hands. "God help me," he muttered, "I'm trapped in an Elmore Leonard novel."

"Well, consider the bright side then. We could be wrong about all this."

Dwight looked up. "You think?"

Richard didn't answer.

"Me either," Dwight said.

"Come on," Richard responded, "all we have do is run reconnaissance. It's not like we're vigilantes. If we spot something suspicious, we call 911. I've got a buddy on the county police force. I'm sure he'd be glad to rush to my aid, wherever I am. And I assume after yesterday you've got some FBI contacts."

"This is a really bad idea, you know."

"Got a better one?"

"Yeah. Let the authorities handle it. The government doesn't always move at garden slug speed."

"Fine. And you'll explain to them you came by the information how? In the course of harboring a fugitive?"

"I don't need to tell them that. All I need to tell them is that I have a strong, well-founded suspicion of what's about to go down. And when and where." He picked up his cell phone.

"Good luck," Richard said.

Dwight punched in Dr. Zambit's cell phone number, knowing his boss probably was awake and hanging around the CDC Emergency Operations Center.

"Zamby," Dwight said when Zambit answered, "I know what this guy Barashi is going to do."

"Who?"

"Barashi, the terrorist. We thought his name was Gonzales. It's not, it's Alnour Barashi, an Arab."

"Whoa, slow down, Dwight. Where are you? How'd you find this out? I thought you'd be home in bed after that CEO gent didn't show up at Hotmouth Harry's. Tell me what's going on."

"Trust me, I know what's going to happen. I can't tell you how—"

"Yes, you can. I can't promote one of your wild-ass hunches to the FBI and—"

"Damn it. You have to!" Dwight slammed the table with an open hand. A cop sitting at the counter glanced in his direction. Dwight raised his hand in apology. "Sorry," he said to the cop. The policeman returned to his coffee and English muffin.

"Look, Zamby," Dwight continued, snapping his words out, "there isn't time. I'm talking a matter of hours." He looked at his wristwatch. "Maybe two."

"Two?" Zambit said it so loudly Dwight had to pull the phone away from his ear.

"Yeah. Sunrise."

"Have you been drinking, Dwight?"

"This isn't a joke, Bossman. I'm dead-ass serious."

Zambit issued a long sigh, then said, "Okay, talk to me . . . against my better judgment."

Dwight spent the next ten minutes giving Zambit the details of how, when and where he expected Barashi's attack to go down.

When he'd finished, Zambit said, "You know, that tale's bizarre enough I almost believe it. But I'd still like to know how you—"

"Not gonna happen, Boss. Can you muster the cavalry or not?"

"Why do I always feel like I'm Wile E. Coyote about to take a header over a cliff when I listen to you?"

"Answer the question. Are we gonna hear bugles shortly?"

Dwight noticed the cop at the counter had taken a renewed interest in him and Richard, and wondered if he'd recognized Richard, or at least thought Richard bore a resemblance to someone wanted for murder.

On the phone, Zambit said, "I don't know. Let me talk to the law enforcement guys here and get back to you."

"Quickly, boss."

Dwight hung up. The cop at the counter was speaking into his shoulder mike and simultaneously keeping an eye on him and Richard. Not a good sign.

Dwight stood. "Be right back," he said, and headed toward the restrooms.

The waitress, who apparently had been overwhelmed by a sudden influx of customers, came flying in Richard's direction with a pot of coffee in each hand. "High test or unleaded?" she said. She hoisted the pots to make them more visible. Tools of her trade held aloft.

Richard declined.

"You didn't finish your breakfast," she admonished. She peered carefully at him, then set one of the pots on the table. She reached out and felt his forehead. "You don't look well," she said. "I'll bet you've got a fever. You need some rest. There's a virus going around, you know."

Richard smiled, took a twenty from his pocket and gave it to the waitress. "Keep the change," he said. "And don't worry, I'll take care of myself."

He, too, had noticed the interest the policeman had taken in him and Dwight. But the cop now sat quietly at the counter, toying with his coffee cup. Richard looked around for Dwight. He hadn't returned yet and seemed to be taking his time.

Richard studied the cop and decided he probably was unsure whether he, Richard, was "wanted" or not. Richard brushed his hand over the stubble on his head. His crappy haircut may have saved him.

Dwight plopped back down in the booth. "Ready to boogie?" he asked.

"Help is on the way, I presume?"

Dwight shrugged. "We'll find out shortly. In the meantime, I guess we'll follow your recommendation and do a little recon of our own. Several of the subdivisions aren't far away."

They exited the Waffle House and stepped into the parking lot, a checkerboard of bright light and dense shadow. The pre-dawn humidity clutched at Richard like a tepid sauna. A young couple, arm-in-arm, laughing softly, nodded as they walked past him.

The policeman trailed him and Dwight into the lot, but moved toward his own car rather than following them to Dwight's Mercedes.

Dwight pulled the car onto the main street. "The cop in there was pretty interested in us," Richard said.

"Well, *you*, maybe. Yeah, I noticed."

"I got the impression he wasn't sure about me, but didn't have any real reason to check me out." Richard craned his neck around to see if the patrol car was behind them. "My guess is he'll probably follow us, then pull us over on some BS traffic stop so he can get a closer look at me and my ID."

"No he won't."

Richard looked at Dwight. "How do you know?"

"He's got a flat tire."

"Really. And how did that happen?"

Dwight adjusted the rearview mirror. "I guess my misspent youth in Newark wasn't all misspent."

Barashi had left his apartment several hours before sunrise, driving carefully on virtually traffic-less secondary roads, following a circuitous route to where he would lay in wait to attack his first target. Despite his confidence that his subterfuge would work, that his attack, or sequence of attacks, would be successful, he fully understood things could go wrong: that he could have bad luck, that he could have miscalculated, that he might have to fight and flee.

He hadn't ignored those contingencies. He'd packed a dozen thirty-round magazines for an AKS-74, a weapon that on full automatic could empty a clip in less than three seconds. He had five fragmentation grenades. He carried a Glock in a shoulder holster under a light windbreaker. He'd tucked a 9mm Heckler & Koch under his seat. Ideally, he wouldn't need to touch the weapons, but if he had to, he'd fight to the death.

At four thirty in the morning he pulled into the parking lot of one of the many megachurches populating north metro Atlanta. The church was less than a minute from his first target. Headlights off, he drove the pickup to the rear of the church's sprawling lot where three rows of short, white buses were parked. The third row abutted a tall hedge. He found a vacant space between a bus and a maintenance truck. He backed the Dodge Ram into the slot and turned off the engine. He would wait here, hopefully unnoticed until first light.

Chapter Twenty-Eight

NORTH METRO ATLANTA
SATURDAY, AUGUST 24

After Dwight and Richard had been on the road about twenty minutes, Zambit called Dwight back.

"I gotta tell ya," Zambit said, "the law enforcement guys here were skeptical as hell when I told them you couldn't identify your source. But that aside, they said they'll get some patrol units out to the subdivisions, but it's going to take time. They have to muster resources first. Local departments are typically on minimum staffing this time of night. Not only that, a lot of their personnel are already deployed downtown and at the airport to guard high-value targets. Bottom line: the forces up where you are are sparse."

"Hold it," Dwight said. He pulled the Mercedes to the side of the road, flipped on the overhead map light and re-examined the paper bearing the names of the subdivisions. "I have an idea. I know where some of these places are—not far from where we . . . I am. I'm already on my way to check a couple of them out. If I see anything suspicious, I'll call 911." He ran his finger down the list. "I'll take a look at Elysian Fields, Magnolia Heights and, uh, Crystal Corners. See if you can vector the cops to the other subdivisions."

"Okay. Hang on. I'll run your proposition past the guys here."

Dwight put his phone on mute and explained to Richard what was going on.

Zambit came back on-line. "Okay," he said. "Your plan has a green light. But if you spot something, instead of calling 911, call the task force duty officer. He'll have direct contact with the patrol cars he's dispatching."

Zambit gave Dwight the D.O.'s phone number, then added, "Ya know, I don't know whether to hope you're right or wrong about this, Dwight."

"Me either, Boss."

As Dwight accelerated away from the curb, Richard removed his handgun from the center console of the Mercedes and placed it in his lap.

"We aren't gonna need that," Dwight said. "All we're going to do is a little early-morning recon. If we see something hinky, we dial the boys in blue and let them do their thing." He tapped his finger on the piece of paper on which he'd written the duty officer's phone number.

"And if the cops can't get here in time? From what you've told me, this isn't a case where the good guys can be just a second or two behind the power curve and come out winners. If this Ebola stuff gets airborne—"

"I know, I know."

"You didn't answer my question."

"I know that, too."

They rode in silence for several minutes.

At five thirty they pulled into Elysian Fields. Dwight eased the car through patches of fog while Richard acted as lookout. They'd driven only a short distance into the subdivision when the glow of headlights appeared behind them, diffuse and dim at first, refracting through a gauzy, drifting mist. After that, they grew steadily brighter and more distinct.

"Turn here and douse the lights," Richard said as they approached a cross street. "Kinda weird for someone to be out and about this early on a Saturday."

"You mean like us?" Dwight said.

He turned, switched off the headlights, pulled the car to the side of the road and killed the engine. Both men slid down in their seats. Whoever was behind them turned, too. High beam headlights bounced off the rearview mirror illuminating the interior of the auto.

"I don't like this," Dwight muttered. He fumbled for his cell phone.

Richard tensed and raised the barrel of the SIG so that it was in position to fire.

Dwight looked at him wide-eyed. "You wouldn't really, would you?" he asked in a harsh whisper.

The approaching vehicle moved around the Mercedes and slowed. A loud slap, something striking the pavement, sounded from outside. Another "whap" followed, this one a bit more distant. Richard chanced a peek over the dash.

"Newspapers," he said. "Those are newspapers landing in driveways. Early morning deliveries. A few homes still get them. Okay to breathe again."

"Good. I was about to turn blue. If a black man can do that."

They resumed their reconnaissance, making a slow loop on the main road that circled an eighteen-hole golf course. They encountered no traffic and began exploring side lanes and cul-de-sacs.

"A quiet Saturday morning in the 'burbs," Richard said.

"Except for us and the newspaper guy," Dwight answered. "Ya know, somehow I can't imagine Ebola here."

"No one could imagine jetliners flying into the World Trade Center, either. Not before it happened, anyhow. So I guess we're forced to imagine this, even anticipate it. Ebola on our front doorsteps. A—what did you call it?—chimera virus. Airborne."

"It's ironic," Dwight said, dimming the dash lights to allow better outside visibility. "First commercial jets, now a microscopic virus. The greatest terrors come from the air."

"No, not from the air, I think, from men's minds." Richard held up his hand. "Hold it." Dwight slowed the car while Richard studied a street sign. "Take a left here," Richard said, "I think this is the road we came in on. Let's check it again."

A heavy, humid haze hung in the air even as the mist began to disperse, but darkness still blanketed the subdivision. Dwight flicked the headlights onto high beam. "It's funny," he said, "as far as I know, the people bent on murdering us have never really articulated a demand or cause, except to kill us."

"Yeah. And we kill them back." Richard sighed. "And then they kill more of us, and we kill more of them. God, it's like a cosmic pissing contest."

Dwight reached the main road outside the subdivision and stopped. "Nothing here," he said. "I think the wild goose is gonna win this one." He turned the car around and headed back into Elysian Fields. He took a right on the road circumnavigating the golf course. "One more loop and we'd better press on."

Richard wasn't listening. "Look," he said softly. His heartbeat kicked into overdrive.

"Yeah, yeah, I see it," Dwight said, his voice strained, tense.

A pickup truck, with only its parking lights on, sat on the side of the road.

Dwight slowed the Mercedes and crept up behind the truck. "Jesus, man. You see what I see."

The truck had a hose assembly—a reel—and a small tank mounted on the rear of its bed.

"Drive by slowly," Richard said. "I'll take a look." He hunkered down in his seat so only his eyes cleared the bottom of the window. Going about

10 mph, Dwight drew alongside the pickup. The writing on its door said "Martinez Yard Care."

"Is it Barashi?" Dwight asked, his voice breaking.

They passed the truck and Richard sat up. "Kermit the Frog could be driving the damn thing for all I know. It's dark, and the windows are tinted."

"Did you see anybody?"

"A figure wearing a baseball hat." Richard wondered if Marty could be in the truck. Wondered if she were still alive. A surge of nausea tweaked his stomach. How could things have gotten so out of hand?

"We need a closer look."

"And just how the hell do you propose we do that?" Richard snapped. "You want me to go tap on the window and ask whoever's in there if he can spare a cup of Ebola? Then if he blows my head off, you'll know we've got Barashi?"

"Easy, man. I'm on your side."

Richard held up his hand, a peace gesture. "Sorry," he said, "not your fault. I'm pissed at myself. Pissed for getting Marty into this mess. Pissed for having to drag you into it. Pissed because I'm so damn helpless. Pull around the corner and stop. Let's think this thing through."

Dwight turned into the next street and pulled to the curb.

"Maybe it's time to call the cops," Richard said.

Dwight shook his head. "I don't know, Rich. The guy could be just some poor Mexican dude waiting for first light to start his day's work. I don't want to come off as Chicken Little on my first call. Hold something over the dome light. I'm gonna run back to the corner, see if I can get close to Kermit."

Richard laid a restraining hand on Dwight's arm. "Stay in the car," he said. "No heroes. Let's just keep an eye on the truck. Chances are nothing will happen 'til sunup."

"Might be too late." Dwight unfastened his seat belt. "You were the one who said we can't afford to be behind the power curve on this one."

"Dwight—"

"Look, I'm the perfect night stalker. Blend right in." He nodded at the interior light. "Cover it." He paused with his hand on the door handle. "If you can manage, turn the car around. Just in case this guy decides to move, we need to be ready to follow. Lights off." He opened the door and slipped out.

"People used to listen to me," Richard said into the darkness.

Dwight dashed to the corner and knelt behind a bush. A startled chorus of crickets ceased its early-morning chant as his knee touched down on the damp, dew-laden grass. A dog barked, baritone and resonant, alert to something non-routine, different.

Dwight quickly realized he wasn't the perfect night stalker, at least not here, not in an upscale, white neighborhood. He was big, black and bald, wearing short pants, squatting behind a bush in the dark.

Someone yelled at the dog to shut up. It didn't.

Dwight stuck his head up over the bush. The pickup, perhaps fifty yards away, hadn't moved. He couldn't tell if anybody was in it or not. It was parked just beyond the ring of illumination from a nearby streetlight.

An exterior light on the house whose yard Dwight was in flicked on. A man in a bathrobe stepped onto the porch. Beside him stood a dog the size of a Clydesdale pony. Dwight shifted slightly to his right, attempting to get out of sight of the man and his pony, yet not reveal himself to whoever was in the truck. He buried as much of his body as he could into the shrub. He figured he probably looked like a 250-pound ostrich trying to hide in the Australian desert.

"Anybody out there?" the man with the Clydesdale called.

"Jesus, like somebody's going to answer," Dwight muttered to himself. He snuck a peek at the truck. It remained parked.

"Who's there?" the man shouted. "I'm going to let my dog go."

For a moment, Dwight didn't know if he were more frightened of the fact that the reincarnation of the Hound of the Baskervilles was about to be set loose, or that there could be a truckload of Ebola-Zaire parked about a chip shot away.

It became a moot point as he heard the distinct sound of a round being chambered into an handgun and a voice from behind him saying, "Don't move."

Chapter Twenty-Nine

NORTH METRO ATLANTA
SATURDAY, AUGUST 24

Richard figured the entire neighborhood probably was awake by now, as the incessant, challenging bark of a dog, probably a very large one, grew more urgent. He heard a shout, a male voice; then a female voice responding, one with authority. The barking ceased. Silence ensued. He felt for the SIG and peered into the darkness, but could see no one.

He snapped off the cover of the Mercedes' dome light and removed the bulb. Leaving the handgun in place, he reached across his body with his left hand and opened the car door. He stepped from the auto, shut the door quickly and stood. "Dwight?" he hissed.

Only the desultory chirp of a tired cricket reached his ears. Enough ambient illumination existed from the street lights that he should have seen Dwight, but the virologist was nowhere in sight. Then, a soft footfall behind him. He whirled.

"Sorry, partner. Looks like I'm a POW." Dwight stood with his hands on top of his head, fingers interlaced, his bulk shielding his captor.

Richard reached for his weapon.

"God, you're such a *Maulesel*," von Stade said, stepping from behind Dwight and leveling a handgun at Richard. "Stubborn to a fault. Just leave the damn pistol where it is."

Richard complied, hope sucked from him like the littoral ocean in the face of a tsunami. He'd been a fool to think he could match up against a cold-blooded, professional killer. Stubborn to a fault? How about stubborn to his death? And Dwight's.

"Hands on your head." She motioned with her gun.

"I can't lift my right arm."

"Yes, I forgot. Left hand then. Keep your right arm where I can see it." She stepped closer, her watchful gaze flicking between Dwight and Richard. Outfitted in khaki slacks and a light blue windbreaker, she appeared almost military. Her manner matched her dress: self-assured and imperious; efficient and professional. A stone-cold killer at the peak of her game.

"Turn around," she ordered.

Richard met her stare, yet there was no real connection, only a vacant look between victor and vanquished. He didn't move.

"Around," she said again, more sharply.

He turned slowly, every muscle in his body knotting. *At least it will be quick. I probably won't even feel it. Just an impact, then nothing. I cease to exist.*

Von Stade removed the SIG from his waistband. "This is illegal, you know."

"A capital offense?"

A scuffling sound erupted behind him, sudden movement. He turned his head. Dwight, on the ground, thrashing. Von Stade crouching next to him, the barrel of her pistol pressed against his temple. "Moron," she said. With her left hand she pointed the SIG at Richard. "I can fire both guns at once if you'd like to keep testing me."

"Why wait for an excuse?"

A car engine started up somewhere near the main road. Somewhere in the distance, a dog barked.

"Get up," she said to Dwight. She stood and backed off, gun at the ready. She motioned for Richard to face her.

Not yet, then?

"You're familiar with Brer Rabbit?" she said, ejecting the clip from Richard's 9mm and extending the empty weapon toward him, butt first.

Richard stood motionless, a cigar store Indian. He looked at Dwight, Dwight at him.

"Brer Rabbit," she repeated, "an American classic. I've actually read it. 'Don't fling me in dat briar patch,' sezze." The words were of the Old South dialects attributed to slaves. They sounded strange rendered in a German accent. She waggled the SIG in front of Richard, demanding he accept it.

He did. The woman clearly had run off the tracks, was cruising with her mainsail at half mast.

"Brer Rabbit, Brer Fox, de Tar Baby," Dwight said, his voice ringing in sardonic mimicry, an early 20th century minstrel. "Law, honey, you ain't heard dem stories by that ole darkey, Uncle Remus?" His words were directed at Richard.

Von Stade smiled, nodded. "Think of me in the Brer Rabbit role, Mr.

Wainwright. Telling you, Brer Fox, over and over not to pursue what was going on at BioDawn. You did just the opposite, of course; pitched yourself into the briar patch. Just like I knew you would."

Richard gaped. "Knew I would?"

"After you accepted the job at BioDawn, I didn't have much time to research your background and develop a profile on you. But from the limited material I was able to get hold of, I could tell you were the kind of man who didn't back off from challenges. Who'd be hands on and involved. To put it bluntly, who'd be my bloodhound."

"Bloodhound?"

Von Stade waited, silent.

Richard understood. "You wanted me to ferret out Barashi?"

She nodded. "I was treading a fine line, between urging you on— reverse psychology—and scaring you off. Turned out you had enough chutzpah for three guys."

"Who are you?"

"Not Veronica von Stade." She slipped her 9mm into a shoulder holster. "The Special Operations Division of Mossad, Metsada, killed von Stade over a decade ago. Her assassination was carried out covertly, and the public never learned of it. Her legend, it turned out, provided useful cover for other Mossad 'black operations'—no offense, Dr. Butler."

"No, of course not. Christ on a crutch, you're Mossad? Israeli intelligence?"

"Technically, the Institute for Intelligence and Special Tasks. Mossad is Hebrew for 'institute.'" She held out an ID card for the men to look at. It identified her as Hadassah Seligmann, a senior Mossad agent. She continued to speak with a German accent, but it seemed more civil, more refined now.

"I don't understand," Richard said. "Why did you need me? Surely you're backed up by the resources of Mossad, and, I would assume, the FBI and CIA."

"I'm not. To tell the truth, I'm not even here. Not officially. This is personal, off the books. Mossad has its hands full at home these days. Barashi is old news. But not to me."

The sky began to morph from black to pale gray. Objects become more distinct as the first scattering of indirect light fell over them. From somewhere above the tattered layers of thinning mist, the high, piercing cry of a hawk greeted the dawn. Much closer to where the group stood, the rattle of a diesel engine clattering to life snatched Richard's attention. The pickup.

"Well, you may be a lot closer to Barashi than you ever imagined," he said, inclining his head toward the truck.

"Checked him out already," von Stade—Seligmann—said. "Scared the pants off him, but he's legit. A Guatemalan with a Green Card. He's got his own yard care business. Just waiting for first light to spray some weed killer on his clients' Bermuda grass. But I assume that, or something like that, is probably Barashi's cover." It was a question, not a statement.

"Maybe you'd better finish your story first," Richard said. He still had not bought completely into Seligmann's abrupt transition from hit woman to Mossad agent. But then again, maybe the two personae weren't really that far apart.

"My car's around the corner, up the street. Let's go." As they walked, Seligmann continued her tale. "Barashi got his initial training in biowarfare from the Russians at a place called Koltsovo in western Siberia in the early 1990s. His intent was to come to the U.S. and covertly, but under legitimate cover, start his own biowarfare program. But on his way to America he made a stop in the Middle East. He assisted Hamas in launching a limited bio-attack on Israel. The weapon of choice was plague bacteria spliced with a gene that makes diphtheria."

"You're kidding," Dwight said. "Super plague with diphtheria toxin. This guy likes floating down the River Styx, doesn't he?" His sandals slapping the asphalt, he strode along the road behind Richard and Seligmann.

"Only this time he got into rapids he couldn't handle," Seligmann said. "The assault was so deadly it killed not only Israelis but the terrorists, too. That was the end of Barashi's assistance to the Palestinians; after that, he disappeared. The Israelis hushed up the attack for fear of triggering a worldwide panic. The U.S. was never notified because of Mossad's concern over the sieve-like security here, America's inability to keep secrets. When Barashi didn't surface again, the Mossad assumed the Palestinians had 'rewarded' him, but I didn't. My hatred burned a little too deeply to assume anything. The Palestinian attack had hit a kibbutz where my family lived. My mother, father and younger brother were killed. I've never been able to let go of that."

"So you kept watching for signs that Barashi had resurfaced some-place?" Richard said.

"After I heard about the BioDawn Gulfstream going down, I got curious about the company. That's when I learned a Dr. Alano Gonzales, a microbiologist, was working on some sort of hush-hush military project. At that point I guess my intelligence officer's sixth sense kicked in. I hopped a plane to Atlanta. 'Extended American vacation,' I told my superiors.

"Only I realized when I got here I'd need inside help to flush out Barashi, if that's who he really was. Gonzales was just too damn low profile and secretive for me to get close to. Which intrigued me even more. But I couldn't just walk into BioDawn, unofficial as I was, and ask what was going on behind the razor wire. That's when I turned to the von Stade-Uncle Remus bit."

"Worked pretty well," Richard said.

"You must be a predictable SOB," Dwight suggested.

"Not really." Seligmann shook her head. "The caper at Diamond Cutters was totally off the wall. I never expected that. Especially with the lady minister."

Richard grabbed Seligmann by the arm. "You were there? You saw Barashi kidnap Marty?"

"I've been on your tail like flies on crap ever since Barashi tried to kill you that night at BioDawn. After that, I knew for certain he was Barashi and not Gonzales. Unfortunately, he got away after trying to turn you into mincemeat at the strip club. But you were my only link to Barashi, and I had to keep you going."

"Had to keep me going?" Richard stopped walking and tightened his grip on the Mossad agent's arm. "What do you mean by that? How did you keep me going?"

"Who do you think gave you the wake-up call, the warning, at the motel?"

"No, no. You meant something else."

Her gaze hardened. "Quid pro quo. Tell me what you know first. What brought you to this subdivision? Why were you interested in a pickup truck rigged for spraying?" She drew a deep breath. "I hope it's not for the reason I think it is." She looked away, as if searching for something distant, unseen. "You know, I'd always hoped if something positive came out of my family's murder it might have been to prove that plague-diphtheria was not viable as a WMD. Unless . . ." She turned to look at Dwight.

"No, that's not what Barashi developed here," he said. "Something worse."

Her gaze darted from Dwight to Richard. "What?"

Dwight and Richard shared in telling the story; Dwight supplying details on the pathology, transmission and weaponization of Ebola; Richard laying out his hypothesis on how and where it would be delivered. When he finished, he handed Seligmann the slip of paper Khassem had given him. "This is Barashi's target list . . . at least his candidate list. We're checking out Elysian Fields, Magnolia Heights and Crystal Corners. The cops are handing the rest."

"I can help," she said, scanning the scrap. She looked up at the lightening sky. "All but out of time." There was something close to despair stitched into her words.

"Quid pro quo," Richard reminded her.

"Yes. My car." They resumed walking. The Lincoln came into sight.

The absurd notion—was it absurd?—hit Richard that Barashi was about to spring from the vehicle and open up on them with an automatic weapon. He tightened his grip on the SIG. Useless, of course. Seligmann had the ammunition clip.

They reached the car. Seligmann rapped on a window, then stepped back.

Chapter Thirty

NORTH METRO ATLANTA
SATURDAY, AUGUST 24

Marty De la Serna emerged from the passenger-side door of the Lincoln.

"Protective custody," Seligmann explained.

"Sure it was," Richard said, fighting to conceal his emotions. He released his grip on the SIG. Two quick steps brought him to Marty. They hugged, an embrace that became a bit more prolonged and fierce than platonic protocol might have dictated.

"Glad you're okay," she whispered. "I was afraid you were going to come out of that happy hooker joint like Humpty Dumpty."

"Glad you're okay, too, Marty. I was worried sick about you." He recalled his dry-heaves outside Diamond Cutters. "Literally."

She stepped back from him and stared at his head. "I love what you've done with your hair."

Seligmann walked over to where they stood. "You're right," she said to Richard. "She wasn't just in protective custody, she was a carrot, something to keep you trotting forward. I didn't want you to give up, loose the scent, after Diamond Cutters. Like I said, you were my only connection to Barashi. Any normal guy would have bailed after being shot, beat up and almost blown up. Maybe you didn't need an incentive to keep your nose to the ground, but I couldn't take the risk." She rested her hand on his shoulder and spoke to Marty. "A real *Mensch*, this one."

"But only a piece of shrapnel away from being a sacrificial lamb," Marty said, her retort sharp and snappish, harsher, Richard judged, than she really wanted it to be.

"Point taken. But he's off the hook now. Job well done. Thank you. All of you."

"And my brother, Jason?" Richard asked, ignoring Seligmann's acknowledgements. "He never was in any danger then?"

"Of course not. I wasn't even sure where he lived. I got the photo off his Facebook page." She walked toward her car. "Tell me how to get to Crystal Corners. You guys can check out that other place . . ."

"Magnolia Heights?" Richard said.

"Yes."

"Wait a minute," Dwight said, "can't you use your intelligence agent status to light a fire under the FBI?"

"I'm not here, remember?"

"But—"

"And tell them what? That I'm a Mossad agent operating without sanction in the U.S.? Let's stick with the plan we've got going. If the list Mr. Wainwright got is the real deal—and I have no reason to believe it isn't—either we or the cops are going to find Barashi. If not today, then tomorrow or the day after. But I have a feeling he's not going to putz around." She settled into the driver's seat of the Lincoln. "Which way to Crystal Corners?"

A pair of doves cooed morning greetings to one another through the evaporating mist. The eastern sky glowed a pale shade of steely orange as the disc of the sun nudged above the horizon.

Marty spoke up. "Look, I'll admit I don't do well in strip clubs. But I can drive a car. And you know the old saw, two pair of eyes . . . If it's okay with Dr. Butler, I'll drive his Mercedes and take Richard. I know my way to Magnolia Heights. Dr. Butler can go with Ms. Seligmann." She turned toward Dwight. "You know how to get to Crystal Corners?"

Dwight nodded and handed Marty his keys. "Take good care of my baby," he said.

Richard and Seligmann exchanged cell phone numbers.

Dwight spoke to Richard. "And you've got the duty officer's number, right?"

"I do. Now let's go find this bastard . . . if the cops haven't already nailed him."

Seligmann tossed Richard his ammo clip. "I don't think you'll need it, but just in case . . ."

"Will you go back to Oregon after this is over?" Marty asked. She drove the Mercedes slowly along Roxburgh Drive, a road circling through the heart of Magnolia Heights, a multi-hundred-home subdivision. A minivan scurried past them, its side-panel sign advertising a catering service.

Richard watched the van disappear over a hill. "After this, I think I'd better retire for real. This is too much for an old man."

"You're hardly old."

"Yes, but I'm probably lucky to be alive. Suddenly golf, fly fishing and widows' casseroles have massive appeal to me."

"So, you're going back?"

There was something more to her question than idle curiosity. He detected it in the subdued timbre of her voice, heard it in a chord that suggested a longing for something never quite realized, something suppressed. A desire, perhaps, to explore what had beckoned before but had been ignored, shoved aside, filed away for future use. But Richard understood how the future slips by, becomes the past before it becomes the present. He wondered how—if—things might be different had he planned to stay for a time. A foolish thought, he realized. Their lives were poles apart. "Yes," he said.

She didn't respond, didn't look at him.

He recalled the photograph in her office, the one of her and her family on the Madison River. "I'll bet the trout in the Deschutes or Metolius are just as big as the ones in the Madison."

She said nothing.

"That was an invitation," he said.

She concentrated on driving, her head craning forward over the steering wheel as if it would help her see more clearly. "Sometimes there're deer in these subdivisions early in the morning. You have to be careful."

"We could go hunting, too."

She turned toward him. "Only with a camera." Her eyes flickered with a restrained flash of her patented smile.

He remained silent, tried to look nonchalant.

"That was an acceptance," she said, a hint of exasperation in her voice.

"I know." He broke into a smile.

A pickup truck passed them going in the opposite direction. He pivoted his head to watch the vehicle. "Oh crap," he said.

"What? What's the matter? Was the truck outfitted for spraying? Could you see?"

"No, it went by too fast. But it looked like there were some kind of rods sticking up out of its bed."

"Rods?"

"Poles or something."

"The truck might belong to a house painter or gutter cleaner. Maybe you saw some ladders."

"Maybe. Turn around. Go after it. Let's get a closer look." He paused.

"I think it's the same model pickup I saw Barashi get out of at Diamond Cutters." Any frisson of elation he'd felt earlier with Marty's return and the revelation that von Stade—Seligmann—was not an assassin, quickly drained from him, replaced by a tiny knot of metastasizing dread.

A pair of joggers, early risers, husband and wife perhaps, bounced by giving Richard and Marty a casual wave. Marty descended a steep hill then climbed back up. A Porsche Carrera growled by going in the opposite direction. As she crested the next rise they could see the truck ahead of them, moving at a leisurely pace.

"Come up behind it slowly," Richard said.

Marty nodded. Her knuckles had turned white from her death grip on the steering wheel.

"Slowly," he repeated.

She tapped the brakes and coasted to within two car lengths of the pickup, a white Dodge Ram. "That's a funny looking rig," she said.

"How so?"

"Those vertical pipes."

He stared at the pipes, four of them mounted on the right side of the bed. Nozzles on their tips. A large tank and what apparently was a motor or pump were snugged beneath the rear window of the cab.

"What's wrong?" he asked.

"I've never seen anything like that around here."

"It looks like spraying apparatus."

"That's my point. If someone is spraying, whether it's fertilizer on lawns, or insecticide on tent caterpillars, they usually drag a hose off a reel and walk to wherever they need to spray. They don't spray from a truck."

"Unless they want to avoid ingesting the spray." Richard punched in the task force duty officer's phone number. He kept talking to Marty as he did. "Keep going at the same pace, pass him, let me get a good look at the truck." A Captain McDowell answered the phone.

"Captain, this is Richard Wainwright—"

"Wainwright! Damn. You're the guy wanted for murder."

"Put that second on your priority list. First is that I think we may have spotted the terrorist here in the subdivision. We need reinforcements. Fast."

"Jesus. What subdivision?"

"Magnolia Heights."

"Hold on."

Richard heard McDowell yelling out questions and commands. Then he came back on-line. "The nearest police unit is about ten or twelve minutes away. I've also got a Detective Jackson whom I've been asked to roust out of bed if we found you. He might get there just as quickly."

"If this is our guy, then I guarantee you we don't have ten or twelve minutes."

"Don't lose sight of him," McDowell cautioned. "I'll give our cruiser your cell number." He hung up.

Marty pulled around the pickup. In the waxing light, Richard got a good look at it. A dirt-splattered sign on its door indicated it belonged to Wilson and Son's Tree Service. Richard cupped his hand over his forehead and didn't risk looking up into the cab as they passed.

Barashi watched the Mercedes come up behind him and then follow at a discrete distance. He parted the duffel bag on the seat beside him so the AKS-74 was within easy reach. He'd debated whether to run a reconnaissance circuit of Magnolia Heights before beginning to spray, and now was glad he'd decided to, just to make sure he wasn't entering a trap. And he wasn't sure yet. The car pulled out to pass him, and he felt inside his windbreaker for the Glock. The car went by, then slowed and signaled to turn into a driveway.

Barashi withdrew his hand from his jacket and, more at ease now, drew a long, deep breath. Only isolated joggers and walkers moved along Roxburgh, a normal Saturday morning in an upscale bedroom community. Nothing to preclude launching his attack. Following Magnolia Heights, he would strike other subdivisions then end his assault with a pass through South Chattahoochee Park. The park was a community gathering place that played host to hundreds of tennis players, picnickers, strollers and softball teams on summer Saturdays. Not many trees, but a bounty of victims.

Inshallah, hundreds of thousands of Americans would be dead or dying within a week. And Ebola would be loose in a nation unprepared. He recalled the country's woeful response to Hurricane Katrina.

Marty wheeled the car into a long driveway, edging slowly toward a three-car garage. The pickup passed to her rear, continuing along Roxburgh. Richard called Seligmann as Marty waited for the truck to disappear over the brow of a hill. Once it had, Richard nodded for her to follow.

Dwight answered the phone. "That you Richard?"

"You and Seligmann better get over here, doc. Fast. We've got a pickup, the kind I saw Barashi driving yesterday, with some kind of customized spraying rig on it reconnoitering the subdivision. Marty says it doesn't look like a typical yard-care pickup. It looks like maybe somebody wants to spray, but doesn't want to get out of the truck to do it. And the cops are ten or more minutes away."

Even through the weak acoustics of the phone, Richard could hear Dwight speaking to Seligmann, then the roar of the engine as the Town Car accelerated away from wherever it was. "Cavalry's on the way, chief. Keep the truck in sight."

"What if he starts spraying?"

"Don't do anything stupid."

"What if I can't think of anything smart?"

"Five minutes. We'll be there in five minutes. Or less. Hang on." The line went dead.

Marty's eyes appeared ready to leap from her head.

"Seligmann and Dwight are on the way," Richard said, hoping to calm her. "We'll just track the truck 'til they arrive."

"And if he starts spraying?"

"I'll think of something stupid to do."

They came up behind the truck again. The pickup slowed as they approached; a vise-like squeeze tightened around Richard's head. He leaned over to Marty. "Stop the car. Get out," he said quietly. "I can drive. I want you away from this. We're in trouble."

"I know we are," she said, barely able to articulate her words. She quivered, a palsy of fear, Richard knew, rippling through her body.

"Stop the car, damn it."

"Don't swear at me. I'm not leaving."

"Listen to me, Marty. Like you didn't at Diamond Cutters."

"I was wrong about that. I'm not about this."

"Okay, use your influence then. We need divine intervention. Right now."

"I'm in sales, not management," she said, then issued a tiny gasp. "He's stopping, turning. What's he doing?"

Barashi was sure it was the same car again. Why? It certainly wasn't a police car. Two people in it. Who? He intended to find out, didn't like the way things were starting to go. He turned left into a driveway, backed out and reversed his course. He pulled the Glock from his shoulder holster, set it in his lap. He passed the car, an older Mercedes, going in the opposite direction. Yes, two people. A man and a woman. The woman driving. She seemed vaguely familiar, but he couldn't place her. The man stared out the passenger-side window, looking away from him. He couldn't see his face. But his carriage and profile were distinctive and familiar. *No, it couldn't be.* "I killed him," he muttered. "I killed him yesterday."

He hammered the steering wheel with the palm of his hand. He was being pursued by ghosts, heckled by sudden self doubts, losing time, falling off schedule before he had even begun. He pulled to the curb and watched in his rearview mirror to see if the car returned. In one sense, it didn't matter. He'd waited long enough. It was time, past time, to attack. He fingered the toggle switch for the pump.

Marty's face drained of color. "It was him."

"You're certain?"

"No mistake." Her answer came out as a rasp.

He picked up his cell phone, dropped it, retrieved it, called Dwight. "It's him," he said before Dwight could say anything. "Where are you?"

"Turning into the subdivision."

"Meet us at the main intersection." He nodded to Marty.

"Has he sprayed?" Dwight asked.

"Not yet. But I doubt he's going to wait. I think we spooked him." He heard Seligmann yelling at a car to get out of her way. Somewhere in the distance, far distance, the wavering wail of sirens challenged the morning stillness.

Thirty seconds later, the Lincoln pulled up to the intersection and stopped. Seligmann and Dwight got out and dashed toward Richard and Marty who stood beside the Mercedes.

"Where is he?" Seligmann yelled before even reaching them.

"Straight down Roxburgh. Right side." Richard pointed. "About a quarter of a mile."

"Is he alone?"

"As far as we could tell, yes."

"Stay here." Seligmann pivoted toward her vehicle.

"Hold it, damn it," Richard said, grabbing at her. "You can't go after Barashi alone."

"Come on, Wainwright, he may be spraying already. I can't wait for the police to get here."

"I wasn't talking about waiting."

Seligmann squinted at Richard, pursed her lips, shook her head. "Enough with the Fearless Fosdick bit, okay. You're a civilian. I may be here illegally, but at least I know what I'm doing. I can handle this. You know I'm good."

"Get real. I don't care if you're James Bond in drag. You're outgunned and overmatched. I may be a civilian, but I was a marine once, too. I know how to handle a weapon and shoot. I know combat procedures. At least it'll be two against one. Let's go."

"Deliver me from hairy-chested men," she muttered, seemingly resigning herself to Richard's assistance. "You're deputized, but I'll make the approach. You, Dwight and Marty are the reserves. Stay about half-a-dozen car lengths behind me. If things go in the tank, I'll holler for help."

Richard hefted the SIG, wondering how effective he could really be with his left hand.

A Corvette approached, then slowed. The driver, a middle-aged bald man, examined the small group. His eyes ballooned upon spotting the handgun. He accelerated away, simultaneously tapping in a short number on his cell phone.

"Don't shoot unless I ask for help," Seligmann continued, ignoring the Corvette. "If you have to fire, make sure the background is clear. I don't want you dropping any bystanders." She stepped into her car, slammed the door. "Lord knows, we're up to our asses in alligators already."

Richard, Marty and Dwight raced to the Mercedes. The chorus of sirens was drawing nearer, but Richard knew they'd be too late.

A small stand of silver maples and sweet gums lay ahead. Barashi eased the pickup forward, his finger resting on the pump switch. *Why all the sirens?* He dismissed them as emergency vehicles responding to an early-morning wreck or fire, a not unusual occurrence in the heavily-populated suburbs. *Still . . .* He eyed the rearview mirror. Nothing. *It's okay. Relax.* He sucked in a deep breath. Ready.

He hesitated, startled by the sight of a young woman, pushing—no, jogging behind—a baby stroller, coming down a driveway just ahead of him and to his right. His finger twitched, paused, resting on the switch. No need to spray them directly, he decided; no need to stir up immediate ire. Let them go. They'll be dead soon enough. He removed his finger from the toggle, touched the brim of his baseball hat in greeting and nodded to the young mother. She smiled, waved, said something, maybe "thank you" or "nice morning," and ran past. He watched her and her child in his side mirror as they moved away from him. *Americans,* he thought, *so open, so casually friendly. Nevermore.*

He glanced once more in his rearview mirror. "Faah," he spat, and clenched the steering wheel, as a big car, headlights on, came up fast behind him. He reached for the toggle switch, but changed his mind and went for the Glock instead. There was only one car, and it didn't look like any sort of official vehicle. No need to panic, to start spraying and running. Yet. Still, he wasn't certain. Had that indeed been Wainwright he'd spotted earlier? Had his mission been compromised? Probably not. The approaching car didn't look like anything the police or military used. But the sirens . . . He placed the Glock beside him, nestling it against his right thigh. The car pulled up to his rear bumper, flashed its lights. Maybe a private security patrol. Barashi stopped the truck.

Chapter Thirty-One

NORTH METRO ATLANTA
SATURDAY, AUGUST 24

Dwight pulled the Mercedes to the curb about twenty-five yards behind Seligmann. From the back seat, Marty leaned forward and spoke to Richard. "Stay in the car," she said softly, then repeated it.

"Sorry," he responded, only half meaning it. He got out, crouched behind the car's door. He held his handgun down, out of sight.

"Nobody listens to my sermons, either," Marty said.

"I can't back up Seligmann from behind a windshield," he snapped.

Marty ignored the rebuke. "The cops are coming. Just cool it. You've done enough."

"She's right, man," Dwight added. "Take it easy. The Mossad chick knows what she's doing. She said she'd let us know if she needs help."

"She needs help," Richard said. "She just won't admit it."

"Oh, yes," Marty said testily, "mister high-and-mighty chief executive knows best. Always hands-on, always in the middle of things."

"Yes. I know, to a fault," Richard retorted.

"To a fault," Marty agreed. She stared straight ahead, arms crossed in front of her, lips glued together.

Seligmann opened the Lincoln's door, remained behind it, leveled her handgun at Barashi's truck. "Federal officer," she yelled. "Show me your hands, driver." There was no response.

"Federal officer?" Dwight said.

"Well, she is," Marty responded, "in Israel."

"Driver, show me your hands. Now."

"Tossing guns out, miss. Don't shoot."

"Don't throw anything out. All I want to see are empty hands out the window."

The door of the truck opened.

"Don't open the door, damn it. Show me your hands."

A handgun flew out the door, clattered onto the street. "Another one coming out, officer."

"Shit. Just do what I tell you."

Richard watched as Seligmann grew increasingly frustrated, antsy. He didn't like the way things were going, either. He brought the SIG up into a firing position.

Across the lawn to his right, the front door of a home opened. A man in ratty blue jeans and a University of Georgia T-shirt stepped out. "Hey. What's going on out here?" He started toward the car.

Richard held the gun up where the man could see it. "Police business," he yelled, "get back in your house."

The man stopped, gestured at the street. "Those don't look like police cars to me."

Richard didn't need this, not now. "But does this look like a police gun?" He whirled and pointed the 9mm at the man.

The resident scurried back into his house.

"That was smart," Marty said.

"I'll let you handle it next time."

Another gun from the truck clunked onto the street and skittered toward the opposite curb. A jogger came down Roxburgh from Barashi's direction, saw the guns flying from the pickup, saw Seligmann with her weapon trained on the vehicle. He wheeled and broke into a sprint, away from the confrontation.

At least one siren had suddenly become quite loud, very near, perhaps within the subdivision. "Good guys to the rescue," Dwight yelled from inside the Mercedes.

"Those are all my weapons," Barashi said, "I'm coming out now."

"Hands first," Seligmann shouted, "and keep your back to me."

Richard knew this was too easy. Barashi would never surrender, never abort his jihad.

"Watch out," he yelled at Seligmann, "don't forget he has grenades." Diamond Cutters.

A hand appeared from the pickup's door. "Getting out," Barashi said.

"Let's see the other hand," Seligmann commanded. "Now."

Richard heard a vehicle coming up Roxburgh behind him. No siren. Not a cop. He turned to look. An SUV. Kids in it. He darted into the street, waving his gun like a semaphore, yelling at the driver to stop.

Richard pivoted to see what was happening with Barashi, saw Barashi's other hand extend from the door, flip a grenade underhanded toward Seligmann. Seligmann saw it, too, got off two shots, then dived for cover into the Town Car. The SUV behind Richard, horn blaring, squealed to a halt.

Barashi's toss, a bit too vigorous, sent the grenade bouncing and tumbling beyond the Lincoln. The bomb exploded in a doomsday starburst of light and noise just past the left rear fender of the car, shredding the trunk and shattering the rear window. It did little other damage beyond defoliating a nearby magnolia and pitting the windshield of Dwight's Mercedes.

The blast wave knocked Richard to the ground. He glanced up, saw large chunks of grass flying through the air as the SUV cut a cookie through someone's front yard. He rolled over, looking for Seligmann and Barashi.

They stepped from their vehicles simultaneously, but Seligmann never had a chance. The ripping stutter of an assault rifle on full automatic filled the morning. Seligmann crumpled back against the door frame of the Town Car, then toppled forward into the street.

Dwight—either out of instinctive concern over seeing a female shot, or in a fit of anger at having his automobile damaged—sprang from his car and darted in a crouch toward Seligmann. He made it only a few steps before another burst from Barashi's assault rifle caught him, spinning him off his feet and onto the pavement.

Richard raised himself into a firing position, kneeling on one knee. Marty screamed at him to take cover. An unmarked police cruiser, blue lights flashing from behind its grill, approached Barashi's truck from in front. Barashi spotted it, dived back into the cab of the pickup.

The police car stopped, siren at full cry. Lieutenant Jackson sprang from the vehicle, shotgun at the ready. He scanned the bodies, Seligmann's and Dwight's, sprawled on Roxburgh's asphalt. Seligmann, quiet, not moving, a handgun next to her. Dwight, quiet, too, a crimson puddle expanding around him like a small pool of sorrow; no weapon near him, only a pair of orphaned sandals.

"The guy in the truck," Richard screamed, "the guy in the truck has an assault rifle. Take cover."

Jackson hesitated, uncertainty registering in his eyes. He glared at Richard whose gun was aimed in the general direction of Seligmann. "Drop your weapon," he yelled, bringing the shotgun to bear on Richard.

"No, no, the truck, in the truck!"

Jackson kept his weapon pointed at Richard, glanced at the truck. Barashi came out in a rush, caught Jackson with a shattering burst of gunfire before the detective could react. The stunned policeman went down like a straw man in a gale. Several rounds ripped into the police cruiser. The siren sputtered to a whimper, then stopped. Barashi spun, ran toward Richard, yelling. "You," he screamed, "you're dead. You're dead."

Richard sighted, squeezed the trigger, squeezed again, and again, and again. Barashi returned fire, emptying the remainder of the assault rifle's clip at Richard in a short, thunderous fusillade.

The leg on which Richard knelt, collapsed. Talons of pain ripped into his thigh as he tilted, then fell heavily onto his right side. Small geysers of blood erupted from the upper part of his leg. Light-headed, disoriented, he didn't understand what had happened. He forced himself to concentrate. No more shooting. Why?

Through a pall of calico smoke, he looked for Barashi. He lay in the street, too, stunned, bleeding from the head and neck, glaring in Richard's direction with unfocused eyes.

Richard stared back, knowing he was face to face with pure evil. There was nothing relative about it. It was total, absolute. And it probably had killed him. Bright red blood streamed down his thigh. He realized now he'd been hit in his femoral artery. He was bleeding to death.

He looked again at Barashi, and Barashi looked back, a trace of a smile slashed across his face. Two men staring. Two men dying. Barashi twitched, rolled to his stomach, forced himself to his hands and knees and crawled toward the truck. He moved only a few feet before he collapsed.

"Richard." Dwight raised his head off the pavement, blood draining from his cheek. Glassy-eyed, he looked in Richard's direction. "Don't let . . . don't let that SOB . . . release that stuff." His words came in short gasps. He started to say something else, but couldn't get the words out.

"Take it easy, Dwight. You'll be okay." He wouldn't be. Too much blood.

Richard recoiled as he sensed a presence next to him. Marty knelt beside him. Her hands trembled. "It's an artery," she said. "Put pressure on it." She handed him a rag. "Press hard, don't stop. Both hands."

"Barashi's still alive," Richard mumbled. Images and sounds around him blurred, whirled faster and faster like a skater tucking her arms in as she spins. A tornado snatched at him and twisted him upward toward the azure void of the dawning day.

"Press," Marty screamed in his ear. "Press."

He pressed. The twister released him, dropped him back to earth. He teetered upright, jammed the rag over the arterial hole with both hands. As long as he didn't have to elevate his right arm, he could do it.

Through a haze of smoke and dizziness, he searched for Barashi. There! Crawling again, leaving a trail of blood; a wounded, humanoid slug. Richard knew Barashi had only one goal in mind now: to release the Ebola.

Where was the other police cruiser? It seemed as if minutes had elapsed, but it probably had been only seconds. A siren, loud, maybe even within the subdivision, cut through the morning air. But it wasn't close enough. Barashi would reach the truck.

Richard turned toward Marty. "Marty," he said.

"I know." She looked around helplessly.

He inclined his head toward the SIG-Sauer. "There's a few rounds left."

"No. Don't make me do this."

Barashi collapsed again, but he was only a few yards from his truck. He stared blankly in the direction of Richard and Marty, then slithered forward again.

"Get the gun," Richard said. "He's going for the pump switch, Marty. The Ebola."

"I can't."

Richard didn't agonize over it, didn't blame Marty, didn't weigh the pros and cons, the personal consequences. He merely released the pressure from his artery and scrambled toward the gun. Blood squirted from his thigh, his life spewing from him like a broken water main. The street and gun rippled and folded in his vision. The weapon faded from view and he flailed wildly for it.

"Don't," Marty said, picking up the gun. "Put the pressure back on your artery." She walked toward Barashi, gun in her right hand.

"You have to shoot him, Marty," Richard said. "Kill him."

She approached Barashi, pointed the gun at him. "Stop," she said.

"Shoot him," Richard yelled.

Barashi fell to his chest, turned to look at Marty, blood draining from a hole in his cheek and a crease in his head. He stared intently at her, then smiled in recognition. He shook his head. "You won't shoot," he said. The words came out choked, burbling, suffused in blood. At least one of Richard's bullets had found Barashi's lungs.

"You're sure?" she said.

"I know you, you're the church lady." Despite drowning in his own blood, he resumed crawling, continued talking. "I've read your Bible. It's a sin to kill. A commandment not to."

"Shoot him," Richard roared.

Marty moved forward, stepped on Barashi's hand. "Stop," she said.

He attempted a derisive laugh, but gagged instead, coating Marty's shoes in a sputum of blood and phlegm.

"Shoot him."

Barashi looked up at her. "Thou shalt not," he said. In a stunningly swift motion he launched himself violently upward, into the truck, knocking

Marty aside, slathering her in his blood.

Barashi's fingers fumbled for the toggle switch, found it, lifted it up. The pump's motor purred to life. He waited for the deadly hiss of the spray, waited for the airborne plague to jet from the nozzles. But beyond the buzz of the pump, there was nothing. Dazed, confused, puzzled, he snapped the toggle down, into the "off" position.

He knew he was dying, struggling for every breath in his last few moments, but he forced himself to concentrate, to reason. He knew with great certainty Allah would not desert him, not abandon him on the threshold of victory, so it had to be human failure, had to be—*I didn't prime the pump!* A half-second more, and the Ebola would reach the nozzles. Barashi's left hand, coated in blood, had slipped off the toggle, but with a fresh surge of resolve he once more reached toward it.

"Don't do it," Marty snapped. She faced him through the open passenger-side door, hand extended, gun pointed at his head.

He looked up, attempting to focus on his tormentor—a child who refused to accept the truth, the hard lesson—but her image swam and danced in the fading light of his brain. "You won't pull the trigger," he said. As he spoke, he sprayed the truck's seat with his own blood.

"You're right," she answered, her voice harsh and filled with resolve. In a sudden, violent motion she smashed the barrel of the gun onto his hand. Once, twice, three times until his arm sagged limply, dangling toward the floorboard.

Barashi didn't embrace martyrdom as an Islamic tenet or believe in the foolishness of beckoning virgins in Paradise. But he did believe fervently in his cause: to rid the world of the scourge of Arab humiliation and degradation. For that, he could become a martyr.

He wriggled his right hand into the duffel bag, feeling for the hard, cold metal of a grenade. The church lady seemed oblivious to his effort, staring only at his shattered and bloodied left hand, the one that dangled uselessly over the edge of the seat.

His right hand, hidden from the woman's view by the folds of the bag, finally touched steel, though the tactility seemed distant and disconnected from his being. A violent spasm of blood-choked coughing seized him, and he lost his grip on the grenade, feared he was going to pass out. *A few seconds, Allah, a few more seconds.*

He found the grenade again, worked his fingers around it, felt the ring holding the safety pin. Using his forefinger, he struggled to pry the ring from the pin, but was too weak to budge it. Yet he knew he must, knew he could. The explosion would shatter the truck and with it the Ebola-filled tank, spraying the lethal virus over a broad radius; an eruption of aerosol death let loose to catch whatever wind currents it could. Let loose on an apocalyptic journey through an unsuspecting American suburb.

The sound of sirens, many of them now, filled his ears, competing with the screams of terrified neighborhood residents, the yowls of hyper-excited dogs and the desperate commands of Richard Wainwright to shoot him.

"Kill him, for God's sake, Marty," Richard bellowed, "he's got grenades in there."

She won't, Wainwright. She can't. He made a final appeal to Allah, looked up at the church lady—suddenly in focus—and felt the ring on the pin begin to give. The woman mouthed something to him, perhaps "I'm sorry" or "help me." Puzzling. Why would she say that? To whom? Then he glimpsed something in her eyes, something that hadn't been there before. And he knew. "I see into your soul," he croaked. "Allah will not forgive."

"The one I know will," she said.

A brilliant flash erupted from the muzzle of her gun.

Epilogue

SUNRIVER, OREGON
FIVE MONTHS LATER

The last of the day's light drained from the western sky, swirling down a distant, ethereal drain beyond the snow-draped Cascade Mountains. Stars annealed on the brilliant blackness of central Oregon's high-desert sky provided the only light for Richard and Marty as they strolled along a footpath through a sparse stand of ponderosa. Moisture from their exhalations formed tiny puffs of condensation fog that quickly dissipated in the brittle December cold. In the middle distance, a coyote yipped, welcoming the night.

"You're getting better with that cane," Marty said. She steadied Richard as they transited a patch of ice.

"It's a walking stick," Richard said, attempting to feign irritability. "The doctor says I'll be able to trade it for a five-iron by spring."

"I didn't know you were that serious about golf."

He thought about the last time he'd played, the last time he was home. "There's a beaver out there that misses me," he said.

"I suppose you'll explain that to me someday."

"It's nothing licentious."

"Well, I've been around you long enough to know that." She paused. "But a lady can always hope." She giggled.

"All talk, as usual."

"I'm good at that."

"So when can I look forward to a sermon at Tommy's church?"

She squeezed his hand. "I'm better off helping Tommy behind the scenes. If I were to preach, you know good and well the focus would be on my media persona—'The Nine-millimeter-Methodist' or the 'Pistol Packing Pastor'—not on my message. Besides—"

Something scurried across the path in front of them, a fox on the hunt, perhaps.

"Besides what?"

"The lease on my apartment in Bend is up in February. I don't know if I'll stay beyond then. I still need to get away . . . I don't know, enter a convent or something, get my head straight."

"A convent?" Richard could feel his metaphorical chain being jerked again.

"Or go to work in a strip joint."

"You're incorrigible. Maybe I should take Hadassah up on her offer."

"Hadassah Seligmann? What offer?"

"I got an email from her the other day. She said if things didn't work out between me and you, she'd find a nice Jewish girl for me."

"Meddling in your life again."

"Somebody has to, I guess."

"I suppose I could . . . if I weren't, as you say, incorrigible. And I'm not."

"Not what?"

"Incorrigible. I'm just confused." She spun him around, made him look closely at her. In the darkness, her eyes reflected only starlight, pinpoints of brightness from somewhere near the outer edges of the universe. "I don't understand," she said. "We ask God for the strength to do something, then ask His forgiveness for doing it. Even with God, nothing is black and white."

He wrapped his arms around her, a gesture that seemed oddly devoid of intimacy, swaddled as they were in heavy sheepskin jackets, and brought his mouth close to her ear. "Let me resolve at least part of your ambivalence then. Don't go. Stay here."

"You're offering to make an honest woman out of me?" she whispered.

"I haven't made a dishonest one out of you yet."

She stood on her tiptoes and kissed him, her hair filled with the aroma of wood smoke. She pulled back and through a small stratus of steam said, "You know, that's the one thing I really don't like about being a minister."

"There's always your fantasy life."

"I gave up on that, remember?"

He took her hand. "Stay," he said. They walked on without speaking, accompanied only by the crunch of their boots on cornflake snow. Despite the penetrating cold, Richard's thoughts drifted back to a sizzling afternoon in Georgia, a day with towers of white cumulus stacked over Atlanta.

He, Marty and a badly wounded but recovering Hadassah—sans earrings and safety pins, her hair brown and straight, not blond and spiky—had watched for the better part of two hours as a procession of law enforcement and federal officials from across North America snaked through the city en route to a memorial service for Lieutenant Jackson and Dr. Butler. Later, they'd watched in tear-distorted silence as Jackson's wife, then Dwight's aged grandmother, accepted American flags from the governor and posthumous Presidential Awards for Heroism from the Secretary of Homeland Security. Small solace.

"I never told you," Richard said, "I prayed for Dwight's grandmother and Jackson's wife at the memorial service."

Marty moved closer to him so that they were shoulder to shoulder. "Was it hard? I mean, did it seem strange after so long?"

"Awkward."

"You need more practice then."

An owl hooted in the darkness.

"Any suggestions?" Richard asked.

"For me. Try some prayers for me. I keep playing that morning back through my mind. Keep seeing Barashi's gaze locked on me, keep seeing his sudden realization of what I was going to do." She turned toward Richard and spoke in a voice husky with emotion. "I know I saved lives, but in the long run, did my shooting him make any difference? Make us any safer? Make any inroads at all against, as the Bible says, 'the principalities of darkness?'"

Richard looked up as a shooting star traced a bright, white trail across the sky. The brilliance was fleeting, quickly devoured by the surrounding blackness. He didn't answer.

"I thought not," Marty said.

Richard stopped, turned, placed his hand under Marty's chin and tilted her face upward toward his. "Don't jump to conclusions," he said. "Sometimes we get overwhelmed by the darkness. But as long as we can muster just a pinprick of light, yes, we can make a difference."

"Even if the light comes from the barrel of a handgun?"

"Even if."

She shook her head. "I don't know."

"As I recall, there was a lot of blood shed in the Old Testament. That's how a nation was built and preserved. That's how God worked among men."

Marty leaned against Richard and buried her face in the folds of his sheepskin. He encircled her with his arms, pulling her into him firmly, as though retrieving something he'd lost.

The owl hooted again, this time drawing a response from another.

ATLANTA, GEORGIA
SAME NIGHT

An empty fast food container, spurred on by frost-tinged gusts of wind, tumbled along a passageway between rows of corrugated steel units at Castle Vault Public Storage near Hartsfield-Jackson Airport. A small figure, collar on his light jacket upturned, hands jammed into his pockets, searched for unit 317 along a dimly-lit passage.

Shivering in the pre-Christmas cold, he found the unit and pulled a piece of paper from his wallet. Clenching a penlight in his teeth, he aimed it alternately at the paper, on which was written a sequence of numbers, and a combination lock on the door. In less than a minute, an almost inaudible click announced he'd succeeded in releasing the lock.

He pulled open the door of the unit and stepped inside. The hum of a freezer, just as the late Sami Alnour Barashi's letter had promised, filled the tiny cubicle. He found a light switch and flipped it on. He walked quickly to the freezer, lifted its door and peered inside.

He was at once both relieved and terrified. Relieved he'd found the stored hope for victory, terrified the legacy of Alnour Barashi and Russia's Koltsovo Institute lived on.

Author's Note

Several years before deciding to try my hand at becoming a novelist, I read Richard Preston's gripping nonfiction page-turner *The Hot Zone,* a book about the deadly Ebola virus.

While most species of Ebola are not transmittable through the air—lucky for us humans—the variant featured in *The Hot Zone* may be. Fortunately, that variant, while fatal to monkeys, is not fatal to humans. Again, lucky for us.

But it got me thinking, What if? What if a brilliant (and psychopathic) microbiologist were able to marry the variant of Ebola not fatal to humans but perhaps transmittable through the air to the form most deadly to humans? That is, what if someone were able to weaponize Ebola? It would be a nightmare aborning. Perfect for a novel.

But breathing life into the story was slow. I'm not a microbiologist. To inject authenticity into the tale required a lot of research. Like most novelists, however, I'd rather write than relive my college days cramming for finals. Still, it had to be done, so for several years I "burned the midnight oil"— not literally—while simultaneously pecking out early drafts of *Plague* (whose working title at the time was *The Koltsovo Legacy*). I also took a two-year sabbatical to complete *Eyewall,* my debut novel.

The research on Ebola and microbiology turned out to be a labor of love since I was truly fascinated (frightened?) by the subject. The Websites of the Centers for Disease Control and Prevention, more commonly called the CDC, and the World Health Organization provided reams of invaluable information and data.

Besides the *Hot Zone*, there were a number of other books that helped me develop insights into microbiology, viruses and the Russian and American biowarfare programs:

Biohazard—The Chilling True Story of the Largest Covert Biological Weapons Program in the World by Ken Alibek with Stephen Handelman

The Dead Hand—The Untold Story of the Cold War Arms Race and Its Dangerous Legacy (a Pulitzer Prize winner) by David E. Hoffman

Germs—Biological Weapons and America's Secret War by Judith Miller, Stephen Engelberg and William Broad

Level 4—Virus Hunters of the CDC by Joseph B. McCormick and Susan Fisher-Hoch with Leslie Alan Horvitz

Virus Hunter—Thirty Years of Battling Hot Viruses Around the World by C. J. Peters and Mark Olshaker

The emergency room scenes in the novel were vetted by my cousin, Dr. John A. McDonald, a veteran emergency room physician. Any errors in the procedures described are mine and not his.

A number of people read and critiqued all or part of the book, and thus guided me through at least five revisions. In the end, it was my editors at Bell Bridge Books, Pat Van Wie and Deb Smith, whose eagle eyes and keen insights got me to the goal line.

But there were others who did some downfield blocking. Novelist Steve Berry, back when he was able to do that sort of thing, reviewed and critiqued—in well-deserved less-than-glowing terms—an early version of the first chapter. Bill Robinson, Sid Moore and Gary Schwartz read ragged early drafts of the novel and gave me both attaboys and figurative slaps upside the head.

My Peerless Book Store writers critique group was invaluable in making *Plague* better. Several members, past and present, read all or much of the initial draft of the book: Mark All, Paul Brussard, Rob Elliott, George Weinstein and John Witkowski. I am deeply indebted to people who volunteer to spend their time that way.

Thanks also to my literary agent, Jeanie Pantelakis of Sullivan Maxx, for believing in me and my work and hooking me up with Bell Bridge Books.

While the characters in the novel are all products of my imagination, there is one, Richard Wainwright, for whom I borrowed the professional DNA of an old friend. I loved the idea of having my hero be a high-integrity

CEO who goes around fixing companies (all fictitious ones in the novel) and who could take over and run almost any kind of operation for a short period.

There was such a person in real life, an old high school friend, Steve Miller. Steve, early in his career, was CFO of Chrysler. From there he went on to spend the next twenty years salvaging a variety of foundering corporations. He met with enough success that he was labeled by the *Wall Street Journal* as "U.S. Industry's Mr. Fix It."

I lost track of Steve over the years, but I followed his professional accomplishments via newspaper and magazine articles. In the meantime, I completed *Plague*, modeling Richard Wainwright's professional life after Steve's, except for the fact that Steve was never in the Marines.

In early 2009, I found out Steve had written an autobiography, *The Turnaround Kid—What I Learned Rescuing America's Most Troubled Companies*. I got in touch with Steve and he sent me an autographed copy. It was a fascinating read. But I was stunned and saddened to learn that Steve's wife, Maggie, had died of cancer in 2006. I'll freely admit that tears flowed as I read of Maggie's death in the book.

The bizarre thing was I had written the death of Richard Wainwright's wife into the novel long before I was aware of Maggie's passing. I explained this to Steve, and trust he doesn't hold it against me.

Here's the good part: The stories for both Steve and my fictional Richard had happy endings. Steve remarried and Richard fell in love.

Art accidentally imitating life.

About the Author

H. W. "Buzz" Bernard is the author of EYEWALL and PLAGUE.

EYEWALL, his debut novel, became a number-one best seller on Amazon's Kindle. Buzz is a native Oregonian and attended the University of Washington in Seattle where he earned a degree in atmospheric science and studied creative writing. He's currently vice president of the Southeastern Writers Association.

He lives in Roswell, Georgia, near Atlanta, with his wife, Christina, and over-active Shih-Tzu, Stormy. If you'd like to learn more about Buzz you can go to his Website: buzzbernard.com; or his author page on Facebook: H. W. "Buzz" Bernard.

Made in United States
Troutdale, OR
07/28/2023

11637572R00140